FIRES OF RAPTURE

Rebecca swayed, and of its own accord, Gordon's hand came out to steady her. As their fingers touched, a lightning spark seemed to flicker between them. The next instant his arms were around her, and he was holding her hard against him.

Beyond thought, Rebecca lifted her face to his and felt his lips brush hers softly. Drugged with the wonder of that delicate touch, she closed her eyes.

His lips moved to her cheek as his hand came up to stroke her neck and move upward through the luxuriant softness of her hair till he held her head caressingly. Then his mouth covered hers again, and she responded as she'd never known she could.

Her body was on fire wherever he touched her...

FIRES
of
RAPTURE

by

LISA BEAUMONT

FAWCETT CREST • NEW YORK

To All My Perfect Men, With Love

LONDON

1775

Chapter 1

"I'm devastated, of course, Miss Blair. It's the cruelest blow to leave you, but a prior commitment at my club, you know."

In the vast gold and maroon drawing room, the strains of a minuet were muted by the crush of brilliantly clad couples moving sedately in patterned sets or strolling arm in arm as they watched all others around them. Near the massive leaves of a wilting palm, a beautiful black-haired girl in a soft yellow gown looked down at the immaculate wig bending over her outstretched hand.

Damn, she thought.

If Ashley Thorpe left now, she'd die of boredom, unless Harlcourt came to her rescue. Thorpe would never haunt her dreams, but his caustic wit was all that had proved amusing this evening. She felt like shaking him with vexation, but smiled brightly as he raised a face full of sorrow. "Naturally, prior commitments must take precedence, Mr. Thorpe," she said and withdrew her hand from his clasp. "We shall all miss you, of course." She turned away, but from the corner of her eye she saw him thread his way through the room and unconsciously she twisted the fan in her hand.

"Rebecca Blair, if you stand up with that man again I will go into strong hysterics." Mrs. Carlsby, her meager bosom trying to puff with authority, wrung her hands as she ran her niece to ground in the corner of the spacious room. "My Letty would never be so brazen in defying my wishes. It's your

9

mother's wild Irish streak coming out in you." She drew a shaking breath. "Mr. Thorpe has neither title nor fortune, and you do not wish your name linked more closely with his. I've seldom been so shocked."

"Oh yes you have, Aunt Honoria. Besides, he told me my eyes were amethysts more beautiful than any crown jewels." The girl's expression was mischievous.

"Oooh. Have you no shame?" Mrs. Carlsby shuddered, then drew herself up as she relished a new thought. "If your father should chance to see you . . ."

"Now, Aunt, you know as well as I that he's halfway across London, gaming at his club again, and the thought of whom I may stand up with at Lady Spefton's ball has never once entered his mind." Rebecca allowed her eyes to rove across the room and tried to hide her feeling of disgust as she watched a group of the new Oxford dandies, who called themselves the Macaroni Club, pose and strut in their polka-dotted breeches and rigidly tight coats. Silly popinjays, she thought. Then her eyes halted on three distant figures.

With suspicious foreboding, Mrs. Carlsby followed her charge's gaze. "No, no," she said hastily, laying her fan on the slender arm before her. "You don't want to be looking in *that* direction."

"Oh?" Rebecca's fine eyes blinked innocently.

Mrs. Carlsby gave her niece a baleful look. Under pressure, she'd promised her brother she would chaperone his lovely daughter through her first London season, but the girl was proving a difficult and exasperating charge. She was stubborn and unruly and refused as often as not to listen to the wise counsel of her elders. Still, it was Mrs. Carlsby's duty to try. "Rebecca, I don't care that Lord Harlcourt is one of the most eligible catches on the market. He must marry money, and *that*," she said with emphasis, "is *one* thing you don't have in overabundance." She looked meaningfully at her niece's low-cut gown. "Besides, he's a gamester and a rake. He would offer you nothing honorable."

"So you've said before, Aunt." Rebecca repressed her annoyance. "Actually, I was wondering about the two men who are with him."

Mrs. Carlsby hesitated, but couldn't resist the opportunity to repeat gossip. "Those two," she said with an attempt at sounding grand, "are provincials, my dear. From *America*."

"What on earth are they doing here?"

"I'm not quite right in the particulars, but I believe there is some distant connection with Lord Harlcourt." She drew a long breath. "You remember Miss Pamela Jenkins, whom we met at Mrs. Trilby's rout last month?" Rebecca nodded, recalling well the softly beautiful Miss Jenkins with the golden curls and the wide, innocent eyes. "I am told," went on Mrs. Carlsby portentously, "that the taller of those two men, the fair-haired one with the near-Adonis looks, has *pursued* Miss Jenkins all the way to London from America. He had used to have an understanding with the girl, and he's mad as a hatter that her father brought her to London to find a proper husband."

"Hmmm . . ." Rebecca made a noncommital sound as at that moment Lord Harlcourt turned and encountered her gaze. Inclining his head, he spoke to his two companions and started across the room.

"Oh, no," Mrs. Carlsby said in a faint voice. "They are coming this way. This is almost worse than Mr. Thorpe. Rebecca, I forbid you to countenance a meeting."

"We have no choice, Aunt," Rebecca replied curtly, "so we might as well make the most of it."

The lazy eyes of Vincent, Viscount Harlcourt, lit up appreciatively as he surveyed the jonquil silk gown with its daringly cut neckline and narrow waist that did a great deal to enhance Rebecca's perfectly rounded figure beneath. The color enriched her big violet eyes, he thought, and set off that raven's wing hair. He smothered a smile. Poetry was not in his line, but there were times when the contemplation of such aesthetic pleasure could almost move him to verse. Pity it was rumored that her father was rapidly losing most of the family fortune at the gaming tables. With a mental grimace he pulled his thoughts back to the matter at hand. His cousin, Gordon Meade, who now stalked beside him, was in a black mood, and it seemed to Lord Harlcourt that Miss Blair, with her lively air, might help to lighten the scowling features. If it was true Gordon had come to London to set matters straight with Pamela Jenkins, he definitely needed to be steered in another direction.

With an expression of frank curiosity, Rebecca watched the gentlemen traverse the room. Mrs. Carlsby's flutterings beside her and disjointed murmurs of ". . . think you so forward," "your fan, miss," "oh, why must he come this way?" fell on deaf ears as she regarded the two tall Americans.

Adonis, she decided, was not quite the proper metaphor for the golden-haired man. His wide mouth held too much of a downward curve, his chin was decidedly too square and his heavy brows too frowning for the classically perfect face. Still, he was very nearly the handsomest man in the room, but for Harlcourt. Besides, there was something about him, some arrogant strength, an impression of energy held in check, that set him apart.

His companion she scrutinized more briefly. He was several inches shorter, and of an even more lithe build, moving like a cat across the floor. Perhaps a good dancer, she thought, but she was not certain she could like a man with such opaquely dark eyes, or with a nose quite that narrow.

Her aunt, not at all pleased with the way this evening was going, was at a loss for words as Lord Harlcourt halted before her, bowing.

Rebecca extended her hand. "Harlcourt, I had not thought to see you here."

The viscount took her fingers and his brown eyes danced in answer to her look. "Ah, Miss Blair. I discovered *you* were coming, and that made all other entertainments in the city appear suddenly dull."

Mrs. Carlsby made an inarticulate sound which brought an even broader smile to Rebecca's face. Rather reluctantly she withdrew her hand, and turning to his friends, she looked up into the most startlingly blue eyes she'd ever seen. Fascinated, she returned their regard as Lord Harlcourt made the introductions and adroitly maneuvered Mrs. Carlsby and the other American, a Mr. Tyson, away.

Gordon Meade, his face still dark from some inner tension, was left to stare down at the black-haired girl who looked boldly back at him. Stiffly, aware he'd been neatly placed, he requested the honor of this dance.

Rebecca's own brows drew together. "You don't have to lead me out, you know," she said in her usual forthright way. "I can see you would much prefer to be somewhere else."

Mr. Meade's eyes narrowed as he assured her she was mistaken. "But perhaps you would rather not be asked," he said succinctly.

With a tiny slap, Rebecca's fan shut in her hand. "I thought only to save you the unpleasantness of having to do a distasteful duty. For my part, I own I'm intrigued since I have never before danced with an American." She laid her hand delicately on his offered arm and they moved to join the set that was forming.

"You say that as though a native of the American colonies is something just come to life from out of a museum, Miss Blair. Surely we are not such oddities in London."

His voice was deep, and Rebecca was not sure if there was a note of humor in it. But since no further exchange was required in the opening of the dance, she shrugged the thought aside. She could see the covert glances of the other girls blossoming into stares of envy as she moved down the set with the tall American. Soon there would be whispered intrigue among mothers and daughters and the inevitable vying for the chance to dance with the handsome stranger. Watching the outcome would at least provide mild entertainment for this so far dull evening.

When the dance ended, Mr. Meade offered his arm with solemnity. Rebecca took it and smiled coquettishly up at him. "You dance very well, sir."

The blue eyes looked blandly into hers. "We *do* dance in the wilds of America, Miss Blair."

"And what else do you do, Mr. Meade?"

"For entertainment? Nothing so barbaric as you would like to hear, I'm afraid."

For just a moment, Rebecca thought she'd seen a softening of the harsh lines in his face, but the impression was fleeting. Her smile turned to a moue which she'd been told was enticing. "You really look quite forbidding when you frown that way, you know."

"I'm sorry," he said shortly, and made an effort to clear his face. "Perhaps you will be so good as to indicate your chaperone's direction. I'm afraid I don't see her in this crush."

The violet eyes beside him grew wide. Never had a man shown an eagerness to be quit of her at the end of a dance. It was such a surprising experience, Rebecca didn't know whether to laugh or to give him a sharp set-down. Even more surprising was the fact that she found her curiosity about him growing. She caught her lip in indecision, and then heard Lord Harlcourt's voice.

"Glad I spotted you," the viscount said cheerfully. "Another moment and Miss Blair would have been surrounded and I'd have lost hope of a dance." He grinned happily at the two of them and tried not to show surprise when the lady's hand was relinquished without a sign of regret. The tall American made a meticulous bow, murmured appropriate words of thanks and melted away.

Lord Harlcourt stared in amazement at that, and was brought to his senses only when Rebecca's fingers tightened on his arm. "You needn't gape so, Harlcourt. You'll draw attention to the fact that my charms impressed your colonial cousin not one whit."

Lord Harlcourt made a hasty rally. "*That* I would never believe," he said roundly. "But he was acting deuced odd."

He felt the fingers tighten once again. "Do we have perhaps part of the explanation?" Rebecca asked softly and nodded toward the dance floor. There before them was the lovely Miss Jenkins, smiling happily on the arm of the Honorable Roland West.

"So you've heard the rumors about Meade and Miss Jenkins." The viscount looked thoughtfully at Rebecca and suddenly steered her aside to join the ranks of the promenading couples. "You'll think me a cad, then, for throwing him at your head. But it seemed a good course at the time." He looked uncomfortable. "I don't know my cousin very well, you see. He's been with me only two weeks. Came by way of Paris. Tyson, his friend, tells me he has the devil of a temper, and has hinted that he's mad as blazes at Miss Jenkins being brought to London. I thought perhaps if he saw there are more beautiful women around he'd stop being so glum and would enjoy himself." He saw his speech rewarded by a brilliant smile and blinked.

"It all sounds very romantic," his partner declared, "except that I don't feel Miss Jenkins is pining for Mr. Meade overmuch."

"Quite. In fact, she's having the time of her life, if you ask me, and leaving poor Gordon to make of it what he will."

"Your cousin, Lord Harlcourt, struck me as a very determined young man. I shouldn't be surprised if he brings Miss Jenkins about."

"Not so sure about that. Her father won't allow it, I hear. He's rich, you see, and is holding out for a title for her."

"Ah, but is *she?*"

Lord Harlcourt looked even more uncomfortable, and his equanimity was not restored by the little ripple of laughter at his side.

"Why, Harlcourt, don't tell me she's turned those lovely eyes in your direction, too?"

"Makes it deuced awkward with Gordon, I'll tell you, Miss Blair. He's quite a good sort, I've discovered. A real sporting man. Though he does have queer turns when he retires to the library to write or to read for hours on end." This time the ripple of laughter called up his answering grin. "Well, you won't find me glooming away over Father's musty volumes. Not when I might be driving in the park, for instance. May I call for you tomorrow afternoon, and take you up with me?"

Fluttering her lashes, Rebecca gave her consent to the notion, and was pleased to feel a tightening in the arm which held hers. So much for Miss Jenkins's pretensions, she thought cheerfully. Aunt Honoria would be appalled, but she wouldn't dare forbid her to go driving with Harlcourt.

As though her thoughts had conjured the woman from thin air, Rebecca found that as she and her partner came round the far side of the room, Mrs. Carlsby was beckoning imperiously from a deep red settee against the wall. Worse, her daughter Lettitia was there too, hazel eyes narowed in speculation as she watched the room full of people. Harlcourt had no choice, Rebecca supposed, but to turn her over to these two harridans, and she resigned herself to her fate as she watched his hastily retreating back.

"Who was that forbidding man you took up with last dance?" asked her cousin as Rebecca seated herself beside Mrs. Carlsby.

"An American, Letty." Rebecca, long used to the spiteful tone of envy in the girl's voice, paid no heed to it. "Have you had a nice time?"

"It would be nicer if you didn't make it so awkward by dancing with only the most improper men in the room."

"Oh, dear." Rebecca tried to look sorrowful. "But you needn't pay any heed to me, Letty."

"I wouldn't, only Caroline Griscomb has just pointed out to me that you are getting worse."

"Am I? How disheartening for you, I'm sure." Carefully, Rebecca kept her voice soft. "But I'm afraid Caroline's opinion is of less than no consequence."

"Really, Becky, sometimes you make me blush for you."

"Girls, please," Mrs. Carlsby said in a faint voice and wondered for the hundredth time how she was going to get through the remainder of the season. Widowed two years ago, she had prevailed upon her brother to take her and dear Lettitia under his roof. But never in her scheming had Mrs.

Carlsby imagined she would be required to bring Rebecca into society along with Lettitia. It was too bad of her brother to be so eager to see his daughter settled. Though, she admitted now with a martyred sigh, he could be no more eager than she. The little hoyden was determined to ruin herself before she could fix the interest of a truly eligible man, and so do her duty by her family. She was so busy leaving a trail of broken hearts in her wake, she never looked seriously at anyone. There was the nice Baron Willingsworth, for instance, who was even now bowing so punctiliously before her. He was obviously smitten with Rebecca, and was quite plump in the purse, too. Besides, he was such a dear man, always so proper about bringing along a gentleman willing to stand up with Letty. Her sigh turned to a simper of delight as she greeted the baron and nudged Rebecca to stand up.

"Miss Blair, I have waited most impatiently for this chance to pay my respects."

The high voice grated on Rebecca's nerves, but she smiled mechanically at the baron's sallow face and nodded at his friend who was claiming Letty. As the baron drew her forward with one wet hand, Rebecca tried not to flinch.

"Here we are, Miss Blair. You look smashing tonight, you know. Didn't want to say so and sound too forward in front of Mrs. Carlsby, but you always do me—all of us who admire you—such credit." The baron practically giggled as they joined the set.

Suppressing a shudder, Rebecca gave him a bright smile and moved down the line, planning her speech of regret should the man ask to escort her in to supper.

From a far doorway Gordon Meade watched the tableau on the settee and was pleased to see Miss Blair hide a grimace of disgust as a foppish dandy pulled her forward. Stifling a yawn, he wondered how late Harlcourt would require them to stay. He feared that this was going to be a long evening, but now that he'd met Rebecca Blair, perhaps not such a tedious one as he'd imagined.

"A decent turnout, eh, cousin?" Viscount Harlcourt handed a glass to Gordon absentmindedly as he studied the throng.

"Very decent."

"You're seeming distracted, Meade. But we'll leave here in an hour and go on to the club. Some high stakes expected there tonight. Thorpe's gone already. We'll be late, but we'll catch enough of the action, I daresay. Your friend seems to be doing well. Two heiresses and an accredited beauty have stood up with him so far. He's casting his eyes at Miss Blair now, I see."

Gordon watched Warren Tyson through narrowed eyes. The man was in his element here, ogling everyone of wealth or beauty in the room, and Gordon could only hope there was no one here stupid enough to be taken in by him. Not since their days in college together had Gordon liked the man. Tyson was the type to smile ingratiatingly as he betrayed his own mother, for he was nearly always in debt and nearly always scheming for a way out.

His mind shifted back to the problem of the letters from the Comte de Vergennes and Caron de Beaumarchais that he was carrying home to the Continental Congress. The hints those letters held of needed arms supplies next year from France were too delicate for any eyes but those to whom the letters were addressed. Yet the letters had been tampered with. And they'd been tampered with here in London. *Who* but Warren would have known where to find them? And for what purpose would he read them? Gordon stilled the urge to slam his fist into the doorframe beside him. He should never have allowed the Congress to send Warren with him to Paris and London, knowing him as he did.

And now there was this absurd story Tyson was putting about that Gordon had followed Pamela Jenkins to London. . . . What sort of perverse motive had conjured that one? He supposed Warren had done it from long-ago jealousy over Pamela, and if Pam had heard the nonsense, she was probably enjoying the sensation it created. Let her.

At that instant Gordon's eye fell on the subject of his thoughts. She was whirling toward him in the set, her face flushed with delight, her eyes nearly glazed with warmth for her partner. Looks like a bitch in heat, he thought, then shook his head. Thank God, the matter didn't concern him. He could actually wish her well now, and be thankful for his own escape from her. Thank God, in fact, for his liberation from any female entanglements.

He continued to watch the couples dancing, and smiled to himself. On the other hand, it was a pleasure to be distracted from pressing matters by someone like the gorgeous Miss Blair. Quite dispassionately, he compared Pamela with the

London beauty. One was a golden ethereal vision, the other a dark enchantress. Rebecca, he noticed, used none of the artful means of enhancing her beauty that others found so essential. Her face was the color of warm ivory, not the sallow mask that face powder produced, and her unadorned hair gleamed blue-black in the bright candlelight. She had a disturbing sort of beauty, he concluded. The wide brow, round firm chin and high cheekbones were lovely, almost as lovely as the enormous violet eyes under delicately arched brows. But it was her full, mobile mouth and her slim, seductive shape, he thought, that would set a man's pulse racing. Add to that her air of coquetry and the defiant tilt to her chin . . .

He'd been too abrupt, distracted, in his dance with the girl. Perhaps he could remedy the matter.

Chapter 2

She was enduring another scold from her aunt because by turning away the baron, Letty had lost her partner too, when Rebecca allowed her feelings to overcome her judgment and snatched at a glass of champagne a waiter was balancing on a silver tray. With a fixed smile, she downed it in the teeth of her aunt's outraged gasp, and looked up to see sharp blue eyes glinting at her above her aunt's bewigged head.

"You have no feelings for your family, you unnatural child," her aunt was spitting furiously. "No gratitude for all I've attempted to do for you."

Appalled that Gordon Meade had witnessed her defiant gesture and was now listening to the harangue, she tried to take Aunt Honoria's arm and lead her away. But suddenly a smooth deep voice overrode her aunt's high one.

"Miss Blair! My luck holds. Will you do me the honor?" Mr. Meade's arm was between them, deftly cutting off the tirade and leaving her aunt with mouth ajar.

Hiding her surprise, Rebecca smiled sweetly and took his arm, but she couldn't help wondering what had made him come to claim her hand. Only minutes ago she would have sworn he was glad to be rid of her. As they reached the center of the room, she studied him from beneath her thick lashes. His clothes, she noticed, were of the finest and fit him to perfection, showing off his broad shoulders and narrow waist to advantage without the padding so many men now affected.

And the white silk stockings encased long well-muscled legs that must be envied by nearly all his peers. She began to wonder just what it was about him that made Pamela Jenkins turn him away. Though if his face was usually so stern she thought she could understand Miss Jenkins's reluctance. Surely he didn't *always* look so forbidding. He must smile once in a while, perhaps even converse.

Testing, she put occasional polite questions to him, and learned that Mr. Meade had, in the past weeks, seen as many of the sights of London as she had, and she was pleased to discover he had been particularly impressed by Poet's Corner in Westminster Abbey and even more by the new British Museum in Montague House, where Sir Hans Sloane's eclectic and enormous collection of objects was on view. On the other hand, he seemed shocked at the sight of Parliament in session, with members lounging on the benches, ignoring speakers, eating food and calling to each other. And he was thoroughly unimpressed by London's smoke-laden air and incessant loud noise.

Happy that she was for once having a real conversation with a man, Rebecca was sorry when the dance ended and said so. Abruptly Mr. Meade suggested that the overcrowded ballroom was becoming stuffy and that a stroll outside would be refreshing. She accepted his arm with alacrity, and sweeping through the tall French windows to the narrow terrace, she cast a backward smile of regret to a young man who'd suddenly come to stalk her, and ignored a frantic signal from her harassed aunt.

The night was warm for May, and the gay lights along garden walks, the scent of spring blossoms and the soft strains of music coming from the small rotunda at the far end of the garden beckoned to overheated couples to enjoy the peace of the outdoors.

Rebecca, filled with a heady sense of freedom, took a deep appreciative breath as they descended wide stone steps to the lawns. "Now, Mr. Meade, you can see that London is not always so heavy with smoke as you claim," she said, looking up at the few twinkling stars directly overhead.

"But we are not in the heart of London here. The people who took these elegant mansions on Grosvenor Square were getting away from the worst of the town air."

"I suppose you are right. But tell me, where do you come from that city smoke is so abhorrent to you?"

Trying to slow his long strides to her leisurely pace, Gordon Meade looked down at the black hair beside him. "I live outside any city, beside the banks of a very beautiful river called the Hudson," he answered. "Right now the river would be high and fresh with spring water, the lilacs would be in full bloom. . . ." His voice trailed off on a reminiscent note.

"You miss it so much, then?" Rebecca stopped beneath a swaying lantern and looked up at the dark face whose high cheekbones were thrown into relief by the soft light.

"Yes, I miss it," the man answered simply, stopping too, and turning to her. "Have we walked too far? Perhaps you would prefer to return to the ballroom?"

Piqued at her partner's willingness to relinquish her once more, Rebecca looked at him sharply. "You may return, sir, if it would suit you better. I prefer the fresh air for a bit longer."

The wide mouth was set in a firm line now. "I would hardly leave you alone in a half-darkened garden. Besides, I feel sure you are not eager to return to Mrs. Carlsby for another scold."

"Really, sir, it is not good manners to admit you realize I behave in a way considered scandalous by my aunt." Rebecca couldn't stop the gurgle of laughter that rose at the picture of her aunt's outrage if she could see her niece now.

"I have a strong suspicion that you rarely behave as your aunt would wish, and that you would be excessively bored if you did."

"I'm afraid you're right." Rebecca sighed. "But discussing my behavior with a man I hardly know is not at all the thing."

"I beg your pardon. We shall now walk as far as you wish."

Rebecca looked sideways at his profile. She couldn't see his eyes. Was he annoyed, or was he laughing at her? She turned and strolled beside him, wondering again why he had bothered to stay by her. She thought of Harlcourt's words about needing to distract Gordon from Miss Jenkins. She ought to be able to do that much. Never had she met a man in whom she had not sparked some interest. Surely Americans were not a different breed.

"Harlcourt said you were in Paris before coming to London," she said, her voice light. "Was it your first visit to France?"

"Yes, it was. An interesting month," he answered noncommittally.

Rebecca was not to be put off again, and questioned him further about Paris. His answers, although civil, were somehow evasive, as though talking of France had brought something else to his mind. Rebecca felt her annoyance growing as they strolled past the rotunda and on back along a more deserted path.

Suddenly before them a flash of pale green skirt showed at the opening of a side path, and within moments they could see Miss Jenkins walking on the arm of the Honorable Mr. West. Rebecca watched the retreating figures throughtfully.

"Ah, Miss Jenkins," she murmured, and felt the tall figure beside her stiffen. Driven by some devil on her shoulder, she continued. "You are acquainted with Miss Jenkins, I believe."

"I am acquainted with Miss Jenkins." Gordon Meade's voice was so low Rebecca had to strain to hear it. Was it anger or laughter he was suppressing? What an irritating man.

The couple disappeared around a bend and Rebecca moved to lean on a tall tree near the path. "Of course. She comes from New York also, does she not?"

"She does," was the curt reply, delivered in the same low voice. The man was standing directly before her now, and she couldn't make out the expression on his face. She sensed, though, that she had gone too far. Aunt Honoria was right; one day her tongue would get the better of her.

Her fan fluttered in her hand, and she tried a small pout. "You are looking very forbidding again. I . . . I think I have offended you somehow," she said rather breathlessly. "I beg your pardon."

He was nearer now, one arm propping him negligently against the tree as he looked down. An unreadable smile curved the corners of his mouth. "Come, Miss Blair, do not disappoint me and hide behind a fatuous facade of coyness. I am fully aware that a story of my past dealings with Miss Jenkins has made the rounds of the ladies' salons in London. You were going to ask me more questions, I believe."

Rebecca's head went up at that. "I was not, Mr. Meade. And I do not know what is being said in the ladies' salons. I heard from Harlcourt just tonight that you have been disappointed by Miss Jenkins, and it was very rude of me to mention her at all. I apologize."

A look of surprise crossed his face, but the unreadable

smile returned in a flash. "Now what, I wonder, prompted that speech?"

"Honesty, Mr. Meade."

There was a soft chuckle as the blond head drew closer, and Rebecca thought that if this was the sort of conversation that would make Gordon Meade smile, his sense of humor was sadly misplaced.

His voice was lazy as he watched her upturned face. "Now *that* is a novel notion, Miss Blair, since I have never yet met a woman of honesty."

"What a very rude thing to say, even if I did deserve it. And I'm sure it is quite untrue," she stated, trying to keep her voice level. The American's nearness was beginning to seem threatening, and Rebecca felt she had put herself at a distinct disadvantage. She pulled herself upright, assuming a haughty air. "I think we have both said more than enough."

"Indeed." Large hands grasped her shoulders, leaning her gently back against the tree again. "We didn't really come down this path for conversation, did we?"

Trying not to gasp at the small stab of fright that went through her, Rebecca attempted to meet his eyes. "You are impertinent, sir."

"Of course. What did you expect from a provincial?" The low chuckle was there again, and Rebecca raised her fan, but her wrist was caught and suddenly his mouth was on hers. Never had a man dared to kiss her on the lips before, and she was so surprised she was still for a moment, wondering at the experience. But then his arms were around her, and the kiss became searching, demanding.

Her moment of wonder gave way to fright, and Rebecca pushed at his broad chest. The man raised his head. "Don't tell me you are surprised, Miss Blair," he said with a sneering note in his voice. "Something of the sort was expected of me, I felt sure." The strong arms drew her forward a fraction.

She tugged back. "You are a . . . a . . . monster," she hissed.

"Is that your response to every man who succumbs to your charms, Miss Blair?"

Never having been taken so literally on her flirting before, she was at a loss for words. And he was laughing at her, making his conduct twice as insufferable. A small voice in the back of her mind said she'd no one to blame but herself for her predicament, but she ignored the voice. Looking wildly over the broad shoulders that seemed to surround her, she saw they were completely alone. Even the muted sounds of the ensemble in the rotunda seemed very far away. His arms grew tighter, and she struggled silently, trying to think of something cutting to say to make him let go.

"No matter," his low voice went on before she could speak. "I am no different from all those admiring dandies who surround you—just perhaps more willing to respond to an invitation."

"To take advantage, you mean," she gasped, and tried to twist away in earnest, but long fingers pulled her chin around and bruising lips were on hers once more. It must be fright and anger that gave her the heady feeling, she thought, and wondered if her ribs would snap under the force of his embrace. When she felt his fingers move to caress the exposed skin of her breasts, she trembled with strange sensations, and almost she returned his kiss. But then she saw his thin smile as he raised his head and a new fury swept over her. With more strength than she knew she possessed, she shoved him away.

Holding herself very straight, she found her voice at last. "If that is the way you treated Miss Jenkins, it is no wonder she fled to a more civilized country," she said in her coldest tones.

There was a moment's charged silence, when Rebecca wondered if he was now going to hit her and thereby cap his crimes. But a lazy smile crossed his dim features. "Don't tell me Harlcourt has not yet shown you his perfectly good red blood? Nor any of the others?"

Rebecca turned away with a swish of her wide skirts. "Lord Harlcourt," she said icily, "is a *gentleman*."

"And I am not. But I find it hard to believe that your beauty has not driven some man to distracted behavior before this. No," and his voice changed to a soft tone of command, "it will not do, Miss Blair, to have you flounce up the terrace steps by yourself now."

Rebecca was walking as fast as she could, fighting down the color she knew to be in her face. "I have no need of your escort, sir," she flung over one shoulder.

"Nonetheless, you will suffer it until we reach the ballroom." A hand caught her arm, abruptly halting her headlong flight. She tried to jerk away, but found herself in a viselike grip, as slowly he paced down the path.

The tense silence lengthened between them, and Gordon Meade watched the girl. So outraged she was now, and yet she'd asked for it, had teased, taunted, flirted shamelessly. What's more, she'd not altogether disliked being kissed. Beneath her haughty air, there was passion, he was sure. If only she'd already been married, things would be a great deal easier. He wondered if she were still a virgin and decided she probably was. That complicated things. However, there were still possibilities. . . .

At the foot of the terrace steps he released her arm and watched with approval as she set a smile on her mouth and put her head high in the air.

Sedately, Rebecca moved across the flagstones at his side. She hoped they looked for all the world like a couple returning from a refreshing and leisurely stroll. But she knew not all eyes would be deceived, and her head began to pound with the effort of holding her anger in check. How dare this provincial lout touch her, she thought stormily, trying to forget the quick thrill she'd felt when first his hands had held her and his mouth had touched hers. He had taken advantage, had passed all bounds of propriety, and had sneered at her into the bargain.

When they reached the door she was practically trembling with fury, but her smile was still in place. "I wish your barbarous country well of you," she said between clenched teeth. "Certainly it will be a pleasure to hear of your return there."

"Well done." The low voice held a hint of amusement.

Flashing a venomous look at his face, Rebecca saw his mouth was lifted on one side and a matching brow was cocked at her. She could have stamped her foot if they'd been alone. Instead, all she could do was raise a shoulder as she turned her back on him.

A smooth voice stopped her as she crossed the threshold. "Can't monopolize Miss Blair all night, Meade. Others must have their turn to enjoy her dazzling company." Warren Tyson, the other American, stood at her elbow. For an instant she thought she could sense an antagonism between the two men, a locking of their eyes, a tension.

Then Gordon Meade was bowing punctiliously. "All's fair . . ." he murmured, and moved off.

Forcing a glittering smile for Mr. Tyson, Rebecca concentrated on keeping her hand from shaking as she took the sinewy arm offered her. She was aware of the fascinated stares all around her, but she ignored them. Surely her face was not so flushed she showed her agitation? And she would not give that dreadful man, whose eyes she could feel still on her, any reason to be satisfied with the underhanded game he had played.

"Your stroll with Gordon was not altogether successful?" Warren Tyson's black eyes looked down on her with compassion, and with a hint of satisfaction, she thought.

"On the contrary," she managed to say lightly, "it was very pleasant."

"Come, Miss Blair. I could see the signs. But never mind. Gordon is chafing at his protracted stay away from home." The soft voice became more intimate. "I, on the other hand, find London utterly fascinating."

Rebecca smiled mechanically, and said something about the need for refreshment. Mr. Tyson had no choice but to go for a glass, and she took a waspish delight in eluding him from that moment on. She wanted nothing to do with *any* American now.

The evening, never very promising, was ruined beyond repair, and Rebecca found she actually welcomed her aunt's signal to leave. Practically running from the ballroom, she caught a fleeting glimpse of Mr. Tyson, his thin features still suffused with annoyance, and felt a small twinge of guilt. But the feeling turned instantly to renewed anger as she spied Mr. Meade beyond, his face a sardonic mask. She wished she could slap it in passing.

Chapter 3

At a late breakfast the next morning Rebecca discovered that her transgressions of the night before, and her embarrassing encounter with the big American were not to be put behind her quite yet. Her father, heavy-eyed and scowling, greeted her rather perfunctorily, and when the servants had left the room he went straight to the heart of the matter with no ado at all.

"Your aunt tells me you were cutting up at Lady Spefton's last night," he began, glowering across his steaming coffee cup.

Rebecca regarded him in silence for several seconds. Long ago she had learned from her mother that the best way to handle Papa when he was in one of his gouty moods was to smile sweetly and say as little as possible. "Oh dear," she answered at last, "Aunt Honoria must have caught you as you came in last night. Did she bend your ear dreadfully?"

"Read me a terrific scold, is what she did. And quite right she was, too. Can't have you throwing your cap over the windmill for some ne'er-do-well like Thorpe. And if you think to bring young Harlcourt up to snuff, let me tell you others have tried before you with no success. Besides, the old viscount didn't leave him sufficiently flush in the pockets to maintain his style, and he'll hang out for an heiress, you mark my words." He leaned back then. "So you'd best make yourself agreeable to some of your more eligible suitors and take your pick of one of them."

Rebecca, sitting with hands folded in the lap of her pale blue morning gown, stole a look at him from beneath curled lashes. "Would you prefer me to encourage Baron Willingsworth?"

"That lump of mutton? I should think not, Becky." For a moment, her father's bluff good humor threatened to break through, but then the scowl returned. "There are plenty of others from all I've heard. Season's nearly over, so you haven't much time left, girl."

Rebecca drew a long breath. "There are still two weeks to go, and then there are the summer house parties and our stay at Bath. And of course the short season in the fall. Surely you will give me that long, Papa."

Mr. Blair peered through blurred eyes at his lovely daughter. Fetching thing she was now. As lovely as his darling Lavinia had been at that age. Could have her pick of nearly anyone on the town. What the devil was the matter with her? He pushed down the stab of pain at the thought of his dead wife, and when he raised his eyes again, his face softened. "See you're married by Christmas, kitten, or we'll both be in this soup with your aunt forever. I haven't the blunt to stand you another season in town, you know."

Rebecca swallowed the question that would have turned the conversation. She'd been going to ask how his evening had gone, but she knew already from his foul mood that he had lost heavily at the tables. Mentally, she consigned her new bonnet to the realm of dreams and smiled sweetly instead. "I'll try to do my best, Papa."

"Of course you will." Her father humphed and sat back. "But that don't include making up to a strange American."

Rebecca gulped. "There were two Americans, Papa. One of them is a cousin of Lord Harlcourt's. I could hardly snub them when they were presented."

"Snubbing them is one thing. Making a cake of yourself in the garden is another, my girl."

Rebecca flushed hotly. "Who said such a thing?"

"Only half of London, according to your aunt. She thinks you should hide your face for shame." His eyes glittered at that, but Rebecca didn't notice.

"Oooh."

"No, don't go into a pet, Becky." He regarded her thoughtfully for a moment. "Seems it really is time you were married. Need a steadying hand on the reins, I'm thinking. You'll require a real man, though." Rebecca stared at him mutinously, but held her tongue. And now his voice took on an almost reminiscent note. "Remember now that Harlcourt had a great-uncle who went off to the colonies over thirty years ago. Took the third viscount's sister as his bride, and killed her off there. But he did well financially, I believe." His eyes regarded her sternly. "This young American will be going back to the colonies some time, so you turn your eyes closer to home."

On that score Rebecca could reassure him with fervor, and her father seemed satisfied. Shortly he took himself off, and Rebecca was left to finish her cold breakfast alone, and to ponder the peculiarities of a fate that would send her a clutch of empty-headed or ineligible young men as suitors in her first season out, and then, after boring her for months, send her a completely odious man to ruin one of the last parties of the spring. Now here was her father insisting she marry *someone* within the next six months. She put her cup of chocolate down. Six months to find a man who didn't irritate her. And the trouble was that the only amusing men she knew were not approved by her interfering aunt. Well, at least the prospect of marriage held some consolation. If married, she could run her own household, could dress as she pleased and see whomever she wanted without the constant censure of her aunt and the old cats who were her friends. She slapped her napkin on the table. She could even choose her own lovers, she thought wickedly, and smiled, not quite certain what that meant, but cheered by the prospect. Then with a shake of her head she brought her thoughts back to practical matters. Since a new bonnet was clearly not in the offing, she'd better go upstairs and begin refurbishing the old straw-colored one.

Opening her bedroom door, she made for the wardrobe, then stopped in surprise. Sitting before her dressing table, boxes and bottles spread in confusion before her, was her cousin.

"Good morning," Rebecca said, knowing without asking what Lettitia was doing here.

"Oh." The thin face turned with a look of calculated thought. "The light is so much better in your room, Becky. I knew you wouldn't mind if I worked in here for a while. Besides, it gives us a chance to discuss the ball." Lettitia's brown curls wagged as she smiled coyly and returned to the contemplation of the array on the table top. "I really don't know if this new cream is going to do all Mademoiselle Hivert claimed. What do you think?"

Rebecca crossed the room and stood behind her cousin, looking at the painted visage in her mirror. "It looks like chalk, Letty. You've a perfectly lovely complexion under that white mud you insist on applying."

"It's not pale enough." The girl pouted, inspecting the caked mass on her face. "You could use some yourself, cousin. You really shouldn't look so—so *healthy,* you know."

"I can't bring myself to put that stuff on me, Letty." Besides, she thought, she rather liked the healthy glow of her own skin, even if it did make her different, or perhaps, she reflected, *because* it made her different. She moved to the side and watched as Letty fingered her patch box, taking out first a tiny black heart shape and then a star.

"I was thinking that perhaps I could try two patches tonight at Vauxhall," Letty said happily, planting the little pieces beside her narrow mouth and near her nose.

"You don't need two. And no, Letty, don't try any more of that lamp black on your eyes. You know it makes them red."

"I don't have black lashes like you, Becky." The small mouth pouted into the mirror.

"You have perfectly nice eyes. Making them red with that blacking doesn't enhance them, I promise."

"It isn't the blacking. I'm convinced it's the candle fumes at the parties that makes my eyes stream."

Rebecca turned away, unable to watch her cousin's experiments any longer. "Perhaps you're right, Letty. By the way, what are you planning to wear tonight?"

"The pale rose, I think." Lettitia's words were barely audible, muffled by her hands working over her eyes.

Rebecca relegated her own deeper rose gown, which she had thought to wear, to the back of the wardrobe, and considered the sea green with an overskirt of white netting. "That will be nice," she answered automatically, and went to find the straw-colored bonnet with fresh resolve to work on it.

There were no callers that morning, a cruel blow about which Lettitia never ceased complaining. That and the fact that Rebecca was churlish enough to refuse a juicy discussion of the Spefton's ball, made the girl quite cross, and by luncheon, Rebecca, who was heartily bored, was glad that the act of putting food in her mouth must stop her cousin's flow of empty chatter and complaint.

It was with a sense of considerable relief that Rebecca saw her aunt and cousin retire to their rooms after the meal. For once she could be on her own for an hour. A brisk walk was what she needed. Finding her maid Sylvie in her room brushing out her clothes, she dragged the girl with her downstairs.

Sylvie had come to London only two months ago to replace old Anna as Rebecca's maid. And never having been far from the shelter of her home at Blair Hall, the girl was still agog at the sights of London and mystified by the belowstairs tales of the people in the metropolis. She was a lively, pretty girl who had grown up with Rebecca at the hall, had even occasionally shared her schoolroom. She had a quick mind and an independent spirit, and she and Rebecca were sincerely attached to each other. All of which made Aunt Honoria thoroughly disapprove, but despite her objections, Mr. Blair had not allowed his domineering sister to send the girl home, and Rebecca had never ceased to be grateful to him for that.

Outside the house she allowed Sylvie to walk beside her, instead of a decorous pace behind. The girl's happy chatter was soothing after a morning with her cousin's snide tongue.

As the two young women prepared to cross Berkeley Square for the second time, Sylvie gave a tug to Rebecca's parasol dangling from one gloved hand. "Will you look at them, miss. The gentlemen across the way." She nodded toward one end of the block. "About the finest young gentlemen I've seen anywhere. Except Lord Harlcourt, perhaps."

Rebecca disengaged her parasol gently and glanced surreptitiously down the square. Strolling easily around the corner were Mr. Meade and Mr. Tyson. Their nearly identical outfits of gleaming boots, fawn-colored breeches and dark coats made them look all the more striking for their differences in coloring.

"I don't know about that," Rebecca answered curtly.

At that instant, distant blue eyes widened and met hers. A corner of the mobile mouth lifted as a slender walking stick came up in quick salute. Abruptly, Rebecca swung her skirts in the opposite direction. "It's time we went in, Sylvie. I must think what to wear riding in the park this afternoon."

Without a backward glance, she fled for the shelter of her own doorway, leaving an open-mouthed Sylvie to keep up as best she could. Not for anything would Rebecca acknowledge Gordon Meade after his behavior of the evening before. There had been not a sign of regret on his face, either, the insufferable brute. With a hand to her mouth, she entered the house, suddenly able to feel bruising lips on hers once more. A mocking smile on a tanned face swam before her eyes, making her pound the parasol on the floor in anger. How dare he enter Berkeley Square at this hour and ruin her one peaceful time! She went up the stairs in a black mood, and threw herself with determination into the contemplation of her wardrobe.

Promptly at five o'clock Lord Harlcourt's dashing equipage was seen pulling up before the marble facade of Blair House, and Rebecca took a hasty farewell of her aunt and cousin. She knew his lordship would not have the horses stand for long while she made her toilette, and so was ready in the hall when the butler opened the door.

To her shock it was Gordon Meade who entered the house first, and his face was more frowning than ever as he bowed. She was on the point of telling him to go away when she spied Lord Harlcourt behind him. The viscount looked as though he'd been landed a hard blow to his stomach, and unaccountably, he was followed by the two grooms who had accompanied Mr. Blair to the races that morning. Rebecca backed a step instinctively as the procession entered the hall and Mr. Meade dismissed the butler. She looked uncertainly at the viscount, trying to ignore the others.

"Is your aunt at home, Miss Blair?" He nodded toward the door of the saloon she had just left.

Suddenly frightened, though she didn't know why, Rebecca nodded wordlessly and preceded the men into the room.

Confusion reigned as Aunt Honoria, flustered by unexpected visitors and the presence of two stable grooms, began to talk in a high-pitched whine, and Letty, appalled at having gentlemen see her without her full "face," tried to scold Rebecca sotto voce.

It took a moment for quiet to be restored as Mr. Meade tactfully led the ladies to chairs and returned to push Rebecca gently onto a gilded bench. She started to brush away his hand, but her attention was caught by Lord Harlcourt who coughed miserably.

In a sepulchral voice, the viscount addressed the room at

large. "I fear there has been an accident." He coughed again and tried to avoid Rebecca's suddenly wide eyes.

"Papa," she breathed. "Something's happened to my father! Where is he?"

At that Lord Harlcourt dropped to one knee beside her and gripped her hand. "Miss Blair . . . compose yourself. I fear we have the most dreadful news."

One terrible shudder racked the girl's frame, then with an awful calm she demanded that he go on. Vaguely, she was aware that Gordon Meade had both hands on her shoulders now, holding her steady. But from that moment things became a blur for her.

The inescapable, central and devastating fact was clear. Her father was dead. The stuttered testimony of the grooms, the hysterical outbursts of her aunt, the distracted murmurs of Lord Harlcourt, nothing could change that fact. There had been a collision with a posting chaise, her father had been thrown from the seat of his curricle and had been crushed beneath the vehicle when it overturned. That was the fact she must digest, must contemplate, must learn to live with.

When strong arms lifted her to her feet, she found herself reassuring everyone in the room, dismissing the grooms with thanks for their aid, requesting that her father's man of affairs be sent for. And soon she could stand on her own, pat her aunt, soothe Letty. Aware now of her own calm, but unaware of what she was saying, she ushered the gentlemen out of the house. And not once in all that time did she see Gordon Meade's face. He was gone as silently as he had arrived, and she had only dim memory of his powerful support through the initial shock of the news. Briefly she wondered why he had come with Harlcourt and remained to stand by them all through the horrible first minutes. His manner was so different from that of last night, she would have been bewildered if the whole question weren't fogged by her grief.

It wasn't until much later that, alone in her room after the first great storm of tears, she was able to really face the news fully. And then she acknowledged how glad Papa must be to have found a way to be with his lost wife again. He'd not been the same since Mama's death nearly five years ago, and she knew it was his grief as much as his antipathy for his carping sister that had driven him to the gaming tables and races every day. She mustn't feel sorry for *him* now. But he'd left her a legacy of a new and frightening reality, and what was to happen to her she didn't want to imagine. Exhausted and inexpressably lonely that night, she fell on her bed without undressing and slept.

The following day did not improve anything, she found, for her aunt, after a great deal of hand wringing and wailing, began to bemoan the loss of their one full London season, and to wonder how either girl in her charge would ever find a suitable husband. "You must realize that we now have to cancel all plans, regret all invitations, bury ourselves in black for poor Geoffrey." She sighed on Rebecca's shoulder. "And dear Annabelle Lofton's ball just a week away, too."

Rebecca, still nearly numb with shock and unable to share her aunt's former delight in the prospect of Mrs. Lofton's ball anyway, found it difficult to make sympathetic noises. Silently, she noted the fact that the main topic of conversation that morning was the lost season, not her lost father, and she felt her resentment of her aunt and cousin grow. Mounting the stairs on wooden feet after breakfast, she left orders that she was not to be disturbed until her father's man of affairs called.

The interview with that gentleman was not heartening. Mr. Bancroft, who had coped with her father's vagaries and extravagances for over thirty years, was unwilling to hazard a guess as to the state of Mr. Blair's affairs. He saw no reason to alarm a mourning daughter, and determined, after one look at the moist violet eyes of the beautiful Miss Blair, to put off any debts and unpleasantness for as long as possible. He took onto himself the arrangements necessary and agreed to have all bills sent directly to him, all the while wondering privately where the money to pay them would come from.

"You have not, perhaps, been able to think what you and the other ladies will be doing this summer," he said at last, glad to have the more sorrowful details behind them, but wondering how he would convince the household to remove to the country.

"I have thought of what we are to do," Rebecca answered in a voice so soft that Mr. Bancroft had to lean forward to hear her. "The season is nearly over anyway, and staying here would only remind my aunt of all that we must now miss. It would seem wisest, wouldn't it, to go to Blair Hall for the summer, and perhaps for longer."

Mr. Bancroft swallowed his sigh of relief. "Very wise, Miss

Blair. Very wise. And you may be assured that I will make all arrangements on that score. I think, too, that it might be best for me to accompany you on your removal, to see that all is in order at the Hall." And to see for myself what economies might be made there, he thought.

Rebecca accepted his offers gratefully, and ended the interview feeling vaguely better now that Mr. Bancroft had entered the picture to stand beside her.

Aunt Honoria and Letty were practically prostrated by the prospect of having to return to Blair Hall, and it took all of Rebecca's fortitude to explain patiently that the delights of the season were shut to them now anyway, that other people would soon be leaving town too. She didn't want to discuss her fears about her father's financial affairs with her grasping aunt, but she found herself forced to hint that they were rather flat in the pocket just now and that removal to the country and the consequent shutting of the townhouse would ease financial burdens. Aunt Honoria, a gleam of dim understanding in her eyes, acquiesced after this, obviously hoping that by pinching pennies now, there would be enough money to reopen the house in the new year.

Letty was not so easily consoled. She didn't dare rant against Uncle Geoffrey's thoughtlessness at getting himself killed during her first season out, but she moped and groaned and worried about her future until Rebecca, who had kept silent for four days, finally threatened to throttle her.

How Rebecca was to survive the removal to Blair Hall with those two she could hardly imagine, but in something of a fog she made decisions, ignored her relations as best she could, and prepared to go home.

Chapter 4

On the golden afternoon in June when the London party wound through a back lane in Berkshire, the only one who seemed to share Rebecca's joy in the sight of Blair Hall was her maid, Sylvie. As the big traveling coach rumbled up the tree-lined drive to the sprawling stone building, the wide-eyed girl grasped Rebecca's hand impulsively. "Oh, miss, it looks just as it always did."

Since Sylvie had been gone from the Hall only two months, the exclamation brought a smile to Rebecca's face for the first time that day. But a hollow feeling began to grow in the pit of her stomach as she realized that now her childhood home was to be shared with only Aunt Honoria and her fussy, complaining cousin Letty.

The sight of her old room, with its gay flowered wallpaper, the high four-poster bed, the walnut dressing table and marble fireplace was her first pleasure that evening, but she soon learned that there was to be little else that would remain as she had known it.

Aunt Honoria immediately began bustling through the house, issuing orders and turning everything upside down. Familiar rooms, cherished traditions, old haunts and easy familiarities were suddenly changed or overthrown. A new formality entered the Hall, and the servants were powerless before Honoria's onslaught. Rebecca recognized what was happening, but felt too alone and downcast to fight the older woman's assumption of authority, even if such a rash act were possible. Once Mr. Bancroft had left for London, she began to feel she was practically a stranger in her own home.

"There will be full livery on any servant inside the house, and more civilized hours maintained in the future," she heard her aunt say one day to a frightened group of servants in the high front hall. "And I will inspect each of the downstairs rooms myself each noon to see they have been properly cleaned."

Rebecca grimaced, thinking of the easy manners of her father and the comfortable life that had been maintained by the perfectly competent servants. She tried briefly to soften her aunt's attitude, but received such a withering look for her attempt that she retreated and said no more.

Her room was now her sanctuary and her lovely filly, Dancer, was her solace. She took to going for long rides through the parks and lanes, fighting to keep her thoughts from straying too far in either the future or the past. A deep grief for both her parents overwhelmed her these first days, and she wanted nothing more than to be alone. To this end, she was pleased to discover that the library was a room her relations avoided. It meant she had a full retreat to which she could escape in hours of need, and though her father's presence was everywhere around her in his comfortable old room, she somehow felt better there. The huge, time-worn desk, the cracked leather chairs, the baize-covered table and the portraits of portly gentlemen scattered among the high bookshelves had apparently earned her aunt's scorn, for she did nothing to disturb the room, and for that small favor Rebecca was endlessly grateful. It was here that she discovered her grief for her parents began to be shot through with a thread of resentment for their leaving her, for abandoning her to the relentless presence of her aunt and cousin. But nothing was going to change her fate for the time being, and she sought only what peace she could find.

As the days grew longer, the soft balm of the country life enveloped Rebecca in a kind of cocoon of retreat. The household settled into a routine unbroken by anything more than the occasional visit of neighbors or outings to church. Although Letty complained of boredom, Rebecca found her life soothing, so soothing she moved through the days unaware of the passage of time, only faintly realizing that her grief was lessening and her interest in the doings of her father's estate was growing slowly. But it wasn't until the first nip of fall was in the air that she began to wonder what was to become of them all. She had not seen Mr. Bancroft in nearly two months now, so knew no more about the financial position they were to find themselves in, and some day they would have to know.

In late August, Lord Harlcourt stopped with a group on its way to London from a week in Wiltshire. Dashing as ever, the viscount was gallant to Rebecca but the girl thought she detected a shade of reserve in his manner, and feared that rumors of her probably sad financial condition must already be circulating. She was conscious of disappointment at the thought, and wondered how much Harlcourt would be swayed by her plight. Surely his interest was deeper than mere money. His presence here must indicate that much. She hesitated to admit even to herself how glad she was to see him, but found she wished she didn't have to wear only dark colors in his presence. Sadly she hoped that it was only Harlcourt's natural tact that held him aloof at present, that kept his conversation from straying from the mundane.

Even when they walked alone in the gardens one evening, the man maintained only the lightest chatter about inconsequential things. Rebecca was beginning to feel it would be better if he left soon, and found her mind wandering from their talk until the viscount said, "Cousin left us last month, you know. I was sorry to see him go, really, but there was nothing for it. He was bent on getting home once news came in June of the rabble in Boston making trouble with our troops."

Rebecca's thoughts jumped back from the brightly colored flower borders along their path. She had heard something about rebellious colonists fighting the king's troops near Boston, and more recently of the blockade a ragtag army had thrown around that city to bottle up the Crown's soldiers in the town. "Your cousin, Harlcourt, didn't come from Massachusetts. Why would he leave England because of a minor insurrection in another colony?"

"Exactly, Miss Blair. Silly way to go on, if you ask me. Though, just between us, I think he'd finally come around to the realization that Miss Jenkins was going on famously without him and had no intention of returning to his country. However, he talked a lot of fustian about a widespread rebellion and about being needed at home. I tried to assure him

38

that with the arrival of our generals Howe, Clinton and Burgoyne, General Gage was going to have sufficient reinforcements to stop this ridiculous play-acting in Massachusetts, and he'd arrive home too late to watch the finish of it all. Not a word of it would he have, though. Gave me a great scold about taxes and quartering of troops and other such nonsense. I don't mind admitting I grew heartily bored with it all." The viscount sighed. "But I do miss him. Good sort, he was. A support in several crises. Lent me money once, and came along that dreadful day we learned of your father." He shook his head. "Pity he had to return."

Rebecca remembered now the support Gordon Meade had given to all of them that day in London, but she didn't want to dredge up memories. As for Lord Harlcourt's sorrow in seeing his cousin depart, she was not sure she could agree, so kept silent. Unbidden, her mind conjured a picture of sunlight on a tan face in Berkeley Square, but the event seemed so very long ago that she could barely bring the picture into focus. No, she was not sorry Gordon Meade was gone from England. She was too preoccupied with what her immediate future held to care about people she'd never see again, so this latest piece of news from the viscount carried no more weight with her than any other she'd received from friends during the summer. Her entire past life seemed far behind her at the moment, and she could not muster sorrow for most of it. She could only hope, now, that Vincent would be waiting when she came out of mourning.

However, when the trees began to shed their leaves and the fall air made for brisk walking, Rebecca tried to bring the future into focus. She knew she had a long winter to endure here with her aunt and cousin, but what was to happen after that? Mr. Bancroft's hints at the time of her father's death had left her feeling vaguely that there might not be the money to set themselves up comfortably in London in the spring. And she now supposed that she had better find out just where they stood. Reluctantly, she determined to write to Mr. Bancroft and request him to come back to Berkshire to call on her. But before she could bring herself to send her missive, the aging man of affairs presented himself at Blair Hall, and the morning after his arrival, requested an interview with Miss Blair in the room of her choice.

Having a vague premonition that this interview was not going to be cheerful, she ordered refreshments to be brought to the library and shut the door firmly on the eager face of her aunt passing in the hall. Her father's man of affairs was in considerable agitation when she finally turned into the room and went to take one of the high wing chairs near the fireplace. He managed to seat himself across from her, but looked as though he'd leap like a startled hare at the first noise.

"I gather, Mr. Bancroft, that you now have a much better notion of the state of my father's affairs," Rebecca began in a soothing voice, trying to quell the nervousness she felt. The man's balding pate bobbed, and he opened his mouth, then shut it again and opened it once more. Rather like a large fish, she thought.

"Miss Blair," he croaked at last. "I have the unhappy duty of informing you that all is not as we would wish in regard to finances." His voice trailed away on something like a gurgle.

Rebecca nodded. "I thought as much." She felt that now he'd begun he would calm himself, and she found her own nerves steadying. "Won't you have a glass of wine? And then perhaps we can go over all your figures."

Mr. Bancroft looked for a moment as though her words had undone the last of his composure, but he braced himself and poured from the decanter at his elbow. After a hasty swallow he began to withdraw papers from the leather case on the floor. "Ahem. I don't know that you want to see all the details, Miss Blair, so I shall try to sort these." His small hands riffled through the sheets.

"On the contrary, Mr. Bancroft, I think I'd best see everything. I've had our overseer bring me Father's books on the estate recently, and at last all those columns and notations are beginning to make sense to me. So if I look at your figures your words will have more meaning."

"But no lady . . ."

"Few ladies find themselves in just my position, do they, Mr. Bancroft? But I assure you I am not lacking in understanding."

"No, of course not." Mr. Bancroft cleared his throat, thinking those violet eyes were suddenly older and sharper than he'd remembered. He spread out books and sheets on the worn desk and they went over them together.

The picture his careful columns revealed was not heartening. It became apparent that Mr. Bancroft had sold odds and ends whenever he could to keep creditors at bay, but that they must now face the fact that her father had left huge debts. Rebecca had known for some time that the Blairs lived beyond their means, but this last season in London at the gaming houses had been the ruin of everything. The extra carriage and two of the horses had gone from the London stables, several servants had been discharged and the bit of money her father had salvaged in the exchange had been withdrawn to pay gambling debts. But there were always more.

Rebecca sat down in her father's cracking leather chair with a thump. "What do we do now?" she asked, her voice steadier than she'd thought possible.

Mr. Bancroft straightened and ran his hand through the fringe of hair above his ears. "We must decide what else may be sold," he said.

"What of mother's portion?"

The elderly man spread his hands in a gesture of despair. "Long gone, Miss Blair."

"I see." Rebecca sat still for a moment. "Then you are saying that we must sell the townhouse."

Mr. Bancroft looked, if possible, even more miserable. He too, sat down with a thump. "I am not convinced that it will bring enough to turn us around," he said at last.

Rebecca's eyes widened. She went back to his sheets and studied them for some time before raising her head slowly. "You are convinced that only the sale of Blair Hall and its dependencies will cover the debts?" she asked then, her voice even.

"I am afraid that is the conclusion I have reached. However, there may be a way of selling some of the land, perhaps a few of the horses, along with everything in London."

The girl turned her chair to stare out the tall window behind her. The morning sun bathed bushes and flower beds with a brilliant light, and the park beyond stood out with amazing autumnal clarity against the backdrop of thick woods beyond. She felt her heart beating faster and swallowed hard to clear the lump rising in her throat. With a jerk she pulled her mind back to the figures on the desk, and briskly she began doing mental calculations of the worth of stables and land around Blair, glad that she'd spent those long hours over the estate books.

"No," she said finally, "we would have to sell everything but the house to clear enough money, and then would be left with no income on which to live. But if the entire estate is sold it will bring a great deal more than the townhouse ever could. We are lucky, I suppose that the estates are not entailed, that there is no cousin to inherit. But I feel we shall have to discuss all this with my aunt. Father took her in last year, you know, and he promised she would be provided for. She has a small income of her own, but I believe it is not sufficient to see to more than her personal needs." She was quite sure she already knew what her aunt's sentiments would be. She was going to be trapped in this inevitable decision.

Mr. Bancroft nodded. "That was the understanding I had from your father." He stared at the slender girl sitting so straight behind the desk and wondered at his own cowardice at coming here. He'd expected hysterics, or at the very least, a great deal of hand wringing, and had not relished the prospect of facing it. But he found himself now wishing Geoffrey Blair had shown half the sense and fortitude of his daughter. This whole mess would not have had to descend on her if he had.

It was hardly a gay time at Blair Hall after that morning interview, but Rebecca found that, now she knew the worst, her spirits actually revived. She had problems to solve, things to think about, hurdles to overcome, and at last she began to shake off her summer lassitude.

She'd been right in her assessment of her aunt; Honoria Carlsby would prefer to live in London at any time, and she obviously saw their present difficulties as a kind of godsend. As far as she was concerned, the sooner the Hall was sold and money freed for their comfort in London the better.

So the following afternoon Rebecca closeted herself once more with Mr. Bancroft and began the heart-rending business of deciding just what must go. It was hard to start, but once into it, she discovered that of necessity, she could harden her heart and contemplate her losses with resignation.

"The furniture in the London house blue saloon was never well-loved," she stated at one point, ideas coming thick and fast now, "so I suggest we sell all of it to clear room for some of our best pieces here. I think, too, that the paintings in the dining room are rather valuable, and so must go. We can replace them with some from the Hall."

Mr. Bancroft made lists with a sense of wonder, and heartily approved all of Miss Blair's decisions.

"Also, I would sell everything in the stables in London except the bay team. I shall bring my Dancer into town, and that is all that will be needed. Letty prefers not to ride, and Aunt Honoria won't go within ten feet of a horse except when necessity demands. That's a great deal of good horseflesh to pay most of father's gambling debts. The furniture should pay his clothiers. And the great sums he borrowed will be handled by Blair Hall and its land. Will that leave us enough to maintain the London house?"

Mr. Bancroft thought it would, but he would have to reach town and discover just what values were. And at the end of two days he heaved a sigh of both sorrow and relief before departing with fervent thanks to Miss Blair.

For the next week Rebecca's head was so full of the drastic plans, she didn't at first notice how much more cheerful her aunt and cousin had become. The prospect of quitting the country, perhaps for good, had obviously restored what good humor the two women possessed, and when this fact was finally borne home to the girl, she decided at least *something* good had come of the difficult decisions she and Mr. Bancroft had made. Though she found, when she began to explain to Aunt Honoria the economies they were practicing, there was a deal of resistance to some of the measures. It was one thing to leave the country and settle permanently in London. It was quite another, the woman pointed out forcefully, to return to town in much reduced circumstances. She was opposed to the sale of furniture from the London house, upset at the thought of maintaining only one team of horses in the stables, furious at the prospective loss of two paintings she had particularly liked. Very soon Rebecca learned not to discuss anything more than necessary with her aunt. But it was not always easy.

"The holidays will be hard for all of us this year," Aunt Honoria said in a doomed voice one afternoon as the three women sat by the fire in the small saloon behind the main hall. "We can't, of course, have the usual festivities here at the Hall, and that will be sad for the tenants too, don't you think, niece?"

Rebecca, who was working dutifully on a piece of tapestry, was glad of the excuse to put it down. "I think Papa would want us to observe customs with the servants and tenants, Aunt. But it is true we won't be able to maintain the usual spirit to which Blair has been accustomed." Her words were automatic, her mind more on the thought that the hard Elizabethan chairs they were sitting on might bring a fair price at auction.

"Yes, I'm sure you're right, dear. But I wonder if some time before the actual holidays arrive we might invite just a few guests for a quiet week with us. I'm sure it would be unexceptionable for us to do so."

Her aunt's tone was so carefully warm that Rebecca was now alert. "I can't think who would want to leave London at this time of year to join us in mourning in the country, Aunt."

"Old friends would understand, dear. We could not provide great entertainment. But gentlemen might go hunting, and I'm sure there are one or two ladies who would welcome the chance to rest for a few days."

Rebecca eyed her aunt sharply. It was unlike the woman to suggest that she put herself out in any way unless there was to be some reward. Could she be thinking that an invitation in November might bring return visits in the spring? Surely that was a bit farfetched. "Did you have someone particular in mind, Aunt?"

"Only a thought or two, dear. Perhaps dear Annabelle. And then we would want some gentlemen to balance things." She tittered unbecomingly. "I had tried to think of decorous souls who would understand our position. Baron Willingsworth would fill the bill nicely, don't you think?" She looked at her daughter, seeking support.

"Oh, yes, Mama. And perhaps Mr. Moorehouse." Letty looked brightly at Rebecca. "And there is Caroline Griscomb. She and her brother would be a good pair." Her cousin's eyes snapped once and Letty flushed, remembering now Rebecca's feelings about her good friend Caroline.

Rebecca sat straighter in her chair. She was beginning to understand the drift of her aunt's thoughts. Matchmaking was never far from the woman's mind, and she now hoped to keep prospects alive by reminding certain gentlemen of the existence of her two charges. Perhaps she thought that Rebecca, after months alone in the country, would find Baron Willingsworth a welcome diversion, and would begin to see his suit in a different light. One could take that thought even further, she realized. If the baron were to make an offer and be accepted, a wedding could be arranged in the summer after their full year of mourning, and then Aunt Honoria

44

would have the Blair townhouse to herself and could concentrate all her energies on getting Letty launched.

The girl shuddered, memory of the baron's clammy hands filling her with disgust, but she schooled her face to a look of smiling sorrow. "I doubt there's time to proffer invitations before the holidays now, Aunt. And you know we might hear from Mr. Bancroft any time. When we do, we will have to begin packing and selling things, and that would make too much turmoil for guests."

"Nonsense, Rebecca." Her aunt's tone had returned to its normal high pitch. "Nothing can be done about the sale of Blair at this time of year. We have been cooped up here for months on end, and it isn't fair. You must . . ." Aunt Honoria spluttered and stopped as her niece stood up, murmuring about arrangements for dinner, and glided from the room so swiftly that the woman was left openmouthed and with the annoying realization that once again her plans had gone awry.

Holding her aunt at bay added to the tension Rebecca felt as their period of waiting lengthened. Christmas was a depressing time, and she was amazed at how she got through it all, putting on a cheerful face for the servants, overseeing the disbursement of gifts and the special banquet for tenants and servants in the Hall.

Then came the dreary winter days when sometimes she could not even escape her thoughts and the presence of her only surviving relatives by riding across the fields and through the long-familiar lanes. Cooped up in the house with Letty and Aunt Honoria, with their sniffles and complaints and speculative gossip, there were times when she wondered how she would ever stand living the more confined life of London with them. Then she would remind herself sternly that she had already stood the unthinkable—the loss of her parents and the imminent loss of her beloved home—so it was likely that she could stand anything else she was called on to bear.

In mid-January came the news from Mr. Bancroft that the furniture and the paintings from the townhouse had been sold and a few debts paid. He now expected to be able to sell Blair Hall within the next months.

As spring struggled to come to Berkshire, several men of affairs were sent to look over the house and dependencies for prospective buyers, but Rebecca, leaden at the thought of losing Blair, managed to be away whenever they came. She could stand the reality of having to leave Blair, she found, but she could not sit by and watch the old place being catalogued and assessed by strangers. Nor could she bear the predatory gleam in her aunt's eyes as the woman went through the house, anticipating the removal of favored objects.

When Sylvie burst into tears one day as she was arranging flowers on Rebecca's dressing table, and admitted that she was weeping because the head groom, who had been courting her for two months, had proved faithless, Rebecca tried to be sage and consoling, though she knew there was nothing she could say to help. Even as she murmured over the shaking brown head, however, she felt a pang of sorrow for herself as well as for Sylvie. Her maid had a momentary disappointment, even heartbreak to struggle with. But when would her own difficulties and burdens ever end?

Chapter 5

"Rebecca, you *aren't* leaving behind the dining room table!" Aunt Honoria's horrified voice made Rebecca jump from her corner where she was packing books into a box.

Slowly the girl straightened, brushing stray tendrils of dank hair out of her eyes and wiping her hands on the broad apron she wore over her simplest black dress. Trying not to let impatience enter her voice, she regarded her aunt steadily. "I'm afraid we must, Aunt. The set that is in the dining room in London suits the room so much better than this massive table would."

"But your great-grandfather . . ."

"I know. But the table really fits the Hall better, don't you think? It should stay where it belongs." Wearily, Rebecca wondered if she would have to defend every one of her decisions. Already there were endless questions about each chair, each candlestand, each tapestry. She longed to point out to her aunt that the decisions were not hers to make and that she was finding it difficult enough without their endless carping. But she supposed that one couldn't talk to one's aging aunt that way, no matter how provoked one was.

Now, as her aunt read her another lecture on the value of family pieces, Rebecca stared stoically out the long window, murmuring politely when the woman drew breath, but hearing almost nothing. The world was so green, and the gardens had at last come to full springtime life. How she longed to go outside, instead of working here in the dust and dark of the far corners of the library. But there was so little time. Mr. Bancroft had said that the new owner wished to take possession of Blair by May first, and now that was only two weeks away.

"Well, I'm sure your dear mother would not at all approve your decision to leave behind her beautiful three-piece sideboard, either," Aunt Honoria was saying as she backed from the dusty room.

Rebecca nodded, and her aunt turned in the doorway with an audible humph. The brisk swish of skirts in the hall indicated she still despaired of setting her niece straight on the proper priorities.

The recalcitrant niece, meanwhile, had to physically stay her hand from hurling one of the books on the desk across the room. Tears started at the back of her eyes as she stared at the now empty doorway, and then down at the box of half-packed volumes. If Aunt Honoria and Letty would *help,* instead of going around badgering everyone and finding fault with everything, all of this might be more bearable. Angrily she brushed back the threatening tears. Much as she'd like to sit down and give full vent to her anger and despair, she simply did not have time.

The shadows were lengthening in the long room when at last she finished her task and stood looking at the half-empty shelves lining two walls. Dimly she was aware there had been voices in the main hall a moment ago. She hoped it was only the parson and that Aunt Honoria would have him in the drawing room so she could slip upstairs without being noticed. She was filthy from all her work and too tired to smile at the worthy man's platitudes this afternoon. So it was with a sense of disgust that she saw the butler's head appear in the doorway. Right behind him was Mr. Bancroft.

With obvious agitation the older man stepped past Meeks into the room. "Miss Blair, I'm so glad you are at home. Forgive me for interrupting you, but I have brought some startling news." He advanced across the room, and Rebecca backed a step.

"As you can see, Mr. Bancroft, I am in no fit state to receive you and dare not shake your hand." She waved vaguely at the box of books and then tried to tuck long strands of black hair back under the mob cap that was slipping down over one ear. The look on the butler's face was so ludicrous, she almost laughed. "Since we are already here, perhaps you could light some candles, Meeks, and then be so good as to bring us tea."

Shutting his gaping mouth firmly, the butler moved quickly to bring lights and then left as Mr. Bancroft proffered apologies once more. Rebecca waved them aside. After all, what did it matter that Mr. Bancroft saw her in this state? She was no longer the haughty, sought-after society belle he had known in London, could hardly even remember her former carefree life.

Hastily she discarded the big apron and went to take a seat at the central table. "Meeks will be back in a moment, and I can see that you would rather not wait to tell me your news. But I suspect I will receive it in better grace if I am seated." For only one heart beat of time she allowed herself to hope Blair was not to be sold after all.

Mr. Bancroft, running his fingers through wisps of hair in a familiar gesture, smiled ruefully and sat across from her. "I came as soon as I could because I have at long last heard from your uncle."

"My uncle?" Rebecca repeated stupidly, and a half-formed thought that Mr. Bancroft was getting too old crossed her mind.

"Your uncle in America."

The girl's head felt as though it were starting a slow spin, and she put her hands flat on the table top to steady herself. "My uncle," she gasped, then blinked hard, trying to focus a suddenly wavering vision. "Oh, my Lord," she said. "Uncle Julian."

Mr. Bancroft nodded brightly and reached out to pat one of her hands tentatively. "I felt sure you'd not thought of him, my dear. And since I did not know if he was even alive, I did not want to mention his name to you until I heard. I'm afraid I have shocked you, though."

"It is a surprise, yes. How odd that I've never once thought of him." She shook her head. "But you said you heard from him. How did you ever find him?"

Mr. Bancroft allowed a complacent smile to crease his face. "I feared my gesture might be futile, but I sent a letter to him in Massachusetts, the last address known for him a dozen years ago. He explains in his letter," and Mr. Bancroft groped in a file of papers on his lap, "that my communication might have been lost forever but that somehow it found its way into the hands of a man who had known him when he first entered the colonies, and who knew he had removed to New York. From there it traveled a tortuous journey to the banks of the Hudson."

"The Hudson?" Rebecca choked. That was the name of the river where Gordon Meade lived, she was sure. "How odd that I met a man only last spring who came from the Hudson River."

"Not so very odd, as I understand it. The Hudson is a very long river. Your uncle owns land not far north of New York City, near a place called Dobbs Ferry. He seems to have done as well as your father thought he would. But here—you must read for yourself." He unfolded two tightly written sheets and spread them on the table before her.

Rebecca looked down at the pages with blurred eyes. Slowly she smoothed them. "Uncle Julian," she breathed. Then looked up as Meeks brought in tea. "Will you pour please, Meeks?" She was suddenly unsure her hands were steady enough.

Mr. Bancroft sat down again. He looked rather like a cat with a cream pitcher, Rebecca thought, and turned her attention to the letter.

"Dear Mr. Bancroft," the cramped, well-formed writing began. "Yours of 30th May reached me only today, and I hasten to send my answer in fear I am already too late. I am, of course, devastated by the news of my brother-in-law's untimely death, and by the thought that my niece has been left nearly alone."

There was more about his recollections of Rebecca as a little girl, then there followed a complicated explanation for why Mr. Bancroft's letter had been so many months on its way to Uncle Julian, and a description of the state of affairs in the colonies. The letter was dated late in February, and at that time rebel troops were engaged in more fighting in Boston. However, people outside Massachusetts were confident General Howe would secure New York City, and would eventually subdue the rebel army from there. With the expectation that the colonial insurrection would be over by summer's beginning, Uncle Julian went on to say that he would like to propose that Rebecca come to him in his new home. "For some years ago I bought a handsome manor house above the banks of the Hudson River, and I find I have need of a hostess. I would like to think my niece would find pleasure in running the house and taking care of her old uncle."

Rebecca gasped as she read these last sentences, and looked up to see Mr. Bancroft sipping his tea still with that cat-in-the-cream-pitcher look on his face. With suddenly shaking hands she picked up the sheets and finished the letter in a daze. Uncle Julian went on to say that he realized Rebecca's own situation and plans might stand in the way of his idea, but he hoped Mr. Bancroft would present her with the notion. He could only assure them both that it was his dearest desire to see his niece once more, and to provide her with a home. In conclusion, he gave more information on how to reach him and stated he would meet any ship that might carry Rebecca to America. He remained hopeful, etc., etc.

At length Rebecca raised her head again and the dazed expression was still on her face.

Mr. Bancroft beamed across the table at her. "Well, my dear. What do you say to that?"

"I hardly know what to say. It's such a surprise. Dear Uncle Julian. Mother used to speak of him with such love. They were quite close, even though he was a great deal older than she. It is very kind of him to offer me a home this way, but I can't help but wonder if he had time to consider his words. He wrote the very day your letter arrived. I'm afraid this is a sweet, but impulsive gesture, and that already he may be regretting his offer."

"I doubt it, Miss Blair. He was always a most kind and generous man. I think you need have no fear on that score."

Rebecca stood up and paced to the long windows behind the great desk. The room was growing chilly without the midday sun, and she rubbed her arms as she stared sightlessly into the spreading shadows on the terrace and lawns. "We must write him quickly," she said without turning back. "Goodness knows how long the next letter will take to reach him, and he will be wondering. I could almost regret the fact that I cannot just disappear into the wilds of America now."

Mr. Bancroft put down his teacup very softly. "I thought you might say that at first, Miss Blair. But consider a moment."

"What is there to consider, Mr. Bancroft?" This time the girl did turn back. "We are in the process of clearing Blair Hall and removing the household to town. I must see to all of that, and settle all of us back in London. There are still debts to be paid and decisions to be made. I cannot go off and leave my aunt and cousin at this point."

His head cocked to one side, her father's man of affairs held up a deprecating hand. "You will say that this is not my immediate concern, but I feel bound to discuss the idea with you."

Rebecca made a gesture of despair. "I don't see what we can discuss."

"The idea of going to America is new to you, Miss Blair. You are still surprised at the sudden appearance of an uncle you'd forgotten. I ask only that you consider his letter again, and that you consider your present situation. I have observed," and he coughed delicately behind his hand, "that your relationship with your aunt and cousin is not the warmest. You feel a duty to them, which is commendable, but you will have discharged that duty once they are back in London where they wish to be. I suggest to you that as far as your *family* is concerned, you have no further obligations. But, of course, only you can know your heart. Perhaps you have other reasons for wishing to remain in England."

Rebecca sat down again, feeling suddenly very weary.

"Of course," the man went on, "one must think of the fact that there is a rebellion on in America. One hopes that it will not spread to the more western land where your uncle resides. But the possibility must be considered. And there is the general danger of a sea voyage. All of these things must be taken into account."

Rebecca smiled for the first time. "Of course."

The man gave one of his rare, thin smiles. "Then you will think about it? We have time yet before we write to your uncle. If I may, I will stay and help with the final preparations here."

"We'd all be most grateful." Rebecca picked up the sheets of paper from the table. "You will want to refresh yourself after your journey. Meeks will show you to your room. We will meet again in the small parlor to go in to dinner in one hour."

Mr. Bancroft bowed as she pulled the bell by the fireplace, and hoped he had done his proper duty by the girl he had become very fond of.

The next morning Rebecca refused to spend the whole of a glorious day inside, and went to get her filly for a ride. Dancer was high-spirited, chafing at the bit as they walked quietly down the drive, and Rebecca felt a sudden twinge of guilt. She hadn't been exercising the filly enough recently. She'd have to give her her head this day. Then she thought of the years ahead when their riding would be confined to the perimeters of Hyde Park in London. How both of them would hate their restricted freedom. Unbidden, the thought came to her that she shouldn't do it to Dancer, and suddenly she was plotting her next correspondence with the new owner. She had managed to secure places on the staff for nearly all of her old servants. None of the people who had served her parents for years were to be turned out of their homes. Surely she could add one beautiful filly to the list! She bit her lip. Already she was planning as though she were leaving England. But in fact she had not given Uncle Julian's letter any more thought. And she didn't intend to agonize over it now.

An hour later, when she came into the hall feeling refreshed after her exercise, she started up the wide stairs to her room and tried not to admire the carved paneling along the walls. It was a game she had begun to play with herself these past weeks. If she did not dwell on the things she loved here at Blair, she would find it easier to part with them. She was nearly halfway up the long staircase and was congratulating herself on looking only upward, when her cousin's voice made her turn her head.

"Oh, Becky, there you are." Letty floated languidly across the hall from the drawing room door. Waving a letter over her head, she draped herself on the massive newel post below Rebecca and smiled up at her. "I've been trying to find you for ages."

Rebecca couldn't summon an answering smile, but she tried to look interested. "Here I am, Letty. And I shall be down shortly, if you'll just let me change out of my habit."

"Oh, I have nothing to say that will take very long, cousin. It is only that I have heard from Caroline Griscomb. She has written a long letter, filling me in on all the latest *on dits* so that I will be very *au courant,* as she says, when we return to London. I will share it all with you later, if you like."

"How nice," Rebecca murmured and started up the stairs again.

"But she does have one startling piece of news I thought you might want to hear right away," called Letty after her. "Lord Harlcourt has finally been caught."

Rebecca turned near the top of the staircase, a puzzled look on her face. "Good heavens, caught at what?"

Letty snickered. "Not caught in that sense, Becky. Caught in marriage! He's to marry an heiress in the fall. Someone whose name you might recognize, a Miss Jenkins."

Rebecca's eyes widened and her hand tightened on the banister. So, she was not even to have the solace of Harlcourt's company in London. Trying to suppress her sudden hurt, she stood very still. "Good for Lord Harlcourt," she managed. "Of course I'm interested in more news. I shall be down directly."

"Just thought you'd want to hear right away, dear," Letty purred and waved the letter again with a satisfied air.

"Of course." Rebecca's voice was barely audible as she mounted the last stairs and turned stiffly down the hall to her room. Without being fully aware of what she was doing, she crossed to the mantelpiece and unfolded Uncle Julian's letter once more.

The massive table in the center of the glittering room was spread with a selection of food the likes of which Gordon Meade had not seen since coming to New York. He eyed the cold ham and tongue, the mountain of mutton, the decanters of ruby claret and the dishes of steaming vegetables, and wished he could feel more hunger and gratitude for this invitation to join General Washington's staff at dinner. But he knew that soon he must face an interview with his commander-in-chief and he feared his proposal was doomed to failure. The late June day was growing hot and Gordon tugged at his tight neckcloth, wishing too he could be rid of the heavy uniform.

Young Alexander Hamilton, captain in the New York artillery, beckoned to him from the table. "You'll need food to sustain you," he said.

Gordon's mouth curved in a tight smile as he heaped his plate and turned to see General Washington halfway across the room nod to him and motion him forward. "It looks as though I don't even get a chance to enjoy the food," he said softly.

"We'll talk later, then." Hamilton moved away, and Gordon followed the tall figure of the general through the room. He was aware of stares of envy from other officers, and felt uncomfortably that he should not have been singled out this way. Corpulent Colonel Knox, for instance, the officer most adhesively attached to Washington, was dogging his heels like a terrier, unwilling to allow His Excellency to be sullied by private conversation with an outsider.

The general climbed the stairs of the Richmond Hill mansion without once looking back to see if Gordon had managed to maintain his pace. Not until they were in the large bedroom now converted to Washington's headquarters did he turn and fix Gordon with his small dark eyes.

Gordon stood before the desk, balancing his plate of food, and waited for an invitation to be seated. Two staff officers gathered papers from a sidetable as Colonel Knox waddled in the door. Through one of the windows there was a magnificent view of the broad Hudson River, invitingly cool and blue under the hot midday sun.

"Colonel Meade." Washington motioned Gordon to a chair and took a mouthful of food. His slightly yellow, pock-marked skin was lightly dusted with powder through which tiny rivulets of sweat were beginning to make their way to his collar. He was only forty-four, Gordon knew, but he looked older. His expression remained grave, even as he chewed. "I'm pleased to see you are recovered from your wound."

"Sufficiently," Gordon answered. "That is why I requested an appointment to see you, sir."

"My afternoon is looking steadily worse, so a talk over our meal will have to do."

Gordon nodded and debated if he should take the initiative in this conversation. Surely the general wondered what he was doing here.

"You know, of course, that General Gates left for Albany three days ago?" His Excellency sat back and dabbed at his mouth with a large square of snowy linen. "He'll have to move quickly to catch up to the forces retreating from Montreal."

"Yes, sir."

"I wonder that you haven't dashed north to join Gates and return to Canada. Or have you had a bellyful of that country?"

Gordon put his fork down carefully. "It was not for that reason that I did not try to join General Gates, sir." He took a deep breath and plunged. "It is because I feel another Canada expedition will be as disastrous as the first, and I hope I can be of more use here in New York."

The general's eyebrows nearly met over his high nose, and Gordon knew he had displeased the commander. General Washington still held hopes of capturing the northern prize, despite evidence that it was impossible. Arnold's march on Quebec had been an appalling failure, costing too many lives. And the loss of General Montgomery after the weary months of fighting along the St. Lawrence had been the death knell, in Gordon's view, for the whole venture.

"You were with General Montgomery from Albany all the way to Quebec. You know the wilderness along the Canadian border, and you are an officer—if reports of you be true—of considerable authority, bravery and initiative." Washington allowed a wintry smile to cross his face briefly. "So what makes you think you would be of more use here in New York City?"

"I attended King's College, Your Excellency. I am familiar with New York and all its environs. And, as your own intelligence has already informed you, the British fleet is even now approaching the eastern tip of Long Island. Tomorrow, or the day thereafter, that fleet will appear in New York harbor. You will, I hope, have need of every man possible when General Howe arrives."

"I already have need of every man I can get, Colonel Meade. Do you have any talent for fortifications?"

Gordon held the general's eyes with difficulty. "None whatever, sir. I had hoped for something more in the nature of a special detachment."

"To do what, Colonel?"

Washington's voice was mild, but his tone aloof. Gordon leaned forward anyway. Here was his one chance for a hearing, however brief, however coolly received. "You will need more eyes and ears, General Washington, when the British arrive. I lost nearly all my regiment between St. John's and Quebec, sir. But I have a nucleus of men whose enlistments were up in the winter, but whom we persuaded to stay on the St. Lawrence with us even after General Montgomery was killed. When I was wounded, they took me home to Albany, but I have them with me now, and they are prepared to form the core of another regiment, or of a batallion, if you'll give me one, sir."

"I haven't so much as a company command to give you, Colonel. But if I had, are you offering your services and those of your men as spies?"

"I do not propose to dress in disguises and slink behind enemy lines, no, Your Excellency. My men are woodsmen and marksmen. I had thought more of general harassment of

56

the enemy when the occasion arose, of intelligence gathering wherever needed. And these operations only for as long as you are entrenched here in the city, defending the island."

"I would not at this time receive authorization from the Congress to commission such a detachment, Colonel. Besides, able officers, especially ones with able-bodied men, are needed here in the city." The general seemed to make an abrupt decision. "Your style, I think, will be admirably suited to that of General Putnam." He rang a bell on his desk, and immediately the door opened. "Major Burr, please have papers drawn up recommending Colonel Meade to General Putnam."

Gordon looked up quickly. Aaron Burr stood on the threshold, slight, handsome, impeccably attired. The two smiled at each other. They had first met in Montreal when General Montgomery had elevated the youthful Burr to the rank of captain. And from there they'd gone back to Burr's former commander, Benedict Arnold, at the seige of Quebec. He and Alexander Hamilton downstairs were among the very young men rising fast in this war. They were brilliant, talented and likable in their own ways, and Gordon was glad to call them friends.

"I'll remember your particular ambitions, Colonel Meade." General Washington stood up, and Gordon felt himself thoroughly dismissed. He winced, but he saluted smartly and marched to the door.

Out in the hall Aaron Burr shook his hand. "Congratulations, Gordon. The rank of lieutenant-colonel appears to sit well on your shoulders."

Grinning, Gordon wrung the younger man's hand.

"And congratulations for managing to get yourself attached to old Put's staff. I've been working on that myself. Ten hours a day copying letters for His Excellency is not my idea of gallant war service. Be glad Washington didn't grab you for his own staff. But then you're not a proper sycophant for him."

Gordon laughed for the first time that day. "One of these times, Burr, your acid tongue is going to be cut out of your head. For God's sake come away from the door. Colonel Knox may have his fat ear at the keyhole, and he'll report every syllable to the general."

"Our commander is not *altogether* stupid, Meade." Burr turned obediently down the hall. "He knows I do not pay him sufficient obeisance, and so will be glad to be rid of me. I suspect his feelings for you are similar. On the other hand, he has need of us. Through our education, and through grim experience, we have picked up a few rudiments of military knowledge. Too few of the officers can claim the same."

"I wish I could convince him of that and force him to give me a solid command."

"In time, Gordon. In time. Come share some wine with me while we set the bureaucratic wheels in motion. Are you billeted in the city yet?"

"Yes." Gordon saw no need to explain he currently lodged with a certain madame in her gaudy house on Murray Street, nearly beside the buildings of King's College. His acquaintance with her went back to his days at that institution, and she had proved a friend on more than one occasion. "I have my men crowded into a boarded-up mansion near the Commons, but the sooner they're out of there, the better."

Burr led Gordon downstairs to an office at the rear of the great house. The halls and rooms were crowded with officers waiting to see the general, with sentries and with staff personnel. Gordon regarded the whole scene with distaste. For a moment he wished he *had* headed north after General Gates. At least he and his men would have been in the woods again, out of the stifling atmosphere that always surrounded headquarters, and out of what he feared was a doomed city. Despite months of preparation, when Howe finally arrived in New York with his soldiers, he would take the place in a day.

As the two men entered the private office, Gordon saw Alexander Hamilton in the hall and beckoned to him. Hamilton joined them as Burr was saying, "I gather you did not come to beg for a place on either Washington's or Putnam's staffs, Meade. Were you for the north again? Did Washington, in his infinite wisdom, shoot down a grander ambition?"

"A much smaller ambition, actually. I wanted a special detachment, a small body of men with which to move freely, and with which to do his dirty work for him. He acted as though espionage and even harassment were dirty concepts."

"Naturally. No one likes to admit spying goes on. So *ungentlemanly,* you know. Anyway, he has his own methods at the moment. Though there will come a time, when the British are crawling over the country behind our fleeing backs, when he will need more."

"I got a feeling," Gordon said almost bitterly, "that he sees this war as some sort of colorful tableau: brightly clad ranks of men facing each other as pretty little powder puffs of smoke balloon from musket barrels."

"Coming it a bit strong." Hamilton spoke for the first time, and the two senior officers looked at him in surprise. "Washington is not so silly as to think war is pretty. He's been in one, remember. He's in a desperate situation and knows it, but he can't get the men or supplies he needs, and spends all his time cajoling Congress to give him more."

Aaron Burr's handsome face looked mocking but sorrowful. "Don't mind him, Meade. He's fastened on His Excellency as the star on whose tail he'll rise, so he feels a bit defensive."

Gordon grinned at Hamilton. "My judgments are premature, I'll grant you. I've not seen our commander ever since I arrived home last July in time to join Montgomery's forces going north up Lake Champlain. And I've not been in New York long."

"You'll learn quickly enough." Burr winked. "Afraid you'll be shocked by the inactivity around here."

Gordon shook his head slowly. "I find, in my advancing years, that there is very little any more that has the power to shock me." Painfully, he thought of all he'd seen in the past two years, from European court society to sickened and dying soldiers in the freezing slush of the St. Lawrence. He'd danced the minuet with a duchess and amputated the arm of a man shot at St. John's; he'd walked in the gardens of stately homes and had dragged a sled of provisions over frozen ground after a horse had died beneath him; he'd eaten at a table where twelve guests were presented with enough food for fifty and suffered months of having fifty men provided with enough food for only twelve; he'd conversed with foreign ministers and done business with war-painted Indians. It was not likely that anything General Washington and the army in New York could show him was going to shock, or even surprise him.

Chapter 6

Planting her feet firmly against the roll of the ship, Rebecca stood on the deck of the French brig, *Andrea*, and stared resolutely out to sea. She had turned her back on the last sight of England's coast, and she now sought to turn her thoughts away as well. But as she watched the monotonous march of gray waves off the starboard bow, she found that memories of these last weeks would not leave her. It seemed that her past life was not to be put from her as easily as the view of a shoreline.

Once she had realized, four weeks ago, that the slim reed held out to her by her almost-unknown uncle was what she had been waiting to grasp, she had been driven by a nearly insane urge to escape the life that had been in store for her. It was hard to believe she'd done it. Her aunt had gone into strong hysterics, of course. But once the woman's mind had encompassed the fact that she was not to be thrown out on the streets and that her charge was removing herself from her anxious care, Aunt Honoria had been almost cheerful, and the few pangs of guilt Rebecca had begun to feel promptly dissipated. It had been a trying time, but it had been worth it.

Dear Mr. Bancroft, she thought. What a burden he had taken onto himself in order to set her free. The poor man would now be the one to deal with Aunt Honoria each quarter. He and Rebecca had settled on a sum to be withdrawn from the estate to pay her ocean voyage and any normal expenses likely to be incurred over the next months, but beyond that the girl had left everything to help pay the upkeep on the London house. Aunt Honoria and Letty could have few complaints. And Rebecca had none at all. The only people for whom she had responsibility at last were herself and her maid Sylvie. Rebecca smiled to herself. Thank goodness for Sylvie and her high spirits. As soon as the girl had learned of Rebecca's decision to leave England, she had practically begged to come along. And it had been Sylvie's enthusiasm that at times had kept her own determination from foundering.

Now Rebecca looked at her companion on the deck and saw that Sylvie was clinging to the rail with whitened knuckles. Her lips were parted and her eyes were wide as she stared down at the great crests and troughs directly below.

"It's beautiful, isn't it?" Rebecca tried to sound bracing.

"Yes, miss."

Sylvie's voice was nearly carried away by the wind, and Rebecca leaned closer. "It is not easy to leave home, I know."

"I'm sure you're right, miss. But I wasn't honestly thinking of that."

"Oh? What then?"

"Them big waves, miss." Sylvie smiled weakly. "I'd best go and see to the rest of the unpacking." And with that the girl turned and stumbled back across the deck to the companionway.

Rebecca watched her go with a puzzled look. What could be ailing the girl? She'd have to go and see soon, but for now the open air was much more appealing than the confines of their small cabin. She let her mind roam across the waves, wondering what Uncle Julian looked like, how big his house was. She realized she'd hardly thought of these questions until now. There had been so much to think of and to do for the past weeks.

"Pardon, mademoiselle."

Rebecca started and gripped the rail as a roll of the ship caught her off guard. A hand came out and steadied her. Brushing wind-whipped hair from her eyes, she looked up at the captain's seamed face.

"It is a good sight, no?"

She nodded. "Lovely, Captain Lefevre."

"And I hope you will continue to enjoy it these next weeks. But for now, mademoiselle, I must ask you to retire to your cabin. My men, they have much to do, and I fear the sight of a beautiful lady on deck is most distracting to them. You understand."

Rebecca had the urge to say no, she didn't understand, but she knew it would be pointless. Reluctantly, she nodded again. "If you say so, Captain."

"My thanks. Jacques will show you the way," and he indicated a wiry little cabin boy a few yards away. "He will also show you to my cabin for this evening's meal. You will honor my table?"

"Thank you, Captain. The honor will be mine." With a sigh Rebecca turned and followed the boy.

Once in the cabin, she regretted the loss of the bracing wind more than ever. The small space was jammed with trunks and boxes and a litter of clothing, and Sylvie, looking very pale, was sitting huddled on the corner of her little bunk.

"What is it, Sylvie? What is the matter?" Rebecca closed the narrow door firmly, and picked her way between the trunks.

"I dunno, miss." Dulled eyes were raised to her mistress's face. "It's just that I feel so . . . so queer." She held her middle with both arms and began to rock back and forth.

Rebecca noted the smudges beneath the dark eyes and the new hollow in the cheeks. "Are you going to be sick?" she asked sharply.

The girl tried to nod as she continued to rock. "I think them waves have done it to me. The movement of this ship is so awful!"

"Oh, dear." Rebecca snatched up the tiny washbasin on the stand between the bunks and pushed it into Sylvie's hands. Then tugging a towel from the drawer, she sat down beside the girl and held her head until the inevitable happened.

Fighting down her own queasiness, she made a face above the bowed head of her maid. So this is how I start my grand new life, she thought.

It was days before Sylvie was truly recovered, and by the end of the week, Rebecca, who remembered starting the voyage in such defiant high hopes, was already heartily sick of the whole trip. Being cooped up with a wretchedly ill person did not lift the spirits, she found. And even her time outside the little cabin could hardly be called exciting. She had discovered the first night that the only other passengers were a stiff-necked elderly gentleman from the colonies who also succumbed to seasickness, and a middle-aged doctor who drank too much and talked endlessly of his new beginning in a new world. The captain was kind, but he was the only one among the officers who spoke English, and Rebecca was already feeling the strain of struggling to talk to the others in her schoolgirl French. She would have given a lot for a decent library of books to read.

She was even getting tired of poring through French fashion plates trying to decide what new gowns might be right in America. The excitement she'd first felt at being able to think in terms of colorful clothes again, now that her year of mourning was over, abated with the realization that she'd have to wait and see how women dressed in New York before she made final decisions. For now, her wardrobe was more than adequate, indeed, rather too fancy for shipboard life, she felt.

At first Rebecca found some solace in dragging Sylvie up on deck for fresh air each day. But the girl would not go near the rail, and soon her mistress found herself promenading alone and wishing she had more space to really stretch her legs. She spent hours staring over the flat horizon, wondering what America looked like, and wondering sometimes at the fact she was here at all. The Rebecca Blair who had danced all evening in London ballrooms a year ago might have wished for change, for more excitement in her life, but she never would have envisioned disappearing into wilds of a new land to achieve her goals. At times like these, though, she needed only to remind herself of her aunt and cousin back in London. Then she would know that whatever lay in store for her was likely to be a better fate than the one she'd left behind.

The days passed slowly and stretched into agonizingly long weeks. For the most part the weather was warm and clear, monotonous in its calm predictability. But at last came a morning when Rebecca, climbing to the deck at her usual hour, found herself enveloped in a swirling gray fog. Happily, she walked across the deck, the ship looking suddenly strange and new in its obscured state. Figures appeared and disappeared among the angles of the ship's planks, and rigging stretched away in ghostly black tendrils above her, floating in and out of wisps of mist like writhing disembodied vines. The whole world seemed wrapped in an eerie blanket of silence. Groping for the rail, the girl stood watching the moving wall of vapor trail past the slow-moving vessel. Even the gray-green waves seemed nearly silenced in the dead world. Occasional breaks in the wall around her offered tantalizing glimpses of more distant water, but the thick atmosphere overhead allowed no hint of the sun's rays. She stayed still a long time, mesmerized, unable to stop trying to penetrate the fog.

At almost the same instant that she heard the distant, echoing cry from aloft, she saw a terrifying ghostly shape loom out of folded curtains of mist. The prow of a great ship, larger than the *Andrea*, seemed to tower for a second, close at hand, before the curtain closed, shutting off the frightening sight. Through the stillness could be heard ships' bells clanging, voices shouting. The mist broke just then and a puff of wind ballooned the sails above her. She felt the *Andrea* heel over on a port tack, and in that instant, the full outline of the other ship could be seen. Then it disappeared again off the stern. Although she was soaked through, Rebecca stood where she was, holding the rail in a paralyzed grip, still waiting for the crash of splitting timbers, the overwhelming crush of the bigger ship smothering her own. Instead, she saw the smallest spark of light in the fog, and heard a faint booming noise. Another breeze caught the *Andrea*'s sails, and the ship heeled harder and sped away.

Only then was Rebecca aware of the feverish activity going on around her. She wished she could ask what was happening, but knew she'd only be ordered below if she spoke. Her legs trembling from aftershock, she made her way back below decks, knowing she would have to be patient, and ask the captain at dinner.

"It was a British frigate we nearly collided with this morning," Captain Lefevre explained to her that evening in a grim voice. "We did not attempt to exchange news because we wish to avoid contact with all such ships. We are a neutral country in this conflict between England and her colonies, but it is known that upon occasion a British warship will feel compelled to press our crews into service if it is shorthanded. I cannot afford to lose my good men, and I do not like to think of them in that life. It is a very harsh one. So," and he gave a very Gallic shrug, "we, how you say, turn the tail and run."

"I see," Rebecca answered thoughtfully, and shuddered at

the memory of that black bulk so near to the *Andrea*. "And must you run from the American ships also?"

The captain smiled then. "There are no American ships of significance to chase us, mademoiselle. The colonies do not have an effective navy."

The girl's eyes widened. She knew nothing about warfare, but she remembered enough history to know that a strong navy had often made all the difference in the outcome of a struggle. "Then how do these colonies expect to engage His Majesty's forces?" she asked.

"Exactly, mademoiselle. But who knows what may have happened since I last heard news of the colonial position. Do not misunderstand. The Americans are an ingenious and a determined people. No one but a madman would have defied his monarch as these Americans have done, one would think. And perhaps they are, many of them, a bit mad. But they do not lack bravery or skills. If they can become organized and can pick good leaders, who knows what they might do? Especially remember that America is big beyond imagining. If all the colonies rebel together, King George will have a hard time trying to decide where to send troops first."

"It would almost seem you admire these rebels, Captain," Rebecca said stiffly.

"Let us say I do not blame them for claiming redress for any wrongs done to them, mademoiselle. But let us not talk of politics. I was merely explaining why we must appear so cowardly when a warship is sighted."

Rebecca was subdued after that day. The incident in the fog had brought home to her the fact that, as far as they knew, the fight was still going on in the colonies. But she convinced herself that it needn't concern her. Uncle Julian's carriage would meet her, and she would go to the safe haven of his home where such insane hostilities would not reach them.

Still, a feeling of relief was mixed with dread on the hot evening of July 8th when Rebecca saw the first hazy blue hint of land. She was approaching New York, and she didn't even know if the letter Mr. Bancroft had sent three weeks before her departure had ever reached Uncle Julian. The letter had gone on a British supply ship bound for New York, but it had been explained to Mr. Bancroft that no one knew the present situation in the colonies. The Royal Governor of New York was last known to have taken refuge aboard a

British ship in the harbor, and it was conceivable that Mr. Bancroft's letter would not get ashore for some time. Rebecca had brushed aside all thoughts of the letter not making it, but now, as she strained to see details of the land they approached, doubts assailed her. She had to tell herself that there were certainly many inns or rooms to be had in the city, and that she and Sylvie could stay at one and send a message to Uncle Julian if need be. But her hasty decision to uproot herself from England had left no time for contingency plans, and she felt frightened at the thought of how alone she really was.

The following morning dawned hot and hazy, and Rebecca took every opportunity to go on deck and watch the low shoreline of what she had been told was Long Island slide by. By early afternoon, all the passengers were at the rail, talking little, each lost in his own thoughts now that the long voyage was nearly over.

Captain Lefevre came down to see them, explaining that thanks to a favorable wind, they would soon be passing through the lower bay, and thence through the Narrows into New York harbor's upper bay. He pointed out the blue bulk of Staten Island looming far ahead, and the marshy land on what he called the Brookland shore. "It has been many years since I have seen this," he said to Rebecca as she stood shielding her eyes against the sun's glare, "and I am glad to be back. It is a beautiful place, no?"

The girl nodded, impatient to catch sight of New York.

"When we pass the neck of water called the Narrows, you will see the city beyond a low island, mademoiselle," the captain went on conversationally. "It sits at the southern tip of an island. To the west flows the magnificent Hudson River, to the east another river called simply East River. It is a rugged land. I have always thought that perhaps some day . . ."

His words were cut short by a cry from aloft. Turning, the captain looked where many hands were now pointing. Ahead, against the shore of Staten Island could dimly be seen a forest of masts. "Mon Dieu," the man exclaimed. "More than I had thought. Pardon, mademoiselle, but I think it is time to consider our final move." He smiled mirthlessly and moved up the ladder to the quarterdeck.

Shouts came from above, and sailors scurried to their stations. Rebecca crossed to the port rail and stared at the huge flotilla of ships that could now be seen clearly. One enormous vessel was coming under sail, and looked as though it meant to move toward them.

At her elbow Sylvie gave a squeak. "It looks like London Harbor," she breathed.

Rebecca narrowed her eyes at the British flag flying high on the approaching ship's main mast.

"Ah, the British fleet has arrived," sighed the doctor behind her, his rummy breath misting the air around them. "Perhaps this means New York is in Royalist hands once more."

Rebecca smiled. This was what Uncle Julian had hoped for, and if it were true, the rebellion might already have ended. So much the better, she supposed.

Her thoughts were interrupted by shouts from the deck above. One of the officers was calling for passengers to go below. Above her, sails were unfurling and flapping in the stiff breeze. The girl looked up and was startled to see a British flag trailing from the mast. Puzzled, she hesitated, but suddenly Jacques, the cabin boy, was beside her, urging her to obey the command. "We must try to outrun them," he was explaining excitedly. Rebecca could barely understand him. "We are small and light and will make it to port. Our flag fooled them into complacency, and they have been sitting awaiting us. But now they seem to know something is amiss. There is a danger they will fire on us, mademoiselle. You must come below."

"Fire on us?" Rebecca looked incredulously at the huge warship slicing through the water toward them.

"They have realized we are not a British ship, and perhaps they mean to board us. We do not wish that. We must reach New York and unload our cargo."

"Why?" Rebecca stood her ground. It was impossible to imagine a British ship firing at her.

"Our captain, he thinks that a British fleet standing out here in the lower bay means New York is yet in American hands, and we must get our cargo through," the boy whispered. Then he tugged at her skirt. "Come now, please, mademoiselle."

Rebecca glared at him. "Your cargo is for the rebels, isn't it?"

The boy nodded in desperation. "Come."

Catching some of his urgency, Rebecca beckoned to Sylvie and followed the boy below. If this ship, in fact, held arms or provisions for the American rebels, it would be awkward for everyone if it were caught by the British.

Cowering in their cabin, the two women waited for the sound of guns firing. They could feel the ship's timbers creak as she moved faster through the water under a heavier load of sail. But beyond that they could make out nothing but the scurrying of feet overhead. They felt trapped and helpless and very thoroughly frightened. But as the minutes dragged by and no report of a cannon was heard, they began to feel hope again, and not a little chagrin at being cheated of their first view of the colony they were to call their new home. However, their main emotion was relief when, some time later, Jacques appeared at their cabin door again, followed by two burly seamen.

"Please, you are invited to come on deck." The boy grinned. "We did well. That warship could not maneuver as we could. We showed him nothing but our stern, and he could not even fire upon us. We were in the Narrows before he knew what had happened." He smiled more broadly. "We are arrived, and these men will take your baggage."

Rebecca let out a long breath. "So, New York is not under British control?" she asked, moving quickly to the cabin door.

"Non, mademoiselle. That is why the fleet lies offshore there. They are come to take the city back into their own hands. The Americans expect the ships to open fire at any time. You will see what I talk about once you are on shore."

Chapter 7

Rebecca hurried on deck, closely followed by Sylvie who was now wide-eyed with apprehension. By the rail she stopped. The arrival of the French ship had obviously created a stir, for knots of people had gathered up and down the wharf and on the banks beyond. She stared over the low skyline of the city where church steeples spiked the afternoon sky, and wondered how long it would take for her to find Uncle Julian. She realized suddenly that she did not know what he looked like after all these years. Her memory of him was hazy at best. She could only hope that *he* would find *her*.

The harbor, which looked as though it had once been a busy place, was now only half full of ocean-going vessels. She could see warehouses by the waterfront whose doors and windows were shuttered. And Jacques had said the Americans expected a British bombardment any time. What if Uncle Julian were not able to be here? Despite the heat she felt the smallest shiver creep down her spine. With an effort she unclenched her fists and managed a smile. "It is not so big as I expected," she said to her maid, "but it looks well enough from here."

"Yes, miss," Sylvie said doubtfully.

Rebecca straightened her back. "We are here now, and I should think you would be glad for the feel of solid ground again," she said more sharply than she'd intended. "I know I will," she added. "Mr. Halscomb must be waiting for us out there." She waved a vague hand and turned resolutely toward the gangplank.

Captain Lefevre escorted Rebecca ashore after issuing orders for the unloading of cargo. "I will see that you meet this uncle of yours, mademoiselle," he said, "and if perchance he is not here, I will see you to proper accommodations. The city is not a place for women alone."

Rebecca followed his gaze and noticed for the first time the trenches dug along the shoreline, topped by an odd flotsam of timbers and tree branches, and the men standing at arms within them. "What does this mean?" she asked. The men were not in any discernible uniform, but they looked disciplined and grim.

"It would seem that an American army is occupying this fair city," the captain answered, "but I can tell you no more than that."

They walked on in silence, and Rebecca began to think she could feel the charged atmosphere of the place. Deliberately she did not look back to see that flotilla of British ships menacing the little harbor.

Suddenly the captain stopped and Rebecca nearly stumbled into him. Coming toward them, arms outstretched, was a tall man in a buff coat and matching knee breeches. His thick eyebrows were raised above a fringe of graying hair at his ears, and his heavy face was wreathed in smiles. "Rebecca," he called, hurrying forward.

The girl could hardly recognize this portly gentleman as the debonair uncle she had known and been told about as a child, but his snapping deep blue eyes were her mother's and she would have known them anywhere. She felt such a rush of relief she could do no more than stumble into his solid arms, sobbing his name.

"Dear girl," he said distractedly, patting her back. "You have come at last. I had not thought your ship would be able to enter the harbor, but obviously you have a captain of skill." He eyed the little Frenchman behind his niece.

Embarrassed by her display of emotion, Rebecca straightened quickly. "Allow me to make our captain known to you, Uncle Julian." She performed the introductions, and regained her composure as the men traded compliments. Then suddenly she was being shepherded toward a handsome brown traveling coach and Uncle Julian was clucking over her in a satisfying way.

As she settled onto the tufted seat and directed Sylvie to her place across from her, Rebecca fought back a second urge to cry. They'd done it. They were here, and Uncle Julian had met them just as promised. Nothing could go wrong now. She had put a vast ocean between herself and the dreary life she had led in England. Few people, she suddenly realized, had the opportunity to begin again. She must be thankful for her fortune and meet her new life with resolution.

With these lofty thoughts in mind, she favored her uncle, who was climbing into the carriage beside her, with a brilliant smile. "I can scarce believe we are in New York, Uncle. I will have to pinch myself to be sure I am not dreaming."

Julian Halscomb lowered his large frame into the seat. Taking her hand he smiled back at her. "It is beyond belief to me," he said. "We will wait until your trunks are strapped on, and then we will go to my inn to collect my things and to have some tea. We will be home by nightfall."

Rebecca sighed happily. How good it was to have a man take charge again. "Have you had to stay in New York long awaiting our ship?" she asked.

"Your letter reached me less than a fortnight ago, and I came almost straight away, thinking the French merchant ship would be faster than the supply ship. So I have been here nearly a week. An instructional week," he added slowly. "My dear, I fear you have not arrived at the most opportune time. Yesterday afternoon the papers were full of the news that the Continental Congress in Philadelphia has declared its intention to sever all ties with England."

"The Continental Congress? What on earth is that? And what does this mean?"

Uncle Julian chuckled, but Rebecca thought there was little mirth in it. "Of course you've no idea what the Congress is. It is an unlawful body of men from all the thirteen colonies. They have taken it upon themselves to set up an alternative government to the Crown. And it means ungovernable forces may be set loose in this country."

"But I had thought the insurrection would be over by now."

"As had I, my dear. But the rebel blockade of Boston was effective. It forced His Majesty's troops out of that city for now. The fleet of warships and troop ships your captain evaded so neatly today arrived here ten days ago, carrying, I gather, thousands of men. Why General Howe, who is aboard one of those ships, has not landed his men on this island I cannot conceive."

"But you think that soon the British troops will enter New York?"

Uncle Julian nodded.

"So," breathed Rebecca, "the rebellion will be over soon." She found the thought somehow promising, having a vague vision of smart lines of scarlet coats wheeling and marching to glory. And afterwards, coming to the balls and fetes prepared for them.

Uncle Julian leaned toward her. "I could wish it were going to be that simple. But many fear this war is just beginning. We can only hope that the king's troops will occupy this city soon. But let me warn you that General Washington, commander in chief of the rebel army, is at this moment here in New York with the Continental Army. They are encamped all around the city, and have given the anti-Royalists great heart. It is unwise, nay, dangerous, to say anything in support of our king. I tell you this so that you will be wary in public places."

Rebecca's soft laugh filled the carriage. "Good heavens, Uncle, you make it all sound so conspiratorial."

"A good word, in fact. But come, we have so many other things to talk of. And I want to show you some of the city as we go on our way." He opened the door of the coach and leaned out, talking to his coachman for a moment. When he turned back, the small lines of worry which had appeared between his eyes were erased. "All is ready, Rebecca, and now I may truly say welcome to New York." His broad smile appeared again, and Rebecca found herself responding as the heavy wheels began to turn under them.

The coach rumbled slowly along a narrow street paralleling the waterfront, and Uncle Julian began to point out landmarks to the occupants. Soon they turned up a very wide avenue, and Rebecca learned they were now on Broad Street. She looked around with interest, noting the few old Dutch houses, their gabled ends fronting on the street. But between these, and the occasional small wood houses, there was evidence of much English architecture that must be new, for the three-story brick buildings looked nearly identical to the newest of the London homes. A few blocks further on they turned west again and halted before a handsome high building.

Uncle Julian assisted Rebecca from the coach. "We will

stay but a short time, long enough for you to refresh yourself, my dear. I confess I am eager to be off, and to show you Halscomb."

Rebecca climbed down, feeling overwhelmed by the sights and sounds of a city once more. "New York looks as though it has been a bustling place," she commented, "but I noticed on Broad Street that a number of the houses were shuttered. Why is that?"

"Some of our wealthier citizens leave the city during the hot summer months, and many more have found it expedient this last year, to retreat to the countryside indefinitely. The reasons are varied, not to be gone into now. I had thought to buy a place here in town myself, but have waited to see what was to become of the city before I did."

Rebecca looked questioningly at him, but he refused to say more, and ushered her briskly inside and to a private parlor.

Less than an hour later they were on their way again. Uncle Julian had been right; the stop had been refreshing. Rebecca felt her interest in this new place growing as they started out once more. Even Sylvie was now leaning forward eagerly, her eyes dancing as they had not for the long weeks of the sea voyage.

It was nearing six, and the shadows were lengthening at last on the heat-laden streets as the coach came to what Uncle Julian called "Bowling Green," an oval park where a gilded equestrian statue of His Majesty George III stood, and turned north once more, this time onto a street called Broadway.

The coach moved into a line of traffic going north, and Rebecca looked with interest at a handsome white house with ornate cornices and Palladian windows behind a screen of lime trees, and at the succeeding mansions that marched up the long hill before them. They passed Trinity Church in a grove of elms as the coach slowed to little more than a snail's pace.

"Traffic is worse than ever," Uncle Julian commented. "Perhaps we shouldn't have come up this way, but I had wanted you to see some of the best homes. Once we're on Chatham Street we'll begin to make better time." He leaned back, preparing to be patient. But in another three blocks the coach came to a full stand. Uncle Julian let down the side window and questioned the driver, but the man seemed not to know why they were halted. For more than five minutes they sat waiting, the heat rising with the particles of dust from the cobblestone street. Despite the open windows, the coach was becoming stifling.

Uncle Julian made a sudden decision. "We cannot sit here and wait in this heat, niece. I suggest we get out and walk a bit and allow the coach to catch us up. At least there is air outside."

Rebecca welcomed the suggestion and climbed down with alacrity. Uncle Julian gave instructions to the coachman, then turned his charges north along the brick sidewalk. They moved beside the snarl of vehicles in the roadway, and within a few paces they could see that groups of people, as well as vehicles of every description, were blocking the way. Around a corner, the reason became obvious. On a vast triangle of open ground, two brigades of the Continental Army were drawn up in hollow square formation. In the center of the square, a knot of officers stood smartly to attention. The streets on all sides were choked with onlookers.

Uncle Julian sighed. "People never stop being fascinated with the troops," he said. "And I wonder what they do here? Retreat is not normally sounded until six thirty. I had thought we'd be past the several parade grounds before the men were mustered out for the evening."

Rebecca gazed at the military formation. Here and there could be seen smart-looking coats of blue faced with buff or scarlet or white. Obviously these were officers, for the great majority of men wore what could only be their civilian clothes, everything from snowy linen shirts and dark breeches to fringed brown homespun over baggy trousers. Surely this was not the army with which the colonies thought to hold King George's troops at bay.

She must have looked her scorn, for suddenly Uncle Julian grasped her elbow. "I have seen that General Washington himself is in that group of officers," he commented. "Let us go a bit closer and see what all this is about."

They edged nearer the soldiers, and now could hear a young officer's voice rising above the hubbub on the street. Someone in the center of the military square was reading the comments of the day to the men. Rebecca could make out little of it, but she felt Uncle Julian's hand tighten on her arm. "He is reading orders from the general," he said softly, "and they include the public reading of the Continental Congress's declaration of July fourth." He moved a little closer. Now Rebecca could hear the officer's voice more clearly, and she made an effort to listen, though she couldn't think why military comments would be of interest.

Talking around them quieted, and in the still evening air, the voice from the center of the square rang out clearly.

"When in the course of human events, it becomes necessary for one people to dissolve the political bands which have connected them with another, and to assume among the powers of the earth, the separate and equal station to which the laws of nature and of nature's God entitle them, a decent respect to the opinions of mankind requires that they should declare the causes which impel them to the separation. . . ."

Rebecca sucked in her breath. It was treason, nothing less, and she felt a bubble of fear begin to rise in her stomach. With horror, she heard the voice continue.

"We hold these truths to be self-evident: that all men are created equal; that they are endowed by their Creator with certain unalienable rights; that among these are life, liberty, and the pursuit of happiness. That to secure these rights, governments are instituted among men, deriving their just powers from the consent of the governed; that whenever any form of government becomes destructive of these ends, it is the right of the people to alter or abolish it, and to institute new government . . ."

She tried to shut her ears, but the sonorous phrases rolled on and on. And suddenly she was listening to an endless list of complaints against her sovereign, complaints couched in the strongest terms, calling King George a tyrant. She could not believe it.

"Oh, it does sound rather grand, doesn't it, miss?" Sylvie's eyes were round as she watched the ranks of men standing so straight before her.

"Hardly," Rebecca snapped. "It sounds . . ." Uncle Julian's hand tightened warningly on her arm. A man beside her turned to look at her. Her chin in the air, she stared him down, but she said no more until the voice at last stopped and well-ordered cheers went up from the soldiers. Under the cover of the noise she looked angrily about her. The crowd was quiet but pleased. "How could they?" she asked Uncle Julian. "How could this Congress say those things about King George? How could they dare to say they want independence from their mother country, especially when all they have for an army is that?" She nodded scornfully toward the military ranks.

Uncle Julian guided her gently back through the crowds. "I should not have brought you to the Commons," he said softly. "This was hardly a place for a young girl just off a ship after a long voyage. These are men's affairs, my dear, and there's no good to come of trying to understand all that is happening here." Rebecca started to say something more, but her uncle seemed not to notice. "Come—Sylvie, is it? We will see your mistress back to the coach. There is yet a lovely drive ahead of us."

Once inside the coach, Rebecca thought to question Uncle Julian further about the outrage she had witnessed, but her uncle remained unwilling to discuss the matter. "Politics, child." He waved a hand airily. "Not the thing to be discussing on a hot evening when we have so much else to think about. Ah, at last we are moving again. And here is Chatham Street. Soon we will be on The Bowery Lane. I do want you to notice James De Lancey's handsome manor off on our right. It is nearly hidden by high brick walls, but through the gate you can see the place quickly. I think it is a very fine house. Just a few minutes now."

He went on chatting as the coach rolled out of the city, and soon Rebecca was interested in spite of herself. Within a short while they were skirting orchards and fields, and had come to the Post Road, the main north-south artery on Manhattan Island. They passed a charming spring-fed lake called Sunfish Pond, and climbed a hill where an old farmhouse belonging to the Kip family stood, and further on, the drive to the country estate of Robert Murray, which was said to be very grand. Yet further, they passed the elegant James Beekman mansion, with its formal gardens in riotous bloom, and could just see the corner of the glass-enclosed greenhouse. Rebecca's head swam with all the names, but she watched the landmarks with fascination.

They went on climbing heavily wooded hills and dipping into long valleys, crossing countless streams and catching occasional glimpses of the evening light on the East River. As they continued north the country became more rugged, broken only occasionally by the neat farms that dotted the island, or by the great estates of the bigger landowners. Running between two steep hills, the road now zigzagged down a sharp grade to a broad valley, and Uncle Julian pointed toward the west. Rebecca followed his gaze and her breath caught in her throat. Across the varied green of the valley the deep blue waves of the broad Hudson were pink-tipped by the last rays of the dying sun, and on the far shore majestic ranks of great cliffs marched beside the narrow banks.

"The Jersey Palisades," said Uncle Julian, a note of real pride in his voice. "There are no finer sights, I think."

Rebecca nodded in silence, overawed by the prospect. Never had she seen anything quite like the steep, evening-blackened masses looming above the quiet river. Soon her view was cut off, though, as the coach passed the tiny village of Harlem and then what Uncle Julian called the Morris Mansion on their right, and traveled up between two massive ridges of wood-topped granite rock. Staring out the window, Rebecca felt something inside her respond to this wild-looking country. Nothing she could have imagined would have equalled the reality of it, and she laughed suddenly for pure joy. An answering twinkle from Sylvie's eye told her that the two of them must have made the right decision to come here. The thought of war, even the thought of England was far away now, caught as they were in the excitement of fresh possibilities.

By the time they crossed the Harlem River at Kingsbridge and turned north onto the Yonkers Road, dusk was descending rapidly. At last it became too difficult to make out the details of the countryside, and Rebecca gave up her vigil at the window. Sinking back beside Uncle Julian, she realized she was exhausted, and now she yearned only for an end to their journey.

Uncle Julian must have been exhausted too, for his voice sounded tired, despite his effort to appear hearty, when he said at long last, "We are here, Becky, and I would welcome you to my home."

They climbed a short hill and came to a stop before a tall white house barely discernible in the shadows. Heavy columns rose from near the ground to support a balcony above, and from there went up to a peaked roof. At the coach's approach, light sprang into two of the long windows at the front, and the wide door was thrown open. Critically, Rebecca eyed the square building, thinking of the warm stone facing on the sprawling mass of Blair Hall. Then she shook herself. Uncle Julian's house was not nearly as large as her own home had been, but it was a very handsome structure, and from what little she could see of the wide central hall, was appointed with elegance. No, it wasn't Blair, but then she'd never expected this New York to duplicate England, nor her uncle's house to resemble her rambling estate.

Despite these sensible thoughts, she found she had to push down a sudden surge of homesickness. It was only that she had been unprepared for the first sights of the colonies, she decided, and for all the turmoil this day had brought. Firmly she stepped from the coach to the broad front steps. She was home now, in a place she had chosen to come and live, and she could only be thankful that with Uncle Julian here, it seemed such a good choice.

WESTCHESTER,

1776

Chapter 8

During the next weeks, Rebecca came to know Halscomb Acres, and was delighted with nearly all she learned. The house itself sat on a low promontory, looking down over two small hills to a view of the Hudson and its majestic western bank. The land behind the house, stretching east past the orchard and southerly woods, was under cultivation, being farmed by four tenant farmers. His was a small holding compared to the great manors all along the Hudson, Uncle Julian said, but he'd never aspired to grand estates, didn't want the running of them, and he was more than content. Actually, he'd not known when he bought the old place how attached he would become. Shipping interests in New York had given him the wherewithal to acquire his country residence, and he now hoped to leave it as seldom as possible. Very quickly Rebecca began to understand why her uncle was so enamored of his land. This was beautiful country, and she could never grow tired, she thought, of looking across at the river and its western shore.

In the first hot July days, Rebecca made herself familiar with the house and grounds, befriended the filly Uncle Julian had presented to her and even managed to come to terms with Halscomb's housekeeper. Mrs. Clark had shown an inclination toward sullenness on the girl's arrival. Having ruled Julian Halscomb's house for nearly ten years, the elderly widow could hardly take kindly to the thought of his young niece coming in to issue orders, and thinking of Aunt Honoria's assumption of authority at Blair, Rebecca was sympathetic. So with all the tact she possessed, she worked on establishing a relationship with Mrs. Clark, and one day she was rewarded with the sight of the large woman standing in the back hall after breakfast, obviously waiting for her.

"I had thought to bring ye this," Mrs. Clark said, holding up a large ring of keys. Even after forty years in the colonies, the hint of a brogue was in her voice, and in times of stress it was accentuated.

Rebecca eyed the keys with interest. "Thank you, Mrs. Clark. That was a nice thought, but I feel sure those keys have been in the safest possible hands since Uncle Julian bought Halscomb Acres, and that they should remain there. I shall ask for them when I need them."

Twisting one hand in her long apron, the woman ducked her head. "Thank ye, Miss Blair."

"In fact, we might use one of them now," Rebecca went on lightly, covering Mrs. Clark's embarrassment. "If you would be so good as to unlock the linen room, I would like to see what is there. Mr. Halscomb has mentioned the possibility of household guests in two weeks' time, and we might be sure we are well supplied."

"Ye'll find all in order, miss. The mending was done in the spring." Mrs. Clark sniffed, her slightly offended manner back in place.

"I don't doubt I will." Rebecca turned toward the stairs. "It is only that I need to count to keep things straight in my own mind. You understand, I'm sure."

A considerable amount of praise for the condition of the linen room was all that was needed to cement Mrs. Clark's grudging loyalty to the new mistress of Halscomb Acres, and Rebecca went for a walk before lunch feeling she had crossed a great hurdle in her new life.

Uncle Julian was not quite so easy to manage. As affable, as considerate and as kind as he was in his vague way, Rebecca found him almost recalcitrant when she questioned him about news of the conflict in the colonies, or about the political situation she must now live with. It was his firm belief, stated bluntly, that women were meant to take care of the home, and that their delicate sensibilities were not to be offended by the more sordid affairs of men. At first Rebecca was amused by this attitude, and was too busy trying to learn the names of the servants and the neighbors to press the matter. But as the weeks passed, and occasional tidbits of news reached her ears, she found Uncle Julian's silence on matters outside his manor a source of frustration.

Despite what she considered a gap in their relationship, they enjoyed each other's company. Among other things they often went for rides together, and one day he took her to meet his tenants, explaining as they passed through a gate at the foot of his drive and turned down a sun-dappled track by the apple orchards, that unlike England, most of the tenant farmers hereabouts paid little more than a nominal rent for the privilege of farming the land. They were a proud and hardworking breed of farmers, and very independent of spirit.

The word reminded Rebecca of the sight of the troops in New York drawn up to hear the Declaration of Independence. "Are they so independent, Uncle, that they would fight against their king?"

"Often," was his short reply.

"Even though you do not approve?" Rebecca was aghast.

Uncle Julian drew rein and sat in silence for a moment, watching a chipmunk scurry for cover beneath a tree root beside the narrow lane. "There are great manors in this colony, held by Livingstons, Schuylers, Morrises, Philipses, where the lord of the manor controls the lives of his tenants. But those are exceptions," he said at last. "I do not have control over the political views of my tenants, and indeed, would not wish it. As for my own beliefs . . ." He looked searchingly at his niece. "I do not discuss my beliefs with many. There are a good number of men who support the Royalist cause in Westchester, and in New York. But there are many who do not. On both sides of the question I have good friends. I have tried to walk a middle road between the two camps, and have only barely succeeded."

"But why should you?" Rebecca asked hotly. "Surely it is not a crime to support your king?"

Uncle Julian coughed. "I so dislike discussing such things with you, my dear. But perhaps you had best know that sometimes it is indeed a crime to speak out for British rule. The New York Provincial Congress has been persuaded by some of its more radical members, and by officers in the military, to 'investigate' many people who have chosen not to take the oath of Association, an oath of support for this rebellion. A number of us from Westchester were required to appear before them late last year, and to explain our reasons for hesitating. It was an uncomfortable time for all of us. I did not take their oath, but I had to swear not to give aid to the British. Now I can only hope that the army will come soon, that the conflict will be as bloodless as possible, and that the entire issue of independence will be laid to rest. Meanwhile, I do want you to understand, Becky, that these are topics not to be discussed lightly, or with anyone you don't know and trust. I hope you understand."

Rebecca's eyes widened. "I understand that this Provincial Congress has taken upon itself the task of terrorizing people into submission to treason, and I think it is a disgrace."

Her uncle turned his horse along the lane once more and shifted his weight in the saddle. "It is not quite so simple. There are many good men in that Congress who speak up for moderation. Some who have gone along with independence have done so most reluctantly, but with a conviction that it is necessary to impress upon the king and Parliament their just grievances."

"When they call out troops to fight their sovereign's army, it doesn't sound very reluctant," Rebecca snapped.

Her uncle's smile was wan. "You would have to know all that has gone on in these colonies since the close of hostilities with the French and the Indians years ago to understand their view, Becky. I cannot help but sympathize with some of them myself. But that is much too complex to discuss. Besides, the Deiters' farm is just beyond that clump of alders." At that he set his horse to a trot, and Rebecca had no choice but to follow. But her mind whirled with the implications of all that he'd said, and for days thereafter she seethed with indignation.

She had little time to brood, though, for her new duties kept her too busy to worry overmuch about politics. The running of Halscomb, she discovered, was a complicated business, with all decisions about the household devolving upon her. Uncle Julian seemed more than glad to give over authority to his niece, and she spent a goodly portion of each day helping Mrs. Clark with the myriad details life on a manor required her to oversee. At first the responsibility seemed overwhelming, but she would learn, she vowed, and she would manage Uncle Julian's lovely little estate as he'd never had it managed before. His steward, the shifty-eyed Earle Evans, might handle the land, but she would slowly take over the great house and the outbuildings and would make her uncle proud.

Despite her duties around the house, Rebecca found that life at Halscomb was not so very different from the one she would have led at Blair. She was still required to entertain all neighborhood worthies, and many of the ladies who came to call these first weeks seemed altogether familiar—extremely well-bred, censorious, superior and sometimes catty. She wasn't sure she would care if she never saw them again, and only for Uncle Julian's sake was she more than civil to most of them. From experience, she felt sure she would fare better with their men.

Her first real opportunity to find out was to come late in August. Uncle Julian, wanting to do things in style, had planned a party in her honor, and Rebecca found herself looking forward to this first full glimpse of New York society with a bouyancy she hadn't felt in a very long time.

Sylvie was the first to notice, during the hot August days, the heightened color in her mistress's cheeks and the new sparkle in her large eyes. "You are excited about this party, aren't you, miss?" she asked once as she worked over Rebecca's black tresses, experimenting with hair styles.

"I am indeed, Sylvie." Rebecca dimpled into the mirror.

"It will be nice, after this past year and all. A change."

Rebecca patted a curl high over her ear, then twisted it around her finger. Something in her maid's voice made her look up at her. "Do I gather you are finding a pleasant change here at Halscomb too, Sylvie?"

"Oh, yes, miss." Sylvie laughed self-consciously. "Do you know there is a school teacher down in the village . . ." She stopped.

"Oh? And you met this school teacher."

"Yes, miss. Mrs. Clark introduced me to him when we went for ribbons last week. His mother is a seamstress, you see. Mr. Adams is a very nice man. He didn't act surprised when I could talk to him about the subjects he teaches, and even offered to lend me some books. He doesn't seem to mind that I am a lady's maid," she added, then blushed. She looked quickly at the mirror, but Rebecca was examining a pot of rouge on the table and did not meet her eye. "I . . . I mean," the girl stammered, "that this country seems more . . . informal than England."

Rebecca looked up at that. "Yes, I know what you mean,

Sylvie." She remembered the easy manner that existed between Uncle Julian and his tenant farmers. There was little deference in the men's attitudes, although they were perfectly respectful. Their wives, too, had seemed to assume a social level almost equal to Rebecca's own. She had been vaguely irritated at first, but was slowly growing accustomed to the lack of servility in America. "Well," she said, pulling her thoughts back to Sylvie, "I hope you see your schoolmaster again. And I think this hair style might be just the thing, don't you?"

"A little more height would be fashionable, miss."

Rebecca pouted. It seemed to her the sweep of curls back from her forehead already towered well over any comfortable height. "I don't think I could bear more. Besides, I must go and help Mrs. Clark now. Mr. Halscomb does not normally entertain in expansive manner, and she is hard pressed at the moment."

Happily, her added labors did not go unnoticed these days. Uncle Julian was practically like a small boy in his enjoyment of the preparations she made. "It is marvelous to see the house looking this way," he said enthusiastically that afternoon when he came upon Rebecca practicing the arrangement of summer blooms in a tall vase. "I always knew it needed a woman to make it look right, and I can't tell you how happy I am that you decided to join me here."

This was the first time Uncle Julian had spoken in so many words of his pleasure in her coming to Halscomb to live, and Rebecca felt a swell of love for her kindly uncle. "I can't tell you how glad I am that you asked me."

Uncle Julian looked as though he'd say more, but instead he patted her arm and wandered outdoors. Rebecca smiled mistily after him. How hard the man was trying to help her remake her life!

On Friday, August twenty-third, the day began under a hot haze left over from a storm of the night before. But by midmorning the sun was sparkling on wet grass and the sky was turning to brilliant blue. Rebecca, inspecting the final dusting of Chippendale chairs and walnut tables in the main parlor, stopped to look out the long windows and revel in the glorious morning. By noon, she knew, the heat would have settled over the land again, but as long as it remained sunny, she didn't care. She could see workmen now, swarming over the side lawn between house and gardens. They were here to set up a marquee for dining tonight, and she would have to abandon her post and go to help Mrs. Clark select the linens that would be needed for the long trestle tables that were going up.

At noon Uncle Julian wandered in distractedly, to find Rebecca placing tall vases of flowers at each side of a great fireplace, and at her suggestion, wandered out again to the stables to seek solace with his horses. He obviously had begun to rue the day he'd suggested this party, and Rebecca laughed as she watched him go. He would be proud tonight; she would see to that.

By three-thirty all was in order, and Rebecca descended the curved staircase to inspect the rooms one last time. She was dressed in a simple gown of palest yellow muslin. The square neckline and wide elbow-length cuffs were edged in snowy lace, and ribbons of the same lace ran down the front of the wide skirt split over an embroidered petticoat. Her hair, waving back over her ears and curled into three heavy ringlets on one shoulder, was unpowdered and glistened from the heavy brushing she'd given it this morning. She looked cool and composed, despite the afternoon heat, and her uncle, standing beside the open front door, drew in his breath as he looked at her.

"You are a feast for old eyes," he said and came to bow his balding head over her hand. "The most perfect ornament to decorate my home. We will make a tour together, and then it will be time to welcome the first of the guests."

Rebecca smiled happily. "I have not anticipated anything with so much pleasure in a very long time, Uncle. I only hope that our preparations meet with your approval."

"How can they not?" Uncle Julian drew her slender hand through his arm and led her across the hall where they peeked in at the dining room. Silver glistened on sidetables, and spotless crystal twinkled on the central dining table set for fourteen. The room, with its handpainted Chinese wallpaper and white wainscoting, rich parquet floor and gleaming mahogany furniture, was worthy of an English country seat, Rebecca thought, and looked with pride on her handiwork.

They toured the other rooms, making sure candles were set in all the brackets and wine was in decanters in the library, then they passed through the high hall again and stepped onto the shaded portico.

"You will meet so many people tonight, Becky, I feel I have been remiss in my duties," Uncle Julian began as he led her down the front of the house to overlook the marquee and gardens. "I should have told you more these past days."

Rebecca chuckled and pressed her uncle's arm. "You needn't worry. My memory for names is quite good. I shan't call people the wrong thing."

"I don't doubt your proficiency, my dear. Still, it would have been easier for you if I'd said more." He shook his brown-clad shoulders. "Also I should explain that you will find men of all political persuasions under this roof tonight. I can only hope there will be little discussion of politics with you ladies present, but if any should occur, you will remember to be very discreet, Becky."

"I will try, Uncle. But surely there will be no rebels here."

"Nearly all coming are what I would prefer to think of as moderates. But there *will* be members of the New York Provincial Congress. One of those men is John Jay, a most impressive and articulate young man, and I warn you, his sympathies are certainly with the rebellion."

"Yet you invite him into your home?" Rebecca stared up at her tall uncle, uncomprehending.

"He is a friend, Becky. And he proved himself to be one when I was examined before the Congress last year. It was partly due to him that I was questioned only briefly and then allowed to return home. He has been in White Plains, where the Provincial Congress is now meeting, having removed from New York in early July, and I will be glad to see him again."

Rebecca felt there was little to be said to that, and marveled at the fact her uncle could straddle the spiked political fence with such seeming ease.

"On the other side, my dear," her uncle went on, "there will be representatives of some of New York's oldest, wealthiest and most influential families, many of whom are staunch in their support of our king."

"I am glad to hear it," she replied with acidity. Then more sweetly she added, "Never fear, Uncle, I shall be the soul of discretion."

He smiled down at her then, and walked her back to the steps. As they descended to the wide drive, they could see two horsemen mounting the hill toward them. Uncle Julian drew her forward. "It would seem our first guests have arrived."

Rebecca looked up, but could see no shade of worry on his heavy features, only an anticipatory gleam of welcome in his dark blue eyes. Perhaps, she thought suddenly, his fence-straddling was not as calculated as she'd assumed. His only real desire seemed to be to remain friends with all and to be left in peace. She remembered the motley army standing defiantly on the Commons in New York. If there was to be war, she would not have anyone mistake *her* allegiance, not if she were the owner of Halscomb.

The horsemen drew rein before them and a groom ran up, catching the bags that were handed down. Then the arrivals swung from their saddles and strode forward. One of the men looked to be about thirty. He was dressed in a simple but well-cut homespun coat of darkest blue, and his dark hair was pulled back from a slightly receding hairline into a smart club at the base of his neck. His gaze was direct and intelligent, and Rebecca thought immediately that she would like him.

Then she looked at his companion, and the shock of recognition made her blink. The tall young man with dark gold hair walking purposefully toward her with an appreciative look in his gray eyes was a younger version of Gordon Meade, the frightening, infuriating and disturbing man whose memory she thought she'd left in London a lifetime ago.

Chapter 9

Her smile frozen on her lips, Rebecca watched the men approach and tried to wrest her mind back to the hills of Westchester.

"I was just now speaking of you, John," her uncle's voice was saying, "and I'm so glad you are the first to arrive." His big hand was outstretched to the older of the two guests, and was clasped warmly in response.

"Nothing to make me blush, I hope," the man said and smiled at Rebecca standing in what she feared was a paralytic attitude.

"Only compliments of the mildest sort," Uncle Julian rumbled and turned to Rebecca. "Becky, allow me to present Mr. John Jay, one of New York's most illustrious citizens. John, this is my niece, Miss Rebecca Blair, newly arrived from England to make her home with me. My fortune is the best, don't you think?"

"The best, indeed." Mr. Jay bowed over the girl's hand. "Your house has never been so graced, Julian. I hope Miss Blair intends to stay a very long time."

Rebecca returned his appraising look. "A very long time, I think, Mr. Jay." She felt a stab of sorrow that this bright and attractive-looking man was on the side of the rebellion.

"Good. Now may I present Lieutenant Alexander Meade?" Jay brought the big blond man forward, and Rebecca froze with horror at the name. Through blurred eyes she could see he was little more than a boy, perhaps seventeen, certainly no older. His features were less chiseled than Gordon Meade's had been, and he lacked those startling blue eyes she remembered, but he had much the same square-jawed look of determination. She put out her hand to him, hoping it wouldn't feel clammy.

He took it without a word, but the admiration on his face deepened as he bowed. The brass buttons on his blue uniform twinkled at her in the afternoon sun.

Uncle Julian shook the young man's hand as Mr. Jay went on. "I know you will forgive me for bringing Lieutenant Meade this evening. He is newly arrived from New York with dispatches for the Congress, and had nowhere to go tonight, so remained under my wing. His older brother, Gordon, is a very dear friend of mine."

Rebecca's body jerked at the name, but none of the men seemed to notice.

"You're most welcome, young man." Julian Halscomb beamed. "But tell me, John, how is Sarah?"

"Very well, thank you. She is staying at the moment with her father in New Jersey."

"A pity she could not be here. But we shall endeavor to keep your spirits up for the weekend."

Thin lines wrinkled John Jay's brow. "I'm sorry, Julian. I had looked forward to this respite from business, but I'm afraid the lieutenant and I must return to White Plains at first light." He hesitated, then said evenly, "General Howe has landed troops on the south shore of Brooklyn."

Rebecca, trying to cover a smile of satisfaction, watched her uncle closely, but he gave no hint of either jubilation or regret. His dark eyes looked mildly at his guest. "Of course you must return in the morning. I am flattered that you felt you could come to Halscomb at all."

She turned away from the group to hide a quick flash of disgust, and was glad to see that more guests were arriving. No time now to think of disloyalties, or even of the frighteningly familiar young Mr. Meade who seemed inclined to dog her footsteps.

During the hour of dressing that followed, Rebecca reminded herself again to say nothing that might embarrass Uncle Julian this night. Then, as she stood still so Sylvie could slip the light mauve skirt of her ball dress over her hooped petticoat, she smiled. This was not an evening to be thinking of politics anyway. It was a time to rejoice in her freedom, to enjoy herself thoroughly and to see that her guests and partners did too. As Sylvie worked on the tiny hooks and eyes at the back of the skirt, Rebecca smoothed the thin chemise over her breasts and plucked at its edging of fine lace. Yes, tonight was for enjoyment. If only it didn't include stays in her bodice, she could feel true satisfaction, she thought, and smiled more broadly as she held out her arms to slip into her confinement.

"You look radiant, miss. And it's all so grand," Sylvie said, struggling to pull the long waist of the bodice into place. "Puts me in mind of the old days at Blair. Does it you, miss?"

Rebecca sucked in her breath as her maid started on the fastenings at the back. "Almost, Sylvie. Tell me, do you ever feel homesick now?"

"Not really, Miss Rebecca. Do you?"

"Once in a while I think of Blair in the early morning light, and I remember my parents. But all that is behind me, and I miss nothing else in England."

"Exactly," said Sylvie with a nod over Rebecca's shoulder. Then she returned to work.

Rebecca looked thoughtful as she stood quietly. She was surprised to realize how true her words were. She yearned for nothing that was behind her. Not even Lord Harlcourt. He had disappeared from her life as surely as though he'd been shot, and her regret had been amazingly short-lived. Here at last, on the banks of the Hudson, she was free of her cares. There was a new world to conquer.

When Sylvie was done, Rebecca pirouetted in front of the looking glass. She could scarcely remember the last time she wore such a gown or dressed for such an occasion. Lifting her breasts, she tugged down on the bodice till it was snug on her hips. Now the creamy skin of her neck flowed down to a deep cleavage which she would have to modify. Carefully, she fluffed the lace ruffle above the bodice until she felt sure that her neckline was, if not totally modest, at least decent. She was glad she had decided against powder on her hair, too, for its dark glossiness was perfect above the pale dress. And at least her hair was merely teased into its heights of swoops and curls, not rolled and cushioned or smothered under a mountainous wig. *She* would not need a head scratcher tonight. Poor Mrs. Carey was already using hers and looked most uncomfortable under a veritable jungle of greenery wound through and over her heavy wig. Rebecca shuddered at the thought of the elderly woman's miserable scalp, and turned her attention back to her finishing touches.

The final touch, she thought, should be a thin band of deep violet ruching around her neck. It matched the long ruffle at the bottom of her skirt and the bands of ruching which followed her neckline and flowed down over bodice and skirt front. Her eyes, now the same color as the accents on her gown, sparkled at her from the mirror. She had enough pink in her cheeks, she thought, and would not have to resort to the rouge pot. She bit her lips to make them more vivid, and they pouted prettily back at her. Yes, she would do. And she would make Uncle Julian proud this evening. Catching up her fan, she walked to the door, practicing the art of making her skirts sway provocatively. She had nearly put the young Lieutenant Meade from her mind. He was an uninvited guest, and would be gone in the morning. With any luck at all, she would never see him again.

However, the lieutenant was among the small party of men standing in the front hall when she came down the wide staircase, and only just in time did Rebecca avoid his proffered arm to go in to the dining room. Seated far from him at the table, she kept her gaze studiously averted from the disturbingly well-known face.

Promptly at seven thirty those of the nearer neighbors who had been invited for the evening only began to arrive. Now, Rebecca knew, came her real test. Could she remember enough from Uncle Julian's chance remarks to single out those representatives of the great families? A De Lancey, a Livingston, a Morris, a Varick or a Philipse was easy enough. But she'd have to remember that Mr. Duane was married to a Livingston, as was Mr. Jay. Goodness, it was nearly as complicated as English society. A new game to unravel. She was in her element, really, and quickly she set about charming the older members of New York's aristocracy. But soon the musicians who had been brought in for the occasion were tuning their violins and the harpsichord, and Alexander Meade was at her side.

"I requested the honor of leading our hostess out for the first minuet," he said, "and received permission from your uncle. May I have the pleasure, Miss Blair?"

Rebecca hid her flash of annoyance behind a demure smile. If her uncle had given permission, she supposed she must obey. Perhaps handsome Mr. Revington, to whom she'd just been introduced, would return for a later dance.

She put out her hand and felt it clasped hesitantly. It was rather like having a giant bear cub attempt to be gentle, she thought, and smiled at the tall boy with more warmth. Suddenly it struck her that Gordon Meade might have looked something like this boy when he was younger, and she wondered if it had been only the faithless Miss Jenkins who had hardened Mr. Meade's eyes, if indeed they'd ever been as honest as those of his young brother. Soon, though, the pleasure of dancing again erased all speculation, and Rebecca gave herself over to the joy of the evening.

Her pleasure could only be enhanced, too, when Mr. Revington came to claim her for the next set. He was a handsome man with strong blunt features and snapping brown eyes, and his mulberry silk coat and embroidered white waistcoat over a deeply ruffled shirt were of the first fashion. He was the most elegant man there, and Rebecca was pleased he had returned to her so promptly. Though she found her composure suffered, when, leaning close, he said, "Rarely has this colony had the good fortune to transplant a perfect bloom from the mother country. The soil in England must look barren without you now, Miss Blair. But our garden has suddenly come to new life."

Rebecca, flushed at his extravagant praise, fluttered her fan and looked around the brightly lit room at all the elegant dresses and smiling people. "Your garden would appear to have done quite well on its own, Mr. Revington."

The man chuckled and led her forward. "But it lacked the essential ingredient to all displays; the perfect centerpiece."

Feeling a bit breathless, Rebecca was glad she had to make no rejoinder, as the dance was starting. Her feeling of giddiness increased when she realized before the dance was over that once again she was the object of envy. She had managed to catch the eye of the handsomest man there, and she meant to keep it. Happily, this last resolution took no particular wiles. Charles Revington paid her all the attention propriety would allow, and Rebecca could see that Uncle Julian, occasionally watching the dancing, was pleased.

By ten o'clock, though, Rebecca felt the need of a rest. Despite the open windows, the long room was becoming stuffy with the heat of the candles and of all the dancers. She wondered if she dared suggest a stroll at the end of this dance, and thought perhaps she didn't, when the music stopped and Charles Revington guided her off the floor.

"A glass of punch would be welcome right now, wouldn't it, Miss Blair?"

Rebecca's full mouth curved into a smile of real gratitude. "My sentiments precisely, Mr. Revington. The evening did not cool the house as much as we'd hoped."

"Yes. This has been one of the hottest summers I can remember, with only just enough rain to keep the crops from drying up completely. I'll be glad when the harvest is in, and I can turn my thoughts to more interesting subjects."

"And what subjects are those, sir?" Rebecca moved her fan languidly and peeked over the top at her partner.

As she'd half expected, Charles Revington took a long breath as he looked at her. Then he clasped her elbow and walked firmly to the long table under the staircase. "I will procure that glass for you, first, Miss Blair."

Rebecca ran a practiced eye over the bowls of punch and cider, and was glad to see they were all full. The wine was flowing freely, and the servants were scurrying down the back hall for refills under the watchful gaze of Mrs. Clark. She stood patiently while her escort worked his way between two broad backs and moved to fill her glass. Beside her at the end of the table a knot of men talked in low but heated voices.

"Washington will move more troops over to Brooklyn," one man was saying.

"I tell you he won't." An elderly gentleman in a high rolled wig waved his wine glass aloft. "This move by Howe may be only a feint. He will come for New York, and Washington is committed to defending the city. The Continental Congress is committed to it."

Alexander Meade's young voice could suddenly be heard over the murmurs of assent. "The Continental Congress does not know how indefensible the city is," he stated baldly. "They are committed to an ideal which mortal men cannot uphold."

"The troops have been fortifying the city for months, young man." The bewigged gentleman splashed wine down his sleeve in his agitation and turned a red-eyed gaze up to the tall blond boy.

Lieutenant Meade's face flushed crimson with embarrassment as the eyes of the other four turned too. But he stood his ground. "Some say the fortifications are useless. Less than useless if the British sail up the Hudson and the East River. They'll fence in our troops as though they were in a cowpen."

"Can't sail up the Hudson, Meade," the first man said. "We've got a barricade across the river near the north end of the island."

Rebecca was sorry she couldn't hear the answer Lieutenant Meade would have given, but Mr. Revington was at her side again, holding out her glass. She smiled ruefully. Obviously these men did not feel the constraints of conversation that Uncle Julian had imposed on his own household, and she'd like to have heard more. In her mind's eye she saw again the great armada of ships off Staten Island on July ninth. Surely if all the troops those ships must have held came ashore, there would be no stopping them wherever they chose to land.

Suddenly unwilling to face the overheated ballroom again, she was glad when Mr. Revington suggested a stroll outside. The evening air was balmy with a soft wind off the Hudson. It was pleasant to walk beside the tall pillars of the porch. She tried to put all she had just heard from her mind, to search for a subject of interest to her companion, but nothing came so she remained silent.

"I could hardly help but hear what Lieutenant Meade said just now," Mr. Revington said at last. He paced along beside her, a thoughtful frown puckering his brow. "And he's right, you know. New York will fall at Howe's first stroke." He turned suddenly. "I . . . I'm sorry, Miss Blair. I should hardly have pursued my own thoughts out loud. There's little more boring to a lady than the constant talk of politics and war. At least that's what my sister says."

"Please don't apologize. I'm afraid I am not at all like your sister, and wish you would go on. You must remember that I know very little about what is happening in this colony. But I am come here to live, only a few short miles above an island which everyone says is soon to be a battleground. You will understand my desire to learn more."

Mr. Revington smiled at that. "I am glad you are Julian Halscomb's niece, for I know full well his Royalist leanings. You won't be shocked when I say that it is so hard to just wait. Those of us who have wished to see the present conflict end in the king's favor have had long anxious months waiting for General Howe to bring his troops down from Boston.

And it has been nearly two months since the first arrived. The nerves begin to stretch thin."

"You would join the army if you could?" Rebecca thought she had now caught the drift of the man's thoughts.

"If they offered me a commission in the army, I would not turn it down, no."

Rebecca opened her fan and, stopping, touched his coat with the edge of it. "I think 'Colonel' Revington sounds most appealing," she said with a twinkle.

The man grinned. "A captaincy would be more than I could hope for."

"Very well, 'Captain' it is." Rebecca's laugh was soft. "And you must promise to defend the homes around Dobbs Ferry to the last man."

"I would station myself at your very door if I could, Miss Blair." An earnest look came over his blunt features, but disappeared as Rebecca laughed again.

"I feel so much safer thinking I might have a personal defender," she said lightly and turned back toward the door. She had not missed the look on his face, and it had occurred to her that a past encounter with a colonial had ended in an embarrassing scene. Tonight she did not want to risk another. She took care, however, to look sorrowfully over her shoulder when a Mr. Thomlinson met them in the hall and claimed the next dance was to be his, and was pleased that her tactic was apparently effective, for shortly Mr. Revington out-maneuvered several determined rivals and managed to make himself her partner for supper under the marquee.

It was a perfect evening for being out of doors, and Rebecca reigned over a long table near the garden that midnight in a glow of newfound contentment. At one point, as she sat sipping her wine and at the same time breathing in the fresh scent of roses so nearby, she looked up the tent at Uncle Julian's table and caught his eye. Amidst the forty people present, her uncle gave her one long slow wink, and she laughed aloud with pleasure. The evening was a success, and she knew she had played no small part in making it so.

Only one little cloud floated on the horizon of her happiness at that moment. She remembered a remark overheard as they had all passed through the wide doors onto the lawn for supper.

"You might as well exert yourself to be pleasant and to enjoy this party, Arabelle," a sharp-featured woman had said to her cowering daughter. "For what with all the talk of fighting, there's no telling when there will be another gathering such as this."

Rebecca found the remark discomfiting, not because she doubted the outcome of any fighting to come, but because she already looked forward to the winter social season. She'd enjoyed tonight more than she'd enjoyed anything in a long time. It would be horrible to think that return invitations might not be forthcoming. But perhaps the British would put a speedy end to things now, and life need not be disturbed so very much.

Chapter 10

The long hot summer spilled over into September, and with its progress came news of General Sir William Howe's success on Long Island. By a night march on little-used roads, his troops had encircled the American position, and there had been a resounding defeat for the Americans. The only fact in which the rebels could rejoice was that in a miracle of command, General Washington had managed to evacuate the remnants of his beaten army and its supplies during the course of one misty night. They'd crossed to the New York shore in a motley flotilla of boats, leaving behind who knew how many hundreds dead and as many more prisoners. The reports that came to the house up the Hudson were of an American army so low on morale that if General Howe chose to press his advantage he could sweep New York clean of rebels with little or no resistance. The wonder of it was that Howe appeared to have called a halt to his campaign, and was sitting in Brooklyn, overlooking his ultimate prize with an incomprehensible complacency. One could nearly hear the collective breath of the people of New York being drawn in to await the outcome of events.

Rebecca found, however, that more immediate matters concerned the good people of Westchester. From Mrs. Carey, who came to call with her plain but vivacious daughter, Millicent, she learned something of the hardships that were being felt in the country due to the blockades of both Boston and New

York. More and more, the ladies claimed, one had to make do with drab homespun cloth for one's everyday clothes, for no new materials were to be had. Old dresses would have to be remade to do their duty again and again, they were afraid. Rebecca frowned at the prospect, and was grateful for the many yards of good stuffs she'd brought with her from England. But she was able to assure the ladies that hoops in London were getting smaller, and that in the most daring circles, bodices were becoming less stiff, sometimes even giving way altogether to the new notion of a one-piece dress where sleeves, bodice and skirt were all attached. She possessed two examples of this new style herself and had Sylvie bring them out to be admired. Millicent, in particular, was entranced, and saw the advantage in using less yardage. She wanted to copy the patterns instantly, and Rebecca, who liked Millicent more than most of the girls she'd met anyway, knew Uncle Julian would be pleased that she had perhaps found the first of a new set of friends.

Depressing though news of shortages was for others, Rebecca was not in dire straits for clothing. She still had a very serviceable wardrobe left from her days in London, and the gowns were not yet out of fashion here in the colonies. However, she'd not had a new creation in many long months, and the sudden desire to wear something different was almost overwhelming. Happily, she turned to the contemplation of her clothes for the season to come.

From Mrs. Clark she heard again that Sylvie's school teacher had a mother who was the best seamstress in the county. This news, coupled with an urge to see the young man for herself, gave her the excuse for a visit to the village, so taking the pony cart, she and Sylvie went to Dobbs Ferry the next day.

Mrs. Adams proved to be a diminutive woman of undetermined age, with thick gray hair and a narrow face that exuded both intelligence and good humor. Rebecca liked her at once and was glad she'd brought with her the yards of embroidered blue silk for the woman's inspection.

"Lovely, lovely," Mrs. Adams exclaimed as the material was unwrapped in her small, spotless parlor. Rebecca, watching her deft fingers hover tenderly over the silk threads on the blue background, realized this woman had not seen material like this in a long time. She didn't know whether she felt guilty for owning such stuffs when others in the colonies could not be so lucky, or glad to be giving Mrs. Adams something new and beautiful to work on.

"The color is perfect for you, Miss Blair, and I know we can conjure the most flattering style. Now, Sylvie, you will help me hold the folds, and will watch and listen carefully." Rebecca looked surprised and the woman chuckled. "Sylvie has expressed an interest in learning my craft, Miss Blair, and I will say she has promise. Now stand very still."

Rebecca did as she was bid, and reflected that neither she nor the shrewd woman before her had any illusions about Sylvie's real interest in this house. However, if the girl could actually learn something of sewing, so much the better.

An hour later, the three concluded the first fitting for the new gown, and Mrs. Adams saw them to the door just as a tall young man turned his long strides up the freshly swept front path. Rebecca took note of the bright pink that rose to Sylvie's cheeks when the young man stopped. His thin face, so much like Mrs. Adams's, split into a crooked smile as he bowed.

"Good day, ladies." He swept off his broad-brimmed hat, and when he straightened, his eyes went directly to Sylvie.

Rebecca, momentarily startled at having her maid addressed in the same breath in which she was greeted, rallied as Mrs. Adams stepped forward to introduce her son. "I knew you must be Seth," she said, extending her hand. "The family resemblance is strong."

"Thank you, Miss Blair," he said gravely, then grinned at his petite mother beside her.

"You are bringing home books, I see," Rebecca went on. "Work for your students?"

Seth looked down at the small stack of books and pamphlets engulfed by his big hand. "Not for my classroom students, no," he said slowly. "The Milton is for my own sinful pleasure, and the others were intended for Miss Tyler."

Once again Rebecca was startled. She watched Sylvie accept the papers with shy thanks, and realized it had been a long time since she'd heard her maid's last name spoken. Quickly she studied the young school teacher again, and noticed that his simple coat was threadbare but clean, his linen spotless. His long face was intelligent and held lines that indicated humor. She suddenly felt very good. Yes, she could approve of Sylvie's young man, and she was glad again for the years she'd insisted on having Sylvie beside her in her studies. The girl was no ignorant lady's maid. Perhaps there was a chance for her with this attractive school teacher after all. She'd have to find more excuses for Sylvie to visit Mrs. Adams's house.

When the pony trap was at the edge of the village, she turned the horse's reins over to her maid, knowing Sylvie was thrilled at the chance to drive home, and picked up one of the pamphlets between them on the hard seat. " 'Common Sense' by Tom Paine", she read, and nearly chuckled aloud. For Sylvie's sake, she hoped Seth Adams wouldn't pass too many high-toned books to her. She opened it idly and began to read.

Two pages later she was trembling with indignation and was reading faster through the appalling paragraphs in which the author attacked the institution of monarchy and the person of King George III in the roundest terms. Only a well-bred respect for other people's property kept her from tearing at the pages in fury. But as she read on, she found the writer's compelling style held her through his catechism of evils and his lists of virtues if American independence could be achieved. When she read, "Freedom hath been hunted around the globe. Asia and Africa have long expelled her. Europe regards her as a stranger, and England hath given her warning to depart. O, receive the fugitive, and prepare in time an asylum for mankind," she shut the pamphlet on her lap and sat, staring at the heavy fall foliage beside the track as they bounced past.

Freedom! The man was talking of anarchy, rebellion, government by ordinary people! But the word "freedom" kept going round and round in her mind. She had come to America, much like countless numbers before her, looking for freedom—her own kind of freedom from her former life. Not political or religious freedom, but freedom nonetheless. Had Sylvie done the same? Had her motives been more than a desire to go on serving the mistress she'd had all her life? But that was absurd. What would Sylvie do in this vast country? And how could either of them be well served by a government of lawyers and farmers and tradesmen? There was an age-old and necessary order to things that required respect for its traditions. This raw land *needed* the steadying hand of the established and experienced government in England, of the unifying deference to the hereditary king!

As the pony trap came to a halt at the great barn door of

Halscomb, Rebecca looked sharply at her maid. "Does your Mr. Adams give you many things to read?" she asked.

"Only two books so far," the girl replied and glanced at the pamphlets clutched in Rebecca's upheld hand. "It is very nice of him, isn't it?"

Rebecca's tart reply was swallowed as she saw Sylvie's bright eyes light up even more at the thought of Seth Adams. "These are not so uplifting as he might give you," she said in a controlled voice. "They are political pamphlets, and I must remind you that you needn't believe everything you read. This top one," and she slapped Tom Paine's handiwork with open fingers, "is a vicious twisting of beliefs held by all loyal and worthy men. I hope this does not mean that Mr. Adams in on the side of the rebellion, only that he is introducing you to the sort of sordid writing these colonies are currently capable of."

Sylvie's face drained of much of its color as she listened, but she bobbed her head when Rebecca finished. "I think that is his intention, yes, miss."

Rebecca sighed. Her temptation had been to confiscate the booklets. But she had never dictated to Sylvie how she must think, any more than Uncle Julian dictated to his tenants and servants. Besides, she had liked Mr. Adams on sight. So she must trust to his motives, and to Sylvie's loyal sensibility. "I can only hope your friend will find more suitable reading for you in future. And you may borrow any of my books, you know."

"But I've already read those."

Both girls smiled at that, and Rebecca felt her own tension ease. "Then go to Uncle Julian's library. It is not at all bad."

The incident was nearly forgotten by Rebecca in the next days, for fall was one of the busiest seasons for the household. Meats, fruits and vegetables must all be prepared for winter storage, and the extra activity meant there were that many more chores for Rebecca to remember and oversee. As she went about her duties, from smokehouse to cellars to kitchen, she found her interest in the running of this colonial estate growing. But when she asked Uncle Julian about the goods coming in from the farms, she found his answers vague and dissatisfying.

"Evans is taking care of everything," was all he would say. "I do not try to keep track of barrels of grain, sacks of potatoes, numbers of pigs."

It was obvious that although he enjoyed his house and land, the running of the place interested him very little. He was always more willing to discuss the sad state of his shipping interests in the city. Although Rebecca listened dutifully, she found she could not be enthusiastic about concerns that did not affect her daily life so directly as the running of Halscomb.

When Charles Revington came to call a few afternoons later, she was glad, however, to throw off her apron and leave the house for a leisurely ride with him along the woodland trails among the steep hills, with only Uncle Julian's oldest groom in discreet attendance.

The golden day and the leaving of chores behind her brought back memory of her last ride on wooded tracts, and after a few minutes of polite inconsequential talk, and a decision to come to first names now, she asked abruptly, "Charles, have you read Tom Paine's 'Common Sense'?"

Her escort, eyebrows raised nearly to his hairline, looked quickly at her, then turned to stare stonily between his horse's ears. "Nearly everyone in all the colonies has read that traitor's hotheaded words, and too many have been swayed by them. The man should be tarred and feathered at the very least. Don't tell me you've seen the pamphlet? Where?"

Rebecca surprised herself by a sudden unwillingness to let Charles know where the pamphlet had come from. If he reacted so vehemently to its writer, how might he take the news that the local school teacher was giving it abroad? "I have heard it spoken of, and wondered about it," she replied evasively. She felt vaguely guilty that Mr. Paine's words had been haunting her for the past days, making her wonder about the righteousness of the rebel cause. A slightly safer subject came to mind. "Do you still find it hard to wait, with General Howe sitting in Brooklyn?"

Startled, he turned again and looked at her curiously. "As hard as ever. Do you feel the strain too?"

"Perhaps a little. And Uncle Julian won't allow me to ask questions about what is happening. It is hard not to hear."

"He is right, of course, but you may ask me anything you like, you know." His voice was soft, and his eyes, traveling quickly over her forest-green riding habit and frilled shirt-front, grew warm as they rested again on her face.

Although pleased at the look he gave her, Rebecca turned her face away so as not to seem too bold. "I have heard," she said at last, "that General Washington's army is demoralized from their defeat on Long Island. I have even heard that his men are deserting him at a wondrous rate. Do you think the rebel cause might just disintegrate there on Manhattan Island?"

Charles's laugh was harsh. "I could wish it would. But the Continental Congress was clever. It chose to commission as field officers mainly local heroes from each colony; people like Israel Putnam of Connecticut, and Thomas Knowlton, and Nathaniel Greene from Rhode Island, and Sullivan and Scott from New York. Many of the militia, who had signed up for short terms of duty anyway, are deserting, it's true, but there are many more who are loyal to their commanding officers, or to Washington himself. I'm afraid we can't count on the army just disappearing down there. No, there will have to be another fight, perhaps several more. The army is not so cocky as it was, I hear, but I would not like to count on its running away forever. I only hope I will be there when Howe delivers the final blow." His voice became fierce, and as though he was aware of it he stopped abruptly. "I think I can see why your uncle refuses to discuss the war. A man can get carried away with your questions. And I did not ride up here today to talk of unpleasant subjects."

Rebecca lifted one perfectly arched brow. "But people can think of little else."

"*I* can think of much else, Rebecca. For instance, the way the sun picks out blue highlights in the curl below your hat brim, or the way your eyes dance when you think a man is about to make a fool of himself over you."

They both laughed then, and Rebecca shook her head in wonderment. How many times had she laughed aloud this last year and more? It was a novelty to be savored.

"What makes you look so surprised? Surely not my heartfelt compliments? I was wishing I could think of something to say to you that you have not heard a score of times."

"You do very well, thank you." Rebecca tossed her head and felt her horse prance beneath her. "In fact, I was thinking what a glorious afternoon this is and how glad I am that you came up to Halscomb."

Her forthright speech made Charles's eyes grow bright. Then he swallowed hard. "We are nearly to the northern boundary of your uncle's land. We had best go back."

On the return ride, he told her of his own lands south of here, and of his family. His father was old and ill, he said, cared for constantly by his mother. His sister was married in

New Jersey, but his younger brother was at home, helping him to run the estate, and would be in a position soon, he hoped, to take over full duties when Charles went off to the army. "I've worked hard toward that end, and I will leave the place in good order," he said proudly, and Rebecca congratulated him, though she felt it wasn't fair that the one man she'd met so far whom she really liked was chafing at the bit to be off to the army. She consoled herself with the thought that that army would be protecting the king's interests here in New York, and that with luck, Charles would never go very far.

Meanwhile, she was assured, she would see a great deal of him, if she would allow it.

Cornelius Bradford's New York Coffee House was doing a brisk business this Saturday evening, and the jovial proprietor obviously saw many such in his future. Since he'd opened the establishment in May, it had become a favored retreat for most of New York's remaining men of affairs and for many of the Continental Army's officers. War brings some men unexpected, but happy, profits.

At a table as far into the corner as they could get, Gordon Meade, Aaron Burr and two others almost had to shout to make themselves heard. Gordon's head was beginning to ache with the effort, and he was growing weary of the ceaseless speculation around them. General Howe, he felt, was an unsolvable enigma. Now that he sat with his army on the Heights of Brooklyn, like a bird of prey perched above the nervous city, it was certain that he would make his move eventually, and worrying about the date was useless. All one could do was prepare for the onslaught, or, as Gordon saw it, get out.

"Been sittin' here like ducks for days, just waitin', an' I'm tired of it," declared Sandy Richards, a captain under General Greene who had plopped unceremoniously at the table just minutes before, but who was more than half drunk already. " 'S good thing you gen'lmen took all the important records and stores up to White Plains early in July." He jabbed a finger in Gordon's direction. "But won't matter much, I guess, if Howe marches into Westchester after he massacres us."

"You forget our esteemed commander is a master of retreat,

Sandy," Burr said mildly. "We will not be massacred here, only routed."

"What the bloody hell is he waiting for, then?" A burly major whose name Gordon had forgotten, banged his large fist on the plank table.

"Sir William he, snug as a flea/ Lay all this time a-snoring,/ Nor dreamed of harm as he lay warm/ In bed with Mrs. Loring," chanted Sandy in a monotonous version of the current ballad making the rounds in the army.

"Oh, do spare us, Richards. No one cares about Howe's bringing that Mrs. Loring from Boston any more. And if her charms really are the reason he is delaying his action against the city, we may have hope yet. The plump Mrs. Loring's husband might do our job for us eventually, and murder the commander."

"Husband's received a commission from Howe," grumped Sandy. "So he'll keep his nose out of his wife's affairs."

"The conversation grows stale, eh, Meade?" Burr's eyes gleamed cheerfully. "I'm going to a party on lower Broadway. Will you join me? Guaranteed lovely girls—alas, not of Mrs. Loring's class, however—and the best food in the city."

Gordon considered the matter. "Perhaps for a while . . ." His sentence trailed off as he watched a fresh group enter the crowded room.

Burr was saying, "On second thought, I don't know that I want competition from a man with your reputation among women," when his eyes followed Gordon's gaze. "Someone you know?"

"Yes." Gordon's face was closed, and he looked away.

"Someone you don't at all care to see," stated Burr, and scanned the knot of men coming toward them. "Is it the fresh-faced lieutenant? Or perhaps the major with his new epaulets?"

Involuntarily, Gordon looked again. Yes, by God, an epaulet on each shoulder showed Warren Tyson had advanced to major. Another miscalculation on the part of the army, he thought, and ducked his head toward his mug.

"Ah, the major." Burr's tone was light as he leaned forward, shielding Gordon from view. The others at their table were singing bawdy songs now, paying no attention to anyone. "An old friend, I presume."

Gordon raised his eyes just to the level of Burr's own. "An old acquaintance. Went to King's together, and last year, to

107

France and England under orders of the Congress. We are not fast friends. Our tastes have never been the same."

"He doesn't like women?" Burr was half laughing.

"That is the only area we could agree on. No, his talents lie too much in the field of gambling and his proclivities too far toward intrigue. I don't care for the company he keeps."

"God, man. You sound like my own puritan ancestors."

"You don't know Warren Tyson." Gordon smiled a tight-lipped smile. "I like a man who can play his cards close to his chest. But this one plays them always for his own purposes, and though I've never been sure, I know I can't trust him."

"Then you need to come with me this instant, for I fear the shock of learning your former colleague is now attached to Putnam's staff along with us will need assuaging in the arms of a fair maiden."

"He *what*?" Gordon half stood in his chair.

"Much too transparent, Meade. Half the room now knows I gave you a shocking piece of information. You would do very badly in espionage. No head for it." He grinned wickedly. "I thought you once said nothing could shock you anymore."

"Only surprise me, occasionally. You took a sinful pleasure in telling me that piece of news, Burr." Gordon shook his head. "It's my fate, apparently, to go on dealing with Warren Tyson. Just as it's my fate to have Washington give Thomas Knowlton the special detachment I asked for back in June."

"Plenty of chances coming for us to cover ourselves with glory, Meade. Don't envy Knowlton his job. There'll be dirty business in it."

"All war is dirty. Anyway, I don't envy him the job, only his freedom of action."

"He'll spend a deal of time dancing on the end of His Excellency's string. And you'll have as much freedom as he when it comes to more fighting. They need officers who can *lead*. Your fate will be to face bullets yet. In fact, your fate may be worse than that, for Washington will soon discover he needs more detachments like Knowlton's."

"But for now, my fate will be to go to your infernal party. You're right; I need distraction. You are *not* cheering company, Burr."

"Scintillating, though, you admit."

For September, the weather was unseasonably warm and close, Gordon thought, as, three hours later, he followed Broadway north toward Murray Street. The city was quieter than usual. Anyone with any sense had found excuses to extend summer stays in the country, or had discovered business in Boston and Philadelphia. If generals Putnam and Greene had their way, the army would have followed the good example set by so many citizens of New York. But Washington had let Clinton and Lee persuade him to consult further with Congress and to continue the ridiculous attempt to fortify the island against attack. One could feel in the still night air that something was about to happen, and Gordon wondered, as he passed Trinity Church, and later the venerable buildings of his old college, just who would be left soon to tell of the mock heroic gesture to hold this key city.

He turned up the alley to the back of the house thinking he'd had too much to drink. He didn't normally indulge in morbid thoughts. At the door he paused to remove his boots. There would be plenty of girls still awake upstairs, but if the lady of the house had retired, there was no sense in waking her as he clumped along the passage. He'd tugged off the left boot when a door down the hall opened, spraying a quick band of yellow light against a floral wall.

"Gordon?" The throaty voice preceded the voluptuous figure to the door. A vision of swirling pink silk beckoned to him and disappeared again.

Half hopping in his one boot, Gordon followed the light and entered an elegant little parlor where brocades and silks and oriental carpets made a rich mosaic background for the still beautiful blond woman standing quietly in the center of the room.

"I have not seen you in nearly a week," she said with a pout.

"It's been a busy time for me, Verona. But my lack of attendance does not signify a lack of gratitude to you."

His speech won a smile, and the woman seated herself on a rose-colored chair. "You may work at that other boot over there." She indicated the chair opposite, and reached for a decanter on the pie-crust table beside her. "I have not had any word today about what is afoot in the city. You must tell me."

Gordon couldn't hide his look of surprise as he sat down. "No one knows more than you, Verona. What's the matter?"

She gave a throaty laugh. "I have been indisposed all day, and this evening left the greeting of our gentleman callers to Sarah. So I have not even heard the usual gossip."

The man declined her offer of a glass of port and worked on his boot as he watched her. Verona's powdered face was nearly as pretty as when he'd first seen it over ten years ago, its greatest asset being her full bow of a mouth. She could tempt a man quite astonishingly with that mouth, he remembered and promptly suppressed his thoughts. She must be nearly forty now, he realized, and doing very well with her small but well-appointed establishment. This might be one of the few clean whorehouses in the city at present, thanks to the fact that she was careful about the girls she chose to service her select customers.

Verona was not her real name, he was sure, but never in their months of intimacy, or in the years of friendship since, had Gordon had the courage to ask how she had been baptized. For all her artful ways, she was a formidable woman. She could be hard and cruel if crossed, as well as warm and loving, and he'd always taken pains to be sure she had no reason to feel offense. He'd been grateful for the chance to stay here this week when quarters became cramped for the army. Comfort was at a premium, even for officers.

"There is nothing to report, really," he said at last, and finished tugging off the remaining boot.

"Howe has *still* done nothing?"

"Nothing. We are kept busy, though, continuing to dig trenches along the eastern shore. And now we've begun stealing anything that can be melted down for bullets. An edifying experience."

"I was thinking today that I should get out some British flags to fly. They will be needed soon, don't you agree?"

"You will stay in the city if the army abandons it to Howe's troops?"

"Where else would I go? Besides," and she gave her throaty chuckle again, "the British will have more money, and more need of my girls after being so long on those troops ships."

"It must be comfortable to be able to be apolitical at a time like this."

"Not apolitical. Practical. But do I detect a note of jealousy in your deep voice, Gordon?" She pouted seductively now, one darkened eyebrow raised in inquiry.

"Do you mean, am I jealous of your freedom to be practical? Perhaps." He saw her eyebrows descend to a tiny frown, and grinned. "Or do you mean am I jealous at the thought of leaving you to the blandishments of suave officers in handsome scarlet coats? Assuredly."

Her mobile mouth formed a kiss. "Good. Then you will perhaps return sometimes."

"If the British land and we survive the fight, we will have to leave the city completely, you know. Returning will not be an easy thing to do."

"Perhaps the British won't stay."

"They need a place for winter quarters. The city would suit them admirably." Gordon's voice was dry. He wondered again how to tell Verona that she should think of leaving town. Some officers were still for burning the place and retreating north, despite the fact that Congress had just ordered Washington not to burn a single building, a judgment which, in Gordon's view, flew in the face of common sense. Besides, he knew Verona was right. Where would she go with her gaggle of girls? Thinking of Verona's safety brought back his worry about his brother, and he frowned.

"You are looking cross, Gordon. You aren't worrying over my safety?"

"Yours and others."

"Which others?"

"Men in the army."

"Ah, you are thinking of your young brother again."

The man nodded. "I should never have let him follow me from Albany this spring. We're bottled up here on this island, and if the British used half their heads they'd realize they could sail up the rivers, surround us and take us to a man. Alex is only a boy. I should have sent him away when I learned we were to remain in the city."

"You couldn't. He's an officer now too. And he is not a boy. He is nearly a grown man. In fact, he is nearly as old as you when you first came to me here." Verona's carefully cultivated accent with its slight French inflection slipped on a reminiscent note, and Gordon wondered for the hundredth time where she'd learned that accent.

"He's a full two years younger than I was."

"And from your descriptions of him, he's a great hulking brute like you. He will take care of himself. You cannot be father and mother to him forever, Gordon."

The officer's eyes narrowed, but he said nothing. His head was splitting from the evening's indulgences, he was tired and distracted with worries. He was not going to discuss Alex any more.

"You grow boring when you become pensive, Gordon. Go to bed." Verona stood up in abrupt dismissal, and Gordon rose gratefully. He was due at headquarters at dawn, and there was precious little dark left to this night.

"Shall I send one of the girls to you? After a party of genteel teasing from the high-born ladies, you perhaps need someone."

"After you, Verona, there has never been anyone here who has interested me." No need to add he was not interested in anyone at all this night.

Verona arched her brows scornfully, but couldn't hide a look of pleasure. "You're getting old, Gordon."

"Perhaps," he said from the doorway. "Perhaps I am."

Chapter 11

It was on the following night, the still-warm Sunday evening of September fifteenth, that Rebecca and Uncle Julian attended a dinner party down the Hudson at the Kents' country home, a handsome stone farmhouse set on a knoll between two steep hills over the river. It was not a large party, but it was lively, and Charles Revington was there, which was the main diversion for Rebecca. They all ate sumptuously at a long table in the low-beamed dining room, and afterward, the ladies retired to a silk-hung drawing room which reminded Rebecca of the maroon and gold decor of the Spefton townhouse in London. That thought brought unwelcome memories of her last ball in England, and she became impatient for the men to join them and distract her wayward mind.

When the men did reappear, the quiet satisfaction on all their faces made her beckon to Charles to join her. "Something has made you pleased," she said as soon as he'd seated himself beside her. "Don't keep me in suspense while we wait for Melinda Kent to begin playing for us."

"We didn't hide our feelings very well, did we?" He laughed. "So I'll tell you. We've just received word that General Howe has landed in New York at last."

"Famous!" Rebecca clapped her hands. She looked up to see others smiling also, even Uncle Julian.

"So you've heard already," her uncle said, crossing the

room. "It is quite a story, and I only hope we continue to get like reports."

"What *is* the story?" Rebecca looked eagerly from one man to the other.

"Soldiers were put ashore at Kip's Bay on the East River this morning," her uncle answered, "and the rebel troops left there to defend the shoreline turned and ran as fast as they could."

Rebecca remembered the sloping land past Sunfish Pond where the Kip farm stood. "So the general has New York," she said happily.

"Well, not completely," sighed Julian. "Apparently General Washington, who had already moved much of his army north onto Harlem Heights, galloped back to turn his fleeing troops, but couldn't rally the men. He had to admit the inevitable and order retreat from the city then, for fear his remaining troops down there would be cut off. I gather that General Putnam managed to clear New York and march his men up the western shore, right past the British troops coming from the east. But the whole rebel army is now stretched across northern Manhattan. General Howe has the city itself, but he may have some difficulty clearing the island."

"The rebels didn't burn the city?"

"No, no. Though it's a wonder they didn't."

Rebecca's eyes glowed. "So, it was just as everyone said it would be. General Howe took New York with hardly a fight. Why on earth didn't he do it before?"

Charles looked as though he'd answer her, but Uncle Julian leaned forward and pulled Rebecca to her feet. "Military tactics are not a fit subject for the drawing room," he said with a twinkle. "And Miss Kent awaits her audience, I think. Let us celebrate by going and listening to her. Quite a good voice, as I remember."

Rebecca fought the urge to say Miss Kent held much less interest for her than the armies' intentions, and tried to remember she was supposed to have easily bruised sensibilities. The men, as always, had closed the subject, and she could do nothing but acquiesce.

The following Sunday, however, even Uncle Julian couldn't stem the tide of talk. It was a lovely, crisp evening, the wind bearing the first real hint of autumn, and he and Rebecca strolled on the wide front porch after their meal, enjoying a quiet companionship they'd both come to treasure. Charles was due to call this evening, and Rebecca found herself dreaming lazily of the season ahead. Already there was a small stack of invitations on the long table in the hall giving promise of pleasures nearly to the Christmas holidays. And Joseph Kent had shown an interest in calling on her this coming week, which would be diverting. He was a stocky young man, nearly as short as she, but he seemed to possess a lively wit, and was appealing in his manners.

She was speculating idly on her wardrobe for all these events when up the drive could be heard the rapid thudding of hooves, and a lone rider burst from among the trees lower on the hill. In the late evening glow she could make out Charles, his dark clothes dusty, his hair tousled, flinging himself from his mount and striding purposefully toward the porch. He tugged at his cravat, straightening it, and smoothed his hair as he took the steps two at a time. Practically skidding, he came to a halt before the two figures near the door.

"I apologize for my appearance," he said, still breathing hard, "but I had a long ride up from Kingsbridge, and did not take the time to stop at home and change because I knew you expected me."

"Kingsbridge?" Rebecca and her uncle echoed his word simultaneously.

Charles grinned and fell into step as the three started down the long porch again. "I was obliged to ride down there for my father, but I expected to be home before this. The trouble was," and his face sobered, "there was a great deal of news to be learned, and I couldn't leave till I'd heard it all."

"Oh?" Uncle Julian, his fingers hooked in his waistcoat pockets, stopped and turned an inquiring gaze on the younger man. "What news now? Has Howe made his move?"

"Inexplicably, no." Charles frowned and stood facing them, his hands playing with the riding whip he still held. "Ever since last Monday, when Washington's army made such a stand at Harlem Heights, he's seemed reluctant to attack again. All he'd have to do is land on the Westchester shore and come right around behind the rebels, cutting them off from all retreat off the island, too."

"Well, if he hasn't done the obvious and intelligent thing, what has he done?" Uncle Julian's voice sounded weary.

Rebecca, looking at the men on either side of her, found she was holding her breath.

"He has done very little. Except hang a spy this morning."

"A spy?" Rebecca's breath exhaled abruptly.

"Yes, a young man named Nathan Hale from Connecticut. A minister's son, if you please. Someone said he was one of Knowlton's Rangers, a special detachment reserved for dangerous duty by Washington himself. It was a great day for our cause when Knowlton was killed last week. He was far too able for comfort. No one seems to know just what this Hale was doing, though it is said he was found yesterday with detailed maps of Howe's troop deployment in his shoe."

"Oh, the poor man," Rebecca said.

"Don't waste any pity on Hale," was his curt reply. "Spying is a nasty business, and those who elect to do the underhanded work know what their rewards will be if they're caught. Though this Hale is reported to have waxed literary at the end. His dying words were 'I only regret that I have but one life to lose for my country,' according to the British captain who brought the news to Washington's headquarters. Very high-minded sentiments for a spy."

"That's from Addison's *Cato*," Rebecca said softly. "But the line is 'What a pity is it/ That we can die but once to save our country.'" She shuddered.

Charles looked momentarily disconcerted as Uncle Julian grasped Rebecca's arm. "I'm sorry you had to hear of this unpleasantness, Becky." He looked reproachfully at Charles. "If there is any more news, young man, perhaps Rebecca would excuse us for a few moments, and then she can return and I'll leave you to talk of more interesting matters, eh?"

"No." Rebecca was surprised by the force of her voice. "Surely there can be nothing more unpleasant than the thought of a young man dying for making maps. What else did you learn, Charles?"

The man shifted uncomfortably. "Your uncle's right, of course. I shouldn't have been so heedless as to blurt out war news in front of you, Rebecca. If you'll give us just two minutes, I shall join you presently."

"Nonsense," she answered, feeling she would stamp her foot in a moment. "I am quite capable of hearing anything else you have to say. Women are hardly so chicken-hearted, nor so feather-brained, as you men would like to think."

Uncle Julian's heavy brows rose, and he scratched the

fringe of hair over his left ear. "If Becky won't take our suggestion, then I suppose she won't. So you might as well finish quickly, Charles."

Clearing his throat, Charles did as he was bid. "The bigger news everyone's talking about is the fact that New York burned two nights ago." Satisfying gasps met this revelation, and he went on hastily. "It wasn't the army. They'd cleared out of the city days before. No one seems to know how it started, though there are rumors it began in many places, all of them under the eyes of rebel sympathizers. By yesterday morning about one third of the buildings were ashes according to a man I met who'd come through the rebel lines from Greenwich, just above the city. Washington and his men are cheering so heartily, you could practically hear them up here."

"I imagine they are," said Uncle Julian quietly. "This will make it harder for Howe and the others to quarter their troops this winter."

"Then they will have to leave the city and come north, won't they?" Rebecca asked brightly.

Her uncle turned to her, but his eyes focused somewhere over her shoulder. "No matter if he does move north, he has to leave enough troops to hold the city and the harbor. New York is the key to the heart of the colonies." Then he brought his gaze back to her face. "Well, perhaps the British will get busy rebuilding. And things will be in fair shape by next spring again. Tell me, Charles, did you hear any details of where the fire spread?"

The men talked for a few minutes, trying to decide from the rumors Charles had heard, which sections of the city had been hardest hit. Uncle Julian seemed pleased at the piecemeal picture they could produce. "It sounds as though Kent's warehouses might have escaped," he said at last. "And if I don't miss my guess, there will be large numbers of officers and men billeted in what's left of New York. Soon wives will come to join them. Trade will return to normal. Kent's should do a brisk business." He smiled for the first time.

Rebecca listened carefully. She was pleased at this prospect for her uncle, for she knew he owned one third of Thomas Kent's business, but she was thinking of more immediate problems. "Surely General Howe will not just sit on the lower half of Manhattan Island, held back by the rebel army in the north? What do you suppose will happen next?"

"What *should* happen next is that Admiral Howe should sail his warships up the East and Hudson rivers, cutting off a northern retreat for the rebels, and his brother, General Howe should push them from the south. They could capture the whole blasted army if they would just move. But the general just sits there biting his nails, and no one can guess his thoughts. No one can ever guess what Washington will do, either. I would think he'd make a run for the Jersy shore if he were smart."

"He wouldn't come up the Hudson shore?"

"I doubt there would be any fighting on land hereabouts, if that is what worries you," put in Uncle Julian. "If the rebels retreat north, they are apt to go along the Connecticut shore, where they can get help. Halscomb is probably as safe a place as any to be. Anyway, we've always been neutral, and there is no reason for anyone on either side of this conflict to harm us."

Rebecca nodded. "And Charles will keep us informed of any new events," she said brightly, "won't you Charles?"

Her friend assured her fervently that he would. "And as for Kent's," he said, "I know of some men who have crossed from Connecticut to Long Island, into the protection of the British army there, and so seen to their businesses in the city. I could ask someone to try to find out about yours and Mr. Kent's warehouse, sir."

"Very thoughtful of you, Charles. I'll consider the matter. I confess I am eager to learn if anything was salvaged. But now, tell us how your father's health progresses. He was much improved last Sunday, I recall."

Taking the hint, Charles talked of his family, and then of the ball to be held next month at his home. Happily, he and Rebecca discussed entertainment for the guests in the afternoon, debating what the weather was likely to be on October nineteenth. Uncle Julian, beaming at the two young people, left them then and tried to refrain from rubbing his hands with satisfaction.

A half hour later, the two stood waiting for his horse to be brought around on the drive. Charles, beaming at all the plans they had made, tucked Rebecca's hand in his arm and walked a few feet along the grass. "Now this, he stated, "is much more suitable conversation for us, Rebecca. I apologize again for the earlier talk of war."

"You remember I don't wish apologies for such talk. Why must I be wrapped in lamb's wool by the men around me?"

Charles looked surprised at her question, and when he answered there was an irritating deliberation to his voice, as though he were talking to a stubborn child. "I am sure that all the men around you hold you in the same high regard as I do, Rebecca. And it is from that regard that we wish to spare you the need to listen to the less pleasant subjects of life."

"Yet the less pleasant subjects of life are all around me. I am allowed to oversee household work, keep household accounts, make decisions of economy, tend to the sick and even witness the slaughter of animals needed to feed us all. . . ."

"Surely not?"

"Occasionally I have done so, certainly. Just as most women trying to maintain a self-sufficient establishment must. And if you, and any other men are wounded on the hunt, or worse, in a battle, who do you suppose will nurse you?"

"The army surgeons," he answered promptly.

"And after they've done their butchery and bandaging and shipped you off to make way for the next lot, who do you imagine takes over the care of all of you?"

Charles was beginning to look around for his horse. "I suppose you are right, that women carry many of the unpleasant burdens. But a gently bred girl such as you should be subjected to as few as possible."

His obvious sincerity touched Rebecca. "It is not that I don't appreciate your attitude, Charles. It is only that sometimes the labor of standing on a pedestal for the benefit of the men around one becomes tiring. Gallantry is appreciated, but for everyday life the feel of firm earth beneath my feet is more comfortable, I assure you."

She squeezed his arm impulsively, felt his body tense, and, surprised, looked up to see his dark eyes fastened on her with an indecipherable look. Slowly his head bent toward her, and as she waited, a sudden memory of another kiss in the dark took hold of her. Would all Americans be so forceful, so knowing as Gordon Meade had been? She suddenly hoped so.

Charles's lips brushed her cheek, but she could feel his arm tremble under her hand. She turned her face so that their lips met, and he drew back as though burned.

"I . . . I'm sorry, Rebecca."

Conscious of acute disappointment, she looked at the ground. "Your horse is here, I think."

Cold fingers groped for hers, tightened on them, let go. "I will see you soon." His low voice was husky, and he turned abruptly away.

Thoughtfully, Rebecca reentered the house.

Uncle Julian's air of preoccupation over the next few days brought back to her the conversation they had shared with Charles on the porch. She was certain her uncle was wondering about his interests in Kent's warehouse and goods down in New York. She considered the matter at great length one day, and finally, as they sat after dinner in the high leather chairs of the library, enjoying the view over thick autumnal woods and bright flowers along path edges, she broached the subject.

"You are brooding about your warehouse in New York aren't you, Uncle?" she began, realizing she was jumping feet first into his affairs, and wondering if he'd be annoyed with her.

Startled, Julian Halscomb looked over from the glass of port he'd been holding up to the fading light at the window. "How did you know I'd been thinking about it?"

Rebecca smiled and tilted her head. "So, you *have* been wondering what happened, and you've heard nothing."

"Nothing."

"Then why don't you go and see for yourself? Charles said he'd heard of men going to Long Island, and thence to New York. It would be exciting for us to see General Howe's army in residence there, don't you think?"

"No, no, Becky," Uncle Julian said hastily. "I would never take you into what is essentially a theater of war, my dear."

"But isn't Long Island firmly in British hands? Surely there would be no danger."

"Perhaps not, but I would never risk it with you."

There was a ring of finality to his words, and Rebecca subsided after that, though she thought Uncle Julian continued to look thoughtful for a long time.

The following week she discovered the fruits of his thought when almost apologetically he explained that he *was* going to New York to see where matters stood with business. Now that the British army was firmly ensconced on Manhattan Island, he needed to get things on an even keel again. He and

Thomas Kent had determined to ride over to Eastchester, and then cross to the Long Island shore with a man they knew. From there it would be quick work to go over to New York from Brooklyn.

Rebecca asked again to accompany him, but wasn't surprised when his answer was no. "You'll be safe here," he said, "and it will make me more comfortable knowing you will be at Halscomb. The Kents have promised to ride up to see you, and I'm sure Charles will be up once or twice. I shouldn't be gone a week. My old mind will be more at rest if I can discover for myself just how things stand."

"Of course, Uncle Julian. And I don't want you to give Halscomb or me another thought. Just be sure to be back next weekend for the Revingtons' ball."

Uncle Julian promised he would, and took a hearty farewell of her the next day, explaining that if anything at all unsettling happened, she and Sylvie were to go to the Kents, only three miles away. Rebecca laughed at his fussy preparations, and kissed him good-bye with the greatest fondness.

It had occurred to her yesterday that here was her chance to see the books on the estate business. More and more recently she had been disturbed by the thought that Halscomb had no firm hand on the reins. Only the other day she had discovered that their inventory of imported wax candles was becoming low, and had realized that they were using the costly lights for their every need. Now that the colonies were determined not to trade with England any more than necessary, the candles as well as other imported goods were not easily replaced. It was high time Halscomb dipped a few score of its own tallow candles to use for every day.

Uncle Julian had not been gone from the house more than an hour before Rebecca was in his office, searching through the drawers for the worn ledgers she knew he kept there. By the following morning she had discovered the disarray that prevailed in the books, and was appalled at the apparent losses sustained by Julian Halscomb in the last twelve months. Things had become shockingly lax around here it seemed. Uncle Julian must have spent all his time brooding over politics and the decline of shipping, and just let Earle Evans run things as he saw fit. It was apparent the man was, with or without help, bleeding Halscomb of money and goods, and it was up to her to stop the process. But she must be careful, for she needed Evans still.

A half hour after breakfast the steward was standing before her.

"You wanted to see me, Miss Blair?" The man's pale gray eyes darted around the desk top, taking in the opened books, then flicked back to Rebecca's face with a look of mild surprise.

"Yes, Mr. Evans, I did. While my uncle is away, he has asked me to see to things here at Halscomb. I am attempting to do just that."

"I understand, Miss Blair." He voice was nearly oily. "But you know, in most ways, Halscomb runs itself. And your uncle will be back in a week or so."

Rebecca, who had been standing behind Julian's desk, sat very deliberately in his chair. "Halscomb may run itself, Mr. Evans, but I am discovering that the way it is running itself is into the ground. Prices paid for peltry this spring are more than double what they were a year ago. There is no record of the hides that should have been delivered after animals were slaughtered for the estate's use. Mrs. Deiter has half the flax she had a year ago, and yet the need for more cloth has increased over twenty percent, Mr. Evans, due to having more servants and one larger tenant family. Shall I go on?"

The man's receding chin receded further as she talked, till he looked like a turkey tucking its wattles back, she thought. His eyes, never steady for long, slid away from her and darted across the desk top again. "Times been hard, Miss Blair. For everyone. You couldn't know about it, bein' newly come from England and all."

"Times may get harder yet, Mr. Evans, if this war drags on. And we must prepare Halscomb for that. We must make the most of every good at our disposal. We will have to redouble our efforts this season."

"With fewer men than ever? We've lost several to the army already."

"We still have enough men—and, may I remind you, women—to get this fall's work done in good order. The army has claimed only those who amounted to little anyway." Except for young Rob, she thought angrily. He'd been a solid, hardworking boy until he'd taken a fool notion into his head to join the rebels in New York. He'd received a most frosty good-bye only last week.

"I hear tell Frederick Deiter's off afore long. An' I'm considerin' signing on myself," he said with a sly look.

"That sounds an excellent idea," Rebecca replied with asperity, "just as soon as the harvest is fully accounted for and the estate is ready to meet the winter. I feel quite certain my uncle will be happy to discharge you at that time."

The underslung jaw dropped and the man spluttered. "You can't speak for Mr. Halscomb. . . . And when General Howe moves on New York . . ."

"The movements of generals do not concern me," Rebecca cut in smoothly, standing up. "The running of Halscomb does. As I am sure it concerns you, Mr. Evans. So, let us together see how we can repair what damage has been done to our inventories. You will meet me at the stable in ten minutes and we will visit the two nearer farms this morning." She began to gather up papers and ledgers in an authoritative way, as she'd once seen Mr. Bancroft do in London. Not until she heard Mr. Evans's footsteps retreat from the door did she realize she'd been holding her breath.

Expelling it at last, she sat down with a thump, her legs suddenly weak. She'd done it. She'd come through the dreaded interview and had forced her will to prevail. Now, if she could only follow through with the tenants. Ruefully, she looked at the neat pile of books she'd made in the center of the desk. For a girl who'd been brought up with no regard for either money or management of an estate, she'd changed a great deal. Her full mouth curved into a sad smile. Perhaps this, not Blair or the London house, had been her father's real legacy to her—the forced learning about things that were supposed to be a man's affairs, but which, she'd discovered, a woman might do just as well. With a pat for the stack of books, she stood up and moved briskly out the door.

The visits to the farms proved rewarding. Rebecca thought she even detected an air of relief on the part of Mrs. Deiter for someone from the big house taking an active interest in the affairs of everyone on the estate again. But the whole day had been exhausting, and her uncle's steward had not made it any easier. The man was obviously resentful of her assumption of authority, and had constantly overridden anything anyone tried to say. She'd had to be curt with him several times, and she feared constantly that he would break into open rebellion, taking the farmers with him. That had never happened though, and now Rebecca looked forward with a martial eagerness to tomorrow's visits to the other farms.

As she led her filly into the barn, and turned her over to a stableboy, she realized how taxing the whole affair had been. If only she could now have a few minutes to herself. Glancing around to be sure no one watched, she gave in to a sudden urge and, hitching up her skirts, climbed the ladder to the great loft above. The scent of fresh-cut hay filled her senses and she stood looking out over stableyard and orchards, soft in the afternoon sun, as she breathed deeply and happily. She felt as she had used to at Blair years ago when she played truant from her studies and hid in the loft of the long barn to dream away a sunny English afternoon until her mother's insistent calls threatened discovery. Only now there was no one to call her to account, and she felt a twinge of sadness at the realization. She had only her own conscience to tell her how long she might stay away from duties, and she was appalled to acknowledge that her conscience was a harder taskmaster than ever a parent or a governess had been.

She turned toward the ladder again, and as she did, she heard a rustle at the back of the loft. A mouse? A cat? She shrugged. But as her feet found the first rung, she looked into the deep shadows and saw a head duck behind a mound of hay.

"Sylvie," she said sharply, "you don't belong up here." She stepped back up to the floor, her hands on her hips and waited as her maid stood up slowly. "Sylvie's face was red with exertion—or mortification—and involuntarily she glanced behind her. Rebecca moved forward. "What—" she began, but the question was cut off as her eye fell on a form lying atop a horse blanket spread in the hay. Incredulous, she stared at the still form while recognition began to dawn. "Rob?" she asked, and picking up her skirts, stumbled through the piled hay. As she drew nearer she could see the awful pallor of the boy's face, the blood-soaked bandage over one shoulder where his coat had been cut away. But Rob was supposed to be in New York! And good riddance to him.

As she looked down at his pain-filled eyes, her anger at what she'd thought of as his defection disappeared. Dropping on one knee beside him, she put tentative fingers to his forehead. "What happened?"

The boy twisted at her touch, glassy eyes swiveling wildly around the loft.

"I'm not certain, miss." Sylvie dropped beside her. "He staggered into the yard a while ago, and Cook saw him from the kitchen. I came out just as some of the stableboys lifted him up here."

"He should be in the house, not up in the loft!"

"We didn't know if someone was after him, thought we should hide him. He was talking when he got here, but most of it didn't make much sense. I think he was with others, going to join the army, when a pack of loyalists from the Livingston manor set on them. I don't know how he got back here alone. We've seen no one else since he arrived."

"But why would loyalists ambush a boy like this?" Rebecca bit her tongue. It didn't matter why. Rob was bleeding into the hay and burning with fever. He needed help. "Never mind. We have to get him out of here. He needs a doctor."

"I was thinking the same, miss. I didn't see his wound until the men put him on this blanket."

"Water," Rob croaked.

Rebecca rocked back on her heels. "Sylvie, go down and have the men hitch a team to the old hay wagon. Then send them up here to carry Rob down. When you come back, bring a dipper of water."

"What are you going to do, Miss Rebecca?" Sylvie was already on her feet.

"I'm going to see he reaches a doctor." Rebecca began tearing at the frill of her thin petticoat, impatiently pushing her skirt aside up to her thighs. Rob's overbright eyes followed her movements.

"Miss!"

"Hush, Sylvie. This is no time to be missish. Rob will not die from the sight of my legs, but he will if the blood isn't stopped. Now go."

She didn't look up as Sylvie scampered across the hay, but bent to pull the tattered homespun shirt away from Rob's shoulder. What she had taken for a bandage was a tail of his shirt wadded against an ugly purple wound high on his chest. The blood was flowing freely enough that the dirty material was not stuck to his flesh, and she removed it with ease, trying not to gag at the sight and smell of the awful carnage. With trembling fingers she tore another length from her petticoat as she crooned nonsense words to the writhing boy. Then she folded the strip and pressed it as hard as she dared against the hole. He panted and tried to turn, but she held on, biting her lip. It was hard to lift his shoulder enough to slip more cloth beneath him, and he cried out when she moved him. But she persisted until she'd tied her wadding securely in place.

By the time Sylvie reappeared, Rebecca was half dazed with her own exertions and could barely hold Rob's head to tip water into his mouth until it began to run down his chin. Yet another length of linen was torn from her poor petticoat then, and she used it to sponge his hot face until the head groom and a husky stableboy arrived to carry him. Going ahead of the men, she and Sylvie piled loose armfuls of hay onto the bed of the creaky wagon and threw more horse blankets over the mound. Rob fainted before he reached his new resting place, and Rebecca, eyeing the lumpy pallet on the hard wagon, though it was as well. She threw in more hay and another blanket till the boy was nearly obscured.

As she began to climb to the front seat, Sylvie, who had gone outside to see that all was clear, came running back. "Oh, miss, Mrs. Kent and her daughter have come to call, and Mrs. Clark already told them you were back. She's looking for you now. And Mr. Charles has arrived too. His horse is being led around here."

Rebecca's foot stopped in midair. "Damn," she said, startling the three people beside her. Her foot stamped to the hard earth floor. "Sylvie, you will have to go in my place. Take Jud here with you, and deliver poor Rob to Dr. Cartwright in the village. Tell him that his reckoning is to come directly to me, not to anyone else at Halscomb." No time to wonder where the money would come from. No time for anything but a hasty retreat to the house before Charles came out looking for her. Rob's rebel views were well known hereabouts, as well known as Charles's loyalist ones. She didn't want them to meet.

"Then you aren't turning him over for being a rebel?" Sylvie asked, wide-eyed.

"Don't be a goose." Rebecca patted Sylvie on the shoulder and nodded to the two men who were shuffling their feet. "Now not a word about any of this." And she ran for the house.

The hour that followed was like a bad dream for Rebecca. Trying to make polite conversation while her mind was on the forlorn figure jolting over back roads to the village was difficult, and attempting to sit on the trailing hem of her riding habit where a smear of rust colored blood seemed to shriek her activities was uncomfortable. She knew all three guests were eyeing her dishabille with interest, but she didn't feel up to excuses, tried simply to fasten their interest on other things. But when Charles said mildly that he had heard some farmers from the Livingston Upper Manor had caught some rebel sympathizers crossing their land last night, she snapped something about civilians hunting people like deer and why not let the armies settle the conflict, which brought a slightly hurt look to his face. She was sorry for her tone, but was too tired to make apologies. She would make it up to Charles on Saturday, she thought, and at last bid them all a relieved farewell. As she'd hoped, none of the party came again to call in the intervening days.

Two days after the startling discovery of Rob in the hay loft, Rebecca rode into the village to see him. He had had a bullet removed from his shoulder, had had a bad day afterwards, but was going to mend now, according to Dr. Cartwright, and Sylvie had persuaded the Adamses to take the boy in for his convalescence. Rebecca sent quantities of food to the little house on the edge of town, and was aware of a real admiration for the doughty little Mrs. Adams and her quiet son who had taken on this new burden without question. They were obviously surprised at Rebecca's aid to a rebel, though, and she found she was at a loss to explain it herself. Except she knew she could not have sat by and let the boy die, whichever side of the war he was on.

The anticipated week sped past after that, and Rebecca hardly noticed the days, so absorbed was she in the new tasks she had set herself. The visits to the other farms proved fruitful, and at last she was making order out of the chaos of the estate books. She hoped Uncle Julian would be proud. She'd even struck a bargain with the teenage sons of Mr. Lovell to buy all the peltry they could trap—at last year's prices. She was looking to the future when, as Uncle Julian predicted, the British reopened trade in New York and Kent's warehouse would need to be filled again.

When Saturday finally arrived, Rebecca awoke with a feeling of anticipation. Today's party was to be her reward after a hard week. These colonies were a demanding place, she'd discovered. If one were to create a good life here without the aid of imported luxuries, one had to be prepared, no matter one's station in life, to work very hard indeed. Surprisingly, the thought was exhilarating. With all her efforts, she'd grown to love Halscomb and to respect the people who lived here more each day.

Smiling, Rebecca stretched and bounced from the bed. Her new gown of blue flower-embroidered silk hung on her wardrobe door, ready for packing. Its full flowing back panels shimmered with silver thread in the early light, and she gazed at it happily. Charles would approve, she felt sure.

Putting on a dressing gown she went downstairs for breakfast, half expecting to see Uncle Julian already at the table. But there was yet no sign of him. Isn't that just like a man, she thought, to show up only at the last possible second, or worse, to forget his social obligations completely. Well, she'd have to get ready and be prepared to leave without him this afternoon if he didn't arrive in time. There was always the chance he would go straight to the Revingtons' from New York. Perhaps a messenger would arrive before she left.

At two o'clock she was tying the ribbons of her bonnet under her chin and trying to suppress annoyance at not having received word from her uncle. She'd ordered the coach, so she supposed there was nothing for it but to leave alone. She sent Sylvie down with her dress box and took a last look in the mirror, smoothing the striped sleeve of her walking dress. The two soft feathers on the brim of her bonnet bobbed as she nodded in satisfaction, then patted a bit of perfume under her ears. She thought she heard the coach coming around the house to the door, and she glanced out the high window over the drive. The coach was in place below her, and the coachman was talking to a strange man in heavy buckskins. The stranger lifted his arm then, and frowning, Rebecca looked across the lawns toward the curve of the drive where it entered the trees. Two more figures could be seen emerging from the wood.

Whoever they were, they would have to be turned away, she thought, and picking up her smart gold-headed walking stick, went out to the hall. Unless, of course, they had word of Uncle Julian. She started down the stairs. And then she heard Sylvie's scream.

Chapter 12

Her legs trembling and her hand unsteady on the banister, Rebecca tried to move faster down the stairs. Sylvie's scream had been bitten off as though her throat were cut, she thought wildly. Clutching her skirt higher she stumbled on, hearing now the hoarse shout of a man, the frightened whinny of a horse, the stamp of heavy shoes on the porch.

She was nearly to the bottom of the elegant staircase when the front door banged back and two burly figures careened into the hall. Rebecca had an impression of brown fringed shirts, high buckskin leggings and muskets trailing on the parquet floor before she shut her eyes in fright. Gruff voices called from outside. She clung to the banister, fighting down a sense of panic. She mustn't faint, or even show her fear. These ragged-looking people could not know the man of the house was away. They must be turned out quickly.

"Now there's a pretty one." A gravel voice crossed the hall toward her.

Rebecca opened her eyes, allowing all the scorn she felt for the speaker to enter their violet depths. Pinning the man with her bright gaze, she drew herself up as straight as she could and descended to the last stair. "The service entrance is at the rear," she said in a clipped voice.

The big man, standing so close, laughed harshly. "Is it now? Ain't that nice, Todd?"

The other moved forward, his small eyes raking down

Rebecca's impeccable figure. "Yeah," he said and a small stream of tobacco juice was expelled onto the edge of the carpet at his feet.

A look of incredulous disgust crossed Rebecca's face, and suddenly her fright gave way to a cold fury. "How dare you walk into this house unannounced," she cried. "Get out."

"Oh, we'll be gittin' . . . by 'n' by," the first man said, not moving, "an' maybe we'll take you along with us. The major has an eye for such as you. He might even reward us for our extra find, eh, Todd?"

"Yup." Another stream of tobacco juice followed the first.

"Who are you? What have you done with my maid?" To Rebecca's chagrin, her voice rose.

"Is that who that was? My, my. She's safe an' sound right outside, lady. If you'll come along with us, we'll show you." He stepped forward and reached out a wide dirty hand.

Without conscious thought, Rebecca's fingers gripped her gold-topped walking cane. Looking into the man's fleshy face, with its stubble of black beard, she felt nearly blinded with rage. "Don't you dare touch me," she hissed.

He grinned, showing blackened stumps among a fence of yellow teeth. His hand came closer.

The gold head of the cane flashed once in the light reflected from the crystal chandelier as Rebecca brought it down with all her might across the outstretched arm. With a yowl of pain, the man staggered back, gripping his arm.

Her eyes glittering with a savage intensity, Rebecca stood where she was, the cane still clutched in her small hand. "Now get out," she said in a tight voice.

There was a commotion at the door, nearly drowning the animal growl of the man she'd hit. Rebecca didn't dare take her eyes off him, but she was dimly aware that more figures crowded out the light entering the hall.

"Todd, Jones, what's going on?" A voice barked from the center of the throng. It was a voice of some command, and there was a sudden silence in the area but for movement of feet. The two men before her turned reluctantly.

"Found this . . . lady in here," one of them said sullenly.

Rebecca's eyes scanned the group. In the center of the mass of brown she picked out a dark blue coat of superfine, its buff-colored facing lying against a waistcoat of the same color and a white linen shirt. Beneath the dark tricorn hat with its cockade of yellow, she saw an aquiline nose and dark impenetrable eyes. Her walking stick clattered to the floor from suddenly nerveless fingers.

Warren Tyson returned her gaze and a thin smile spread across his face. He stepped forward a pace, distancing himself from his ragged crew. "Miss . . . uh, Blair, I believe?"

"Mr. Tyson," she gasped. "How . . . how did you come here?" She eyed his coat again, fearing she already knew the answer. She'd seen others like it on the Commons in New York the day the rebel troops were drawn up for the reading of the Declaration of Independence.

"I might ask you the same question, Miss Blair." His voice sounded harder than she'd remembered, but his manner contained the same feline grace she'd first seen in a London ballroom more than sixteen months ago.

Rebecca lifted her chin higher. "This is my uncle's house," she stated. "I have come here to live."

"I see." Warren Tyson's voice was thoughtful as his eyes took in the wide hall with its long walnut table beneath the stairs, the oriental carpets, the gilded sconces, then returned to Rebecca. "And where is your uncle now, Miss Blair?"

"He . . . he should return shortly. I was on my way to a party not far from here. So if you and . . . and these men could return tomorrow, I am sure he would talk to you then." She didn't want to ask him why he was here. She didn't want to know. His uniform, and his unruly pack of men filled her with foreboding. She wanted only to find Sylvie and escape.

"Major!" A voice called from the doorway, and another uniform entered the hall. "Begging your pardon, sir, but we've discovered two wagons and a stable of horses. . . ." The voice stopped as the newcomer took in the scene before him.

"Very good, Lieutenant. We'll discuss your find shortly." Warren Tyson, who had not taken his eyes off Rebecca during the exchange, smiled in mock sorrow now. "I'm afraid, Miss Blair, that you will have to forego the pleasures of the party. In the name of the Continental Congress, we will have to request the use of your horses."

Rebecca steadied herself with a hard grip on the banister. "The use of our horses?" she repeated, panic welling again. She swallowed hard. "For what purpose, Mr. . . . Major Tyson."

"For the use of General Washington's army, Miss Blair. He is rather pressed at the moment, trying to bring his men out of New York. Wagons and horses are in too short supply. The need is immediate."

"You can't make off with our horses," Rebecca blazed.

"The deed is already done." Warren Tyson's voice sounded syrupy, and Rebecca regretted having dropped her walking stick. It would make a memorable welt across that smug face. But she couldn't stoop over for the stick now. She didn't dare let go of the banister, and she felt somehow that she should remain up on this stair where her height was equal to that of the arrogant major.

Her eyes snapping, she stared into those black depths coming closer. "Uncle Julian will have something to say about that."

"But Uncle Julian is not here, as you just testified."

"He will be soon, and I've no doubt the Provincial Congress would listen to his complaint. Mr. John Jay is a friend."

"I will remind you, Miss Blair, that the Provincial Congress of New York is under the authority of the Continental Congress." He now stood directly before her. "Besides, our information is that the owner of this house is a Tory sympathizer. The Congress and General Washington will approve heartily of the steps we have taken."

"But I do *not* approve. Nor will my uncle, and those horses and wagons belong to him. You may be sure that your Congress, your general and anyone else of authority will hear about this."

"In due time, Miss Blair. I look forward to meeting your uncle. Where did he go?"

"That is no concern of yours." Rebecca started to say more, but just then a tearful Sylvie was brought through the door by one of the brown-shirted men. Sobbing her mistress's name, the girl darted away from her brawny guard and ran to the stairs.

"Oh, miss, they've taken the horses right away from the coach, and they've taken Luke right with them. There are hordes of these awful men all around."

Rebecca caught the girl's hand and pulled her up the stairs to stand behind her. "Yes, I know, Sylvie. But you are all right?" Her maid nodded and cowered back against the banister.

"Send your maid upstairs."

Rebecca glared at Major Tyson. "I'll do no such thing."

"Then I will have one of my men carry her up," he announced, unperturbed.

Rebecca gasped. "If any one of your filthy men lays a hand on Sylvie I shall have him whipped within an inch of his life," she declared hotly. Then she gasped again. Standing just inside the door, one of the men who'd first attacked her was grinning and holding her blue silk ball gown up in front of himself, making shuffling little parodies of dance steps and rolling his eyes in high glee. "How dare you," Rebecca spat.

At that Major Tyson did turn. "Todd," he barked, "bring that here." The man shuffled forward and mincingly handed skirt and bodice to the major. With a lazy smile, Tyson surveyed the gown. Then he brought it to Sylvie's trembling hands. "Very nice. In fact, just the dress for dinner, don't you think Miss Blair? We will look forward to the pleasure of seeing you in it this evening."

Eyes the color of stormy winter seas met his. "You have stolen private property, your men have defiled our hallway, all of you have played your disgusting games. You will now, Major, remove yourself and your filthy friends from this house." Far too angry and humiliated to feel any fear, Rebecca's voice rang out, and she had the satisfaction of seeing several of the men by the door take a backward step.

Opaque eyes only inches from her face became hooded as she talked, but a hand shot out and gripped her wrist painfully. "Pity you feel that way, Miss Blair," Tyson's soft voice said without a trace of sorrow, "for I find I've taken a fancy to this house and its occupants." Still holding her wrist, he flicked a glance at Sylvie, rooted to the stair above Rebecca. "Take that dress upstairs, Sylvie," he said as softly, but with a knife edge to his voice, "and do not return until you are called for."

"No!" Rebecca choked as his grip tightened even more and she was brought halfway to her knees. With a look of terror at what was happening to her mistress, Sylvie began to back up the stairs, the blue dress trailing from her hands.

"That's right, Sylvie," the major encouraged her, and Rebecca heard soft snickers from behind him.

With the hand that had been all this time clutching the banister, Rebecca struck at him. He snatched her arm and she felt it would be twisted from its socket in retaliation. She fell back against the banister, and heard a low laugh in the center of the big hall.

There was a sudden deathly silence, through which a soft voice said, "A touching scene, Major, but you will have to continue it later. There are to be no women . . ." The voice stopped as Rebecca, free of the painful grip at last, pulled herself upright and looked into brilliant blue eyes that flashed in anger.

Her throat closed as she stared at the one face she had thought never to see again. For what seemed an eon their eyes locked, and Rebecca felt faint with disbelief. Then Gordon Meade moved and his face seemed to grow harsher. "You are staying here, madam?" he asked, his voice cold and imperious.

It was all Rebecca could do to nod.

"Stroke of good fortune, wouldn't you say? But I remind you I saw her first." Major Tyson stepped possessively closer to Rebecca.

"Lieutenant Meade," the vividly remembered voice snapped, "you will see the lady to her room, and return to the porch."

Alexander Meade stepped through the doorway, a look of horrified resignation on his face.

"Major Tyson, your report." Gordon Meade walked out the door without a backward glance.

Suddenly, miraculously, the hall was empty but for three people. Warren Tyson, letting go of her wrist at long last, shot a venomous look at Meade's departing back, then glowered at Rebecca. "Until later, Miss Blair," he said with something like a growl.

Rebecca didn't move, could only look at him with eyes still dilated with surprise, and then he was gone and Alexander Meade was beside her, his face crimson. "I'm s-so sorry, Miss Blair," he stammered, as though somehow with a few words he could erase the events taking place. Then he recollected his orders. "The colonel asks that you allow me to escort you to your room," he added hastily, and moved to take her arm.

Rebecca jerked away from him, rubbing at her sore wrist. "The colonel?" she asked. "So your brother is a colonel in this rebellious army?"

"Please come with me," Lieutenant Meade was looking nervous. "You will be safe upstairs, Miss Blair."

"Safe! From this pack of wild dogs who have taken over my uncle's house?" Rebecca's laugh had more than a tinge of hysteria.

The tall young lieutenant looked miserable but determined.

He picked up her walking stick from the floor, took her elbow firmly and turned her up the stairs. Once more she was held in a grip that brooked no resistance, and dazed, Rebecca allowed herself to be propelled to her room. Lieutenant Meade stiffly tried to assure her she would be all right, then backed awkwardly from her door. Rebecca ignored him. Her heart was thudding with the shock of all that had happened, and her mind kept repeating "he's here." She shook herself and looked around. Sylvie was sitting on the edge of the bed still clutching the blue ball gown, and looked so relieved to see her mistress that Rebecca patted her arm. Then she crossed to the window.

The coach was gone from in front of the house, and in its place several saddle horses stood cropping grass at the edge of the drive, their reins trailing negligently on the ground. A number of the brown-shirted men could be seen among the trees near the road, but there was no sign of any of the officers. They were probably making themselves comfortable in the drawing room or in Uncle Julian's library, Rebecca thought, and banged her fist on the windowsill. How dare they simply walk in and take over his house this way? When he returned . . . Her thought came to an unhappy stop. When he returned, what? What could he, a vague old man, do against this company of soldiers? They could burn the place around his ears, and Uncle Julian would be powerless to stop them. Even if he had the support of the male servants and the tenant farmers, the men of Halscomb would be woefully outnumbered.

Charles! She pulled away from the window and began pacing the broad polished planks of her floor. Surely he was wondering already where she was? He would come for her, to see that she was all right. The flash of hope that thought brought was gone before it could be enjoyed. Charles was host at his own party this day. How would he explain a sudden disappearance to find a guest who simply hadn't shown up? And even if he could get away from his other guests, even if he was worried, knowing she was alone at Halscomb, what could he do, arriving by himself to confront a group of armed rebels? She turned and paced back to the front window again, her fist hitting her open palm.

"Oh, miss, what do you suppose they are going to do?" Sylvie's trembling voice came to her as she walked.

"Do? Lord, I don't know, Sylvie. I can't even think why they keep us here." She had a sudden inspiration. "Colonel Meade may be trying to decide right now. We're certainly useless to them. Perhaps they will escort us to the Revingtons' and leave us there. It would be the easiest way to dispose of us."

This hopeful reflection was interrupted by the rumble of large wheels on the drive. Rebecca looked down once more to see the two farm wagons from the barn lumbering down the track, the farm horses straining in the harnesses. Tied on behind one of the wagons was her own filly and two more of Uncle Julian's good saddle horses. The wagons themselves were piled high with sacks of grain, barrels of foodstuffs, tools and implements. Rebecca's nails dug into her palm as she watched in impotent fury this looting of Uncle Julian's barns. The team usually reserved for the coach now came into view, pulling the landau. A large escort rode behind the little procession. Was the house to be stripped of all but furnishings? It was as though an army of barbarians had invaded the countryside. But this was 1776, not a long ago time of barbarians, and from all she'd heard, even this rebel army was commanded by gentlemen. Thieving could hardly be considered a gentlemanly occupation, but surely Colonel Meade and the other officers would go no further than that? She thought of the little black eyes of the first men to enter her house this afternoon and shivered. How much control did the officers have over their men? Enough, she hoped, and flung herself into the chair before the dressing table.

She and Sylvie looked at each other in silence, neither wanting to voice the fears that swirled through their brains and clutched at their insides. At last Sylvie stood up quietly and began smoothing the dress Rebecca had been going to wear in such high spirits this evening. Slowly she hung it back in the huge wardrobe. Rebecca said nothing.

It was perhaps an hour before the two women heard heavy steps outside the door, and a soft knock. At a nod from Rebecca, Sylvie opened the door cautiously, her eyes enormous with fear. Lieutenant Meade coughed and stepped over the threshold with obvious reluctance.

"Miss Blair," he said, "I have been delegated to ask you to dress for dinner in an hour's time." He stopped, and drew a deep breath, his eyes avoiding Rebecca's raised brows and set mouth. "It is requested," he rushed on, "that you wear the gown you had planned for this evening. I will return to escort you." He began to back from the room.

"Lieutenant Meade." Rebecca's voice, clear and chilly, stopped him abruptly. "You will explain, please, why we are being kept in this house."

Circles of fatigue beneath the gray eyes looked somehow incongruous in the boyish face at the door. "There are no horses to take you anywhere, Miss Blair. And at present, we'd as soon not advertise our presence in the neighborhood."

"Surely some of our servants have already raised that alarm, Lieutenant."

"Possibly. And tomorrow we will have to forage for more horses and wagons. Perhaps at that time . . ." He stopped, and Rebecca wondered if he were under orders not to talk to her. His face was red and miserable, and she might have felt sorry for him if she hadn't been so angry.

"You have an odd way of showing gratitude for Halscomb's hospitality to you last summer, Lieutenant Meade," she said, and had the satisfaction of seeing his face go nearly white.

"Believe me, Miss Blair, I didn't know that this . . . anything," he finished lamely. "I will have to come back in an hour." He turned and practically raced from the doorway.

Rebecca sat in tight-lipped silence as the shadows of the afternoon lengthened in the room. "Miss?" At last Sylvie approached her. "If you are to dress for dinner . . ." The girl began lighting the candles on the dressing table.

"You needn't bother." Rebecca's voice was flat. "I'll not dress on orders from anyone, least of all from these so-called officers, Sylvie."

"But, miss, if that colonel or that major said . . ."

"I don't know who issued those absurd orders, Sylvie, and it wouldn't matter if I did. I will not be bullied in Uncle Julian's house. They can keep us prisoners here, but they cannot tell us what to wear or say or think."

"If you say so, miss." Sylvie sounded less than convinced, but she retired to the edge of the bed again, to await the lieutenant's return.

Rebecca's black mood did not lighten as the minutes stretched on, and she tried not to think of the entertainments she and Charles had so carefully planned and that she had now missed. She tried not to think of her situation at all, since nothing made any sense. She had only one fact to dwell on: that she was being detained in her home by a man she had once detested for his insolence and had hoped never to see again. What an ironic fate that he—and Warren Tyson—

would reappear in her life at this time and in this place. She could not rid herself of the thought that Gordon Meade's presence was like that of a horseman of the apocalypse. When he appeared disaster soon followed. She might be powerless to turn aside calamity, she decided, but she would not bow her head to it and allow him the gratification of seeing her cowed.

When Alexander Meade knocked on the door just one hour after he'd departed he could not hide the surprise he felt on seeing Rebecca, back as straight as a poker, eyes flashing with anger, sitting in a chair in the same walking dress she'd had on all afternoon.

"Uh, perhaps you need a bit more time, Miss Blair," he hedged, his unsure stance at the threshold looking almost comical. "I could make your apologies until, say, half-past."

"You may make my apologies, yes," Rebecca replied in an even voice, "for I shall not be coming down to dinner. If all the servants have not been stolen, murdered or run off, you may have someone bring me a tray."

Lieutenant Meade opened his mouth, then shut it again. He glanced at Sylvie, who refused to look up, and back at Rebecca. Finally he cleared his throat and tried to square his shoulders. "There are not many servants, no, Miss Blair. Some seem to have left for the village. And some went with the wagons. But regardless of the servant count, my orders are to escort you to the drawing room."

He looked miserable but determined, and Rebecca realized that as long as he wore his uniform, he would try to carry out his orders. It was possible that he was enough like his brother to pick her up and carry her from the room if he thought he had no alternative. The picture of this boy-man carrying her, kicking, down the stairs, to dump her like a sack of meal at the colonel's feet, brought her out of the chair.

"Is Sylvie allowed to go to the kitchen?" she asked.

Lieutenant Meade looked startled. "Of course."

"Very well." She swept down on him so quickly he nearly stumbled trying to stand aside.

Chapter 13

A fire was going in the drawing room, its fresh flames not yet combatting the evening chill of the October air, and holding only a few of the room's shadows at bay. Rebecca stood in the center of the long room, refusing her impulse to cross to the fireplace, and refusing to acknowledge the man who unfolded lazily from her uncle's favorite chair near the hearth. Instead, she watched Alexander Meade light candles on a round table then leave, and tried to keep her hands from clenching at her sides.

Major Tyson's lip curled in distaste as he surveyed her attire. "Not quite suitable clothing for entertaining a guest at dinner, Miss Blair," he drawled, and straightened a fine lace cuff below his coat sleeve.

"Uninvited guests do not merit consideration of dress," she retorted, looking at him for the first time.

"But I sent ample notice of our intention to remain and enjoy your hospitality, and expressed a desire to see you in your ball gown."

Rebecca allowed herself one quick glance about the room. There was no one else present. Did that mean that Warren Tyson had been left in charge of her and of Halscomb? She nearly shuddered, but collected herself in time. In her one meeting with this man she had not liked his too-smooth manner, his sly innuendos. It seemed as though the thin veneer of gentility he had worn in London was now rubbed thinner by the power of the epaulets on his shoulders. Somehow she knew, too, that to show him her scorn and dislike would only amuse him. So she looked at him dispassionately and said clearly, "You may save your expressions of your wishes for your men, Major Tyson. They are nothing to me."

The dark eyes narrowed, but the thin lips curved unpleasantly. "It would seem, Miss Blair, that for the moment, you are under the 'protection' of the Continental Army, and you may find it more comfortable to obey orders."

"I am not in the army, Major," Rebecca snapped, forgetting to maintain her cool composure. "Nor am I one of your camp followers."

"We shall see, Miss Blair, we shall see. But I will remind you that you *are,* at least, our prisoner."

"Too strong a word, Major, I think."

Rebecca whirled at the voice. Gordon Meade stood just inside the room, his face in shadow, his arms crossed in a relaxed attitude. He was not looking at her, but at the fire. It was obvious he had been there these past moments. "I seem always to be interrupting your . . . er . . . lively conversations. But I gather dinner is served," he said mildly.

Warren Tyson stood stiffly, facing his superior officer. "I was not aware we would have the pleasure of your company this evening, Colonel."

"I went only to talk to the tenant farmers and others in the area, Major. Since many of my men are still here, I can think of nowhere else I could be tonight." Colonel Meade's voice was soft and without inflection, but Rebecca sensed that there was a charged current between these two men. No matter. She was glad only of the fact she was no longer alone with Warren Tyson. Responding to Gordon Meade's bow, she stalked past him to the dining room.

To her chagrin the table, leaves removed to make it a more comfortable size, was set with some of the best crystal and china. And there were only two places laid. Mrs. Clark was standing at one end of the room, and her eyes grew rounder in her wrinkled face when she saw the three silent people enter from the hall. The colonel went to her, and after a low-voiced exchange, she scurried out to return with another place setting.

Rebecca watched the preparations with a wooden face, but her mind was whirling. What was Mrs. Clark doing waiting on table? Where were the other servants? Staring stonily at a cream soup now set before her, the girl began to eat with mechanical movements. She would not ask questions or converse with her captors, would not show she condoned their presence at the table.

Her self-control was in vain, however, for Gordon Meade ignored her, and kept up such a flow of talk about dispatches, orders and movement of supplies that Warren Tyson could do nothing but listen and answer his colonel. Feeling oddly deflated, Rebecca chewed and swallowed without tasting any of the courses that Mrs. Clark served. By the time dessert came, though, she was tired of staring at the Wedgwood plates set in succession before her. Hoping they were too engrossed to notice, she lifted her eyes just as the major said, "Why not make this house our headquarters for the time being? It sits nearly atop the roads to White Plains and down through Yonkers, and it has a view of the river."

Gordon Meade fingered a goblet on the table before him and his eyes flicked to Rebecca as she watched him under lowered lashes. "A view of the Hudson does us little good at this time. The British troops, if they move by water, will be more apt to come up the East River. We need stay in this area only long enough to collect anything else of use to the army."

Rebecca looked down. "I'm sure," she heard Tyson say, "our charming hostess would be devastated at our departure." His eyes seemed to burn holes through her as he spoke, but she didn't look up even then.

"We won't disappoint her for now," the colonel said softly. "I need this house for a few days, anyway. I'm sorry, Miss Blair," he added. Too startled to stop herself, Rebecca looked at him squarely. "But to show our intentions are not all dishonorable, I will give you these." A sheaf of papers was extracted from inside his coat and laid on the table before her. Puzzled, Rebecca picked them up, ignoring the cough meant to cover Major Tyson's snicker. They were papers stating that horses and wagons would be returned to Halscomb after doing service for the Continental Army.

Rebecca read them through quickly and dropped them on the table. "I've no doubt these are worth nothing more than the paper and ink it took to produce them," she stated.

A muscle at the corner of the colonel's mouth tightened, but his voice was mild as he said, "You may even be right. Nonetheless, our intentions are to have your property returned to you."

"Does that include the servants who have apparently disappeared?"

"We have had little to do with the servants, Miss Blair. Though I gather from your inestimable Mrs. Clark that some of them disappeared at the first sign of my men, and that others declared an intention to join us."

There was no answer to be made to that unpleasant statement, so Rebecca returned to her dessert. When she put her spoon down, she thought to make a cutting remark about retiring to the privacy of her own room, but Colonel Meade stole her line with breathtaking brevity.

"If you are done, Miss Blair, you would perhaps be good enough to retire to your room."

Furious at her loss of ground, the girl sat still. "Is that an order, Colonel?"

"A request, Miss Blair."

"I am not used to such requests in my own home, sir."

"Would you prefer that I make it an order?"

"I am even less used to being ordered," she snapped, and met his steely look with blazing eyes.

"Perhaps you would choose to stroll before retiring." Major Tyson was on his feet, his silken voice cutting between the two antagonists.

"I think Miss Blair will find the sanctuary of her room more to her taste," said the colonel and stood also. At the sound of the chairs scraping on the floor two corporals appeared in the door. "Please escort our hostess upstairs," Gordon Meade said to them, his eyes never leaving Rebecca's flaming face.

"I am capable of finding my own way," she hissed and practically jumped from her chair.

"Nonetheless, you will allow these men to aid you."

Rebecca, remembering the same cool tone of command used on her in a garden in London, felt hot rage consume her. Pasting a smile on her mouth, she turned a shoulder to the colonel, just as she had once before, and looked sweetly at Major Tyson. "If I may accept your kind offer, Major, I will find a walk in fresh air very agreeable at this moment."

A look of pleased surprise crossed Tyson's face fleetingly, and then he moved to offer his arm. With a swift glance at Gordon Meade's set expression, Rebecca took it. The colonel would learn that she was not to be commanded into submission to any man's whims.

Soon she wondered what price she was to pay for her small victory, though, as the major led her out the front door and steered her down the wide steps to the drive. The cool night air felt good on her hot cheeks, and she was glad at first for the cover of darkness, but within a few paces the chill autumn breeze cut through her dress and she began to shiver. Doggedly she walked on, determined to endure anything for the few minutes it would take to drive home her point to the arrogant rebel colonel who had taken over Halscomb.

When they were well away from the house, Rebecca could see a row of tents pitched on the side lawn where just weeks before a spreading marquee had sheltered a glittering party of diners. Beyond, a small fire built before the stable illuminated dimly discerned shapes of many more men. So they were billeted in the barns too, she thought, and clenched her jaw at the realization of how completely Halscomb had been invaded.

"I thought most of your men had gone with the wagons," she said at last, wondering when she could turn back.

"Less than half left today, Miss Blair. We are secure here, as you see."

"Yes," she said and tried to make the word neutral.

"This is a lovely estate. It is no wonder you came to America to live," the major went on, drawing her arm further through his own.

Rebecca stilled her impulse to pull free. "Yes, it was lovely," she said slowly.

Her companion seemed not to notice the barb in her voice. "And it has been made much lovelier by your presence, Miss Blair. What good fortune that I found you here. I look forward to a closer acquaintance."

Rebecca could not see his face well, but she had an impression of cat's eyes looking at her hungrily. She shivered again, and said in a voice rather too loud for intimate conversation, "I find the air too cool after all, sir, and must ask that we return to the house."

Her arm received a small squeeze. "Of course."

They stopped, and Rebecca turned to retrace her steps, but suddenly found herself held fast against his coat. Cold fingers lifted her chin with a jerk and bruising lips found hers. Repelled and frightened, she twisted away. "Major Tyson," she gasped, tugging free of his hands.

"Merely hoping to help warm you, Miss Blair," he said, and the hint of a smile was in his voice. "The nights grow cold at this time of year. You are new to our country, and do not know how chill the rooms can get. You may find need of some extra warmth on a long autumn night."

"You forget yourself, Major." The girl began to walk briskly back up the drive, the fast pace and her own anger warming her as his arms never could.

She was still flaming with indignation when she mounted the steps and came face to face with the colonel standing in the shadows of one of the wide pillars. As Major Tyson caught up to her, Gordon Meade stepped forward. "A pleasant walk, I hope," he said quietly. Two more shadows detached themselves from the gloom of the porch. "Now, perhaps you will accept the escort of these men to your room, Miss Blair." Rebecca nodded wordlessly, and he turned away without another glance at her. "Major, you will join me briefly in the library, please."

The men stood aside as Rebecca entered the house, and she heard the sound of their voices receding in the hallway. Silently she mounted the stairs between her guards, but once in her room could not resist slamming the door in their faces. She leaned against it a moment, stilling the trembling in her limbs, and listened to the muffled voices and tramp of feet down the hall.

"I'll put my money on the major for that girl," chuckled one man.

"Colonel ain't likely to allow it."

"D'ya s'pose he'll take her for himself? He's a stickler most times, though I hear tell off duty he's a devil with the women. Girl as pretty as that would turn *my* head if I was a high 'n' mighty officer an' had the choice."

The voices faded down the stairs and Rebecca drew ragged breath. The leering suggestions made her heart hammer, and she hugged her arms to herself to regain control. Her imagination was getting the better of her. With a crooked smile, she pulled herself upright. Lewd voices were not a danger, only a nuisance. The troop of rowdy soldiers in this house was under the command of strong officers who would see that order was maintained. She hoped.

She walked into the room then to see candles lit, her night things laid out and a fire burning, giving the white and green room the appearance of safe comfort. Sylvie was at the wardrobe, straightening clothes and hanging away the last of this morning's discarded dresses.

"Oh, miss, I'm glad you're back," the girl said, and smoothed the folds of a gray muslin skirt. "The kitchen was nearly empty. Most of the staff have just disappeared, though Mrs. Clark and Cook say many will be back. Mrs. Clark actually *likes* that Colonel Meade. Imagine."

"Imagine," Rebecca echoed drily and removed the jacket of her walking dress. "Are there soldiers all over the house, too?"

"I didn't see any but one sergeant who brought water in to Cook. They're all out in the barns or by the rose garden." Sylvie made a face and shut the wardrobe door with a click.

"Well, I'm glad to hear they're not billeted in the house at least. And we may see the last of them in a day or two."

"That's not the way Cook heard it, miss. She says the men are talking about staying here to guard the roads, and to help guard the rear of General Washington's army."

Rebecca looked thoughtful a moment, then shrugged. There was no sense repeating what the colonel had said. She'd have to wait and see. If only Uncle Julian would return! "Sylvie, I think it might be best for both of us if you slept in here tonight," she said casually. "Mr. Halscomb should return by tomorrow and then we shall see how long the soldiers are to stay."

The girl nodded and stooping, began to drag a pallet from under the high four-poster. She'd slept on this same mattress for several nights when they'd first come to Halscomb before a room was prepared for her in the back wing.

"I'm afraid your trust in your uncle's return is misplaced, Miss Blair."

Rebecca whirled, as once again Colonel Meade's voice spoke from behind her. "Do you always enter rooms without knocking?" she cried.

"More often than not," he answered, and walked across to the fireplace. "Thank you—Sylvie, is it? Please drag the pallet closer to the fire." He watched as a startled Sylvie did his bidding with fumbling hands. "That's fine. Now you may retire. Miss Blair won't need you any more this evening."

Sylvie's large eyes dilated, and she looked at her mistress in confusion.

"The colonel is mistaken," Rebecca said in a low voice.

"I am rarely mistaken," Gordon Meade contradicted her

and with a slight smile took Sylvie by the arm. "That will be all, thank you." Firmly he propelled the girl out to the hall, then closed the door and turned the key, ignoring Rebecca's outraged gasp. Dropping the key into his waistcoat pocket, he came back into the room.

"How dare you," Rebecca choked, and flew at him, snatching at the pocket where the key lay.

The colonel slapped her hand from his waistcoat and she scratched at him, tears of rage starting from her eyes. He grabbed her arms and shook her till she stopped struggling, then held her still. "Calm yourself, Miss Blair." His voice was hard, commanding again.

She glared up at him, pulling against his grip, but said nothing. He let her go then, and she backed away, fear beginning to creep through her fury. "Wh-what are you doing?" she faltered. The voices of the soldiers outside her door seemed to resound in her brain.

"You have shown that I cannot trust you to obey an order. If I told you to keep your door locked tonight, you would promptly leave the room. So I have decided to stay here."

"Stay in my room?" Her voice rose on a note of hysteria, and she reached out to steady herself against the bedpost. Realizing it was the bed he intended to use, she drew back as though she'd touched a burning brand.

Gordon Meade noticed the movement and a half smile tugged at his mouth. "Your worst fears are not to be realized tonight, my girl," he said, and began tugging off his heavy coat. "That is precisely the reason I am staying here." He hung the coat on the back of a chair and went to prod the pallet on the floor as Rebecca stared at him, appalled. "This seems quite comfortable enough," he commented, and removed his waistcoat. Then unbuckling his sword, he sat down on her chair.

Rebecca watched his actions in a daze. She felt as though all this must be happening in some other house far away from her. She stared in horrified fascination as he untied his neckcloth and flung it down on her dressing table. Somehow her mind wouldn't dwell on what he was doing. "What did you mean my trust in Uncle Julian's return was misplaced?"

"Simply that I found out from a stableboy where your uncle went. If he ever reached the city, he is unlikely to be able to retrace his steps. A great deal of Washington's army is between us and the Long Island shore now, Miss Blair." The man undid his cuffs with maddening deliberation, then bent to his boots.

"You cannot force me to sleep on that pallet," she said softly, trying to control her voice. "You cannot stay in here."

His eyebrow rose quizzically, but he concentrated on the boot.

"You will have to answer for even more than your troop's invasion if you do. I have friends, and they will come to rescue this house. When Charles learns of this . . ." She stopped, unable to think of a threat awful enough to utter.

"Charles?" The colonel stopped in mid-pull and looked up at her. "Do I take it you have a handsome knight who will come charging to the rescue?"

"He will come," she stated with a certainty she didn't feel, "and he will not be subject to your orders. He is not in your unlawful army."

"Ah, a loyalist. I shall have to take care that the wondrous Charles does not make it to Halscomb's door."

Rebecca's eyes dilated. "You wouldn't *shoot* him?"

"If it would distress you so much, perhaps not." The colonel stood up, and the corner of his mouth twitched once. "But for tonight I feel we are all safe. Good night." And without so much as a glance in her direction, he walked to her bed and threw himself down.

Rooted to her spot, Rebecca watched as he lay, unmoving. It was as though her mind were suspended in some previous time, had not yet encompassed the events of the past minutes. But slowly awareness returned and as she tried to focus her thoughts on the long form lying carelessly on her sheets, she realized she had not dreamed the bizarre happenings. A nearly unknown man was asleep in her bed, and she was standing in the center of the room like a witless post, waiting for him to wake up. He was clearly exhausted now, but when he did wake up, what then? A tingle of primeval fear moved down her back, and she looked around wildly. His coat and waistcoat still hung on the back of the chair, and she began to inch across the floor toward them, all the while watching the man on the bed. When she was close enough to touch the buff material of his pocket, she stopped. What would she do once she extracted her door key? Her mind whirled as her eyes lit on his sword, hanging easily at the other side of the chair. It looked heavy, a solid weapon. But could she draw it from its sheath without making noise? An image of herself, sword held high, standing over the sleeping man, made her grit her teeth. Even if she could do all that without a sound, she doubted she could wield the sword effectively enough to kill him before he could move against her.

As though her thoughts might have awakened him, she glanced at the bed again. Still he did not move. Now she felt bolder, and a plan began to form. Carefully, she lifted her skirts and untied her petticoats. The rustling sounds did not penetrate his sleep, and she stepped out of the confining yards of material, leaving them in a heap on the floor. Then, silently, she withdrew the key from his pocket and blew out the candles on the dressing table. On tiptoe she went to the wardrobe and got a long dark cloak. She held her breath as she tied it on, then moved to the bedside and took up the candle there.

Gordon Meade's arm was outflung in sleep, and she could see the deep blue circles under his eyes. He must be exhausted beyond imagining, she thought, and noticed that the hard lines of his face were softened now as he slept. She had never seen a man asleep before, and she had to resist a temptation to watch. Backing away from the bed slowly, she took the candle to the door and inserted the key. The lock gave with a click that seemed to echo around the room, and Rebecca froze with her hand on the handle. But still the officer slept. Snuffing the candle, she opened the door quietly and slid into the darkened hall.

Chapter 14

A thin shaft of light sliced across the floor at the bottom of the stairs. Someone was still awake down there. Rebecca darted past the upper newel post and turned down a long corridor into the back wing of the house. Mrs. Clark, Cook, a maid and Sylvie all had rooms in this wing, and Rebecca stole along the wall, feeling for the doorknobs. She passed the first and groped on till she encountered the right one. Softly she turned the handle, but the door was locked. Wise girl, she thought, at the same time her exasperation mounted. How was she to rouse the maid without waking the household? Softly she rapped on the door, but there was no answer. If Sylvie had heard the sound, it had probably frightened her half to death. Rebecca knocked again and thought she heard a movement behind the door. Putting her mouth to the keyhole she spoke softly. "Sylvie. Let me in please." She felt as though she'd shouted her words in the echoing silence that followed. "Sylvie," she hissed again, and this time she heard steps come toward her.

"Miss Rebecca?"

"Yes. Let me in, please." There was a click and a creak of hinges as the door opened just enough for Rebecca to squeeze through to the little room.

"Oh Lord, miss, are you all right?" In the dark Sylvie's horrified whisper seemed magnified to the sound of a bugle.

"Shhh . . ." Rebecca closed the door silently. "Yes, Sylvie, I am. But I have to get out of this house."

"But the colonel . . ."

"He is fast asleep. There is someone downstairs in the front of the house, so we can't use the main stairs. I want us to escape together because you know the village better than I. Could we go to the Adamses' house, do you think?"

"Yes, I suppose so." Sylvie's voice faltered.

"You're sure of them aren't you?"

"Oh, yes. It's not that, miss. I was wondering how to get out. Mrs. Clark told me a man was to be posted at the back door by the stairs. We've no exit."

Rebecca bit her lip in frustration. She tried to think of other doors in the house. There were several, but if the stairs were watched, there was no way to reach them. Yet how could she turn back? The thought of slinking back to her room to await Colonel Meade's awakening made her chew her lip in earnest. She crossed to the window and looked out. Below, a slanting roof over her uncle's office and a tall beech tree blocked her view of the herb garden and orchard beyond. As she watched, a few leaves drifted lazily through the moonlight onto the roof. They fell noiselessly a few feet away, and suddenly she had it!

"Sylvie," she said, her voice full of excitement, "get your cloak. We are leaving by the window."

"Miss Rebecca!" Sylvie was half laughing, standing beside her now. "How do we reach the ground?"

"The roof slants down, and from its edge it can't be more than nine or ten feet. And there's that tree. It grows right next to Uncle Julian's office. We've climbed copper beeches before, Sylvie. They have lots of branches. We should be able to use it. Even if we can't, the drop won't be a long one."

"But what if somebody sees us?"

"We're on the opposite side from the barns where the men are sleeping. No one will see us."

"They may have guards or sentries or something."

"Perhaps. But I'll take the chance. Once we're on the ground, we circle the wall of the herb garden and then we can enter the fringe of trees by the orchard. We'll work down near the road that way."

"Oh, miss, when we climbed trees, we were little. And the last time I nearly broke my arm." Sylvie hadn't moved, was staring at the skeletal branches outside.

"You're stronger now," Rebecca said impatiently. "And we *must* get out of here. I won't share my room with a rebel officer. And I don't like either of us here in this house alone, with soldiers all around." She let the implication of her words sink in for a moment, then tried again. "Will you get your cloak, or do I go alone?" She began to lift the sash.

With a scurry of footsteps Sylvie was across the room, snatching her cloak from a peg behind the door. When she returned Rebecca had the window open and was tugging up her skirts. Squeezing the maid's arm, she climbed out and down to the roof below. The air had grown even colder, and she was glad of the cloak she wore, but its billowing folds were going to be a nuisance. Thank heaven she'd left the petticoats behind at least. Pulling skirt and cloak high, she held the mass of material in one arm and inched down the slope of the roof. Sylvie followed close behind. As she'd hoped, the trunk of the tree was only inches away from the eaves and a handy network of branches stretched down toward the ground. She crouched and reached for the tree.

"If there's a man below, I will die of shame," Sylvie whispered.

"If you make any noise and bring the soldiers running, you really *will* die of shame, I assure you," Rebecca whispered back and maneuvered off the roof. She felt her skirt catch on something and tear. But Sylvie loosened it, and then was reaching for the tree above her head.

Leaves rustled on the ground as a squirrel or chipmunk scurried among the tree roots. A clock chimed somewhere in the house, and Rebecca froze at the sound, her feet planted between branches, her arm hugging the trunk. Then all was quiet and she moved down to the next limb. Far away a man's voice called out and someone coughed. The sounds were from the stables, and she hoped the men there made enough noise among themselves that they couldn't hear the rustle of clothes and the snap of twigs from the beech by the office. She was glad when her feet encountered no more branches, and slithering down against the trunk, she gripped a branch and swung into space. Miraculously, her toes touched the earth and she dropped almost silently among the leaves. Then Sylvie stood beside her and the two listened intently for any movement nearby, trying to still their panting breath. But for a faint breeze sighing in drying leaves, there was nothing.

Blindly the two groped for each other's hands. Rebecca

nodded toward the low bulk of the garden wall and tugged Sylvie forward, away from the protective deep shadows by the tree. Moonlight dappled the narrow lawn as the girls darted across to the wall and crouching, ran along it, hands brushing its rough surface. They slithered past the near corner and stopped.

Rebecca looked around her slowly, trying to get her bearings, exploring the darkest pockets of ground beneath trees, beside rocks. She saw nothing move. Over her right shoulder the mass of the big house loomed toward a starry sky, all of it black but for ribbons of dim light which probed the night outside the long library windows. Who kept a vigil in her uncle's leather chair? She didn't want to know. She had accomplished the hardest part of her escape. Now she must steel herself for the endless stumbling walk through unknown fields and woods to the village. If they followed the length of wall, it would lead them nearly to the tiny grove of sumac bordering the orchard. Once there, they could decide their best route.

"I don't see anything, miss. But what if someone is coming from behind?"

Rebecca felt her spine tingle, but she pressed Sylvie's hand reassuringly. "Don't look back. We'll end up in quakes if we do. We will reach those trees and we will run. No matter what, just run, Sylvie. Once in the shadows you can't be seen in that brown cloak."

Bent over, she moved forward, her maid beside her now. Near the end of the wall, they broke into a run. They were passing a towering oak, nearly to the clump of sumac when Rebecca's foot caught in a root. With a small cry, she stumbled. Sylvie stopped, but Rebecca waved her on. "Run," she whispered, and staggered to her feet.

Her cloak had hooked on something. Desperately she jerked at it, but the hem was held fast. With trembling fingers, she untied the ribbons and dropped the heavy weight from her shoulders. Her ankle was turned, but she could stand. She took two staggering steps and felt her heart skip a full beat as a voice called, "Halt!" Footsteps seemed to thunder across the hard ground. She pulled up her skirts and ran. Sylvie was already out of sight, hidden by the dense foliage only yards away.

"Stand, I say," the voice shouted, and another set of running steps joined the first. A shot rang out, and Rebecca tripped once more. Sprawled on the ground, she wondered hysterically if a bullet had hit her. But she felt no pain, only devastating fear and frustration.

"My God, it's a woman." A gruff voice was right above her.

"So 't is." Another voice joined the first. "Proper sight she is, too." Rough hands pulled her to her knees, and she looked up to see the dark shapes of two soldiers standing over her. A third came up as she cowered on the ground. "Lookee what we got here," the second man said to the new arrival, and in the moonlight Rebecca saw a broad grin spread across his face. The three gaped at her, and she became horrifyingly conscious of her bedraggled appearance. One sleeve of her dress was torn nearly off from her fall. The hooks on her bodice were ripped free at the bottom, and her skirt was in tatters. Without the concealing folds of her cloak she must look a fright.

"What're you doin' here?" the first man asked and prodded her with his foot.

Rebecca drew back. "Don't touch me," she said and realized her voice was thin, frightened.

"Hear that?" a dark form asked. "She says not to touch her, boys. An' us without so much as a glimpse of a woman these past weeks. Let's get a look at her." A hard hand caught her hair and jerked her head back. She stared up into a pockmarked face with heavy jowls and the stubble of a rough beard. Tears of pain and terror started in her eyes, but she said nothing.

"Colonel's asleep with *his* lady. Wouldn't do to wake him yet. So let's ask questions after." One of the others shouldered her tormenter aside and grabbed for her arm.

Rebecca struck at him and cried out at the jerk to her hair. Callused fingers were at her throat, tearing at her bodice. Others tugged at her skirt. Desperately she twisted and kicked. There was an oath and she was flung down. She thought she heard a distant voice as her head hit the ground, and she screamed.

Suddenly there was a grunt and a sharp command. The hands let go of her. She lay still a moment, unable to believe she was free of the hateful tugging and mauling. Another command and she was hauled to her feet. Holding her bodice together, she stood, swaying, and tried to see what was happening. From beside one of her attackers stepped Major Tyson. Now, in the distance behind him, she could see one of the long library windows was open to the side porch. He must have heard the shot, she thought dully.

The major peered narrow-eyed at her, his chin jutting forward like an accusing finger. " 'S a lady, boys," he said, his tone unnaturally high. "B'longs here." He waved an unsteady hand. "Fall back." Reluctantly the men did as he ordered. "All the way back," he snapped, and gave a bark of laughter.

The three soldiers looked at each other and then began moving off slowly. Rebecca, who had thought her mind gripped in stupefying fright, suddenly realized the officer was drunk. His breath reeked of Uncle Julian's best brandy as he moved closer and grasped her arm, pulling her to him. "A real lady," he sneered. "Only ladies don' usually sneak around in the dark." Appalled beyond words, Rebecca looked at him dumbly. "Do they?" he snarled, shaking her arm. Then he jerked her toward the house. " 'S matter?" he asked in a vicious voice. "Gordon not please you enough? You running away from him? Shouldn't do that. Told you I was here."

Rebecca shuddered and stumbled over the grass beside him, too sickened to speak.

"Though don't know now," he went on in alcoholic rumination. "Used goods not what I'd had in mind. On other hand . . . always did admire you!"

Without thought, Rebecca jerked away from him and began to run. Like a frightened hare she zigzagged down the lawn, hearing the clink of his sword as he ran behind her. The trees that had seemed such shelter only minutes before were endlessly far away now. She glanced at the house, wondering wildly if there was somewhere inside she could hide, and saw a tall figure outlined in an open library window. She swerved as the figure moved.

Seconds later another set of hands pulled her up short. She fought them, but she might have struck a tree trunk for all the good it did. Behind her she heard Major Tyson's panting breath as he drew to a stand. Shivering, she stopped struggling, her mind clouded with despair.

"Devil of an hour for a stroll," was all her captor said, and spun her back toward the house. Half carrying her, he walked steadily to the door. "Major, you may retire," he called above her head.

"Hell I will," choked Tyson. "You lost her, Meade. Men found her running off from back of the house. Seems she doesn't prefer your bed."

The grip on Rebecca's waist became painful, but the steps remained steady, and she found herself propelled across the candlelit room. At the far door she was halted. Over his shoulder, Colonel Meade said softly, "Good night, Major." To Rebecca's overstrained nerves, his voice sounded dangerous. Clutching her tattered dress even closer, she was swept forward once more, and pushed up the staircase. With a feeling of being disconnected from all reality, she wondered if the colonel was going to kill her now.

In her room she was released to stand, dazed, by the bed while Colonel Meade shut the door. "The key?" he asked pleasantly, and held out his hand.

She shook her head. "I . . . I must have dropped it in Sylvie's room."

His eyes narrowed. "What were you doing there?"

"It's how I got out. The window." She slumped against the bedpost, reaction to the events of the past hour making her knees buckle.

Gordon Meade stared at her in disbelief. "The window, by God. With your dutiful maid dangling you from a bedsheet, no doubt."

Rebecca shook her bent head. "There was a tree beside the roof."

"I wasn't aware that tree climbing was normally listed among a lady's accomplishments."

Despite her exhaustion Rebecca rose to the bait. "I wasn't aware that stealing and taking a lady prisoner were among a gentleman's accomplishments. Besides, I find it hard to believe you know much about a lady's accomplishments anyway."

"More than I usually care to know," he answered shortly and began moving about the room.

Once more he shed his coat and boots by her dressing table, and when he was done, sat surveying her bedraggled form. She flushed, knowing the picture she must present, her dress nearly in shreds, her hair matted with leaves. Behind his head she caught a glimpse in her mirror of trailing black waves framing a smudged face where a scratch made an angry line down one cheek. She bit her lip and turned away, wondering where she could hide. Perhaps Sylvie's room. He didn't know yet, apparently, that her maid had disappeared into the night. Had Sylvie seen all that had happened? Rebecca prayed hastily that the girl was all right and had reached safety in the village. And if she had, what then?

There was little hope that a handful of local men would arm themselves with pitchforks to do battle with a company of soldiers, and so liberate her from her prison. But what was to become of her now she couldn't imagine.

Behind her the wardrobe door opened and she heard a great rustling of material as the colonel rumaged among her clothes. "There." His deep voice held a certain satisfaction. "Put this on. You look half dead with cold and fright."

Rebecca turned slowly and found him holding out one of her heaviest chemises. Flushing all over again, she stepped backward. Colonel Meade threw the snowy garment on the bed in a gesture of impatience. "Put it on," he repeated. "I'm not going to stand gaping at you like a yokel. The sooner you get warm and lie down where you were supposed to, the sooner I can get back to bed." He went to the fireplace and, taking up a poker, began stirring the embers.

Rebecca picked up the chemise and retreated to the far shadows of the room. With trembling fingers she undid the last hooks of her bodice and skirt and dropped the ragged dress to the floor, all the while watched his stooped back anxiously. Quickly she slipped the night dress over her head and when its soft folds fell to her feet she let go her breath for the first time. So, the tired colonel had seen this whole ghastly episode only as an annoying interruption of his much-needed sleep. There was relief to be felt in that reflection. And he had kept his back turned while she undressed. With a certain feeling of bravado, she went to the washstand, splashed cold water on her overheated face and dried herself carefully. She did not look behind her as, with great deliberation, she made her way to her dressing table and began brushing her hair.

Gordon Meade stood beside his bed, his fingers prepared to pinch out the candle he held, and watched the lithe figure move about the room. The unconscious grace of Rebecca's upraised arms as she pulled at tangled masses of glossy hair took his breath away. Too bad he was too exhausted to appreciate her charms as fully as they deserved. What he did appreciate, with a surprised start, was the girl's courage in the face of all that had happened to her today. Most women would have been weeping and moaning long since, begging his protection, crying to be sent away, or worse, to stay close to him. Not only had she done none of those things, she'd tried, foolishly but valiantly, to escape him. He cursed the ill fortune that had brought his men ahead of him to this elegant house where a beautiful girl stood lone defense. Under any circumstances it would have been a lamentable situation. But to discover that the lone girl was the gorgeous London flirt to whom he had once made satisfactory but improper advances, was an ironic twist that he didn't feel up to admiring. He had apparently misjudged Rebecca Blair when he'd thought her an empty-headed society belle, though he remembered that the day of her father's death she had already shown him she had strong character. At the moment, however, he had more than enough troubles without the added responsibility for the headstrong girl's safety.

If only she'd shown some common sense, she might have been all right, but her scornful defiance had inflamed half the men in his command, and now he didn't dare leave her side until he could get his men away. The girl was a nuisance. What's more, the situation would become a tangle if he didn't take hold of himself. He'd just told her with high-minded scorn that he wouldn't gape at her like a yokel. Yet here he was staring at the sumptuous curves so tantalizingly outlined by the softly hanging material as though he were a randy schoolboy. He watched her cross to the pallet and creep under the covers, and slowly his fingers closed on the flame. With a muffled oath at the pain, he flung himself down again and tried to concentrate on all that had to be done on the morrow.

Chapter 15

Faint watery light seeped over the windowsill and across the floor to tickle Rebecca's eyelids, and she came awake with a start. At first her eyes, burning with lack of sleep and with unshed tears, seemed to deceive her as she looked at the grate on the hearth where cold embers lay in a bed of gray dust. What was her head doing on a level with the hearth? She moved and felt the straw of her mattress shift under her. With a jerk, memory returned and she lay rigid, listening. Cold air seemed to envelope her in a cocoon of silence broken only by a bird calling far away. As quietly as she could, she lifted her head and looked at the bed, half afraid she'd see Gordon Meade's sharp blue eyes watching her expectantly. But there were only rumpled bed clothes to speak of his presence. Clutching the quilt to her chin, she sat up and peered around the room. Coat, boots, waistcoat, sword, all were gone. It was as though the man had never been here.

A wild hope surged through her and she jumped up, dragging the quilt. Half stumbling, she ran to her front window. Leaden skies and frosted grass met her anxious gaze. In the distance, a gray-blue line of white-tipped waves rolled beneath brown fall-bare cliffs. But nothing else moved.

Perversely, she stamped her foot. All those awful men coming and taking over Halscomb Acres, looting, making her a prisoner, disappearing as swiftly as they'd arrived, and they'd had to choose the day of the Revingtons' ball to do it!

Now she'd missed what was probably the best party of the season, would have to explain to Charles her unannounced absence and had suffered endless humiliation at the hands of a group of ill-bred, leering, disgusting men. It was all too much to bear.

But thank God it was over. She stomped back to her wardrobe and began hauling out clothing. She supposed she'd better go find Mrs. Clark and survey the damage that had been done. Pulling out a dark rust-colored India cotton trimmed with simple beige ruching at the neck and hem, she slipped on a petticoat and looked around the room. Those sheets, for instance, would have to be changed at once. She suppressed the thought that seldom had she seen a man who wore such snow white linen, whose clothes were so immaculate. Regardless, only heaven knew where Colonel Meade had slept before he used her bed.

Swiftly she dressed and tied her hair back with a wide beige ribbon. There would be so much to do. She'd have to find the papers Colonel Meade had left her for the horses and wagons and put them on Uncle Julian's desk. And she'd have to see the place cleaned up for his return. She thought of the soldier who had spit on the hall carpet and clenched her fist. Someone would have to go to the village and retrieve the servants and find Sylvie. Poor Uncle Julian would be undone if he saw all that had happened in his beloved home. She could only hope the colonel had been wrong when he'd said her uncle could not get back here through the rebel army. She prayed he was safe and on the road even now.

Out in the hall she heard distant voices and darted to the stairs in hopes that some of Halscomb's men had returned. But at the bottom of the staircase she stopped. If servants had come back, they hadn't yet begun the job of erasing dusty bootprints, and there was even what looked like an old blanket flung into the corner by the front door. She'd have to get people organized. But first she needed food. She'd eaten little during last night's tense dinner, and she felt famished.

Briskly, she crossed the hall and opened the dining room door. Then stopped in her tracks. Seated at the table were Major Tyson, Lieutenant Meade and two other men. At her abrupt entrance all of them got to their feet.

"Miss Blair, are you all right?" The young lieutenant came around the table toward her, but she waved him back. Her dismay was so total, so deep that she must have looked physically ill.

"I had thought all of you gone," she managed in a tight voice.

The lieutenant halted, looking nearly as dismayed as she. "Only some of the men, Miss Blair. My brother took a party to General Washington this morning. I'm afraid you have not seen the last of us yet."

She realized his solicitude was profound, and with a sinking heart thought of last night. The whole company must know the colonel had stayed in her room, and they could all draw only one conclusion. She wanted to scream it wasn't so, to wipe that awful look of worry from Alexander Meade's face, to smack away the sneer on Warren Tyson's mouth. Instead, she turned to the sidetable laden with food and took up a plate. Carefully, she heaped bacon and hot cakes and eggs on her dish, and when Mrs. Clark bustled in with another pot of steaming coffee, took a cup to be filled. Then, with her chin high, she looked squarely at the old woman. "I will carry this food to my room, Mrs. Clark, and will remain there for the day. Please be so good as to see my other meals are brought there. I find this company uncongenial." She watched the housekeeper's mouth fall open, then turned and stalked back up the stairs.

When she'd done with her breakfast, her temper improved a bit, but a bleak feeling set in. Why did the soldiers have to stay here? What if Charles should ride up to see if she was all right and discover the house swarming with rebels? If he wasn't shot outright, what would he think of her? That lowering thought reminded her of Sylvie's plight, and she worried all over again about what had happened to the girl.

As the morning wore on she grew restless and bored. She was now unused to long inactivity, she realized. Pacing the spaces between furniture and windows, she wished she hadn't announced her determination to remain confined to this room. But where could she go anyway? A brisk walk outside would lead only to more encounters with the rough men who surrounded her.

At lunchtime there was a solid thump on her door which made her jump. Apprehensively she opened it to find Lieutenant Meade balancing a large tray and a wine bottle.

"I thought you might find some wine fortifying," he said with a red face. "Mrs. Clark is busy downstairs, and I can find no sign of your maid, so I took the liberty of carrying your tray."

"Thank you," she said in icy tones, and stood back to let him in.

He put the tray down and rubbed his hands nervously, trying to keep his eyes from straying about the room. Rebecca watched him in silence, knowing he was thinking of his brother's presence here, and feeling her anger and embarrassment rise.

"I'm sorry about your maid," he gulped. "She must have run off."

"She did," Rebecca answered, and volunteered no more.

"Oh." The lieutenant looked crestfallen, and then determined. "You w-won't be disturbed again," he stammered at last, and gave in to his impulse to glance at the bed. When he saw the pallet on the floor near the fireplace he couldn't quite hide his start of surprise, and Rebecca smiled grimly. "G-Gordon may not be back till late. I'll t-try to have one of the other rooms made up for him. Though I don't know if he'll like that," he added with boyish candor and flushed all over again.

"Your brother's likes and dislikes are of no concern to me," Rebecca stated flatly. "And I would appreciate it if you would see that he does have a room of his own."

"I'll give him mine," the lieutenant said in a rush, and backed through the door.

Rebecca bowed her head in acknowledgment, and saw him stumble away. Following him out to the hall, she decided she would go to Sylvie's room and find her key before she sat down to lunch. It would make her feel more secure if her door were locked while she was in her self-imposed prison. But nowhere in the plain little room could she find the key. She gave up the search and went back to her lunch, reflecting that it probably didn't matter anyway. For now, the lieutenant was obviously watching that no one bothered her. But tonight? It probably would make no difference if there were *two* locks on her door if Gordon Meade wanted to enter the room. Though perhaps he would not try to force his way in. He was certainly not interested in sharing his bed with her. So perhaps he'd be grateful for a room of his own. Why she should feel the smallest sense of pique at that bright thought, she couldn't imagine, and furious at herself, she sat down to eat.

During the long afternoon she was glad that she had two books from the library downstairs to keep her company, but the inactivity and uncertainty of the day began to tell on her spirits. By nightfall she felt heavy and sullen, more resentful than ever of the rebels, more worried than ever about Sylvie, Uncle Julian and even Charles. There had been no sign of any visitors, no one on the drive all day, and her isolation was weighing on her nerves.

When the rap on her door indicated the evening meal had arrived, Rebecca had to force herself from her chair to go and meet whoever was there. She found that it was Mrs. Clark, still puffing from her climb up the stairs. The girl was so glad to see her, she dragged her into the room and took the tray from arthritic hands.

"My lands, it's so gloomy in here," the woman said as she gave up the tray and stood wiping her fingers on her broad apron. "Let me light some more candles, miss. You'll ruin your eyes." She looked with distaste at the book overturned on a small table, and bustled about, bringing light back to the high-ceilinged room.

Rebecca nearly laughed with relief and peeked under the covers at the dishes brought to her. Lentil soup, fresh slabs of bread and a big bowl of mutton stew full of vegetables and swimming in thick rich gravy made her nostrils quiver.

" 'Tisn't fancy like," the housekeeper apologized, standing beside her now, hands on ample hips, "but 'tis what the officers wanted, them bein' out all day in the brisk air."

"The soldiers who left this morning are back, then?"

"Came in near an hour ago. The colonel's been in the office working ever since. Never knew there was so much paperwork to be done in an army."

"Nor did I." The girl's voice was heavy with scorn as she picked up the wine glass on the tray. "Have you heard from Sylvie, Mrs. Clark?"

"Mercy!" A pudgy hand flew to the woman's mouth. "I clean forgot to tell you. A boy came up from the village this afternoon. Said he'd been sent with a message for you. Sylvie is fine, and was worried half to death about you. I told him to say you were all right. Though how, I don't know, with all that carrying on last night. What your uncle would think of such doings I hate to imagine, miss."

"Happily, he'll know nothing about any of it, Mrs. Clark."

Rebecca filled her glass from the bottle left at lunch. "Though I think he would applaud my attempt to escape."

"Maybe so." Mrs. Clark looked hard at the girl. "You *are* all right, aren't you, miss?"

"As all right as a prisoner can be. Don't worry, Mrs. Clark, Colonel Meade never laid a hand on me." Rebecca took a sip of wine, noting the housekeeper's look of relief.

"Glad it is that I am," the old woman said with feeling. "Not but it's what I would expect from that one." She nodded emphatically. "Now I must be off. I know you don't approve, but 't is good to be taking care of lusty young appetites downstairs. And most of 'em are little more than boys doing all this dirty work."

"If they'd stayed home where they belonged, none of us would be in this mess," Rebecca snapped. Then added in a calmer voice, "Thank you for the food."

"There, there." Clumsily Mrs. Clark patted the girl's arm and waddled from the room, removing the dishes left from lunch as she went. The door closed behind her and Rebecca sat down with a thump. Well, at least eating would give her something to do.

By the time she was done, she saw that full night had dropped like a massive black cloak around the house. Finishing her second glass of wine, she shivered as a gust of wind off the Hudson rattled the panes in the windows. The room needed a fire. She stared at the dark well of the fireplace with longing. How did one build a fire? Perhaps someone would think to come up and light it for her. As soon as she'd had the wistful thought, she pushed it aside. No one was coming. She'd have to warm herself as best she could. She considered putting on a cloak, then thought of the warmest one she owned probably still caught in a tree root outside. She stood up and began walking back and forth, beating her arms to get warm. This was ridiculous. And what if the colonel did return this evening to her room? Would she have to undergo the same mortifying scene of scampering out of her clothes as he stared stonily at an opposite wall? Better to be ready to dive for her bed when he came in—if he came in.

Her fingers had grown clumsy with the cold, but she managed the tiny buttons and hooks with fair speed, and soon stood clad only in her heavy chemise once more. Darting to the wardrobe, she took out a midnight blue velvet gown and wrapped it around herself. That was better. The awful sense of urgency left her as partial warmth was restored, and carefully she put away her dress and returned to the dressing table.

In the candlelight the gown made her eyes look nearly as dark as the velvet, and the closely tied waist, wide soft lapels and tight sleeves were very becoming to her figure. More becoming than she liked. But it was the warmest thing she had for around the house. Two small hooks held the gown close under her breasts, and the wide V of the neck allowed a lovely triangle of ruffled chemise neckline to show. The soft swell of her breasts was just visible at the line of the ruffle, and Rebecca eyed her bare throat nervously. Perhaps her hair could save the situation. She sat down, undid the ribbon at her neck, and began brushing the long locks.

Watching the strokes of her brush in the mirror, she grew dreamy. Rarely in the past two years had she had so much time to be utterly alone. She admitted now that she had savored at least part of her solitude this day. Here at Halscomb she was usually busy, and always at home in England there had been Aunt Honoria and Letty sitting with her or barging in on her. There had been endless rounds of mindless entertainments, designed to coax all of them from their lethargy brought on by boredom. What a vapid existence that had been, each day regulated by the rules of polite society, each hour accounted for on gilt-edged calendars.

"Boredom has its compensations, though," she said aloud to the mirror. "We were usually warm, at least." And she dropped her brush on the polished mahogany.

Stiffly, she marched to the fireplace and looked down. There were only three logs left in the wood basket, and they all looked enormous. Kindling lay in the corner beside them, and another box of chips sat on top. She tried to remember a time that she'd watched a fire being built, and realized she'd never paid much attention, had always just assumed it would be done for her. Obviously she should have added fire building to her new list of accomplishments. What a helpless ninny she was!

She rubbed her cold hands together and decided common sense would dictate that the chips went on the grate first, then kindling. But she'd no idea how much of each she should use. With an air of desperation she began piling things into the fireplace. The logs proved to be just as heavy as they looked, and when she'd wrestled one out of the basket, she nearly dropped it edge-on on her careful pile of kindling. Heaving and panting, she finally got it in place with a thud, realizing as she did so that she was kneeling on the edge of the ashes. "Damn," she said, and rocked back on her heels.

"What a very unladylike exclamation."

Rebecca whirled and nearly lost her balance. Gordon Meade stood in the center of her room looking at her with the first real hint of laughter she'd seen him display. "Why must you always sneak into rooms?" she snapped, acutely aware of her undignified position.

"This time I knocked," he replied, "but you were so busy at your Herculean labors you didn't hear, so I came in to see that you were all right. Obviously you are, though I wouldn't vouch for your gown." He smiled then, displaying remarkably white teeth.

To Rebecca, the smile looked full of wolfish delight at her predicament. With what hauteur she could muster, she picked herself up and brushed at the clinging ashes on her skirts. "If you'd really had a single thought for my welfare," she said waspishly, "you'd have sent someone up to build a fire. The water must be frozen in the pitcher over there." She waved toward the washstand, trying to distract his gaze from her sorry condition. His eyes didn't move. In fact they seemed locked on her, and she stepped away to break their hold.

Gordon shook his head at her movement, and made an effort to control his thoughts. Though that wasn't going to be easy, he reflected, having walked into a room to find one of the most beautiful girls he'd ever seen looking so adorably disheveled and swearing like a guttersnipe in a well-bred voice. Just as he'd quelled the urge to laugh and snatch her to him, she'd turned around to show huge violet eyes stormy with annoyance, but pleading for help, and he'd nearly choked on his own breath. He stared at the black hair tumbling over the magnificent dressing gown, and with an effort looked away from her, reminding himself sternly that this gorgeous creature who didn't know how to build a fire was also a clever and resourceful girl who hated rebels and was daring enough to try to escape by climbing out a second-story window. It might have been better for both of them if she'd succeeded, but once caught by Tyson and the others, he couldn't have left her to their mercies. He felt his exhaustion and his irritation returning with these thoughts, and he stripped out of his jacket, flinging it at the chair. Without looking at the girl again, he went to finish the fire.

Rebecca stood quietly in one corner and watched him as he worked. She had not missed the changing of his moods, and she wondered at them. For just the briefest instant she'd seen the light in his eyes as he looked at her, and she had felt inadequately clothed. It was one thing to have a man look at you that way on a dance floor; it seemed quite another to stand undressed in a bedroom and encounter that look. Nervousness made her want to break the silence between them.

"I would have managed to get that lit, you know," she said. He didn't answer, and she crossed her arms, staring daggers into the back of his blond head. "Do you know yet when you will be gone and we will be left in peace?"

The colonel looked up then. "No," he said over his shoulder. "I received orders today to stay in the neighborhood as a rear guard for the army. So I cannot give you a satisfactory answer."

"The 'neighborhood' is a large area. Surely there are other places to stay. You and your men will eat us out of food before long, and I hate to think of all the light fingers that have gone through this house already."

Meade fanned the sparks he'd ignited and stood up as the fire sprang to life. "There has been no theft that I know of, Miss Blair. But we all give thanks to you for the meats in the smokehouse, the vegetables in the cellars, the preserves on the shelves, yes."

"That's called 'living off the land,' isn't it?" Rebecca flared. "But what of the people you've robbed of food and left in their empty homes when you've gone?"

"We will not use all your stores. But I must remind you there is a war on. These men have had to leave families to fend for themselves too, families with a lot less than you have. And the men, most of them, don't even have heavy coats against the coming cold. Some don't even have shoes." His voice was edged with anger, and Rebecca's own wrath rose to meet it.

"Then they should have thought twice before participating in treason."

"There's no good to come of our standing here arguing. I'm tired." He crossed to the chair and began unbuckling his sword.

"So am I," Rebecca fairly shrieked. "How do you suppose it is to sleep on a hard pallet, and then be kept in your room all day?" She was aware of the license she was taking with the truth, and realized soldiers must rarely sleep in feather beds, but she was beyond caring what she said.

"Leave off, girl," Meade said wearily, "or I'll let you take your chances with the other men in the house."

Rebecca eyed his movements and felt her frenzy mounting. "What are you doing? You're not staying here again! Your brother said . . ."

The colonel's sword belt slapped against the chair with a crack. "Alex is a young fool," he said in a hard voice, "and you're to keep your flirtations to yourself around him."

"How dare you!" She gasped. "This is *my* home, and you've no right . . ."

"Leave it, I say." His voice seemed to strike her physically, and she drew a shuddering breath. "Count yourself lucky I'm so fatigued, or I'd be driven to spank you for your spoiled ways."

She gasped again, and wished she could scratch his handsome face. But some deep instinct told her he meant what he said, and that he was capable of nearly anything, including throwing her out the door to face Major Tyson and the others. Fuming but silent, she stood rigidly watching him remove his waistcoat and boots. Then he went and stoked up the fire and blew out all the candles but the one nearest her on the washstand. For such a large man he moved with a surprising grace and silence, but even from yards away he exuded a power that was physically daunting. The full-cut linen shirt couldn't hide broad shoulders and big arms, and when he'd removed his stock, the open shirtfront revealed curling hair on a chest bulging with muscles. Rebecca shivered and backed further into her corner. If this man really lost his temper, he could snap her in two like a large twig, she thought, and felt like a trapped hare watching a fox circling close. Incongruously, the memory of his mouth on hers sparked in her mind, and she felt her breath coming in short gasps. It was only fear, she tried to tell herself, and reached behind her for the wall.

To her surprise, he lay down without another word, and soon she thought she could detect his deep, even breathing. Not until then did she dare move, for she could hardly see the large form among the shadows of the bed. Very quietly she undid her robe and put it on a hook. Without it she felt more exposed than ever and considered making a dive for her bed on the floor. But as she took up the candle, her eye fell on his sword draped again over the back of her chair. How much more secure she would feel with the great weapon in hand! She moved silently to the chair, put down the candle and grasping the hilt, tested the play of the blade in the scabbard. The weapon was well oiled and slid freely in her hand. With only the faintest of slithering sounds, it came out of its long case, and she realized that it was too unwieldy and heavy for her to use effectively. But she clung to the thought that it represented security. If the colonel should wake up and . . . Carefully, she lifted the sword to her right shoulder and took up the candle. Then on tiptoe she crossed to the bed, put the candle on the table, and looked at the rumpled form lying there. His face was turned toward her, tense even in sleep. What demons must haunt his dreams, she wondered as, shuddering, she leaned over to blow out the candle.

A stockinged foot came up and caught her such a blow in the side she was knocked against the wall. With a snarl Gordon Meade was up, one hand at her throat, the other gripping the wrist that held his sword. A twisted bronze face pushed up to hers. "Is there nothing you would not dare, you hellcat?"

Chapter 16

Rebecca choked, trying to draw breath, and clawed at the strangling hold on her throat. Blue eyes, now the color of dark metal, bored into hers. Then slowly the hand began to loosen on her neck. She saw that it was with an effort he was pulling back from killing her, and the knowledge made her knees buckle.

Shifting his grip to her shoulders, the man shook her till her head felt it would snap off and she heard the sword clatter to the floor. "Bitch," he spat. "Would you be so stupid as to kill your passport?" He slapped her then, bringing hot tears to her eyes.

She threw herself against the wall, horror holding her upright, animal fear mingled with raging fury pumping in her veins. "Touch me again and I *will* kill you," she sobbed.

"You damned fool," he blazed. "Do you know what I would do to a man who tried a stunt like that? Shall I describe it to you?"

"Don't you dare," she raged back. "I only wish I *had* killed you."

"And what did you propose to do then? Run to my brother for protection?" He raised his hand again and Rebecca flinched.

"Damn you," she whispered. "You arrogant, bestial . . ."

His hand dropped to her neck and with a rip her chemise was torn open. "Bestial?" he snarled. "You mean like the men who caught you on the grounds last night? My dear, you don't yet know the meaning of the word."

With a cry, Rebecca tried to cover herself and dart past him, but his arm shot out and snatched her back, tossing her against the wall like a rag doll, one hand cupping her face like a pair of tongs. He kissed her savagely, and she kicked at him, but his grip didn't slacken. She bit him then, and thought he would strangle her as he drew back with a growl. His furious eyes raked her exposed breasts and returned to her face.

Her head pressed against the wall, Rebecca stared back at him in silence. She felt a hand circle her breast and follow the line of her side to her hip, and she shivered. "No," she whispered. "Please."

Suddenly he released her and she staggered. For one charged moment their eyes locked, and then with an oath he snatched up his sword from the floor. Rebecca leaned on the table, waiting for the blow. But the man spun away from her, grabbed up his coat and boots and flung out of the room, all before her brain registered the fact that she was not to die now.

She stumbled the two steps to the edge of the bed and sat down hard. Her neck felt raw and red, her lips felt bruised, and her body was tingling with reaction. For a long time she sat, staring at the dancing fire in the grate, holding the pieces of her chemise together and waiting. She heard the muffled chime of the clock downstairs and the crack of a log on the fire. At last she turned, and pulling the covers over herself, curled up against her pillow and allowed the first tears to come.

Twice during the night she awoke with a start, thinking she heard a noise in her room. The candle had long since guttered into oblivion, but the dying coals of the fire showed her no one was there. Toward morning, she slept deeply.

The sun was high and bright the next day when a tap on the door brought her awake once more. "Who is it?" she called, and rubbed her eyes against the piercing light.

The door opened and Mrs. Clark's round face peered in. " 'T is your breakfast, miss. The colonel ordered it up to you. Seemed to think ye'd eat like his men, for he heaped the plate himself just now as he came through the kitchen."

Rebecca scowled and started to sit up, but thought better of it as she remembered the tattered condition of her night dress. "Thank you, Mrs. Clark. I think all I feel like is strong coffee, though."

The woman put the tray down and started from the room. Near the door she stopped and looked at Rebecca closely. "You are feeling all right, miss?"

"Oh, yes. Just lazy, Mrs. Clark," Rebecca lied, feeling the aches and bruises from the last two nights.

"Good. It's difficult for you, I know," the woman said enigmatically. "Colonel's not in the best of moods this morning. He took a party out foraging for the army. I don't envy anyone in his way today." And shaking her head, she left.

Were those words meant to convey some sort of warning? Rebecca wondered, throwing back the bedclothes. She looked down at the ripped chemise. Well, the colonel's temper was no longer petrifyingly fearful. She'd experienced its full force, she sensed, and it was comforting to know that the man stopped short of murder. It was just as comforting to know he stopped short of rape. She could have done little to stop him last night, and he'd certainly been mad enough to do her harm. So what had halted him? She remembered his taunting kisses in the garden the first time she'd ever met him. They had been full of a restrained fire, even then. Last night his kiss was more frightening, more forceful. And yet he'd stopped. . . . The man was a mystery. But, she thought vehemently, not a mystery she wanted a hand in solving.

She swallowed some porridge and nibbled at the toast dutifully, but she felt restless and not at all hungry. The coffee sent warmth flooding through her, and soon she began to think of all that she should be doing today. Looking in the mirror at her disheveled condition, she decided the first order of business was to bathe. The water was icy but she knew there was no one to bring her a hot kettle, so she did her best, and soon felt much better. The act of dressing and fixing her hair was restorative too, but she eyed her wardrobe ruefully. There were a number of gowns she couldn't wear without aid in dressing, since they hooked up the back. It was a dilemma she'd never before considered and she fingered a gray and black taffeta longingly. She would miss Sylvie more as the days wore on, she feared, but she wouldn't have the girl return here now. A lady's maid did not even have the dubious distinction of a lofty station in life to protect her from lecherous advances of the soldiers. Not that Rebecca's situation as mistress of this house had done her a great deal of good. Still, Sylvie might have fared even worse.

She was searching for her sewing basket to mend her chemise when there was another knock. "Yes," she called, and went to the door.

It opened to reveal two unfamiliar young men in brown homespun, and she stepped back involuntarily. One of them, a freckle-faced boy, made a gesture toward his forehead. "Pardon us, Miss Blair. We're under orders to come and see if you would like to take some air." He shifted his feet uncomfortably as his companion stared woodenly at the far wall.

It was on the tip of her tongue to tell them what she thought of their orders, but she realized it was fruitless to snap at these boys. Besides, the lure of the outdoors was too great. "I don't suppose there is any way I could ride a horse?" she asked.

"Afraid not, miss. None of your nags is back from White Plains yet. Would you rather we came back another time?"

Rebecca could see that they both wished they'd been detailed to some other duty, and she wanted to tell them she wished so too, but she just smiled. "If you will wait a moment, while I get my cloak . . ." The heads bobbed, and she retreated to wrap her oldest brown wool around her shoulders.

As they went down to the front door, Rebecca saw no signs of more soldiers, but she noticed that the house looked more orderly. The hall carpet seemed to have been cleaned and the old blanket was gone from the corner. A vase of bright chrysanthemums stood on the long table under the stairs, and the girl wondered when Mrs. Clark had had time to arrange them. Colonel Meade certainly liked his headquarters to be comfortable, she thought with a grimace.

The day was as lovely as it had looked from her windows and she drank in the crisp fall air with its smell of dry leaves and turned earth. She might have enjoyed a long walk in the golden sun, but she found the two young soldiers following a discreet distance behind her disconcerting. It was one thing to have footmen follow you through the streets of London as you laughed and chatted with friends, went in and out of shops, piled their waiting arms with packages and forgot they were there most of the time. It was quite another to walk in solitary splendor across wide lawns, hearing two sets of stolid footsteps echoing your own. Though there was no one about, she felt ridiculously conspicuous. Soon she gave up and returned to the house.

To her surprise, her room had been cleaned when she came in. The sheets were changed, the pallet was back in place beneath the bed, the furniture was dusted. It gave her a lift to see it, and she wished she could thank whoever had done the work, though she reddened at the thought that it might have been soldiers fingering her things. Still, it was obvious that the colonel's lady was to be well treated now. She glanced back at the two boys at the door, waiting to be dismissed. Was this why she was suddenly encountering such deference? She was considered the personal property of their commanding officer, and must be treated with respect? If only they all knew how things really stood between Colonel Meade and herself! Stiffly, she thanked the two soldiers who had stalked her so faithfully, and watched as they practically ran into each other in their relief at the discharge. Closing the door behind them, she was further surprised to see the key restored to the lock. Did this mean she was to be given not only respect, but full privacy at last? She wondered.

The afternoon was spent in the office, wrathfully pushing aside saddlebags and stacks of papers so that she could finish her work on the books. How dare the rebel officers make so free with Uncle Julian's desk? Her fury was not helped, either, when she went to look for the steward and was told he'd not been seen today. She had an awful suspicion that she would not see Earle Evans again, now that rebels were in the house. Slamming the books back into the drawers, she stalked upstairs as the sun, dipping toward the Hudson's cliffs, cast long golden beams across the floor. Her hands on her hips, she looked around her spacious room, thinking. It was much too convenient for the officers to have her shut away upstairs. Undoubtedly Colonel Meade would have ordered her locked in if she hadn't saved him the trouble by imposing imprisonment on herself. Therefore, it was time to reassert her independence from his orders, she reasoned.

Taking great care, she dressed in a daffodil taffeta gown that evening, thankful that the modish dress had rows of buttons up the front of the bodice. Without help, she couldn't possibly do anything dramatic with her hair, and she was almost glad. Instead, she brushed it and tied the sides into loose waves meeting in the back of her head, then plucked tendrils loose to fall before her ears. The effect, she knew, was better than any of the rolled and padded styles so fashionable at the moment. Picking up her fan and gloves, she stalked out the door with the light of combat in her large eyes.

Two unfamiliar officers stood in deep conversation by the dining room table, but broke off as Rebecca swept regally into the room, and stared in open appreciation at the vision who had come to grace the evening meal. The girl smiled dazzlingly at them both, and they leaped to hold her chair, stammering introductions.

"Please do not let me disturb your conversation," she said, sitting down and arranging her skirts carefully.

" 'T was nothing of importance, miss," the officer with one epaulet, signifying he was a captain, assured her.

A moment later, Alexander Meade walked in and stopped in surprise. "Why, Miss Blair . . ." he blurted. Hastily he collected himself, trying not to stare at her. "We are honored."

Rebecca inclined her head graciously. Yes, she thought, this evening she would show Gordon Meade she was not to be repressed. "You have had another busy day?" she asked, and patted the chair next to hers invitingly. The wicked thought that Colonel Meade would be enraged to see her sitting beside his young brother flitted happily through her head.

But all her efforts were in vain, for Gordon Meade did not appear for dinner. By dessert, Rebecca was feeling very put out, and ate the last of her meal in moody silence, thinking the only thing for which she could give thanks was the fact that Major Tyson was absent also.

In her room once more she undressed with impatient motions and donned the velvet dressing gown. Someone had lit a fire this evening, and all might have seemed normal if she hadn't had a churning feeling at the pit of her stomach. Was the colonel going to come sneaking in here again, demanding a right to her bed, alternately insulting her and ignoring her, as he had the past two nights? And would he tonight find something else over which he could lose his temper, and perhaps his control? She sat down abruptly. There was nowhere to hide, no way to be sure last night's scene was not repeated. Then she remembered the key in her door. She ran across the room, turned it in the lock and leaned on the door, suddenly out of breath.

Voices came up the stairs, and she flattened herself against the wall, her eyes riveted to the handle of her door. The voices were nearer now, and she recognized one as Major Tyson's. Her teeth clinging to her lower lip, she waited. The men said good night. Footsteps came along the hall, paused outside her door. Slowly the handle turned.

Rebecca wanted to scream, but her throat was closed. She knew, as though there were windows in the panels of the door, that Warren Tyson stood in the hall, trying to enter her room. Suddenly, illogically, she wished Colonel Meade were here. The strange catlike major would not dare to try the handle of this room if he were. She watched the brass knob twist and then slowly return to its resting position. There was the softest chuckle, then the footsteps moved on.

The girl drew a ragged breath and inched away from the wall. The silence of the house descended, but she stood in the center of the room for several more minutes, listening. Then at last she sat down and opened her book.

An hour passed and her eyes grew heavy. No sounds came to her as she half attended to the story. Was the colonel in the house tonight? Vehemently, she told herself she didn't care, hoped in fact that he was gone for good. With deliberate actions, she made ready for bed. When she'd blown out the candles and turned to the big four-poster though, she found that the darkened room seemed remote and empty. In just two evenings, Gordon Meade's presence, his forceful energy, had somehow impressed itself on this chamber, and Rebecca suddenly felt a small thrill of worry. At last she was truly alone here with a large group of men from the Continental Army camped just outside her door. If their colonel had left them, what was to become of her?

It was a dream-tossed night, and the girl awakened once more to Mrs. Clark's knock with a feeling of being only lightly rested. Grudgingly she opened the door to her breakfast, then retreated back to her bed.

"You're looking pale today," Mrs. Clark commented as she followed with the tray and placed it across the girl's legs. "Shall I say you'll not be wanting to go outside this morning?"

"I don't know," Rebecca answered, lifting covers off eggs and sausages. "I can't stay inside the house forever. Perhaps later I'll take some exercise."

Mrs. Clark nodded. "There be few men about today, miss. The colonel's sending them all over the countryside."

"The colonel has returned then?" Rebecca took a deep

swallow of scalding coffee and choked on the pain in her throat.

"Left near dawn, he did. Would you like me to come up and help you dress later? I know it's gone hard with you."

Rebecca considered the offer. Mrs. Clark had her hands more than full, coping with the squad of officers staying here, and her arthritic old legs did not need an extra climb up the stairs. "Thank you, Mrs. Clark, you are kind. But I find I can manage on my own."

"Well, then . . ." The woman wiped her hands on her apron in a characteristic gesture. "I'll be off. The rooms will all need airing today, and there's a deal to be done in the larder if we're to continue feeding so many hungry men." Grumbling, she went out the door and shut it firmly behind her.

Rebecca chewed thoughtfully on a sausage. Then, taking a more cautious swallow of coffee, she put the tray aside and got up. Without Earle Evans to see to things, there was a lot of work to be done. But she knew she would not be allowed off the immediate property. The business on the farms would have to take care of itself until Uncle Julian returned or the rebels left here. At least she now knew where things on the estate stood, and today her energies would have to be channeled back into the household. The linen room, for instance, was fast becoming chaos with all the officers using everything in Halscomb's stores. She'd have mending to occupy her for days, she thought with a grimace. And later she and Mrs. Clark would turn out the library.

It was well into the afternoon when Rebecca, tired and coughing from the dust of the books, decided fresh air was necessary. Opening a door from the room, she went out to the side veranda and walked around to the front of the house. Almost immediately her two escorts of the previous day were upon her, requesting permission to accompany her as she walked. Wearily she granted it, and moved out on to the lawn. To her left she could just see the end of the herb garden and the spreading oak where she'd fallen the night of her attempted escape. Hugging herself, she set her back to the sights. A brisk walk down along the fence to the bottom of the drive would clear her head, she thought, and set out with a determined pace. When she reached the road she paused. This walk was really a self-indulgence, and she should go back to the house now. She turned to start back up the drive and heard the clop of hooves beyond a far bend. Hesitantly she waited, shielding her eyes, wondering who came this way.

Almost immediately two riders came into view and Rebecca could make out Gordon Meade in the lead. She hadn't seen him for nearly two days and, annoyingly, her heart thudded as he rode toward her. How straight and proud he looked in the saddle! He had seen her, so she stood still, wondering what sort of words they could now exchange after their last meeting. In front of his men, he would not be likely to apologize for his actions that night, but would he give her some sign that he realized he'd lost his odious temper for nothing?

She watched the big brown gelding trot heavily onward and saw that both horse and rider looked tired to the point of dropping. Gordon Meade's blue eyes were narrowed and heavy-lidded as they met hers. Then his hand went to his tricorn hat in quick salute, and he rode on past. Rebecca stared at his retreating back in disbelief.

"What a rude, arrogant, self-important, bullying man," she said softly.

"Miss?" One of the soldiers was behind her, looking worried.

"Not a thing." She smiled, and strode purposefully back up the drive.

The following day was a near repeat of the previous; full of hard work, but empty of the presence of the commanding officer. Rebecca returned to taking meals in her room, no longer willing to face the colonel if he should return to dine. She had been thoroughly angry at herself for feeling strangely crushed by his curt salute yesterday afternoon, and was now determined to keep to herself, grit her teeth and simply await the day the soldiers would leave Halscomb in peace.

177

Chapter 17

Two more days of imprisonment nearly drove Rebecca insane, but her stubborn pride made her maintain her resolution to occupy herself mainly in her own room. And no one came to disturb her. There were no more footsteps stopping at her door in the evening, no sudden appearances of the colonel in her room. Only the two young soldiers detailed to escort her, and Mrs. Clark, came to her door. She helped with chores in scullery, kitchen and linen room, and walked out twice a day in the herb garden despite the fact that the weather was turning cold and bleak. Otherwise, she had no contact with the rebel soldiers.

On Thursday evening, five days after the first arrival of the rebels, she went down the back stairs to fetch her evening tray. Mrs. Clark met her in the hall, and with anxious looks around, pulled the girl into the darkness of the pantry doorway.

"Another message arrived just an hour ago, miss. From that Mr. Adams and from Sylvie, it was. They say your Mr. Revington was mad as a hatter when he heard what had happened here, and went off to join the British army. He hoped to be able to lead good British soldiers against the nest of vipers in this house, was how Mr. Adams put it. But he says we can't count on it because General Howe, now that he has landed troops at Pell's Point, is finally marching on Westchester. Mr. Revington and the British will be busy chasing the rebel army for a time, he thinks. And glad I am of it, may I say. Don't know how I'd face Mr. Halscomb if fighting came to our door and this house was harmed."

The quick flash of hope that began was extinguished with the news that the British were on the other side of the county. If Charles had joined them, he'd have no choice but to go where he was ordered, and she couldn't hope to see him here. For a moment she had a vision of Charles and Colonel Meade facing each other in the hall, swords drawn. Inexplicably, her stomach lurched at the prospect. For whom did she feel this knot of fear? Then she shook her head. Colonel Meade was the bigger man and an experienced soldier. It was likely he'd make short work of Charles Revington if they ever fought. It was as well Charles was nowhere near Dobbs Ferry and Halscomb.

"Thank you, Mrs. Clark," she answered at last. It was comforting, at least, to know that Sylvie was still safe.

The day was to continue to hold surprises, Rebecca discovered, for shortly after dinner Alexander Meade appeared at her door to announce that the main body of the troops had left Halscomb.

"The main body?" Rebecca stood with hands clenched, wondering what this could mean.

"The colonel took most of his detachment to White Plains to join General Washington."

"Is he expected to return?"

"I don't know, Miss Blair. I thought I should tell you that for the time being, at least, most of the officers and men are gone."

"And yet you remain."

"Yes." The single word held considerable bitterness. "The colonel ordered me to stay behind. This is still our headquarters. Some of us must remain to guard it."

Rebecca frowned. "Then who was left in charge?" Her heart gave a jump of fear. If Major Tyson was in charge here . . . The thought couldn't be completed.

Alexander Meade flushed. "I am, Miss Blair."

"Congratulations, Lieutenant." She tried to keep her voice light.

"The colonel didn't want to do it. But he *had* to take the more experienced officers, and he was determined to keep Major Tyson far away from here. There's going to be a battle soon, I know. He doesn't want me in it." The bitterness was more apparent now.

Through the wave of relief she felt at learning Major Tyson was gone, and that the colonel had pulled him off deliberately, Rebecca was aware of a certain sympathy with both the Meade men. "Have you ever been in battles before, Lieutenant?" she asked softly.

The young man avoided her eyes. "Only on Harlem Heights, and then I was kept in the rear. Gordon's the one who's been doing the fighting, covering his name with glory. He won't give me a chance."

"He's a good deal older than you. Perhaps he wants to be sure you get your chance when you're his age."

The lieutenant's mouth compressed. "I just came to let you know how things stand, Miss Blair, and to tell you I will be patrolling tonight."

Rebecca sighed. "Thank you." She watched her door snap smartly shut.

She saw little of Lieutenant Meade in the next two days, and gathered from Mrs. Clark that he was occupied with scouting and with trying to replenish their larder with stores sent by his brother from the commissary. For that much, she felt grateful. But her gratitude was magnified tenfold when, on the crisp afternoon she looked out a back window, she saw the tall lieutenant ride up to the stables with two saddle horses in tow. Running out to the barn she was overjoyed to discover she wasn't imagining things; both her filly and Uncle Julian's favorite gelding had been returned to their stalls.

"Where did you find them?" she asked, her face eager and radiant.

Alexander Meade sucked in his breath as he turned to her, and suddenly thought he would commit murder if it would make Rebecca Blair look at him that way again. He only wished he could claim the credit for bringing the horses home. "Th-the colonel sent them back," he stammered, and wished his brother in perdition.

"But you rode over to White Plains to get them, didn't you?" Rebecca stroked the glossy neck of her mare, oblivious to the turmoil inside the young man.

"Well, yes," Alexander answered at last, thankful she chose to give him a share of the glory.

"You don't know how I've longed to ride." Bright purple

eyes lifted to his. "Thank you," she breathed. "I'm going to change right now."

"Well . . ." Alexander thought of all he should be doing, and consigned every duty to the same perdition as his brother. "The colonel's orders were, you are not to ride alone. There are deserters and thieves behind every army, and even though we're miles away, I don't know who might be in these woods. I'll have to ride with you if you go." He held his breath for her reaction, and nearly burst his lungs when she gave him a dazzling smile.

"I can be ready in ten minutes." She laughed with joy and, picking up her skirts, ran for the house.

Alexander saddled her horse and, though he knew Gordon hadn't meant him to be Miss Blair's escort, for the first time blessed one of the colonel's orders. He felt weak with the knowledge that he was about to ride alone with her, and wondered again at his brother. Gordon had made it look as though he'd claimed Rebecca for his own, but Alexander had seen the pallet on the bedroom floor, was sure that Gordon had not bedded the beautiful girl, and felt certain that she was not overly fond of the colonel and his high-handed ways. Therefore, Alexander reasoned feverishly, as he led the horse from the stall, Gordon had established no rights. Though why he hadn't was a mystery. He'd always had any girl he wanted. How could he pass up Rebecca Blair? Had he really escaped bewitchment? Perhaps he had, but he'd be the first Alex knew of who had managed to. He considered Gordon's past successes, trying to decide what it was that usually made women fall at his feet. Perhaps it was his cool, often sardonic manner. The lieutenant straightened his hat and tugged at his cuffs, trying to assume a nonchalant attitude.

True to her word, Rebecca was back in ten minutes, dressed in her forest green riding habit, and Alexander was hard pressed to maintain his negligent pose as he helped her mount. He could only hope her delicate hand on his shoulder couldn't feel him trembling.

But Rebecca was so absorbed in her pleasure at riding once again, she noticed nothing. "It's a glorious afternoon," she stated happily as they walked their mounts down the track to a far meadow. Alexander didn't answer, and she looked at him, suddenly conscience-stricken. "I've taken you away from duties that are urgent, haven't I? And you were too kind to say so."

The lieutenant felt his head spin as he looked at her luminous eyes. "Nothing is more urgent at the moment, Miss Blair," he said with perfect faithfulness to his inner feelings. She nodded, accepting his word, and they rode in silence while they gave their horses their heads.

At last they drew rein, and reluctantly turned back to Halscomb. "That was perfect!" Rebecca smiled. "And you are looking less unhappy, I think. Have you resigned yourself to your brother's orders to remain here?"

"I can't help thanking him for giving me the chance to serve you, Miss Blair. . . ."

"But . . ." she prompted.

"But I can still wish that when a battle does come, I might be there."

"Why are men always so eager to go off to battle and be shot at?" Rebecca thought of Charles and shivered.

Happy that she seemed to have included him in the category of men, Alexander tried to think of some way to answer her without sounding either pompous or vainglorious. "I suppose we don't think of the dying part of it," he said lamely.

"I suspect your brother did think of it when he ordered you to stay here."

"Perhaps." Alexander looked away from her. "But how can I prove I'm no child if he never lets me near the ranks? He's babied me ever since our parents died. He thinks of me only as his little brother, too young to be of any use."

"And yet here you are, a lieutenant, and at a young age."

"I am *not* so young. I'll be eighteen in a few months."

"Too young to be killed, surely."

"Gordon was my age when he went off for two months into the wilderness with the Indians. That was every bit as dangerous as being in the army."

"Why did he go off with Indians?" Rebecca's nose wrinkled.

"For the sheer fun of it," was the bitter reply. "But he wouldn't let me do the same thing. Said the only Indians he could really trust were too far west now."

"Did he do that sort of thing often?"

"No. Just that one summer. That was before he came down to New York to study law." There was a hint of pride in the voice now, and a touch of awe. "That's where he met John Jay and others who got him involved in the state assembly later. After that it was Philadelphia and finally Europe. All the while leaving me with tutors at home." The bitterness was back, and he stopped, his jaw clenching.

Rebecca was overwhelmed with the urge to know more. "Where is home?" she asked.

"Up the Hudson, near Albany." The lieutenant's face relaxed as he thought of the stone house on the high rolling bank of the river, the parklands and the forests. Unable to stop himself, he described it to her.

"It sounds lovely," she said when he halted, embarrassed. "It's a wonder either of you ever left it."

"Oh, Gordon says he's going back there the moment this war is over. He loves Laurel Manor more than most things in life. And he can afford to now. He's had his adventures. I hope to go back too, someday, but I've had a bellyful of being imprisoned there. I'm not like him. I don't want to study law, but I do want to see something of the world the way he has."

"He managed to see a bit of the world, I gather, when he followed Miss Jenkins to London." Rebecca felt a tiny stab of annoyance at the thought.

Alexander's eyes opened wider. "Followed Pam?"

"Didn't he?" Rebecca's heart skipped a beat.

The lieutenant chuckled. "He'd stopped following her long before he left for Philadelphia where he was asked by Congress to go to Paris and London. And lucky he was to be free of her. I'd have shot him myself if he'd brought Pam to be mistress of Laurel. She was neither smart nor capable enough for Gordon."

Rebecca was surprised by a momentary sense of elation. But then where did the story about chasing Pamela Jenkins come from? How Gordon Meade must have been laughing at her that evening in the garden in Grosvenor Square when she had tried to nettle him with talk of Miss Jenkins. She felt her face grow hot with the memory.

"No," Alexander was saying, unaware of her reaction, "it's been a long time since women have played any important part in Gordon's life. He doesn't trust them, says they're all scheming." He gasped, suddenly conscious of what he was saying, and started to stammer a disclaimer.

Rebecca waved his words away. "I'm aware your brother has little love for women, Lieutenant." And I'm not surprised, she thought, that he finds them all scheming. Any man who looked like Gordon Meade must have encountered more than his share of feminine wiles. Most men would enjoy that prospect, though. So what made Gordon Meade different? A tight feeling in her chest made her angry. Her urge to learn more about the colonel had ruined a nice ride. She needed to put the arrogant man far from her mind.

During the next days, Rebecca redoubled her efforts to return to her former life at Halscomb. Several of the servants had now reappeared, so she was no longer as needed to help do the hard work. Nor was she as restricted as she had been. She could not ride alone or go into the village—always Alexander or another man watched her outdoors—but she could come and go on foot within Uncle Julian's immediate domains much as she ever had. She and Sylvie exchanged messages freely now, and she learned that Rob was healing nicely under Mrs. Adams's care. In another few weeks he'd be right as rain again. Rebecca asked that he return to Halscomb, but in a short message Rob thanked her for everything and expressed renewed determination to join the rebel army. General Washington needed him more than ever, he said. Short of help on the estate, Rebecca was annoyed at the boy. He wanted to be like the rabble she'd seen here—barefoot and threadbare with only their ideals and their worship of General Washington to eat on long marches? Puzzled and infuriated, Rebecca yet wished she could meet this general who could command such determined loyalty against all odds.

Sylvie, it seemed, was happy at the Adams house, though she offered to return to Halscomb immediately if need be. Rebecca urged her to stay away. She feared that Meade's detachment of men might show up again at any time, and she didn't think Sylvie, with her pert and pretty looks, should be here to welcome them. She missed Sylvie sorely though, and found that without callers, without someone to talk to besides the lieutenant, who was as often away as he was at home, boredom had set in again. It didn't help that her confines had widened these past days; she was as much a prisoner as ever, and she resented the fact bitterly. She took care not to show her feelings to Alexander Meade, though. She could hardly blame him for her predicament; he wanted to be here no more than she wanted him. Besides, he exerted himself to be pleasant, even thoughtful, and she liked him. They had come to first names at last, agreeing that it was ridiculous to stand on formality under the circumstances. After all, they were allies of a sort.

She was more than halfway through her second week of confinement when Rebecca felt an overwhelming need to stretch her legs. There had been a frightening day of thunderous sounds on the twenty-eighth, sounds which Alex had said were cannon. They'd all kept close to the house for two days, fearing the fight might come their way. Then, on the night of the twenty-ninth, it had rained, leaving the world leaden and wet. As a result, she had not been out for three days, and she needed exercise. The wind had fallen this morning at last, and the world looked newly washed. A light frost silvered the grass in the fields and tipped the gay autumn leaves with white.

Donning high walking boots and her heavy cape—restored miraculously, like her room key—she set out after breakfast in hopes that a brisk walk would sweep the cobwebs from her mind. She'd spent too many hours worrying over things she couldn't help, and she needed to escape. Activity was what she craved. Even danger would be better than the present monotony. Kept within the bounds of Halscomb, she thought she'd go mad. If only she knew Uncle Julian was all right, that Charles was all right . . . that Gordon Meade was all right. With a start she pulled her thoughts away from the tall colonel. What was the matter with her? Tugging the hood of her cape close, she marched through a shallow glen and climbed to a meadow where the sun sparkled on brittle leaves and golden grasses.

It was there that Alex found her, standing still, watching two cardinals whose bright spots of color danced and twirled through the half-bare branches of a twisted oak at the edge of the glade. Reluctant to break the quiet mood of the place, Alex walked softly through the grass until he stood beside the girl. Her very nearness made him ache, but his mind was divided among urgent matters. "You shouldn't have gone out without leaving word," he said, trying to make his voice low and authoritative. "I've searched everywhere for you."

Rebecca looked up, startled. "Have you? I'm sorry. I just needed to get out."

Her pout of contrition made Alex clench his fists to keep from touching her. "You'll have to go back, Becky. I'm riding toward White Plains today, and want to know you are safe before I leave."

"Is there news? You're looking nearly as forbidding as your brother."

"Yes, there's news. That cannonade three days ago was a battle in White Plains, and Washington lost some ground. The man who told me said the armies were just sitting yesterday, eyeing each other. But there may be more action, and I won't stay here, knowing that."

Rebecca took his arm. "Was the colonel there?"

"I imagine so." Alex looked sulky. "But I am sure he's all right. He leads a charmed life. Only one wound in all those months in Canada, and he survived occupied New York."

They were walking toward the trees as they talked. "The colonel was in New York after the British took the city? To do what, burn it?"

"I don't know. He pushed me into the retreat with Putnam's forces, while he, with his special commission from Washington, stayed on. He won't talk about it."

Rebecca tilted her face up. "How disagreeable of him," she said. Then she laughed. "You may not leave in such a black mood, Alex. I'll race you back."

The lieutenant gaped at her. "You can't run in those skirts."

"You'd be amazed." As she spoke, Rebecca snatched up a handful of leaves and stuffed them down his coat. He bellowed with outrage as, whirling, she picked up her skirts and ran for the woods. At the fringe of trees she glanced back to see Alex pounding after her. Laughing again, she turned and ran headlong into an outstretched boot.

Gasping with shock, she jumped back to avoid a horse's stamping hooves, and looked up to see Gordon Meade's dark face above her. His blue eyes glinted at her, but he didn't move in the saddle as his horse quieted. Her first flash of relief, even of joy at seeing him disappeared under his gaze. Alex pulled up a pace behind, and involuntarily Rebecca stepped back toward him.

Gordon had ridden across the fields that morning, wondering at his need to return to Halscomb. It was a desire to be sure his headquarters and his brother were safe, he told himself, that took him past the house now. Washington had withdrawn the troops to higher ground around North Castle during the night, and had scattered Gordon's men over the landscape before dawn. The colonel was ordered to go west, and Halscomb was, after all, to the west.

As he'd ridden through the early light, his mind had

turned, unbidden, to the beautiful girl who was imprisoned in the house. Why had he not sent her off to her loyalist friend, or to some other neighbor this past week? She was an encumbrance none of them needed. He thought of the last time he'd been with her, the night she had tried to kill him, and now wondered for the tenth annoying time why he hadn't taken her then. She had been going to kill him with his own sword, and so deserved any fate he meted out. Besides, all his instincts told him she was a passionate woman, and God knew he desired her. So why had he stopped? Surely it wasn't chivalry that had taken him from the room. That moral nicety had deserted him this past year of marching and fighting, of witnessing brute force, agony, defeat, death. Was it then some deeply buried sense of self-preservation, a fear that he might embroil himself in some emotion he could not easily escape? But that was nonsense. Rebecca Blair meant no more to him than the countless other women he knew. He had considerable respect for her courage and her high spirits, but he wanted no entanglements. Furthermore, hauntingly beautiful though she was, she was also an enemy and worse, a distraction. If Washington was going to continue to insist he hold Halscomb, he'd have to get rid of the girl now, send her to that Charles she was sure would protect her. Her lover? He ground his teeth. No matter. She'd be out of his hair, away from his men. Especially he wanted her away from his brother. Alex was clearly becoming besotted, and was setting himself up for his first pain of love. If Gordon could help it, it would not be Rebecca Blair who inflicted that pain.

He had come through the woods in time to witness the scene in the meadow. The still fall air had brought their last words to him, and he had not missed the intimate gesture of entwined arms as they had walked. So engrossed did they seem in each other, they would have walked into him without noticing if Rebecca hadn't behaved in such a hoydenish fashion and run pell-mell into his horse. The urge to stick out his boot and catch her had been overpowering, and now he sat, glaring at the two miscreants menacingly.

"I wasn't aware your duties included chasing your charge through the grounds, Lieutenant," he said in a cold tone.

The boy's face reddened. Woodenly he answered, "No, sir."

"I wasn't aware your duties included searching us out,"

Rebecca said hotly. She saw the colonel's eyes snap dangerously, and afraid his wrath would fall more heavily on his brother, added, "Alex came out to herd me back to the house. I had gone out without telling him."

"You are referring to Lieutenant Meade, I take it?" The voice was remote, frightening.

Trying to keep from shaking, Rebecca said softly, "I am referring to your brother."

But the colonel wasn't even looking at her. His eyes locked on the lieutenant. "You will straighten your uniform. Then you will return to the house, where you will await me in the library." He pulled his horse aside and made room for the two to pass.

Alex jerked at his jacket and looked at Rebecca.

"Lieutenant!" The voice was a thunder clap.

"Yes, sir," Alex answered sullenly, and took Rebecca's elbow to steer her forward.

Outraged, Rebecca considered hanging back, but something told her that the colonel was prepared to take his riding crop to them if they didn't march as ordered. Furious, she stalked through the woods beside Alex. In the charged silence she could hear the creak of saddle leather, the clop of the horse's hooves on the damp ground as Gordon rode behind them. Her back tingled with the feeling that the colonel's steely eyes were on her, and she wished she could claw at them.

They encountered no one near the house, and inside all was silent. The servants must be in the kitchen wing, and the soldiers out by the barn. A sense of guilt and a sudden feeling of protectiveness made Rebecca follow Alex into the library. She couldn't let him face his brother alone.

The boy, his back rigid and his face still flushed, went to stand by the tall windows. After a while he looked back. "You'd better leave, Rebecca," he said with what he hoped sounded like firmness.

"Your odious brother does not frighten me, and besides I am the cause of your being in disgrace."

"This is not a child's game, Miss Blair." Gordon stood in the doorway, light framing his tall form, making him look bigger, more menacing than ever. He still held his riding crop, and it slapped against his boot with a decisive sound. "You will oblige us by retiring to your room."

"But Alex . . . the lieutenant . . . has done nothing wrong," Rebecca began, fear and anger maddeningly mixed in her voice.

"Miss Blair!"

Rebecca flinched as though his riding crop, not his voice, had hit her. She would face him down, she told herself, if the act wouldn't get Alex into even deeper trouble. But she sensed both men wanted her gone. Meeting the colonel's eye with a look of fury, she walked slowly out of the room and up the stairs.

She wanted to throw something, smash something. How dare that man lie in wait outside, order them about, frighten them, treat them like misbehaving children! How dare he ruin a lovely morning! She realized she'd been looking forward to his return, and he had destroyed everything. Practically crying with rage now, she stood in the center of her room and clenched her fists against her eyes.

There was a knock on her door, but she ignored it. She couldn't let anyone see her until she'd gotten hold of herself. The door opened slowly and heavy boots sounded on the plank floor. Hastily, Rebecca went to a window. "What is it?" she asked shakily, not turning around.

The footsteps crossed the rug and came to a halt behind her. "I came to apologize for upsetting you," the familiar deep voice said.

Rebecca was conscious of a wild urge to fling herself on his chest, and she gripped her hands harder. She wished she could wipe her eyes, but she didn't want to betray her emotions by the gesture. "I was not upset," she managed, still staring sightlessly out the window.

"Then for angering you." The voice held a tinge of amusement, and Rebecca's fury flared anew.

"That you did," she stated. "You are abominable to treat me, to treat your own brother as you did."

Brown hands gripped her shoulders, turning her. He'd left his coat downstairs, she noticed, and his snowy linen shirt was open at the neck. The triangle of golden hair swam in front of her as his hands seemed to burn her arms where they held her.

"Discipline is . . ." His voice stopped as she struggled to meet his eyes. Gordon looked at the amethyst pools blinking at his chin, and felt all his stern words slip away. She was trying so hard to cling to her outrage and to face him with hauteur that his chest contracted. Her black hair, tumbling around her shoulders now in wild and beautiful disarray, brushed his fingers and he longed to take hold of a shiny lock. God, what am I doing? he thought and tore his hands from her shoulders.

Chapter 18

Rebecca swayed, and of its own accord, Gordon's hand came out to steady her. As their fingers touched, something as elemental as a lightning spark seemed to flicker between them. The next instant his arms were around her and he was holding her hard against him.

Beyond thought, Rebecca lifted her face to his and felt his lips brush hers softly. Drugged with the wonder of that delicate touch, she closed her eyes. His lips moved to her cheek as his hand came up to stroke her neck and move upward through the luxuriant softness of her hair till he held her head caressingly. Then his mouth covered hers again and she responded as she'd never known she could.

Her body was on fire wherever he touched her and her legs would scarcely hold her upright. Never had she experienced sensations like this, yet always she had known it could be no other way. She had tried to dream of Harlcourt's or Charles Revington's kisses, but always a shadowed face, a pair of powerful hands, a tall lean body had intruded on her efforts. There was only Gordon, and he was holding her at last. She didn't dare open her eyes, for if the image dissolved, she would surely go mad. She clung to him, her fingers not even daring to explore his back, his neck, for fear any movement might break the spell.

His voice, muffled in her hair, was rough. "I tried to tell

myself I was coming back here just to see the house was safe. . . ."

His hands cupped her face then, lifting it. Slowly she opened her eyes. He was there! He was real, not an illusion, a product of her yearning imagination. Surely he wanted her with the same intensity as she wanted him.

His eyes, usually so brilliantly blue, became suddenly as dark as midnight, his face as hard as a mask. Fearfully, Rebecca touched his cheek. He was at war with himself, trying to pull back from a dangerous precipice. If he won now, she might never see him again. Her mind screamed the thought. Gordon's eyes closed, and gently he began to push her away with shaking hands.

Desperately she sought for something to say, something to make him stay, to bridge the gulf of war, of duty, of defiance that was between them. Despair and longing made her ache, and she held his hand to her face. "Gordon," she whispered, knowing there was no other word.

Through his fingers she felt the shudder that racked him.

Oh God, why not, Gordon thought, his will dissolving in the whisper of his name. Her response just now had been unbelievable, and he hadn't held a woman in weeks. His body throbbed with the need for release. She was willing, ripe. And they were in the middle of a war. Who knew where he'd be tomorrow. Even as he ran the litany of rationalization, Gordon tightened his fingers on her face. The thought that this girl had just been caught in the act of enslaving his own brother he pushed to the far recesses of his mind. He knew he was lost to the moment, to his own body's urgency, and he ceased to care. Slowly his fingers unhooked her bodice.

Rebecca stood perfectly still, her own tumultuous emotions nearly paralyzing her. She didn't know why she'd won, knew only that her blood was pounding, that his fingers scorched her neck, that for the moment at least, he would stay.

As his lips caressed her shoulder she felt her skirt being unhooked. Almost she drew back, but his hand moved to her breast and his mouth was over hers again. His touch was feather light, making her shiver, yearn for more. A corner of her mind tried to tell her that she should be afraid of what was happening, that she would be ruined, but she couldn't stop the arch of her back, the curl of her fingers in his thick hair. She was in exquisite torture and not all the wisdom of the world could help her.

192

"You shouldn't be so beautiful," he murmured as somehow her bodice fell to the floor and her chemise was tugged down.

She wanted to say the same to him, but couldn't speak. Her breath seemed locked in her throat where her heart was jumping. Deftly now, he undid the last fastenings of skirts and petticoats. The man was too practiced, she thought in a daze, and was covered with embarrassment as clothing dropped to a heap around her feet. Automatically, she tried to cover herself.

"No, let me look at you." His voice was a soft command, and he backed a pace.

Shy and trembling, she stepped out of her encircling skirts and closed her eyes. There was a sharp intake of breath, then a rustle of movement and Gordon was holding her again. His chest hair tickled her breasts, his lips burned her eyelids, her mouth. Her head swam as he picked her up and crossed to the bed. He was beside her then, his hands searching for her most sensitive places, his lips teasing one nipple till she strained against him, moaning. When his body moved over hers and he entered her, even the sharp pain couldn't stop her ecstasy, for after that there was only a wave of sensuality that carried her to a crest of unbearable joy.

Not until they lay spent and satisfied did she dare to open her eyes. Gordon sprawled beside her, his arm cradling her head, his face relaxed, sleepy, his long body stretched contentedly on the rumpled quilt. Hesitantly she touched his face and saw his lips curl into a lazy smile. His eyes were closed, and Rebecca knew he was only half aware of her. Still filled with the wonder of what had happened, she wanted to bring him back, to make him think of nothing but her. She stretched against his hard body and snuggled further into the crook of his arm. His hand toyed with her hair absently, but he still didn't open his eyes or speak. Instinctively she knew she had no power over his thoughts now. His need had been satisfied and he had other matters to consider. Feeling suddenly chilled, she pulled the edges of the quilt over herself, and fell asleep wondering what was to become of her.

It was hunger, she realized, that woke her at last. Her body felt so torpid, though, she didn't want to move. Slowly she became aware of the bruised feeling between her legs, and memory stabbed through the haze in her brain. Hardly daring to breathe, she reached out beside her, but felt nothing. Throwing back the quilt, she stared at the empty bed and suddenly felt an unreasonable urge to cry. Her body told her it had been no dream, and now her mind registered the fact that Gordon was gone from her as swiftly as he had come. She would have to face and sort out her tumultuous feelings alone.

In an agony of embarrassment, joy, hurt and a throbbing ache of indecision, she got up and washed herself, barely aware of what she did. Dressing hastily, she sat down to brush her hair and stared at her face in the mirror. Her eyes were still heavy, but their depths began to smolder as she picked up the brush. He *used* me, she thought stormily, and dragged the bristles through her hair till it hurt. The next moment she propped her chin on her hand. But he had been so tender . . . he must have felt as she did. He couldn't have made love to her that way without caring. Then, where was he? She remembered the knowing skill of his hands and shivered. Hers was not the first body he had coaxed to the heights of delirium, and the agonizing thought came to her that it might not be the last.

Her need for reassurance overpowered all other thoughts. Jumping from the chair, she fled the room and ran down the stairs. If she could see him, watch his eyes for even a moment, she would know if what had happened had any meaning for him.

At the library door she slowed her pace. The round central table, the long oak desk, the leather chairs, the high shelves of books all gave back her gaze in the midday sunlight coming through the long French doors. There was no one here. She whirled and went to the drawing room to find the same emptiness. More slowly now, she canvassed the other rooms downstairs. The office looked newly cleaned. No papers, no saddle bags, no leather cases were strewn about to speak of recent occupancy. An unreasoning fear took hold of her, and she ran from the house, making for the stables.

A boy Uncle Julian had hired just last summer was cleaning tack beside the massive door as Rebecca skittered to a halt and peered into the gloom, trying to see if the horses were in their places. She could not see beyond the first stalls, but that was far enough. Colonel Meade's horse was not there.

"Andrew." She addressed the boy, who looked up with wide dull eyes. "I see the colonel has gone out. Did he say where, or for how long?"

The boy nodded, and held up a gleaming bridle for her to admire.

"That's a good job you're doing. Where did the colonel say he was going?"

Andrew lowered the bridle to his lap and thought for a moment. "Scouting," he said at last with a happy grin.

"He went alone?"

"No, miss. He and two officers went, oh, a half hour ago."

"Did he say when he'd return?" Rebecca felt her breath catching, and was glad Andrew was the only one in hearing.

"That he didn't . . . I don't think." The boy worried his memory. "No, he didn't," he stated with finality. Then his eyes lit up. "But there're three men back o' the barn, if you need a soldier, miss."

"Thank you, Andrew, but it's nothing important." Rebecca waved the problem away and walked slowly back to the house.

Mrs. Clark and Cook were seated at the heavy old table in the kitchen, enjoying their luncheon and a good coze when Rebecca entered. Summoning a smile, she waved them back to their seats when they tried to get up to serve her. "If I may just steal some bread and a ladle of that wonderful-smelling soup, I shall be grateful."

"Why, of course, Miss Blair. And let me cut you some ham." Mrs. Clark, whose eyes seemed suddenly shrewd, watched Rebecca saw at the fresh bread on the long cutting board.

"No, thank you. This will be fine." Rebecca ladled soup quickly, anxious to avoid the gaze of these two older women. Perhaps it was only her imagination, but she thought she'd seen them exchange a knowing glance. Unable to make up her own mind as to whether she felt shame or rapture, she wanted no one else making the decision for her.

Hastily she left them and went to sit in the small morning room and gaze out past the withered rose gardens and lawns where the army tents had been and the ground was now streaked with patches of trampled earth. Most of the company was in White Plains, she supposed, and the few guards who remained must be billeted in the barns. Feeling her hunger once more, she ate, trying to keep her mind only on the food.

She was still sitting there when Mrs. Clark came to find her to say she'd seen the dining room set for dinner, and hoped Cook's good roast wouldn't be spoiled by the men coming in late this night.

Rebecca turned a flushed face to the housekeeper and spoke in a voice that was husky. "They left no instructions?"

"Only the hope they'd be back for dinner, miss. But they had food with them in case. I was just wanting to let you know."

The woman backed from the room, her eyes averted, and Rebecca sighed. Was she being censured by Uncle Julian's faithful servant? She couldn't tell.

With care, she dressed in the yellow taffeta gown for dinner. She'd made her mind a blank, suspended all emotions, speculations. Only the glow she could feel suffusing her skin kept reminding her of what had happened this day, and as she descended the stairs once more, her heart began to thud painfully.

The dining room was still empty, four places set at the well-polished table. Rebecca wandered out of the room and went to wait in the library. From there she should hear any booted steps in the hall. So as not to appear eager, she searched among the shelves and took down Dr. Johnson's novel, *Rasselas*. Better to put her mind to a more useful occupation than anticipation of the first sight of the tall, lean man who had reduced her to putty in his hands, molded her to his desires and so casually left her to harden alone.

For half an hour she sat, every third word on the printed page registering on her brain. The shadows in the room had long since turned black beyond the narrow pools of candlelight around her, and she felt as though her heart had lodged forever in her stomach. When Mrs. Clark walked quietly into the room to say she'd better eat the dinner that had been prepared, Rebecca nearly dropped the book, she was so startled by the voice.

"Very well," she said without enthusiasm, and felt her spine straighten as she watched the woman's stiff form retreat from the doorway. Other people's disapproval had always served only to set her back up, and although her behavior with Gordon Meade today was certainly more worthy of censure than anything she'd ever done, Mrs. Clark's sudden coolness angered her.

She tasted nothing of the food set before her, but ate doggedly, determined to act natural, to seem as though it was nothing to her if the officers never returned to this house.

When she'd finished at last, she forced herself to go and compliment Cook on the meal and to discuss food for the morrow. That worthy tyrant of the kitchen received Rebecca's words with fair grace, but watched her so narrowly that the girl thought she would scream before she could escape.

Restless and brooding, she needed to move about. So snatching up a shawl from her room, she went down to the front porch and paced in the crisp air. Sudden visions of ambush, of fighting among the hills nearby, of Gordon lying in a bed of cold leaves in the dark, made her mouth grow dry. She shivered and entered the hall again.

In the bright candlelight, she blinked, thinking she was hallucinating. Coming down the hall were Gordon and Alex, deep in conversation. He looked so tired, she thought, and caught a ragged breath.

Gordon looked up at that instant and stopped in midstride. For a fraction of a heartbeat she met his eyes before his heavy lids half obscured them, and her pulse raced. He'd forgotten nothing. And he had returned.

Then his voice said casually, "Good evening."

Her throat, still dry with fear for him, wouldn't allow her to speak. Silently she nodded, and became aware that Alex had glanced at his brother and was now staring at her. An expression of pleasure at seeing her faded slowly, was replaced by a whitening around his mouth and an uncharacteristic narrowing of his gray eyes. As though undergoing a metamorphosis, his face hardened and hollows appeared beside the wide cheekbones.

Gordon, standing so near the lieutenant, had seen none of this, she thought. "You were out for a stroll?" he asked.

Rebecca's voice returned to her. "Yes. There is enough dinner left over for you. It can be warmed." She found her gaze traveling between the two uneasily.

"We had some food, but could use more, don't you think, Lieutenant?" Without looking at Alex, now wooden beside him, Gordon turned back down the hall. "I will ask Mrs. Clark to have something brought to the library, and will get the maps from the office. Join me in five minutes, Lieutenant."

It was as well he did not wait for a response because his brother gave no sign of having heard him. He'd never stopped watching Rebecca, and slowly the hard lines on his face were dissolving into a look more like hurt bewilderment.

He has guessed, she thought resignedly. He had only to

look at me and he knew Gordon and I were no longer enemies.

For the second time this day, she had to face this sudden knowledge on someone else's face, and Alex's look of pain did what no amount of disapproving stares from Mrs. Clark and Cook could do. She felt exposed and in the wrong. She had deliberately ignored the signs of Alex's infatuation, assuming they would dissipate in time. She had never meant to treat him as anything but a friend, but somehow her casual intimacy with him had led him to believe there could be more. She must now make him understand she cherished his friendship, but that a friend was all he'd ever be.

Hoping her convulsive swallow wasn't obvious, she took a step forward. The rustle of her taffeta sounded loud in the tense silence. "You had a long ride this afternoon?"

Alex's eyes bored into hers and in a swift movement he was before her, gripping her shoulders. "How could you, Rebecca?" His whisper seethed with youthful emotion.

Almost blandly she met his look. "What? Eat without you? It was growing so late, you see. . . ."

"You know that's not what I mean," he hissed, his fingers tightening.

"You're hurting me." Rebecca pulled away and the boy dropped his hands slowly.

"I'm sorry, Rebecca. I wouldn't hurt you. But I know something has happened. Did he . . . ?"

"Alex." The girl put a hand on his rigid arm. "You know . . ."

At the back of the hall a door shut with a bang, and loud footfalls came toward them. Rebecca drew back.

"Mrs. Clark's bringing food in a moment, Alex. Shall we go to the library? Miss Blair will excuse us, I'm sure." Gordon's voice was devoid of inflection as he moved to the door of the room. His dismissal of her was complete, Rebecca thought, and watched deflated, as Alex went stiffly to his brother. With a small bow to her, Gordon closed the door.

Rebecca nearly stamped her foot. Always she was shut out of talks between men, and at this moment, she wanted nothing more than to sit quietly and watch Gordon, to savor the knowledge that he was safe for one more day. Then she thought of Alex's black mood. Now was not the time to be near the lieutenant. She must be content with the fact that they were both back, and after all, their dinner couldn't last all night.

Up in her room she hugged herself. Gordon would come to her again. She'd read that certainty in his eyes as he'd walked in. And then the hours of loneliness, of worry, would drop away, and she would feel the strong protection of his arms, the excitement of his touch. Practically dancing, she undressed and put on the midnight blue robe.

The fire was going, the candles lit and the bed remade. All was in order, she thought as she looked around the big room, suddenly made warmer, more beautiful by her memories of Gordon here with her. On tiptoe she went to the door and set it slightly ajar. She wanted the thrill of hearing his boots approaching. Then carefully she arranged herself in the chintz-covered chair near the fire and took up her nearly forgotten book. As the minutes dragged by, however, she was forced to admit to stiffening limbs, and abandoned her careful pose. Tucking her feet under herself, she curled up and read each word of *A Midsummer's Night Dream* with concentrated precision.

Almost, she became engrossed in the play, but a corner of her mind must have been straining for the sound of his feet, for before he reached the door, her heart had leaped to her throat and the book had become a leaden weight in suddenly hot and trembling fingers.

Chapter 19

He came just as she'd pictured him, his linen shirt open, his pale hair clubbed at his neck, his hard body poised on the threshold, one dark hand on the door. He'd washed, she saw, for a bead of water still glistened on his forehead below a stray wave of gold that curled on his brow. Suddenly shy, she smiled tremulously as he closed the door and moved into the room. But her smile melted as she saw his expression.

Darkened eyes held hers until he reached the center of the floor where the soft lights picked out stern lines around his mouth and tight cords in his powerful neck. His arms were crossed on his chest now, the sleeves of his shirt rolled to the elbow exposing knotted forearms that looked tense. His eyes scanned the room, then lingered on her form, traveling slowly from her hair to her folded legs. She blushed, unhappy under his scrutiny.

"Very artful," he said with the same lack of inflection as he'd had downstairs. "Perhaps I should be flattered by such a welcome. Though the pretty picture is somewhat marred by the bare toes at the hem of your gown."

Blushing more furiously, Rebecca looked down at the offending foot and automatically covered it. She realized, too, that the deep V of her robe's neck had fallen open, nearly exposing one creamy breast to his view. Quickly she pulled the top of the material together at her throat. She was suddenly, unaccountably, mortified.

"You needn't cover up for *me*, sweetheart." His voice was almost sneering now. "After all, *I've* tasted your charms."

"Oh!" Rebecca's free hand flew to her mouth.

"But what if I had not been the one to push open your conveniently cracked door just now?" His voice went on inexorably. "I envision Alex confronting this view in a different manner, don't you?"

Her hand fell away in surprise. *"Alex?"*

"Or have you already tantalized him with voluptuous visions such as this?"

Nearly choking with anger, Rebecca raised her head higher. Her eyes blazed. "How dare you insinuate that I would . . . would cast lures . . ." Her voice cracked, horror flooding her.

"Self-righteous wrath is most becoming, Rebecca. May I, by the way, take the same liberty of calling you by your given name that you gave to Alex? I feel sure you can't object, *now.*"

The girl gazed at him as though at a coiled snake, and saw a mocking smile come and go on the handsome face.

"But that was not the subject under discussion, was it? I believe you were asking how I dare to question your behavior toward my brother. So I need, perhaps, to remind you that the two times I came across you this day, you were on, shall we say, obvious terms of intimacy. It would seem that you made good use of my time away from this house, despite the fact that I had warned you to keep away from Alex."

The urge to cower in her chair evaporated in a blinding flash of fury, and Rebecca jumped to her feet, still clutching both the book and her robe. "You are despicable," she cried. "Just because you are a man of base instincts, you attribute the same to all others."

"My dear Rebecca, where you are concerned all men have base instincts, especially when encouraged."

Her cheeks flaming, the girl glared at him. "At least you admit that Alex is no longer a boy. Yet in all other things you appear to treat him as one."

For the first time Gordon moved. He looked, she thought wildly, as though he were going to throttle her. "He is my younger brother." It was obvious that he kept his voice low with great effort. "I just lost a dozen good men in battle. I saw boys younger than Alex writhing on the ground, their guts spilling over their hands on Chatterton Hill. Is *that* the definition of being a man?" His voice rose despite the effort. "Well, I won't let him be that much of a man yet. I need him now, though. The army needs him. And I'll not have him fuzzy-headed from mooning over you."

Sickened by his words, Rebecca still could not control her own hurt and anger. "So you will set Alex an example. *You,* of course, never lose your head over anything."

"With you, I lose my temper, not my head. I warned you to leave Alex be, and now I'll have to remove him from your influence, take him with me back to North Castle, just where I did *not* want him to be."

Gasping at his rough words, Rebecca was close to tears. "I did nothing, I tell you. We are friends."

"Friends? And yet that dress tonight allowed us both the most provocative view of a few of your charms, sweetheart. Is that how you expect to remain friends with Alex?"

Rebecca's eyes dilated until they hurt. How could he say such vicious things? Never, now, would she admit that she'd worn the dress only for him. "You would prefer that I go to dinner in sacking to the neck? It was one of my many evening dresses," she cried.

"I look forward to viewing the rest of your wardrobe, then." The sneer was back. "But if you need to cast your net so far and wide, I must insist you throw it toward older fish."

Nearly blind with fury, Rebecca hurled the book at him. It took him in the stomach, and he bent under the force of the blow, but in the same movement he grabbed her, nearly pulling the robe from her shoulders.

She twisted in his grasp as tears of rage and bewilderment finally spilled over the brims of her huge eyes. Lean fingers snatched at her chin, forcing her head around. She scratched at them, but felt her face lift in spite of her will.

"You really are a hellcat," he growled as she kicked his booted leg.

"Don't touch me," she stormed, and slapped at his arm, trying at the same time to pull her robe together.

"How could I resist?" Viselike hands gripped her arms, holding her rigidly still. "The invitation was so obvious." His eyes roved down her scantily clad body.

"Not for you!" Rebecca spat between clenched teeth. Fervently she wished she had his sword here. How could she ever have let this beast touch her, make love to her, reduce her to mindless jelly? She hated him, and she'd kill him now if she could.

Her face must have registered her thoughts, for he let her go abruptly and, reaching behind her, removed the fire poker from beside the chair. It spun across the rug to the far wall, and Gordon grinned wolfishly. "Nonetheless, the invitation was tendered," he said, mocking her now with her helplessness.

Backing a pace, he sat on the edge of the bed and removed his boots. Rebecca watched him, transfixed by indignation. But when he pulled his shirt over his head, she came to life again. "If you think I would let you come *near* me now," she began, her voice harsh with fear and horror.

Gordon cast down his shirt and looked around in feigned surprise. "Have I mistaken the situation after all? Is there someone else hiding in the wings? Or was it really Alex you were so deliciously awaiting?"

Her hands to her ears, Rebecca flew across the room. She had to get out, get away from this cruel and frightening man. She was nearly to the door when his arm caught her and flung her back. She twisted from his grip and found herself pushed against the wall.

"I could kill you," she hissed.

"So I gathered once before." He stood, pinning her shoulders against the plaster, surveying her dishevelment. "And if you weren't so enticing, I would consider returning the sentiment. As it is . . ."

Rebecca struggled, but couldn't free her arms. The hook below her bodice had snapped as he'd thrown her back, and she could feel the robe gaping open nearly to her waist. Bending her head, she tried to hide her breasts with her glossy hair, and at the same time, tried to move closer to him.

Surprised, he let her come, his grip less tight on her arms. They were nearly touching when she caught her breath and brought her knee up toward his groin. Almost she managed to hurt him, but just in time he doubled over and one forearm smashed into her raised thigh. She groaned with pain and renewed fear, and butted at his chest. "Let me go," she cried.

"And be murdered for my kind deed?" Gordon's voice was hard, unrelenting. As were his hands when he jerked at the front of her robe.

She heard threads pop loose and snatched at the material falling away from her sides. But he slapped her hands down and jerked again till the waist gave way and the entire garment slipped to the floor. She twirled and felt herself captured and held against him. She kicked backward at him and beat at the arm encircling her waist. Then he was lifting her like a fighting child, carrying her across the room. He tossed her onto the bed and she bounced up, hissing and spitting like a cat. For a poised moment she saw his broad chest above her, saw the curl of his lip and the light in his eyes. Then he was on her. With one hand he pinioned her wrists above her head, while with the other he unfastened his pants and kicked them free. She writhed beside him, anger at him and at the quick waves of heat spreading over her body making her dizzy.

His lips teased her neck, her breasts, her belly. Then his free hand stroked her outflung legs. She tried to kick him again, but her attempt was feeble. His hand had moved up between her legs and his fingers were setting her on fire. Moaning, she burrowed into the soft quilt to escape him, but he followed, his body now covering hers. He let go her hands, and cradling her chin, he kissed her as he entered her. Of their own volition, her lips responded, her hips moved to meet him. Half hating herself, she gave up the struggle and abandoned herself to her overpowering need of him.

Spent once more, Gordon lay on the bed, watching the shadows flicker on the ceiling overhead. He felt the soft body beside him quiver once, and slowly he turned his head. She was lying very still, almost rigid, and her face was averted, but by lifting his head he could see one tear moisten long lashes and roll silently down her cheek. Torn by a desire to hold her and a memory of fury at her, he lay clenching his hands behind his head and trying to master his thoughts.

A sense of guilt and an overwhelming anger hounded him. All day he had not rid himself of the feeling that he should never have taken the girl. He'd known she was probably a virgin, but heedless of consequences he'd let his better instincts be overruled.

He'd once before made this mistake, and had paid for it in bitter months of worry. Pamela had acted like this girl; half innocent, half wanton. He'd given into his own urges, only to discover she'd used her body to trap him. Agonizing over the fact she'd been a virgin, he'd finally done the gentlemanly thing. He'd asked her to marry him, and had suffered under the look of triumph in her eyes. But it was that very act of nobility that had brought her father to the decision to leave for England. No matter that the Meades were an established family of considerable wealth. Mr. Jenkins had greater ambitions for his only daughter. What a fearful time that had been, wondering if he'd made the girl pregnant, wondering what the outcome of the father and daughter struggle would be. He'd hated to admit even to himself his relief on learning she was going to London and their ties were broken.

Never again would he do anything so foolish, he'd vowed. Yet here he was, a scant two years after his bitter lesson, lying beside another beautiful girl who had been innocent. The anger welled, and he allowed it to flood his mind. He was angry at his own stupidity, yes. But he was angry at Rebecca and all other women too. He was even angry at Alex for falling for the wench. All his efforts to protect Rebecca in this house, to protect Alex, had been for nothing. He'd tried to make it abundantly clear that Rebecca Blair was the property of the commanding officer, and it had been his own brother who had defied him. Now the boy was set on a defiant course, just when they could least afford to be at loggerheads!

With a jerk, Gordon got up. Wrathfully he began snuffing out candles around the room. It was true she was a hellcat. She'd set brothers against each other, had driven yet another wedge between him and Warren Tyson, had complicated his life and had even made it hard for him to think only of his duties. To top it off, she was a Tory, wishing to be free of the rebel army, worrying over returning to her Charles Revington. From Mrs. Clark he'd unwillingly heard more of the handsome Charles who was now in the British army, and had gathered that Rebecca was on the brink of marrying the man.

On this last thought he pinched the flame on the dressing table and returned to the bed. These were useless reflections, he realized, as he watched the shivering form huddled on the far side. The thing was done, not once but twice. She'd have a hard time explaining herself to her Charles now, and it was all his fault. But he couldn't undo it, and he couldn't stay to play the game out. He was off at first light. The thought made him annoyingly sad. Carefully he pulled back the covers, wishing for the first time he hadn't lost his temper with her. He'd had enough control to know he hadn't hurt her when he made love to her, but it had been no way to say good-bye. He lifted her into the center of the bed. She looked up fearfully when he moved her, and the planes of his face hardened even more at what he thought was reproach in her eyes. Yet he crawled in beside her, snuffed the candle, and curved his long body around hers. She stopped shivering in a few moments, and soon he could hear even breathing as she slept. Once she moaned softly, and he stroked her hair till she snuggled like a child against him and fell back asleep. Against his will, he lay awake a long time, savoring the feel of her velvet smoothness, wondering where he would be lying now if there had been no war.

For four days Rebecca saw no sign of either Alex or the colonel. She had, after their night of furious passions, awakened once again to an empty bed and a confusion of emotions. Despair had been dominant. She hadn't known what to make of Gordon's action last night, why he had been so angry. But she was too well accustomed to male admiration not to know there'd been at least a hint of jealousy in all his scathing words. The roughness with which he'd subdued her had been in such contrast to his tenderness thereafter, she didn't know what she was to make of him or of her own churning thoughts. She couldn't deny that for all her anger that night, she'd melted at his touch, had wanted him again. And desire was still there after four bleak days of no word from him. But he was a soldier driven by the needs of his army, impelled to put all but his duty aside. She'd clung to that thought at first, and only slowly had admitted that he seemed, too, a man untouched by softer feelings. He might be compelled by the impulse between them to make love to her, but she had no reason to believe she had really reached his heart.

As for herself, she must try to pick up the pieces. She had fallen into an age-old trap, had given herself to a man who dominated her senses, but whom she had no reason to love.

As her days returned to the same dreary routine, watched over by a strange lieutenant with the face of a belligerent bulldog, she forced her mind away from the colonel and concentrated on the running of the house, always with the thought that now His Majesty's troops had claimed victory at White Plains, her own freedom might be at hand. And when it was, perhaps Charles would come for her. The consideration of how she would face him now she pushed to the back of her mind. If he still cared . . . If together they could find Uncle Julian . . . Somehow she would put back together the scattered shards of her life.

Only at night did she suffer her thoughts to turn to the tall man with whom she'd first experienced her body's passion. And then, for brief times she couldn't control, she missed him, worried about him, wanted him back.

It must be, she thought, waking for the second time this night, that her body's torment was causing her mind to play games. For Gordon was suddenly standing over her, his hand shielding her from the glare of a lantern, his features satanic in the shadowed light. Throwing her arm over her eyes, she willed the teasing image to disappear. Then his hand touched her shoulder and she dropped her arm, her heart leaping.

"It is nearing morning," he said, his voice hoarse with fatigue. "You must dress quickly."

Sudden fear pulled her to her knees. "What's happening?"

"Nothing. Yet." He put the lantern on the table and began pulling things from the wardrobe. Her warmest dress, a deep brown wool, hit the bed and her cloak followed. She noticed he was wearing the long, heavy, fringed linen shirt often favored by field officers when in action.

"Then what . . . ?" Her voice trailed away at his quick savage look.

"I'm taking you out of here. The redcoats left White Plains last night. I've been dogging them these past hours. They are heading for Dobbs Ferry and the Yonkers road, and some may cross the Hudson here. But I can't be sure yet. They may spread all over these shores. You can't stay here alone to welcome them." As he talked he tugged a valise from the shelf of the wardrobe. "Pack any essentials in here."

Round-eyed, Rebecca watched him, barely taking in his words. "You came back," she said in a whisper.

He paused, but didn't turn around. "I'm clearing this house. Orders from headquarters." He set the valise on the foot of the bed, then fingered the brown dress. "Hurry, girl. I'll help you dress. Then I must get the others."

Her heart jumped as she climbed from the bed and his narrowed eyes watched her pull on her petticoats. Exhilarated by the nearness of him, she almost laughed when she felt his big fingers fumbling with the buttons down the back of the dress. "I will *not* hire you as a lady's maid," she stated in a choked voice, lifting her hair for him to see better.

"Your maid! Where is she? You'll need her." He finished the last button and spun her around.

"In the village."

"Damn." He let her go and scooped up her cloak. "I can't take you there. Here, put this on, do whatever mysterious things you ladies do to make yourselves feel presentable, pack that bag and be downstairs in ten minutes."

He was gone as he finished speaking, and Rebecca stared at the open valise in bewilderment.

Knocking on doors as he went, Gordon headed for the back stairs and the kitchen. The first faint rays of a cold morning sun were spreading on the tile floor as he rummaged for food. The fire was banked on the hearth and he hesitated, wondering if there was time to cook something. Knowing women, he thought there was. Rebecca would be up there making agonizing decisions about what to bring with her, and he'd have to drag her out in the end. Quickly, he uncovered the coals, tossed on kindling and swung the kettle over the fire. He'd get hot coffee at least.

"Here now, what's amiss?" Mrs. Clark entered the big room, her gray hair standing up around her head, her apron untied and flapping in her wake.

"I'm sorry to wake you so suddenly, Mrs. Clark, but we must leave Halscomb."

"Well then, you'd best be going about your business, and let us go about ours. You'll have food before you go." Cook appeared at the housekeeper's elbow and nodded agreement, eyeing the hearth with disfavor.

"There will be little time for one of your breakfasts, I'm afraid. You are leaving too."

"Leave Halscomb? Whatever for?" Mrs. Clark looked comical in her sleepy indignation, but Gordon couldn't appreciate the humor at the moment.

"The redcoats are marching this way, and they may come here. I cannot leave you."

The two women considered his words, and Gordon felt his impatience mount. Then Mrs. Clark's mouth set in a firm line. " 'T isn't likely the two of us will go gallivantin' about the countryside. We were here when you came, and we'll be here when you go. We have a charge to take care of the old place till Mr. Halscomb returns, so you can set your mind at ease and know you won't be slowed by us." She cocked her head and her expression became almost sly. "Miss Rebecca now, is another matter, mayhap."

"Miss Rebecca *must* leave. You can see that." Gordon considered arguing with the two ample forms before him and decided to save his breath. Instead he thought quickly. "There is a pony trap in the stables, I will leave a horse hitched to it. If you change your minds, or if there is any real trouble, you can leave in that." He knew they had friends throughout these hills as well as in the village. He thought it was unlikely they would come to harm in any event—unless the redcoats burned the house. But with all of his troops out of here, there'd be little reason for that. It was well known hereabouts that Halscomb was a loyalist household held forcibly by the rebels. No, this redoubtable team would survive. If only he could leave Rebecca with them. He'd racked his brain for an idea, for any haven to take her to. But it looked as though North Castle was it.

Mrs. Clark was clucking, shooing him away from the cupboard. "We'll wrap you some food. Mind yourself now."

Gratefully, Gordon left them and went to check that the horses were rubbed down and resaddled, that the men had cleared the barns. Alex was there, supervising grimly as the men scurried. Without explanation, Gordon gave the orders to hitch Julian's saddle horse to the pony trap, saw Rebecca's horse led out from her stall, and with a brisk nod, left them to it.

Back in the house, he stuffed final papers in a saddlebag and propped it by the office door. Then he went to be sure nothing had been forgotten in the front rooms. As he emerged from the drawing room, the front door banged open. A man in ragged homespun stumbled into the hall, his musket trailing a streak of mud on the polished floor. His hair was matted and a thick growth of new beard sprouted from his haggard face.

Wild eyes spied the colonel and the man waved frantically behind him. "Redcoats," he shouted. "Took the pickets five minutes ago. Coming up the drive."

Gordon waved him through the house to the stables, and as he did he saw Rebecca on the stairs, the battered valise clutched in one white hand. Her large eyes followed the man, then sought Gordon's. "Redcoats," she echoed faintly.

"That's what our friend said." Gordon ran to the library, threw a look around, and darted back to the stairs. "Rebecca . . ." He stopped. She was standing on the bottom step, in the place he'd first seen her two weeks ago. Her face was drained of all color and her hand gripped the banister in a convulsive gesture.

"Charles," she said in a whisper, and turned disbelieving eyes up to his.

Chapter 20

Through the open door Gordon saw a horse pulling up at the steps. The rider's high black boots, white breeches and scarlet coat with its shiny brass buttons, bright facing and stiff collar left little doubt as to his military identity. Rebecca's Charles was now a British captain.

"Saved at last," he said mockingly, and reaching out, tugged her toward the library door. "No sense in being a target in your moment of joy. Stand here where you'll not be in the way. Pity I have to rush off, but you're safe now."

Rebecca snatched at the door frame to keep from falling, and watched him throw her a casual kiss as he turned on his heel. He had nearly rounded the newel post when Charles Revington, his sword drawn, burst into the hall, calling for surrender.

Charles saw the other man's eyes flick to Rebecca and he checked. "Thank God," he breathed, and spun back to his adversary.

But his brief glance had been all Gordon needed. Sword in hand, the colonel faced him. "Sorry, old chap, but I'm afraid I can't oblige."

"My men are surrounding the house, Colonel. I'm afraid you have no choice." Triumph and anger were in the heated voice.

"Perhaps we can come to an understanding, Captain." Gordon's look was cool, his stance easy, almost careless. "You are here for the girl. I am happy to deliver her to you, safe, as you see." He smiled wickedly and backed a pace, ignoring Rebecca's gasp.

"Not good enough, Colonel. We'll clear this entire rebel nest, and you'll pay for making Rebecca a prisoner." Charles lunged forward, sword on the ready.

Moving like a large cat, Gordon sidestepped and swung around the newel post. Nimbly he jumped to the first stair and his sword described a low arc as the other slashed after his spinning form. There was a clash of steel echoed by a small cry from the girl in the doorway. Neither man gave any sign of hearing. Gordon retreated two steps up, forcing Charles to follow. When the captain was on the second stair, hard against the wall, Gordon made a classic feint, the heavy sword seeming as light as a fencing foil in his hand. Charles countered, but his guard was high. For an instant the two hung suspended, Charles's heart exposed to certain death. Rebecca's knuckles whitened on the door frame. Then Gordon's sword hand touched the banister, and in a flash he hurtled through space and was gone.

With an oath, Charles shoved off the wall and pounded down the hall in pursuit. Desperately, Rebecca followed, calling his name, but the man heard nothing except his own shout of rage. Out the rear door of the hall they ran, but Gordon's long legs had given him the advantage. He was already in the saddle when the captain charged past the corner of the house. Rebels were scattering in every direction, some on horseback, some on foot. From the wall of the herb garden shots rang out and a soldier by the barn flung up his arms and fell from his stamping horse, a mask of blood spreading over his face.

Rebecca screamed, but her voice was lost in the shouts and confusion. She saw a brown shirt appear by a tree in the orchard, and the whistle of a musket ball reached her as she watched a scarlet-coated figure tumble out from beside the garden wall. Gordon was calling to his men, riding back and forth between the barn and the orchard boundary.

Dear God, he'll be killed, Rebecca thought as she clung to the trellis on the house corner and fought down a sudden nausea of fear. At that instant she saw Charles by the barn snatching at the horse of the dead rebel. The beast snorted and stamped away, but Charles held him grimly till he could catch the stirrup and mount. Gordon saw him at that moment, and wheeling his horse, rode for the fringe of wood back of the barn. Men were pouring from the orchard now, running for the herb garden and the side lawn beyond. The redcoat firing had stopped. Perhaps they were all dead. Rebecca could spare no thought for them though, as she watched Charles ride like a madman behind Gordon. From the corner of her eye she saw a brown figure drop to his knee nearby and raise his long rifle.

"No-o-o . . ." Rebecca shrieked, but her call was drowned in the explosion of the gun. The redcoat behind Gordon swayed in the saddle and toppled slowly to one side. With no thought to her own safety, Rebecca ran forward.

Gordon had swerved at the sound of the rifle, and looked back to see Charles falling. His horse reared as he pulled him around and caught at the head of the captain's maddened mount. Charles's leg was caught in the stirrup, his body trailing beside pounding hooves. Clinging to the other horse's bridle, Gordon flung himself off his mount and threw his weight to one side. The horse skidded to a halt, his head nearly pulled from his shoulders.

Alex appeared beside his brother and bent swiftly to free Charles's foot from the stirrup. Gordon wasn't even watching as he held the horse steady and scanned the landscape around the orchard.

Rebecca was beyond the corner of the barn when her own pounding heart halted her. More men were running up and she saw Warren Tyson dismount beside the colonel. Gordon was bending over Charles now, and Rebecca jammed one fist in her mouth to keep from calling out.

"He'll live," she heard Gordon say, "but we can't care for him." He looked up at the circle of men. "Major, you arrived in the nick of time. Your men have cleared the garden and orchard. We'll finish here. You and two others take this officer down to the Dobbs Ferry Road and leave him for the redcoats to find. We'll meet at McHenry's farm a mile down that lane." Gordon's arm indicated the track behind the orchard.

Tyson's dark eyes narrowed, but he sketched a quick salute. Jabbing at the chests of two burly soldiers beside him, he snapped out orders and turned to get his horse.

Rebecca sank back against the barn wall. She didn't know if it was relief at hearing Charles was alive or horror at the order to abandon a wounded man beside a road that made her legs weak. Through blurred eyes she watched the men pick the captain up and start down through the woods.

Gordon gave more orders in a low voice, and the other men melted away. Now he and Alex stood alone, holding their mounts, looking at the house.

"Where is Rebecca?" Alex asked suddenly.

"In there. Too bad her Charles was wounded. She might now be on his hands instead of ours."

"Rebecca *knew* that man?"

"Was going to marry him, from what I can gather." Gordon's eyes still moved restlessly, surveying the trees and fields.

"And yet you . . . ." Alex choked. "And now, after you've had your way, you're willing to abandon her to a redcoat's care?"

"What the hell would you like me to do? Carry her off into the clouds?" Gordon's eyes blazed at his brother's livid face. "Or perhaps leave her in *your* care?"

"It'd be a bloody sight better than any care *you* give her," Alex fairly shouted.

Gordon's face suddenly showed his exhaustion. "Shut up, Lieutenant. We have work to do, and then we'll worry about the girl."

Rebecca drew her first breath in a full minute. The words had acted like a freezing waterfall on her shrieking nerves. She remembered all too vividly Gordon's mocking voice, offering her to Charles's keeping. As long as she'd been able to convince herself Gordon cared for her at least a bit, she'd been able to scorn her own moral conscience. Nothing had mattered when she was with him. But the abrupt realization that she meant nothing to him, was only a nuisance to be dispensed with, made her feel humiliated and defiled. Sagging against the rough barn boards, she heard the deep voice instructing Alex to round up the men in the fields and to see if there were any prisoners. The colonel was going to the front of the house and would cover the rose gardens, see that all was well inside. They had to move out. Captain Revington might not have acted on his own hook.

Rebecca's head snapped up at that. She realized that all the ghastly events at Halscomb had happened in less than a quarter of an hour. At any second more fighting might erupt around the house.

It was at that moment that Gordon noticed her. "My God.

What the hell are you doing?" he fairly bellowed. "Trying to get killed?" Before she could bring her choked voice to answer, he was coming toward her. "Get back in that house, you fool."

Rebecca pulled back from his reaching hand. "You have work to do," she managed. "I'm going, never fear."

His blue eyes searched hers for an instant, then he nodded. "Now."

She bobbed her head and stepped away from the wall. At that he was gone.

When he and Alex had passed beyond the barn, Rebecca paused. The morning seemed unnaturally still. No birds called in the trees or meadow; they'd flown at the first gunshot. Just as she now wished she had. Better, perhaps, that she had never heard Gordon's words to Alex, had cherished her ridiculous hopes. Though the rude awakening would have had to come sometime, surely. Gordon had given her warning of it in the front hall when he sighted Charles.

Charles! She jerked upright. Wounded, maybe bleeding to death, the man was being taken to lie by the verge of the road, possibly until he died alone and untended. All other thoughts left her mind as the horrifying image filled it. Picking up her skirts, she ran to the barn.

Two horses blinked at her in the silent gloom. Her mare, fully saddled, munched hay contentedly in an open stall, and Uncle Julian's gelding shifted restlessly in the harness of the pony trap. She didn't stop to question why the big horse was hitched to the contraption, just blessed her luck and swiftly led him to the door. If she needed to carry Charles to help, this was far easier to manage than getting him into a saddle. The only trouble was she'd have to follow the lanes, and who knew how many companies of soldiers would be marching on back roads? She'd have to take that chance, she decided, and biting her lip, climbed into the cart.

The track was deserted, and away from the orchard, birds could be heard once more. Her heart jumping at every sound, Rebecca urged the horse forward, but the animal was unused to a harness, and he balked constantly. Frustration finally brought the tears that humiliation and pain had not summoned, and Rebecca flung herself off the perch and ran to take the gelding's head.

It was hard to stay on the narrow lanes, yet try to follow the direction Major Tyson had taken through the woods, but doggedly the girl pulled the horse onward, always moving down the long slopes toward the Dobbs Ferry Road.

When the overgrown bypath wound past a cluster of beech trees and spilled out onto the highway, Rebecca halted and backed up. Dense undergrowth around the bend they'd passed offered the concealment she needed, and quickly she tied the gelding to a sturdy log. Then shivering despite her heavy cloak, she crept forward once more till she could see the ribbon of road clearly. There was no movement, no thud of tramping feet, no rumble of carriage wheels, though the dirt of the road was heavily churned. Cautiously she stepped out from the trees and looked up and down the short stretch of road. Nowhere did she see a splash of scarlet against the dun browns and soft grays of autumn. Back among the trees again, she moved a hundred yards along the roadside, convinced that it was this hollow in the hills that Major Tyson had headed for. Still she saw no sign of the wounded captain. But now her straining senses picked up the unmistakable beat of movement on the highway. The distant clop of hooves, rattle of muskets, thunder of wheels grew louder even as she tensed. The sounds were coming from the east. They could mean nothing but soldiers on the march.

A violent fear overtook her and she ran, stumbling and clawing through the woods back to the cart. The thought of meeting a company of soldiers in this deserted place made her fingers clumsy as she tugged at the tied reins. The horse threw up his head as she freed him, and tried to back away from her terror. He twisted between the slim shafts of the cart and attempted to kick free of the contraption. The girl wondered how she would get him to move again, and wildly considered leaving him, but knew she'd be even more helpless on foot. Desperately she went to work on the buckles of the light harness.

Agonizing moments passed as she fumbled the big horse free of the cart. She could hear voices now, and the tramp of many feet. Trying to keep her voice soft, soothing, she talked to the horse, quieting him as she climbed on the big log and gathered up the long reins. Then hitching up her trailing skirts she flung herself across his back.

The lead soldier in the long redcoat column stopped in surprise as just ahead, a powerful bay horse bolted from among the trees and galloped down the road, a low figure wrapped in a flying cloak clinging to his back. For an instant the two stood out against the upward curve of the dusty highway, then swerving abruptly, disappeared through the woods on the other side.

When they emerged in a grassy sward far from the road, Rebecca used the last of her strength to slow the large animal. She had not thought, as she'd thrown herself onto his back, of anything but returning the way she'd come. She wanted only to avoid the soldiers. But she'd had no control those first frantic moments, and the horse had taken his head straight for the road. Once on it she could do nothing but try to hang on and to turn him through the first opening she saw in the bordering trees. Now, as they walked slowly across the crisp grass, she realized her way back to Halscomb was blocked by the column of marching men. Not for hours, perhaps, could she return there, and she didn't want to return alone. There was no knowing who would be at the house now.

She checked her horse to take her bearings, trying to remember where they'd been on the road. She was sure if they turned west once more, they'd find the village almost directly below them. And Sylvie was in that village. There was even the chance that Charles was there, that Major Tyson had disobeyed the callous order to dump him by the roadside like a discarded shoe, had taken him instead to certain help. She would find out.

Resolutely she urged the horse forward again, and tried to push away worry about what was happening at Halscomb. Gordon Meade had made it clear she was the last person he wanted around him now, and had acted with barbaric ruthlessness toward an officer of the king. He deserved any fate he met this day. Tears streamed down her cheeks unchecked as the big bay picked his way down a deer run toward safety.

Gordon made a wide sweep around the house, but found no sign of more of the redcoat captain's troops. When he came inside, Alex met him in the hall and reported that five prisoners were even now marching under guard back toward North Castle. That left just four of them to meet Major Tyson at the McHenry farm. Gordon nodded, slinging the saddlebag he'd left by the office door over one shoulder.

"There's just one thing," he said slowly. Alex looked at him sharply. "We will stay close and we will go carefully." A grin tugged at one corner of the colonel's mouth. "I sent Tyson on the errand with Captain Revington because it occurred to me it would afford him an ideal chance to join the British."

"To *what?*" Alex's mouth fell open.

"You've never had the least suspicion? Well, I have. And I'm not alone—now. The man has too many sutler friends, too many urgent calls of nature at inopportune times, too many excuses to be where he needn't. I can prove nothing, but if I'm right, he just might take this golden opportunity. However, at the same time, he may inform some zealous redcoat officer of our meeting place at the farm."

Alex looked dazed. "Then why don't we bypass the farm and head straight back to headquarters?"

"Because Tyson is a major in the Continental Army, and if I'm wrong about him, I'd leave him in a pretty spot. Also, he has two good men with him who may or may not be loyal to us."

"Good God. And there's Rebecca."

"Yes. There's the girl. Another reason for us to go very carefully. If we can get to North Castle intact we can leave her with an officer's wife, I'm sure. But first we have to reach the army."

His brother's face was full of resolve. "We're off. Where's Rebecca?"

Gordon shrugged. "I sent her back here. Found her out by the barn. But she may not have come in. You look upstairs. I'll check the kitchen."

A few minutes later the brothers met again in the hall. Neither had seen any sign of the mistress of the house. "She's outside still," Gordon stated. "Call the men out front around to the barn. I'll meet you there."

But nowhere was there a trace of Rebecca. Precious minutes were lost searching the gardens before Gordon thought to see if her horse was in its stall. It took another minute for him to remember the pony trap and Julian Halscomb's big bay gelding. Alex, entering the barn at that instant, heard the colonel begin to swear with a profanity the boy had seldom encountered. Then the man was past him, leading Rebecca's filly, growling to all of them to mount and ride. "She's gone," he snarled, "and could be any damned place in these hills."

One of the soldiers studied the ground. "Cart wheels going off that way," he said softly.

Gordon stared at the tracks, barely visible in the dusty

barnyard. He sat still for a long moment, then with a wave of his hand he gestured the men forward, following the faint ruts. They lost them almost immediately, but across the meadow the same soldier's sharp eyes saw signs that led them into the trees. Only a good woodsman would have made it possible to discover the abandoned cart twenty minutes later. They could hear the sounds of an army passing nearby, and Gordon sent a man forward to the road to have a look while he stood beside the forlorn pony trap, trying to hold back the horrible images that the sight conveyed. Alex, watching the pain on his brother's face, knew with the suddenness of a religious revelation that Gordon cared about the missing girl, and that Alex's own feelings about her were vastly less important than his feelings for his brother. He didn't like the knowledge, but he faced it squarely, standing still and thoughtful beside his colonel.

The soldier who'd been sent ahead was back almost instantly. "Whole bleedin' army out there," he whispered, gesturing past a tall clump of bushes. "An' the horse's prints show he went right out onto the road." The soldier's eyes shifted away from the colonel as he said this last, so he missed the jump of the man's jaw muscle and the steely look that came into the brilliant blue eyes.

Alex gasped, but said nothing as he saw his brother's face. Softly the four men backed their horses and stole off up the track again. When they were well away from the road, Alex pulled his horse up beside Gordon's. "What do we do now?"

"Do? We go to McHenry's farm."

"But Rebecca may be on that road. . . ." Alex began.

"With her friends. Maybe even now nursing the gallant captain." Gordon spurred forward, and Alex, frowning with thought, had no choice but to follow.

Justin McHenry's farm was a small holding in a hollow between low hills where a thin stream meandered westward to the Hudson. The crude house and outbuildings were scorched hulks on this hazy November morning. Mr. McHenry had been unwary enough to declare himself hotly in favor of the king, and had been burned out of his homestead in the summer by local "patriots" who were seeking vengeance for the burning of two patriotic farms nearby. McHenry counted himself lucky that he had left with his family and meager possessions in time, and he had since set himself up in the village as a jack of all trades. His farm lay fallow now, a place fit only for the mice and foraging animals.

Circling the slope of hillside directly before the farm, Gordon stationed his three men beyond the road, well concealed in the undergrowth, and carefully he approached the half-burned barn. The clink of a bit made him draw rein, his rifle at the ready. But as no further sound came to him, he dismounted and followed the line of the crumbling fence to the angle of the barn wall.

Silently he stepped around the corner, and confronted Major Tyson and his two men standing nervously by the major's horse.

"Colonel Meade." Tyson's voice was nearly a purr. "No doubt held up by the fair Miss Blair."

"You saw the captain to the Dobbs Ferry Road?" Gordon's tone was low. Relief at finding Tyson here, at the thought that the man might not be a traitor after all, was tempered by the reflection that now he and the army would have to continue enduring the unpleasant major's company.

"Of course. Though there was no one yet to receive him."

"Good. Your men will have to ride double. We have only one extra mount." He doubted Rebecca's filly could carry the men far, but perhaps far enough to get them all out of the neighborhood. Politely he stepped aside for all of them to precede him. He still preferred not to have Tyson at his back.

He collected his horse, and up the road Alex and the other two joined them. The two burly soldiers on foot looked skeptical, but obediently they mounted the prancing filly Alex led. Major Tyson showed surprise at not seeing Miss Blair, and was answered with a curt, "She chose to make her own way." He looked annoyed at that, but Gordon ignored him. Slowly, the little procession made its way out of the clearing.

Twenty paces into the woods, shots rang out. A horse reared as a soldier screamed and fell. Gordon jerked his mount into the trees, firing across the road as he went. A flash of red showed beside a stone wall and he yelled a warning to Alex, riding behind him. The patch of red disappeared. Clamping his knees tight, Gordon held the reins in his teeth and frantically reloaded the long rifle. There was a shout, the high-pitched shriek of a horse, more firing. Smoke hung in the air, and a horse hurtled past him. Tyson was waving his gun and yelling something, but at that instant a deep voice commanded them to stand. Gordon fired at a man on the road, saw Alex being pulled from his saddle by two redcoats, and spurred back out of the trees. He was nearly on the men, his horse's hooves slashing viciously, when something slammed into his chest. For an instant he was suspended upright in the saddle as more firing filled the air. Then he was falling, his horse somersaulting beside him. His shoulder hit the ground, the horse rolled onto his legs, and his already glazing vision picked out Alex's agonized face. Then his eyes closed.

NEW YORK,

1777

Chapter 21

The scent of lilacs hung heavy in the early evening air as the last golden rays of sun picked out dazzling white flower clusters at the tops of the tall bushes beside the brick house. Rebecca cast a lingering look around the enclosed garden, sorry that she could not stay to enjoy the sunset, for long streaks of heavy clouds crisscrossed the still blue sky, promising a pink and gray light. Her eye roved over the flower beds along the back fence and fell on the bench half hidden behind the tiny rose arbor.

"Sylvie!" Rebecca leaned through the doorway into the narrow passage. "You left your sewing again."

Her maid, who had nearly reached the stairs, turned back, the color suddenly leaving her face. "Oh, it's nothing important, miss. I'll go and get it soon."

Rebecca noted the startled, almost guilty look. "For someone who has recently discovered the avocation of seamstress, you are very careless of your work, you know," she said sharply. "It may well rain soon. Please go and get the material. I'm sure Mrs. Adams's sewing case is out there too."

An almost mulish look crossed Sylvie's face. "Very well, miss. But do let me set your bath first. You haven't much time to dress now."

Looking thoughtfully at her, Rebecca walked down the hall. Sylvie's eyes fell just as her mistress said, "All right.

But be sure you don't forget. And do not be so careless in future."

As she settled herself in the warm bath, Rebecca sighed. The strain of living in this house, of worrying almost constantly, was telling on all of them. She must learn not to be so snappish. Anyway, a part of the strain was lifting now that Uncle Julian was better.

She sank further into the soothing water, memory of the past seven months flooding over her, and for once she did not push it away.

As clearly as though it had happened *this* morning, she could see the hazy autumn sunlight glinting on the windows of the Adams house as she rode tearfully into the yard that fateful day last November; could see Sylvie running out the back door of the cottage to catch her as she tumbled from the big horse. They had all been so kind to her, but those had been frightening times: hiding in the root cellar with Sylvie when Seth spotted redcoats coming to the door; worrying over Halscomb and the people left there when news came that a detachment of the king's troops had claimed the house; hearing that the Kents' place had been burned and the Revingtons, fearing the same from rebel marauders, had abandoned the old stone house and fled to New Jersey. She'd realized then that she had nowhere to go, that the only option left to her was to find Uncle Julian. She couldn't stay on at the Adamses' small house. They had no room and little enough food as it was, especially with Rob still staying there.

After lengthy conferences, it was decided Rebecca would go to New York, and Sylvie would go with her. Rebecca, knowing Sylvie's heart now belonged to Seth, had protested this last decision, but to her surprise, they'd all been adamant that Sylvie accompany her.

It was a nightmare journey, first down to Kingsbridge on foot, and from there in an overladen wagon carrying vegetables to the Royalist troops on the island. Rebecca had posed as the surly driver's wife through the ordeal while Sylvie sat uncomfortably on the rear of the wagon. The roads were in confusion, redcoats marching toward Manhattan, rebels disappearing as fast as they could, people barring their doors along the way. But they'd come through unscathed, and the driver must have been well paid, for he took them, after many inquiries, to the very door of Thomas Kent's house in Queen Street.

Relief at finding Uncle Julian safely ensconced with Mr. Kent in his city residence had so overwhelmed Rebecca that she had hardly noticed at first that her uncle looked a great deal older. But soon it was brought home to her that Julian Halscomb was very frail. Great coughs racked his once large frame, and rarely did he leave his bed. Her conviction that if she could find Uncle Julian, all would somehow come out well in the end, had wavered for the first time since leaving Dobbs Ferry. But Rebecca was made of sterner stuff than even she knew, and instead of giving way to despair, she'd thrown herself into a new role of nurse to her uncle and mistress of this house.

Thomas Kent had welcomed her with open arms. Word about the burning of his country house had already reached him, and he knew his family was safe with his brother in Yonkers. He was resigned to his loss and determined to rebuild at the first opportunity. On that first night in this elegant house, he'd explained that he and Julian had found their warehouse intact, and had quickly reestablished contact with merchants and suppliers around the city. The British were delighted to discover another loyalist importer, and already a ship was on its way to the West Indies for cargo. Profits were to be had in this city. Unlike the rebels, the redcoats had money to spend. But Julian, once he discovered his return route to Halscomb had been cut off, had fallen into despondency, had contracted an inflamation of the lungs, and had barely been able to move this past week or more. It would mean everything to him, to both of them, Mr. Kent declared, to have Rebecca here. The war would not last forever, and meanwhile there was money to be made in New York. When Julian recuperated, all of them would do what they could to recover their former lives.

But Uncle Julian did not recover. For anguished months Rebecca, with Sylvie's help, nursed him and ran the house, living always with the thought that if something happened to him now, they'd be truly adrift. And always Rebecca blessed Sylvie for her sacrifice in coming to New York with her.

The long winter had been made endurable by distractions, of course. The shortage of housing had forced British officers into quarters in what private homes remained after the fire. Those that had been shut up were reopened for the army's exclusive use. Where owners were in residence, extra rooms were requested. Two officers had shared the spare room here, and their presence had afforded the only amusements of the cold months.

At first Rebecca had tried to discover what had become of Charles Revington, but when Captain Trumbull had pointed out that since she knew nothing of which regiment the loyalist had joined, and therefore inquiries would be exceedingly difficult, she'd been forced to give it up.

Forever at the back of her mind was the question of what had become of Gordon Meade. But she had no way of ever discovering. That chapter of her life was as closed to her now as the former chapter in England had been. She was firmly entrenched behind British lines, and it was unlikely she would ever hear Colonel Meade's name again. She'd tried to tell herself that was precisely what she wished, but knew with a hollow feeling, that a dull ache would remain with her for a long time to come. She could only try to ignore it and attempt to rebuild her life yet again.

The water in the bath had grown nearly cold when Sylvie entered the room once more. "You have little time to dress, miss," she said, startling Rebecca from her reverie.

As the girl moved about the room, laying out clothing, Rebecca watched her. Sylvie had become something of a mystery these past seven months, and Rebecca supposed it was because her maid's mind was so often back in the village of Dobbs Ferry with Seth. She'd obviously been in touch with him too, for when the news had come last December that the redcoats had burned Halscomb, it was Sylvie a few days later, who had been able to assure them that Mrs. Clark and Cook and the others were safe, though she wouldn't say how she knew. The awful news about his beloved home was what had kept Uncle Julian from recovering, Rebecca was sure, and to lift his spirits, she'd had to pretend that the fire hadn't been so bad, that Halscomb could be restored. She'd known though, that there was nothing left of the gracious house that had welcomed her to America so warmly, that had captured her imagination and led her to work and scheme as she never had before, that she had hoped to make into a self-sufficient, even profitable estate, and the knowledge had nearly crushed her.

"Mrs. Allen says there will be twelve for dinner tonight." Sylvie shook the folds of a green velvet dress. "The officers are having a number of friends in, some of them from a battalion newly come from New Jersey. General Howe is rumored to be leaving the city soon, and Captain Trumbull says he doesn't know how much longer they'll be here to entertain."

Rebecca took the large towel handed her and stood up. "Did Uncle Julian send word whether he'll join us?"

"He says he does not feel up to it."

Rebecca nodded and stepped out onto the floor. "I suspect the evening will be a long one, and it would be too much for him." She felt a headache coming on, thanks to the dredging up of old memories, and wondered how she was to get through the long hours herself. Captains Trumbull and Pierce, who had been billeted here all winter, were pleasant men, always solicitous, but their company held little excitement for her. She wondered what their new friends would be like.

Captain William Trumbull, middle-aged, stocky and given to talking in abreviated sentences, was standing in the hall waiting for her when Rebecca descended the stairs resignedly an hour later. "How lovely our hostess looks tonight," he said with heavy gallantry as he came forward to offer his arm.

The girl dipped a curtsy. "You're kind to say so, Captain, when you know this is the same dress I have worn nearly all winter. It has been gratifying to see the ships coming into harbor this spring, to know new goods will soon be available to all of us." It had been gratifying too, she reflected, to receive from dear Mr. Bancroft just two weeks ago, the money needed to pay for the new finery she needed. Uncle Julian's resources had been severely depleted by the war, and a great deal had been lost at Halscomb. Realizing she couldn't live on Thomas Kent's largesse forever, Rebecca had sent a plea to her father's man of affairs during the winter, and had been pleased to learn that his management of the remnants of Mr. Blair's estate had allowed extra money to come to America. Now that ships from the West Indies were putting in to New York, Uncle Julian's fortunes were changing, but she could not have been sure of such luck during the cold months of wondering if her uncle would live to see this spring.

Delicately, she laid her hand on the captain's arm, and allowed him to lead her to the drawing room. The Chippendale settee covered in gold brocade, the graceful Hepplewhite chairs with their serpentine top rails and inlays of satinwood, the bureau bookcase on one wall near silk-hung windows and the handsome handwoven needlepoint carpet in shades of gold and green and ivory, all glowed softly in the shimmering light of the wall sconces. Thomas Kent was making the British officers most welcome this night. The windows were closed against the night. Winter had clung tenaciously this year, and although it was May, a small fire fought the cool air in the room.

Four officers stood as Rebecca entered on the captain's arm. She'd met them all before, and she greeted each with a smile.

"Larger party this evening," her escort whispered as she completed her rounds. "Several more coming, and I think you will find there is a most pleasant surprise."

Obediently, Rebecca looked inquiring, though in fact she was only half attending him.

"Yes, a pleasant surprise," the man repeated with a smug look as at that very instant voices could be heard outside in the hall.

Rebecca stood by the settee as a tall man with narrow shoulders and a permanent stoop entered the room. The others moved forward to greet him, slapping him on the back, congratulating him on some feat Rebecca couldn't make out. She wasn't looking at him now, anyway, for crossing the threshold, tassled sash crimson against the snow of waistcoat and breeches, scarlet coat fitting perfectly his trim body, was Charles Revington.

He hadn't seen her and Rebecca, glad now of the captain's sturdy arm under hers, stood watching him, trying to compose herself. His face looked older, she decided. Fine lines creased his cheek and brow, and there was a set expression that had not been there before. War aged all men, she thought, but thank God it didn't necessarily kill them. She felt a large weight lifting from her heart at the sight of this man she'd worried about for seven interminable months.

And then he saw her. For an instant he stood stock-still, his fine brown eyes registering shock and joy, and Rebecca realized Captain Trumbull had kept his "surprise" for all parties concerned. Thomas Kent had spotted Charles too, and shaking his head in wonder at the sight of his old neighbor, he began wringing the younger man's hand as though it were a pump handle.

Without taking his eyes off Rebecca, Charles smiled and returned the pressure of Mr. Kent's hand. Then gently he extricated himself and crossed the room. "Trumbull, you're a cad," he chided softly. "He never let me know, Rebecca, that the fairest flower in Westchester was safe under this roof."

The girl extended both hands to him, her eyes filling with tears of gratitude for his safety. "He never told me either," she said, "and I fear he's very proud of himself."

Captain Trumbull coughed behind his hand and grinned boyishly. "Did warn you there was a surprise, you know. Ah, there's Rosefield." He moved away, exhibiting a surprising delicacy.

For a long moment she and Charles looked at each other. Questions tumbled about in her head, but she could find expression for none of them.

"I thought never to see you again," Charles said at last. "I feared that rebel colonel had spirited you off to whatever corner of hell he came from."

Rebecca started at his harsh words, but she kept hold of his hands. "And I was afraid you had died somewhere along the Dobbs Ferry Road."

"Perverse of me, wasn't it, not to let the rebels kill me yet." He smiled for the first time, and for the first time, Rebecca could see the Charles she had known last fall.

"Wonderfully perverse," she answered with a twinkle. "But how did you manage it?"

"The wound was shallow, and the army found me only a short time after I was dumped by the roadside. So I fear I can take little credit. I was whisked off to New Jersey to recuperate, and have been there, one place or another since. I was transferred here just last week. But tell me how *you* came to be in New York."

The girl hesitated. She'd only just gone over all this ground in her head. To put it in words so soon after seemed a double burden. So she started with how she'd run from Halscomb to search for him, and gave the briefest of summaries for the rest of the tale, saying only that friends had been kind and gotten her to the city.

"And your uncle? I don't see him tonight." Dropping her hands at last, Charles looked swiftly around the room.

"He's not been well this winter, but is now recuperating. I think he's not up to parties yet, though I know he would welcome a brief visit from you."

"I shall return tomorrow and pay my respects. Besides, now that I know you are here, nothing could keep me away." He looked at her searchingly. "You can't know how glad I am

231

to see you here, Rebecca, to know that you left Halscomb that morning. And I am most flattered that you went in search of me. It was a dangerous thing to do." He paused, and a note of bitterness crept into his voice. "I sincerely regret not being able to carry you off to safety as I had planned."

Rebecca squeezed his arm impulsively. "You walked into something very like a trap. There was nothing you could do. But I have always wanted you to know I appreciated the concern for me that prompted you to come to my aid."

"I nearly went mad those two weeks you were in rebel hands, knowing there was nothing I could do to get you out of there until I had command of enough men. But I underestimated that colonel in the end. I should not have demanded his surrender; I should have run him through."

"And yet he did not try to kill you," Rebecca nearly whispered, and knew instantly that she'd said the wrong thing.

"You think I thank him for my life?" Charles's face flushed nearly as crimson as his coat. "I nearly had him and he slipped away. He'd taken over Halscomb and held you prisoner. The great Colonel Meade ended up going free at the last moment to rampage around Westchester at will. I wanted that man!" Charles's fist slammed into an open palm. "And instead I let him get away. But if ever the opportunity arises again . . ." His voice trailed off as his eyes glazed with remembered fury. Then he shook his head. "I can only be thankful that you too got away before the devil burned the house around you."

Rebecca, whose stomach had given an uncomfortable lurch at the mention of Gordon's name, found she couldn't let this remark pass. "It was His Majesty's troops who burned Halscomb," she said gently. "No doubt because the Continentals had been there."

Charles's eyes refocused abruptly. "I find that hard to believe."

"Nonetheless . . ." The girl spread her hands. "But let's not talk of that. Have you seen your family in New Jersey? I heard they had reached there safely."

"Yes, I saw them only last month, having finally learned what became of them. They survive in a crowded farmhouse with my sister's family, afraid to go home now that Westchester is a near wasteland with both sides struggling for every head of cattle, every inch of ground. Another victory for the rebels, this driving off of my parents from their home of two generations."

"I'm glad they are well, at least," the girl said quickly. "Now tell me about your adventures since you got your wish and joined the army."

"Too much time was lost in bed for me to have had many adventures," he answered.

"Then you will tell me about that." Deftly, Rebecca steered Charles down the room, hoping to make the conversation more general. His sudden vehemence had clouded her joy at seeing him alive and well. But perhaps he would return to his easier ways once the surprise of finding her in New York had worn off, and with it the unwelcome memories of their last sight of each other.

Chapter 22

Charles Revington was at the house in Queen Street as often as his duties allowed, and slowly Rebecca grew used to the older, more bitter version of the young man who had courted her the year before. The bitterness, though, softened as Charles seemed to settle into the comparatively luxurious life of the city. Winter quarters in the small towns of western New Jersey had not afforded either comfort or entertainment. And although he wished, he said, to be in the forefront of the summer's campaign, he could hardly be anything but grateful for the respite his transfer to New York offered.

"I cannot help chafing a bit at being left behind when General Howe removed from the city," he declared one morning in late June when he discovered Rebecca walking in Mr. Kent's garden and came to stroll beside her, "but I expect General Clinton has his own plans afoot, and we will not be kept inactive forever."

Rebecca laughed. "You do not expect me to clap my hands at that prospect, surely. I am most contented with your present orders, Charles, and cannot pretend otherwise." She stopped and brushed an imaginary fleck of dust from his immaculate lapel.

Charles smiled at her, and his face softened more than usual. "I must admit that the distractions offered in the city are nearly enough to take a man's mind off his duty," he said, catching at her hand.

Rebecca tried to feel a thrill at his gesture, and almost succeeded. "Then what have you planned for today?"

Her companion feigned surprise. "I had thought my services were bespoken. You said you needed to shop, and I have presented myself this morning to act as your escort to whichever emporia you must visit."

Rebecca did clap her hands at that. "Charles, how famous. I didn't really expect you to act so much the gallant. But I shall hold you to it, I promise."

"And well you may. But you will also promise to bring your maid and a man to escort her, for they will have to return with your purchases when you are done. I am taking you on to a reception at Jones's this afternoon."

Rebecca dipped low before him. "As you say, kind sir."

Fifty minutes later the little procession left the brick house and turned right on the cobblestone street. Only a few blocks away, toward the bay, there was a wasteland of charred rubble, the remnants of buildings burned in the fire of last September. The British had made no attempt to rebuild the ruined blocks, and now miserable souls lived in makeshift shelters among the ruins, cooking over open fires, scratching out the poorest existence. Rebecca knew of the ghastly conditions in such areas of the city, as did everyone, but today she turned her face resolutely toward the handsome streets where the life of fashionable, military and mercantile New York still moved at a busy pace.

She'd had her own privations this past year, with the loss of her American home and her removal to the city, and had spent a long winter with scant numbers of ill-fitting clothes. Many a time she had thought longingly of the dresses and materials lost at Halscomb, and today she was going to set about replacing some of what she missed. For now, her cares and the somber months of worry were behind her, and she intended to make the most of her freedom. Another time she would acknowledge the plight of those less fortunate than she.

Relishing her prospects, she'd dressed carefully for the occasion. Her black hair framed her oval face in ringlets beneath a chip straw hat covered in delicate artificial flowers. Her dress of lilac panniers over an embroidered underskirt, the tight bodice a darker hue trimmed with ruching to match the skirt, was most becoming, she knew. Unfortunately, it was one of a kind in her wardrobe. Today she would remedy the situation.

And remedy it she did, with an extravagance she'd rarely shown before. Charles was the soul of patience as she fingered and looked, discussed and worried and finally decided on materials, laces, shoes and hats.

"Oh, Charles, my appetite for lovely things knows no end today," Rebecca declared joyfully as she ran her hands over bolts of striped taffeta, glossy satinet, delicate muslin.

"You'd think you had worn nothing but homespun all your life." He laughed, following her.

"Very little better!" She pouted. "I came to the city in a drab wool with nothing else to my name, and there was little opportunity all winter to do more than have two hasty gowns made up. If I ever see the dark green velvet again I shall scream. For months it was all I had to wear to dinner."

Charles frowned. "You should never be without clothes that become you," he stated and reached for a bolt of crimson silk. "This for instance."

Rebecca frowned at the color and finally decided it would not be right. "I have already exceeded the limit I set for myself, anyway, and must make choices of a more delicate nature now."

Smiling, Charles retired to a chair at the front of the store to wait for her to conclude her spree. It wasn't long before she reappeared to give him a dazzling smile as reward for his tolerance. Then happily she piled Sylvie and the footman high with boxes and bundles, and sent them on their way with a distinct sense of well-being.

It was the first such expedition she'd had since her season in London, and she enjoyed herself thoroughly. Nothing could cloud this day of celebration. The promenade through the throngs on Wall Street and around the garden at the ruined Trinity Church, and the reception at Judge Jones's house all added to her sense of euphoria, especially since she knew she would return to Queen Street to find Uncle Julian at table for dinner. Her world was righting itself at last, and memories of brilliant blue eyes and strong arms around her had to be locked away and somehow forgotten.

She'd determined nothing would shadow her enjoyment of life now, and very little did. Charles was her attentive escort to innumerable functions through the warm summer, and she could have asked little more of him than that he put aside his consuming desire for revenge on the rebels. It was a fire that burned in him, sometimes making him moody or sullen if he heard of a rebel success in the field, sometimes erupting in heated discussions with brother officers. Rebecca tried to ignore these spells, reflecting that it would take time, but that with the winning of the war—as surely His Majesty's forces would do by the end of the season—he would feel vindicated and would put aside this passion. For her own part, she tried to think of politics and war news as little as possible in a determined effort to enjoy herself. She knew she was blooming under the flattery of attentive young men, was looking her best and acting as carefree and happy as she had in long-ago London. So why didn't she *feel* as happy as she seemed? She supposed that that too would simply take time, time to recapture her old mode of existence. Accordingly, she threw herself ever more heartily into the role.

It was on a warm evening in very early September that a crack at last appeared in the exuberant facade Rebecca had steadfastly maintained.

She was attending an assembly ball just doors down from Mr. Kent's handsome house, and was anticipating a lively evening, for news had spread of General Burgoyne's continued advance southward from Canada, and the army could feel victory within its grasp. General Howe, having chased Washington for two futile weeks in June, had returned to Staten Island, and from there had sailed in July, presumably to take Philadelphia at last. The spirits of the troops remaining in New York were high on expectations, and their revelry reflected their mood. Rebecca could not help but be caught up in it.

The ball was a glittering, crowded affair, bright with the throng of scarlet tunics and ladies' finery, and General Sir Henry Clinton, now commander in New York, was the honored guest. Rebecca whirled through every dance, laughing and flattering her admirers, but she wished she could recapture the once heady sensation that came with making myriad men her slaves. It seemed to her she had lost more than her virginity in Westchester. She'd lost much of her innocence as well. Perhaps that was for the best, though, since Charles was exhibiting signs of jealousy when she talked too long with another man. Now, for instance, he had captured her for two dances in a row.

"You know," she said softly, as Charles brought her to the edge of the floor at last, and she looked down at her new polonaise gown of blue silk embroidered with twining flowers, "this dress is a near duplicate of the one I had made for your party in October. I thought it would be nice to wear it for you at last." She twirled to show him the gown, and was surprised to see the scowl that crossed his face before he murmured appropriate words of admiration. Oh dear, she thought, I've said the wrong thing again, made him think of that time and the rebels.

But Charles seemed to recover quickly, for his eyes lingered on her face with a warmth that made her almost uncomfortable. Taking her hand, he led her out of the spacious drawing room to a secluded spot at the rear of the hall. The fresh air was welcome, and Rebecca tried to say so, but Charles cut off her remark abruptly.

"Rebecca." He clasped his hands behind his back and paced the narrow hall. Then whirling, he returned to her and caught at both her hands, squeezing her fingers painfully. "You must know, must have known this past year, that I have . . . have held you in the highest esteem."

Her eyes dropped under the heat of his gaze, and she wondered, in an agony of mixed emotions, what was coming next.

"This damnable war has made it impossible for us to go on as we might have back at home. It has even made it impossible for me to tell you now of the strength of my feelings." He dropped her hand, turning to stare out the darkened window beside him. "I don't know how much longer I shall be in New York. Burgoyne's advance toward Albany has so far been successful. At any time Sir Henry may march north to meet him, and I will go with him." He looked back. "When we do go north, we will close the Hudson to the rebels. We will seal New England off from the other colonies, and we will have the end of this conflict in sight. When that happens, Rebecca, I will be in a better position to speak. If all goes well, I will return, and I will ask you to be mine."

With difficulty, Rebecca focused her eyes on his face. For a moment his features had changed, had wavered before her, altering to a tanned face with hard lines beneath golden hair. Angrily, she blinked and Charles's familiar face came back.

She tried desperately to summon elation at his words while she smiled at him. "We all wish for nothing but an end to this war," she managed. "And you know I want little but your continuing safety."

"Then you will be here when I return?"

"Where else would I go?" Her voice was bantering, hiding her turmoil. How could she tell him she'd already belonged to another? She could not, and hastily she put aside the thought that she was playing him false. She was not the first girl to find herself in this uncomfortable predicament, and like so many women before her, she could try to pick up the pieces with another man. She would school herself to think only of trying to make Charles happy. Looking at him now, she knew she already had.

"Rebecca," he said huskily, and leaned forward eagerly to plant a kiss on her forehead.

She turned her face up and saw the look of surprise in his eyes before his arms went around her and his lips met hers. Obviously, he had meant to give her a chaste kiss, but as she swayed toward him, his control seemed to loosen, and he devoured her mouth with a hunger that could only come from long waiting for this moment.

At first Rebecca was nearly as eager as he. Her body, she suddenly realized, had been starved too long. But as his arms tightened and his lips became more demanding, uneasiness took hold of her. She could not hate his kiss, but she could not answer it. Disgusted with herself, she tried to break away, but Charles held her ardently. His kisses rained on her eyes, her cheeks, her hair until he said brokenly, "You are the most beautiful, desirable creature I've ever seen. The thought of waiting for you, of knowing that half the men in New York would do nearly anything to snatch you away from me, makes me desperate."

"Please," Rebecca whispered, and pushed gently at him. There were voices on the stairs. Someone was coming up to the hall, and would put a stop to his fervor.

Charles let go of her so fast she nearly staggered. His face was flushed as he tried to straighten his leather stock. "I'm so sorry, Rebecca. I should never ... You will forgive me, I hope."

"Of course I forgive you, you goose." Rebecca's voice was half amused, half exasperated. She realized he'd taken her lack of response for maiden shyness, and she felt her own cheeks flame. Perversely, she could think of nothing but the fact that Gordon Meade would not have made any apology. He would have snatched her away to an even more secluded spot, or he would have laughed and whisked her, still trembling, back to the ball.

Charles noted her heightened color and tried to apologize once more, but Rebecca shushed him, nodding toward the stairs. Turning, she walked down the hall in time to see three more officers before the drawing room door. She didn't look at them, tried to bypass the group until she heard Charles say, "Well met, Major. I'd hoped you would come this evening."

At the pressure on her arm, she turned and looked up to see Warren Tyson's surprised eyes fasten on her.

It required just one incredulous second for her to take in the silver and gilt officer's gorget half covered by the lace under his black military stock, the bright scarlet of his new uniform, before her eyes, open and inquiring a moment ago, narrowed and darkened with disbelief.

The major recovered first, and bowing low he subjected her to a mocking smile. "We seem fated, Miss Blair, to meet at each new stage in our lives."

A delicate brow lifted at him, and there was no answering smile. Rebecca's mind was whirling even as she felt her old repulsion return. "This is certainly a new stage for you," she answered and ran her eye slowly, deliberately over his uniform.

A sly look came and went on the aquiline face. "It seemed prudent, not long after we all left Halscomb, for me to openly declare my allegiance. Surely the thought pleases you."

"The thought of a turncoat, sir? Hardly."

Black eyes snapped in anger, and she felt Charles's hand close convulsively on her arm, but Rebecca was beyond caring. Warren Tyson had been a major in the Continental Army. He'd been in Gordon Meade's command just last fall. And now here he stood, preening himself in a staff officer's uniform of Sir Henry Clinton's regiment. And from what he'd just said, he'd been a loyalist all along. But how had he come here? Who had he betrayed in his peculiar service to his king? Her skin grew cold with a sudden dread.

Charles and the other officers were trying to cover the embarrassing confrontation with light social talk, but Rebecca heard none of it. "Over which bodies did you take this step, Major?" she hissed.

Tyson leaned close, his mouth sneering and his eyes raking her insultingly. "Only that of my esteemed colonel, your old friend, Miss Blair. And you?"

If he had bayonetted her in the stomach, the blow could not have been more powerful, but with a superhuman effort, Rebecca kept from crying out. Charles's hand held her upright as she struggled to hold her face immobile. She knew Charles had heard, knew Tyson was watching her in his catlike way, knew she must not betray anything here.

She might almost have won her battle if Charles hadn't at that instant exclaimed, "Are you saying that Colonel Meade was done, for, Major?"

Tyson smiled wickedly. "When last seen, he lay in his own blood, his horse atop him. Regretfully, we found we were pursued and had to bid him a most hasty farewell."

Charles's grin was the last straw. With a strangled sound, Rebecca pulled free of his hand. She coughed once to clear her throat, then took a deep breath and held it. The effect was as she'd been taught by her mother long ago. A semblance of composure settled over her for the time it took to say, "If you'll excuse me for a moment, Charles, I shall return." Shakily she mounted the stairs behind them, and hoped she looked as though she was going to repair a ruffle.

Knowing she could not face any inquisitive glances, she did not go to the repairing room, but blindly opened the first door she came to. The bedroom was dark but for a faint trail of silver light from the window. With great deliberation, she closed the door, crossed to the window and leaned her forehead on the cool panels of glass. The pain was spreading through her chest, up to her head, and the images of trees, houses and the night sky wavered and dissolved into countless collages of Gordon smiling down at her, reaching for her, bending to kiss her. With a horrible clarity she remembered that last day at Halscomb, the abrupt awakening, the hasty packing, the wild thudding of her heart at just seeing him again. She could recall his every look, his every word, and her own heartbreak at realizing he cared so much less than she. The final scene of that fateful morning was replayed in her mind's eye. She recalled the spin of events, and even the rough feel of the barn boards at her back. She could hear Gordon saying, "Too bad her Charles was wounded," Alex asking, "Rebecca *knew* that man?" and Gordon answering with carefully controlled carelessness, "Was going to marry him from what I gather."

The images blurred as she choked on a sob. How headstrong, how foolish she had been. Gordon had thought she wanted to be with Charles still, had offered her to him because of her supposed betrothal. How could he have been so blind to his affect on her as to think that? And how could she have been so stupid as to let her self-pity consume her? If she had obeyed him that day and returned to the house, had gone with him . . . But would that have saved his life in the end? He was a soldier. She could have no control over his actions, his duty. He would have died whether she'd clung to him or not.

Dry-eyed now, she listened to the sigh of night wind against the window. The military band downstairs was playing a lively air. Voices floated up through the floor, the door. She would have to go back soon. Charles would be wondering where she was. And he mustn't see that anything was wrong. It he suspected she'd been upset by the news of Colonel Meade, he might suspect more. And right now she couldn't face that. He had just made what amounted to a declaration to her, and she had just determined to have him when he asked. Now, more than ever, she must hold to her decision. She would shut away the memories of Gordon in the most secret places of her heart, would teach herself to love Charles. Resolute but unsteady, she opened the door to the hall.

"Rebecca. I was beginning to worry." Charles pressed forward to greet her at the threshold to the drawing room.

Her eyes were dazzled by the sudden light, but she could tell he noticed nothing wrong. He was smiling, almost jubilant, and from somewhere had procured a glass of brandy. He brandished it aloft. "Permit me to drink a toast to our newest liberation."

She blinked as he drew her into the room. "The evil colonel is dead. Your tormentor, my nemesis is gone, and we may rejoice. Though I must be sorry it was not my own hand that dispatched him. Come, have a swallow."

Rebecca shook her head, not trusting her voice.

"Ah well, I shall swallow for both of us." He took a long drink, obviously not his first. "And here's another to Major Tyson, who has done me a service this night." He swallowed again and leaned toward her conspiratorily. "He has solved the mystery, and I am most grateful, you know."

Rebecca stepped back. "Mystery?"

"Hmmm . . . yes. Seems I had the wrong man."

"What do you mean?" she whispered, anguish and revulsion at his words making her dizzy.

"Provost Marshal Cunningham told not long ago of a rebel officer named Meade who has been a prisoner here in New York since late last year. Seems the man refused to give his parole, stating he would attempt escape whenever an opportunity arose." Rebecca's heart had stopped for two full beats as Charles talked, and she knew her hand had gone cold in his. But still he seemed to notice nothing, caught up in his own exultance. "Meade did try to escape once last winter, and nearly killed a sergeant in the process. Made the provost so mad, he had the insolent rebel tossed into jail to share the fate of private soldiers. Just yesterday I learned the rascal was in North Church, and was trying to decide whether to go and see him for myself. But now Tyson assures me this Meade is not the devil colonel at all, but his younger brother captured at the same time the colonel was struck down. I need think no more about it, and I cannot be sorry."

Apparently she was numbed to any fresh shocks, for she could return Charles's look calmly. "I take it I am to congratulate you on all the news," she said.

"Assuredly. It is an old score settled, and now I can think only of winning the war—and you, my dear Rebecca."

She smiled stiffly. "I'm sorry, Charles, but I must ask you to escort me home. I found the damage beyond the means of the repairing room upstairs."

Charles's face sobered instantly. "Of course. And I shall wait while you change your gown, if you wish."

"No. I feel I have danced enough for tonight, Charles. If you would be so good as to pay my respects to our hostess, I will wait in the hall." She smiled sorrowfully at his puzzlement and very carefully left the room.

Chapter 23

For several days Rebecca lived in a haze of suppressed emotion, insensible to life around her. The control that had brought her home that night, that had allowed her to smile and thank Charles for the evening, had cracked completely once she was alone in her room. She had given in to a strangled storm of weeping which had left her feeling limp and hollow. Too many times she had faced loss in her young life. She had lost her parents and her home, the bases of all her security. She had lost the girlish hope of marrying Lord Harlcourt, and with it the possibility of remaining in England. She had even lost what security she'd discovered in America, and but for Uncle Julian, would now be alone and homeless in this new land. But the loss of Gordon had the feel of an ultimate disaster. She acknowledged now that although she'd lost him in a sense the morning she'd fled Halscomb, she'd always harbored the knowledge that he was with the army, that his vitality and strength was not so very far away. She'd unconsciously drawn her own strength from that knowledge and from her unacknowledged love for him. Now her secret prop was gone, and she ceased to care what became of her.

Others did care, though, as she was reminded by constant inquiries about her health during the following day, and slowly she learned a kind of dull acceptance, though she found it difficult to respond to anyone with more than automatic civility. At first she had Charles turned away when he called, though she knew she could not continue to do that for long. She just wanted time to readjust to her new reality, but she was aware she would not be allowed to do it alone. So she was not surprised when Charles, overriding the protests of the servants one day, came into the garden and found her.

"You have been ill," he exclaimed, crossing to the bench where she sat watching a woodpecker work patiently at retrieving his noonday meal from the bark of a tree. The hollow rat-a-tat of his strong bill had soothed her, made her unaware of Charles's approach.

Now she looked up. There was a bouyancy to his step, a brightness to his eye that seemed in such counterpoint to her own low humor, she almost smiled. "I'm afraid so. But it is nothing serious," she added, seeing the concern on his face. "I shall be right in a few days. Tell me how you have been," she asked listlessly, wishing vaguely he would go away. He'd frightened off the woodpecker, and she missed the even tattoo of the bird's beak.

Charles sat down beside her. "There has been a battle in New Jersey, outside Philadelphia," he said. "General Howe put Washington to flight again. Now, if he'll only follow up, we'll snare the gentleman from Virginia once and for all."

The girl nodded and looked at the last roses clustered on the arbor vine. The softest pink they were, with pale ivory centers. But now their edges were beginning to curl and brown. Never mind, there were several buds starting. Perhaps one more display would be unveiled before the first frost.

"With Howe's victory yesterday, we are in a fair way in the west," Charles's voice was continuing. "Now Burgoyne must move forward. The losses at Bennington in August were embarrassing, but he can still slice down the rebels if he'll only act decisively."

Rebecca turned her head slowly. She knew she should attend Charles more closely, but she could feel no interest in his talk of generals and battles. "Yes," she said, hoping the single word would suffice.

"Forgive me, Rebecca. I did not mean to tire you with news of the army. I came to see how you are, and instead have lapsed into talk that should be reserved for the officer's mess."

"I'm afraid I am not as attentive as I should be."

"From the look of you, it's no wonder. Oughtn't you to be in bed, not out here in the garden?"

"Perhaps I should be. Though the sun feels lovely."

Charles jumped up. "Let me help you inside. Then I promise not to disturb you again until you are well."

Rebecca allowed him to help her up. He walked her to the house, and she watched him leave then with apathetic eyes.

It was midmorning. Perhaps Uncle Julian would be up. She would go and see. His color had not been good these past few days. All through the hot weather he had seemed to improve. Though he'd never returned to his former strength, he'd at least been on his feet occasionally, had taken regular meals with the rest of them in the house. But the first hint of cooler weather had seemed to sap his strength.

At her uncle's door she stopped to listen. There was no sound. She knocked softly and at last heard his voice bidding her enter. He was sitting in a Windsor chair near the window, a robe around his legs, and his heavy face looked gray in the harsh morning light. As he raised his head, a coughing spell seized him, and it was some moments before he could speak.

Rebecca hurried to pour a glass of water from the small pitcher on the table, and gave it to him when his hand was steady enough to hold it.

"Thank you, child." Her uncle looked at her with watery eyes and dabbed at his mouth with a large square of linen.

"This is the first I've heard of your cough in months." Rebecca's concern brought her to her knees beside him.

" 'Tis nothing much." He put a quaking hand on her shiny hair. "You are going to do something entertaining today?"

The girl shook her head. "Nothing today, Uncle. I thought perhaps I could read to you, or we could play chess."

"Ah, is Charles on duty, then?"

"He was here earlier."

"Good." Her uncle's head dropped to his chest. When he raised it again, his eyes had something of their old warmth. "It is the greatest good fortune that he was brought to the city, wasn't it, Becky?"

She nodded.

"You know, last fall, I'd rather hoped . . . But the war did get in the way of things, didn't it?" A look of pain crossed his face, and she knew he was thinking of Halscomb.

"A temporary setback, only, Uncle Julian. Charles says

there has just been a British victory in New Jersey, and that General Burgoyne still marches south on the upper Hudson. I think he expects an end to all this by winter. We can hope to return to Westchester in the spring—a warm thought to hold us through cold months, don't you think?"

Julian Halscomb nodded, but his eyes avoided hers. She wondered how much he really knew about the destruction of his home. "And by spring," he said slowly, "you will perhaps be a blushing bride." His hand moved gently to her cheek, and she felt it tremble.

"If you mean to ask if Charles has declared himself, Uncle Julian, I will tell you he has said he wants to wait until the war is over."

"Why?" There was an urgency to his voice that surprised Rebecca.

"I imagine it is because he doesn't know where he'll be sent at any time, and he prefers not to leave me alone before we even have a home."

"And you, Becky? How do you feel about waiting? You do wish to marry Charles, don't you?" He leaned forward, his other hand groping for hers, and a second spell of coughing caught at him.

When it was over, Rebecca tried to make her voice light. "I marry no one until you are well again, Uncle Julian. Who else would give me away?"

"There is Thomas. No, child, waiting can be a great mistake. You must follow your heart, and take your opportunity for happiness while it is before you. What if the war does not end as predicted?"

Rebecca bit her lip and looked down. "We won't know about the war for a few months yet. It *may* go as we wish."

"And then you will have Charles?"

"I've told you, dear, that I won't leave you."

"I want you to be happy, Becky." Her uncle's voice sounded exhausted. "I have little to give you now that Halscomb is burned. Charles will do well by his land. He can care for you in comfort. Besides, I have the strong impression he loves you very much, hmmm?"

"I couldn't say. But there really is no need to worry over my matrimonial prospects today, Uncle. Shall I bring the chessboard?"

"That would be nice." As she moved away, his voice followed her. "You haven't met another who interests you more, have you?"

"No, Uncle." Rebecca returned and placed the small board on the table beside him, trying to ignore the pain inside her.

"Then you will think about Charles, and the possibility of hurrying him a bit?"

"I'll think, Uncle. Now, we start a new game today, and you, as the victor in the one last week, must allow me to consider my first move."

It was early that same evening when Uncle Julian's words about following your own heart returned to Rebecca. She was standing by her window, gazing at nothing but the pale mauve sky when a movement below caught her attention. It was Sylvie, coming to the door from the garden, and her hands were clasped tightly as she walked. Rebecca frowned as the girl disappeared from view. Sylvie had been in the arbor with her only minutes before, and had been mending a small tablecloth with the quick dainty stitches Mrs. Adams had taught her to perfect. Yet here the girl was, entering the house at last, without her sewing. Really, she was more absentminded all the time, no matter how often she was told. Evidently her mind was more and more in Westchester, where her heart so obviously was. It was then that Rebecca remembered her conversation with Uncle Julian. Sylvie had been gone from Dobbs Ferry for ten months, too long a time to be separated from Seth. She'd not been given the chance to take her happiness where she found it, had come instead to support Rebecca in a strange city. Something should be done for her.

While she waited for Sylvie to appear, she considered the problem, and by the time the maid knocked on her door, Rebecca had a solution. Without preamble, she drew Sylvie into the room and launched on her little speech.

"And I shall obtain a pass for you from Sir Henry himself, if need be," she concluded. "You deserve at least some time away from the city."

Sylvie listened to her mistress's concern for her with ever-widening eyes, but now she smiled gently. "Thank you for your thoughts, miss, but I won't leave you."

"Why ever not, Sylvie? You haven't changed your mind about Seth have you?" Rebecca searched Sylvie's pert face, noticing that as fresh and young as it still was, there was something about it that was more mature. Perhaps it was the slight tightening of the muscles beside the rosebud mouth, or a certain almost wary look in the large brown eyes.

"No, I have not changed toward Seth. And he still loves me, I know. But he understands that I must stay here." The girl's hands were twisting together as she talked, and she suddenly seemed aware of the fact, because she lowered them to her sides and held them very still.

"Then why won't you at least go for a visit?"

"I can't explain, Miss Rebecca. But I can't leave New York just now."

The girl looked as though she'd burst into tears in a moment, and baffled, Rebecca put her arms around her. "All right, Sylvie, I'll say no more. But I want you to think about it. You aren't happy here. I can tell that just by the way you look."

Sylvie stepped back and smiled in a genuine way. "New York is a fascinating place, miss. I know all sorts of people here. It's not as though my life is dull." Her eyes twinkled now, with an almost secret amusement.

Rebecca was more baffled than ever. "I'm glad," she said stiffly.

"Will you be dressing for dinner?" Once more Sylvie was an efficient lady's maid, smoothing the bed, taking the cloak to hang it in the wardrobe.

"I don't know." Rebecca felt tired again.

"You really ought to, miss. You're not eating properly. And you've hardly spoken to anyone for days. Your uncle has been better, hasn't he? You shouldn't take on so."

Watching Sylvie bustle about, Rebecca had the urge to cry and be comforted. She'd not told anyone of all that had happened at the ball the other evening, of the news of Gordon's death, and she wished she could just once pour out her heartbreak. But what was the use? No one here in New York even knew of her relationship with Gordon. Besides, all of it was behind her now, and she'd resolved to have Charles once the war was over. There was no going back, and there was no good to come of pining. "All right," she stated suddenly. "I think the new green satinet would be right this evening. But, Sylvie, before you get out my clothes, would you *please* retrieve your mending from the arbor?"

The smile on the girl's face wavered. "Oh, I'm sorry," she said and cast a hasty look out the window. The soft mauves of sunset had turned to gray as the last glimmers of light faded above the rooftops. "I'll go right now." She smiled again. "I *am* glad you decided to go downstairs. You were coming on to a prison pallor, all cooped up here in your room till today." With that, she practically bounced out the door.

Her words jolted Rebecca. Prison pallor! She looked in the mirror and saw Sylvie was right. Her outing in the garden this morning had restored some color, but she did look pale. It was then that she remembered Alex, and she sat down with a thump.

Alex was in a prison here in New York! When she'd heard the other night, she'd been so caught up in her grief over his brother, she'd completely forgotten what Charles had said. And Alex was not under house arrest like so many officers; he was in the North Church prison with enlisted men where conditions were known to be horrid. In fact, what was it that kind Mrs. Sinclair had been saying just a few weeks ago? Something about how badly she felt for the men held in squalid prisons, and for the poor relatives who'd come to try to help them. "Standing outside the prisons for hours, waiting to be allowed a glimpse of their poor men, hoping to hand over a crust of bread or some meat. Ragged souls they all are in those places, and the wives and friends little better, with so few rooms to let in the city. It's a wonder that any of them, prisoners or wives, survive."

Rebecca stood up and paced the room. Alex was in one of those awful places. How could she have forgotten? There was nothing she could do about his brother, but there must be *something* she could do for him! She'd have to try, both for the sake of her friendship with Alex, and for the sake of Gordon, who had loved his young brother and would want her to try.

She considered going to Charles, but rejected the idea. Even if there was anything he could do, he would not welcome the suggestion that he help a rebel. What of some of the other officers? The trouble was that most she knew well enough to ask a favor were no longer in the city. Besides, she should find Alex first, discover his true circumstances. He was an officer. Surely he might be exchanged? Might even now be on his way back to the rebel lines. How was she to find out?

When Sylvie returned, Rebecca was still pacing, stewing over the difficulties.

"Is something wrong, miss?"

Rebecca eyed her with sudden interest, and Sylvie stared back in surprise. "Yes. Yes, something is wrong, Sylvie. You said a few minutes ago that you had friends around the city."

The girl nodded, wariness apparent on her face.

"Can your friends find out anything about rebel prisoners?"

Sylvie made a show of lighting candles and getting out her mistress's combs and hairpins. "What sort of thing about prisoners, Miss Rebecca?"

"Sylvie, do you remember Lieutenant Meade? He was at Halscomb last fall with the colonel and his company."

"Yes, miss, I do."

"I learned the other evening that Alex,—Lieutenant Meade, —is in prison here in the city. The North Church was what Mr. Revington said. Do you know anything about it?"

The girl's face puckered in distaste. "Only that those are awful places, miss. I feel sorry for any man put in one of them."

"Yes, I've heard that too. I want to know more. I need to know if the lieutenant is still there. Is there any way you can find out?"

"I honestly don't know, Miss Rebecca. They have visiting hours at those places, but who goes to visit besides the relatives, I couldn't say. I will ask, though, if you like."

"Yes, please. I would like very much." Rebecca sat down and allowed Sylvie to start on her hair. She realized she'd hardly thought of her own misery all day, and she suddenly felt better.

It took nearly all her fortitude to wait patiently through the following day. She did not see Sylvie from midmorning until evening, and could only hope the girl was trying to discover news of Alex. She was grateful that Charles merely sent around a note saying he would call again in two days' time, and hoped she would be recovered by then. She didn't want to see him just yet. There were more pressing things on her mind.

When Sylvie did appear that evening, she announced that Lieutenant Meade was still in North Church, according to the list of prisoners there, though her informant had never seen the lieutenant himself. It was on the tip of Rebecca's tongue to ask who this informant might be, but she thought better of it. If Sylvie wasn't going to volunteer the name, it was not up to her to pry. What mattered was that she now knew Alex was still in the city. She thought of asking Sylvie to go to the jail to see him, but realized she couldn't send the girl alone. Nor could she send one of Mr. Kent's loyalist servants as escort to visit a rebel prisoner.

"Sylvie, are you willing to go to this prison with me, to find the lieutenant?"

"With you? Oh, Miss Rebecca, I don't think Mr. Halscomb would like you to go to that place."

"He doesn't have to know anything about it. No one in this house has to know. Lieutenant Meade was kind to me when I was a prisoner at Halscomb. The least I can do is try to see him while he is a prisoner here. He may need things—food or clothing. Are we allowed to take him anything?"

"People do. Though I think they must be careful not to let the sentries see. They might take the things away again. I've heard that the soldiers rob the prisoners of anything they can find."

"Then we will have to be careful." The light of combat was in Rebecca's eye as she smiled thoughtfully. "But right now all I want to do is see him."

"What would Mr. Charles say if he found out?"

"He need know nothing either. You will come with me tomorrow, won't you?"

"Well, I . . ."

"Oh, thank you, Sylvie." Rebecca seized her maid's hands and gave them a quick squeeze. Suddenly she was relieved Sylvie had refused to leave New York. She didn't think she could have gone to the prison alone. But once she had learned what could be done for Alex, she promised herself, she would see Sylvie returned to Dobbs Ferry. She felt better every moment.

From the corner of Fair and William streets, Rebecca surveyed the crowd on the low steps of North Church. The heavy oak doors were closed fast, and the people stood quietly waiting. Sullenly, they stared at the line of sentries before the portal. Some were as ragged as Mrs. Sinclair had claimed, but a few were clad in decent, even sumptuous clothes.

"Do the doors open at a specified hour?" She moved closer to Sylvie and drew her old cloak more tightly around her brown wool dress.

"When the soldiers come with food. Big barrels they bring, of rancid meat and hard biscuits, or a terrible stew I'm told."

Rebecca made a face and walked to the fringes of the

252

throng. Close up the group took on individual features. Here an old woman whose wispy hair stood up like a halo around her pink scalp sucked nervously on toothless gums; there a man stood aloof, a look of nothing but curiosity on his face; beside him a young woman whose face was pinched with anxiety, wrapped her arms around a small boy who complained of the wait.

Behind her she heard a muffled oath, a grunt and the tramp of heavy feet. Two soliders lugging the barrels Sylvie had described followed a corporal to the steps and the crowd parted silently to let them through. The corporal banged on the oak doors with the butt of his rifle and slowly they opened as an audible sigh went up from the group outside. Rebecca moved up the steps with the others, Sylvie close beside her.

Inside the entrance to the church, the soliders put down the barrels and a hulking sergeant came to stand before them as they removed the heavy lids. From the gloomy light behind him, Rebecca could see shadowy forms pressing forward eagerly, bearded faces and sunken eyes all turned to those barrels.

"Gi' us some room ye filthy scarecrows," the sergeant shouted into their ravaged faces. "Stand back I say." He slapped an ugly length of chain against his hand and the crowd of prisoners shifted backward silently. When quiet had descended all around, the sergeant ordered lines to form, then stood back almost reluctantly, allowing the soldiers to begin ladling out the rations.

Stiff with horror, Rebecca felt herself being pushed farther up the steps. The sentries were standing aside, letting the people into the doorway to mingle with the prisoners. As she drew closer, the stench of the place assailed her and she nearly stumbled. *This* was where Alex Meade had been kept for months?

"Jem? Jem?" A woman's high voice cracked as she pushed past Rebecca and flung herself into the arms of a prisoner in line. "Oh, Jem, I thought never to find ye."

The man folded her to his shrunken frame and bowed his head wordlessly over her capped head.

Rebecca looked away, trying to shut out the sounds of such reunions all around her.

"Shall I try to find him for you, miss? I think I'll know him if I see him. You wait here by the door." Sylvie pulled on her cloak, trying to stop Rebecca.

"No." Her mistress's voice was almost savage. "If he's alive in such a place, I shall find him."

She stepped further into the dimly lit church till a soldier barred her way. Through blurred eyes she scanned the lines of prisoners still shuffling toward the barrels, but not one looked like the handsome young man she'd known. Beyond the soldier she could see rows of straw pallets across the floor, some still bearing their occupants under thin blankets.

"You mustn't stay in here," Sylvie said beside her. "The jail fever . . ."

Impatiently Rebecca shook off her hand and turned to the first prisoner she saw. "I'm looking for Lieutenant Alexander Meade," she said softly. "Do you know him?"

The man looked at her with red-rimmed eyes and shook his head. But he caught at another prisoner's arm with clawlike fingers. "Alexander Meade. You know 'im?"

The second prisoner nodded with disinterest, his eyes fastened on the barrels by the door. "Crazy Alex." He spat into the dirty rushes on the floor. "Officer, but he wouldn't give parole. So he gets to take his chances with the rest of us."

"Where is he? Could you tell me please?" Rebecca touched the man's arm tentatively.

He looked down at her hand with surprise. "Dunno. Over there, I s'pose." He waved his tin plate toward the other side of the door.

Carefully, Rebecca stepped back behind the soldiers and barrels, trying to ignore the smells and sights before her. She edged to the far side of the lines.

Then she saw him, and her stomach lurched.

Chapter 24

Alex stood in the wavering line of men, his dark blond hair long and dirty, his face gaunt and remote. His once fine linen shirt hung in tatters on his thin frame, but he stood straight and tall, holding his tin plate in one hand. His other arm was around a dark-haired man who leaned on him heavily as he labored for breath. Alex's threadbare coat drooped from the man's bent shoulders, and he shivered despite its protection.

Rebecca gulped, fighting back quick tears at the sight. "Alex," she said and walked slowly toward him.

His dulled eyes swiveled slowly, looking for the voice. When he saw her he started and wiped the back of his hand over his face. "My God, Rebecca." His voice was the only thing about him that seemed still strong.

She stopped before him, searching for something to say that wouldn't sound foolish. They stared at each other for a long moment. Awkwardly, Alex shifted his plate to his other hand under his comrade's shoulder, then he reached for hers. Rebecca gave it to him and they clasped fingers silently.

"I've come to see what I can do for you."

His grin was a mockery of its former self. "Unless you've brought a wagon of muskets and swords," he whispered, "there is little you can do. You shouldn't be here. Where on earth did you come from?"

"I live on Queen Street now. My uncle and I are staying with a friend. Halscomb was burned last December."

The gray eyes narrowed, and Alex moved ahead in the line. Rebecca followed. "How did you find me?"

"By chance. I heard an officer named Meade had refused his parole and been sent here. Sylvie found out you were still here."

Alex looked over her shoulder and nodded at her maid, hovering close. "It was good of you to come. But there is little you can do, Rebecca."

"Is this all they give you to eat?" Rebecca waved at the barrels.

"A feast today, I assure you."

"I'll bring you food."

The man who still slumped against Alex's side looked up at that. "Food?" he said in a cracked voice.

"Yes," Rebecca replied firmly.

"Oh, miss. I'll bring anything." Sylvie came closer now. "Officers sometimes visit the prisons. You might be seen."

"And what if I am?" Rebecca's gorge was rising steadily as she watched the poor wretches around her. "I had no idea . . ." she said softly, letting her voice trail away.

Alex cleared his throat and shuffled ahead a pace. "You have heard about Gordon?" he asked, avoiding her eyes.

"Yes. What happened Alex?"

"It was that morning we cleared out of Halscomb, after we couldn't find you." For a moment she read reproof in his eyes. Then he lowered them again. "Gordon thought you had gone to the redcoats, seeking protection. We followed the tracks of the pony cart, you see, and found it abandoned. Your horse's prints had gone onto the road."

"But I went to the village, not the army."

Alex searched her face for a long moment, then nodded. "I knew . . . But we couldn't follow any more, so we went to our rendezvous with Tyson and his men. After we'd met them there was an ambush in the woods. Five of us were taken prisoner. One of my men was downed instantly. Then Gordon was shot. There were men all through those woods. The redcoats thought there were more of us around, so they drove us off then." His voice took on a singsong quality, as though he'd gone over the brief version of the story many times in his mind. "Major Tyson must have been exchanged immediately. I don't know what happened to his two men. Sanders and I tried to escape when we were near New York on the Yonkers road. After that we were tied up, and when we reached the city he was brought here. I don't even remember where I was taken. They talked some gibberish about my giving my word not to escape. I was half crazy over what had happened, and refused." A lopsided grin split his face.

Rebecca nearly blurted the news about Warren Tyson wearing a new uniform, but checked herself in time. No need to add to his anger, his troubles now. "And later you tried to escape, I hear."

"Yes. They didn't care for that. Bad luck that fat dog of a provost marshal was nearby at the time. He flew into a rage and had me thrown in here."

"How long have you been in this place, Alex?"

"I don't know. Five months, anyway. Sanders came down with the jail fever. We couldn't save him. Never even enough water."

"Alex. You must give your parole. You can at least get out of here."

"Never." His eyes hardened. "I will escape whenever, however I can."

"But you might be exchanged."

"Yes, and I might wait a year for the privilege. I won't wait another winter, not here, not in any other jail."

"How could you possibly escape from this . . . this place?"

"I'll find a way. Others have. I must get out, Rebecca. I don't know what happened to Gordon that day. I think, I feel that if he were really dead as the others thought, I'd *know*. But I don't know. I have to find him."

Rebecca turned away. The lump of nausea that had been forming in her stomach ever since entering this place was rising to her throat. Alex was sick, starved, almost wild-eyed. Perhaps this hope for his brother was all that had kept him alive in here. How stubborn he must be to cling to his determination. How like Gordon!

They were standing by the barrels now, the last in line, and the soldiers were ladling impatiently, anxious to escape the reeking prison. Alex's plate received a wooden biscuit and a piece of unrecognizable meat. With a slam, the lids were replaced on the barrels.

"Aw right. Everybody out," hollered the sergeant, the chain slapping at his hand again.

"I'll bring food tomorrow," Rebecca whispered and felt the pressure of Alex's hand on her arm saying thank you.

The soft September breeze was pleasantly cool as it riffled the leaves on the heavy trees and sighed among the brambles beside the narrow trail. Birds twittered high in the branches and small forest animals made noisy protest at the passage of the five horses plodding wearily down the steep wooded bank. At the bottom of the hill, a small stream gurgled happily among rocky outcroppings, and the horses plunged forward thirstily. Their way had been long and dusty until this last hour. The cool of the woods and the sight of water was welcome indeed.

Gordon Meade dismounted and looked around him warily. It was more from habit that he scanned the stream banks than from any real need, but still he did not order the other four out of their saddles until he was quite sure they were alone.

"A likely spot for a rest. We've made good time, Colonel." Corporal Johnston squatted beside Gordon on a flat rock, and dipping cupped hands into the cold water, drank gratefully.

"We'll not be stopping yet, Corporal." Gordon stood up. "There's a farm just downstream. No sense in having someone see us now."

The corporal leaned back on his heels and squinted into the westerly sun until he could make out the low stone wall angling up the far bank through a fringe of trees. "It's late in the afternoon. Not likely anyone'd be around."

"A child, coming to fish for supper, would be enough. We'll top that next hill and then see."

The corporal looked around regretfully. "All right, men," he called in a low voice, "back in the saddle."

There were some grumbles as the men hauled the horses' heads clear of the water and mounted again, but Gordon wasn't listening. His mind was on the miles of forest track that lay ahead, and he was wondering how soon he could rejoin a road.

Back near Peekskill he'd welcomed General Putnam's armed escort. There were marauding bands of citizens as well as hungry men from both armies in Westchester. They were laying waste to the countryside in search of food, or in reprisal against those they considered wrong-thinking people, and they were not above attacking groups of travelers. But up here nearer Fishkill Gordon doubted the need for such protection. It slowed him down. General Putnam had made it clear that Gordon was to stop at nothing to answer the summons from John Jay, had even issued fake orders to account for Gordon's absence from the army. However, the old man hadn't said what Jay wanted. Perhaps he didn't know, though the twinkle in his eyes last night showed he relished whatever he *did* know. Gordon wished he could share the general's enthusiasm, but he wanted nothing more than to reach Jay and discover what it was that had made him call for aid. After that he would sleep. He was tired, and his shoulder and chest were beginning to throb with a nearly forgotten ache.

Spurring his horse through the stream, Gordon consulted the map of the country that was in his head. He would rejoin the road to the east of them in another three or four miles. It would be growing dark in a couple of hours. No sense in floundering around through these rocky hills at night.

"Another mile," he urged the men. "Then we stop."

"Colonel, there's a farm downstream. We could get some vittles there, I'm thinkin'." A weasel-faced soldier eyed Gordon plaintively and then peered through the trees as though he could see a cooking fire from here. His mouth hung open, already tasting the family's evening meal.

"You'll eat in Fishkill." Gordon gave the man a withering look, and the slack mouth snapped shut. "Move your horse."

It took more forceful urging to get the men going after the promised rest, but they soon realized the colonel was in no mood for stalling. The last miles were covered as fast as the troop dared to push its mounts in the gathering dark. And the reward was a decent meal at an inn on the outskirts of the little town. Gordon saw to their bellies and left them to wait cheerfully for his return.

John Jay was not at his lodgings. He'd gone to a dinner arranged for some of the members of the Committee on Conspiracies. Gordon hesitated at that news, but finally asked the direction. John's meal could wait till he told Gordon what his summons had meant.

At a handsome clapboard house set back in a grove of maples, he asked for Mr. Jay, and was ushered into a tiny rear parlor by an incurious woman who left him without ceremony. He paced the dimly lit room, feeling his stomach growl, and wished he'd done more than snatch at a mug of ale and a single leg of chicken back at the inn.

"Gordon! Why, you still have the dust of travel on you, man." John Jay, dressed in a beautifully cut coat of deepest brown velvet over a waistcoat of white corded silk, advanced through the doorway with outstretched hand. As Gordon took it, smiling, Jay shook his head. "I didn't think to see you till tomorrow. But you're a welcome sight, Colonel Meade."

"I'm sorry to pull you away from your dinner, John, but it has been a long day, and you did say it was urgent."

"Do not be sorry. We keep country-hours around here. We are quite done, and the ladies await us in the drawing room. They will not miss me for some time yet."

"When you leave *any* gathering you are missed, John."

The shorter man cocked his head and his smile broadened. "I'll never know why you chose to take a commission, Gordon. You would have done very well as a diplomat. Your talents are wasted on the army."

"Not completely, I hope."

Jay laughed at that. "Touché. Not completely, no, if all I've heard of you since '75 be true. But come, let us walk outside. The fresh air will do me a great deal of good after an exceptionally heavy, if delicious supper, and you are dressed to withstand the autumn chill." He took Gordon's arm and steered him back down the hall to the front door. "Now tell me," he said as he closed the latch firmly behind them, "how you get on."

"Well enough. How is Sarah?"

"Splendid. But you haven't come all this way to hear about her. Let us talk instead about you."

They were at the side of the house now where a wide path led past tall flower borders to an artfully arranged woodland garden among the tall maples. The pleasant cool breeze of the afternoon had picked up, moving the branches high overhead in ghostly patterns across the path. Low clouds scudded near the treetops, blacking out the ribbon of moon every so often, throwing the men into dark relief against the columns of trees.

"You are better," Jay stated when they'd cleared the angle of the house. "You walk without a limp."

"Yes. It was not long after I saw you in March that I managed to rid myself of that."

"And have you rid yourself of your demons, too?"

"I have no demons. Only an honest hate for a man."

"And a woman?"

Gordon missed a step and halted. He remembered now that he'd told John about the ambush, about his suspicion that Rebecca had informed on him. At the time, John had argued that Warren Tyson was the most likely culprit. He'd never trusted the major, and although Tyson had been caught in the trap along with Gordon that day in November, he'd been exchanged promptly and then disappeared. There had been no doubt in John's mind about where Warren had gone. As for Rebecca, he'd tended to put her disappearance down to disorienting fear. Gordon had been unconvinced at the time. His worry over Alex and his hatred for Tyson had made him view everyone involved in that unlucky day in the same light. He'd had sober months to reflect now, though, and his wild suspicions about Rebecca had faded into a dull acceptance of her defection. She'd had reason to run from him, heaven knew. She'd even had some reason to inform on him, he supposed. He simply tried not to think about it any more than he had to.

"Hate? No," he said slowly now. "Indifference would more accurately describe my feelings toward the lovely Miss Blair." And that's very close to the truth, he told himself. "But our good Major Tyson's another matter." He resumed walking beside his old friend. "If he's done what we think, he lives up to all the promise he displayed during our years at King's, doesn't he?"

"He does. And he has."

"You have learned something?"

"Warren Tyson is now a major, no less, on Sir Henry Clinton's own staff."

Gordon was silent. There was no sense in saying aloud all the dirty names Tyson deserved, or cataloging the man's probable crimes. He'd be preaching to the converted, anyway. John had known Warren in college too, and had borne him no love even then. "It is a pleasure to be on opposite sides at last," was all he said.

"A pity, though, that we could not hang him on our side." The clouds moved, and through the trees a sliver of moonlight fell on John Jay's tight-lipped smile. "And now, tell me if you've heard anything about Alex."

Gordon stopped again. "Nothing. In all these months, nothing. I traced him only down the Yonkers road, as you know.

He disappeared there. But then, I haven't your spy network to inform me."

"Exactly so. And I have, quite by chance, finally discovered your brother's whereabouts."

"My God." Gordon gripped his friend's shoulders. "He's alive? Where is he?"

"He is in New York. And I must suppose he is still alive, if he hasn't done something else foolish."

"What do you mean?"

"Only that I learned, in discussing matters with a loyalist spy we uncovered, that Lieutenant Meade had been imprisoned in the city late last fall and had tried to escape. That charming man, Provost Cunningham, got wind of the fact Alex nearly killed one of his sergeants, and removed him from his quarters. Where he was taken I don't know, but one supposes, I'm afraid, that it was to less comfortable circumstances."

"When did all this happen?"

"During the winter."

"God, he could be anywhere now." And please God, don't let it be on one of those prison ships in the harbor, Gordon thought in agony.

"Yes, but my loyalist friend felt it likely that he was jailed within the city still."

Gordon took rough hold of himself. "I appreciate this intelligence, John. But you could have sent it in a message. You didn't call me up here from Peekskill just to tell me about Alex, or even about Tyson."

"You never were a fool, Gordon. If this war ever ends, I hope I do not have the misfortune to argue a case opposite you. Shall we turn back here?" The two circled past a small pond in a narrow glade and returned to the path. "You know General Gates has moved into position up the Hudson, at a place called Bemis Heights?"

"Yes. I know the area."

"As you also know, some of our best units have been removed from the defense of the Hudson to join Washington in New Jersey. We have only Gates and his forces between us and Gentleman Johnny Burgoyne now. And Putnam's small force at Peekskill. You are as aware as I that our position is weak if Clinton moves out of New York and marches north to join Burgoyne. We'd be caught like a walnut in a nutcracker if Sir Henry took us by surprise. He must not take us by surprise."

Gordon remained silent. He knew all that Jay was saying. There was obviously more.

"Most men would expostulate at this point, begin telling me all that should be done to avert the catastrophe."

"But you are not finished yet, John, and you are not concerned with my opinion."

"Not so, old friend. I value your opinion, but it is true that an opinion is not what I need at the moment. We must have information about Sir Henry's intentions. Last June the British caught one of my men. He was hanged in New York. We had to go to ground for a bit. But we remained confident, for I have some excellent men in the city. They are perfectly placed, and for the most part have every reason to be there. Most of them live and work there, which makes it difficult for them to leave with information for me. I had another man who discovered ways to move in and out of New York . . . I wish I'd found out how. But last week he failed to arrive when expected. I have to assume something has happened. I need to keep the information coming. General Washington, General Gates and General Putnam must have anything I can find out. Will you go to New York for me?"

Gordon evinced no surprise at the request. He'd worked with John Jay before, once even in disguise behind British lines. He knew the subtlety of Jay's mind, and he knew the success of the spy ring Jay was still running. So he didn't waste time asking how he could be gotten through the British army in Westchester, or where he would go when he arrived in New York. "I'm still known in the city," he said instead.

"By not so many as in the old days. And you would take care not to frequent former haunts that might still be open."

"You played me like an old trout, John. You held out Alex's imprisonment like the choicest fly."

"I did. And I did it because I know your distaste for espionage. You are willing to do anything dangerous, even in the dark of night. But spying has a taint to it that most men of upright character deplore. I fear I'm sadly depraved, for I see the necessity of it."

"It is the strategy of the game that appeals to you." Gordon smiled in the dark, but his voice was tired. "You didn't have to cast your best bait. I would have gone for you anyway."

"I wanted to be sure. I'm sorry."

"For what? For calling on one of your friends when you think you need him?"

"No. I know I could always do that. For using Alex. Especially when I can't even hold out the lure of seeing him. I still don't know where he is."

"I'll find him." The low voice had a hard edge to it that John Jay had rarely heard.

"I don't doubt it. And I wish you luck. But nothing must stand in the way of your coming out again."

"I will come out again."

Jay paced silently then, until they were nearly to the porch steps. "If we can get the information we need, can be prepared when Clinton marches north, we may even be able to stop him from joining Burgoyne. Gentleman Johnny, left on his own in the north, may yet lose his fancy army. If we can eliminate him from the contest, we may at last persuade the French to enter the war."

"The French waver only slightly now. It will take just one decisive victory to pull them in with us."

Jay nodded, rubbed his chin, then looked up. "Things are arranged for your travel. Several good men between here and New York will get you through."

"I assumed so."

"But have you a place to stay in the city? I can take one more chance and force the man you will contact to keep you but, understandably, he would rather keep his distance."

Gordon thought of Verona, and wondered how far she could be trusted. "I'll manage."

Jay nodded again. "But remember there is that option for you. Come to my rooms in the morning. I will give you money and instructions. You have a clear road into the city. From there you are on your own."

The tall man bowed mockingly, and they shook hands. "I'll rouse you before dawn."

His friend grimaced. "Very well. Oh, and Gordon, if Alex will give his parole, if it's still possible for him to do so, I will see pressure is exerted to bring about his exchange."

Gordon pressed more tightly the hand he still held.

"I nearly forgot," Jay went on in what sounded almost like a sly voice. "I heard well over a month ago too, that Miss Rebecca Blair now resides in New York."

His hand was dropped as though it were a contagious thing, and Jay watched with interest as the other stiffened before him.

"Till dawn," Gordon said softly, and melted smoothly into the shadows around the house.

Chapter 25

Rebecca stopped at the door to the drawing room and tried to back a step. "I beg your pardon, Mr. Kent. I had not realized you had company."

"Ah, my dear. Come in, come in. You're just in time. Won't you stay and pour tea for us?" Mr. Kent rose from the settee, and at that instant a scarlet-clad figure in a low-backed chair stood up. To Rebecca's horror, Warren Tyson made his bow.

"We would be honored, Miss Blair," he murmured, watching her from under half-closed eyelids.

"Thank you," she said, feeling stiff, "but I was about to go up and see my uncle."

"Surely you can pause long enough to welcome our new guest." Mr. Kent's voice was jovial, but it held an undertone of command.

Obediently, Rebecca crossed to the round table where the tea service was spread invitingly. The two men resumed their seats, and she tried not to look at them as she lifted the cover on the heavy silver pot to check the strength of the brew. Thankfully, it was ready to pour. She lifted the first cup to Mr. Kent's outstretched hand and willed herself not to shake as she poured the second. The major crossed to her table and his hand closed over her fingers when he took the proffered saucer. She recoiled and very nearly spilled the tea.

"You *are* going to welcome me to this house, aren't you, Miss Blair?"

"It would seem Mr. Kent has already done so." She kept her tone carefully neutral, but his next words left her speechless.

"I think it more fitting for the lady of the house to greet her newest guest, though. Especially since I will be living here for an unknown period of time."

Rebecca could only stare at him and then at Mr. Kent.

"A pleasant surprise, eh, Rebecca? I gather from the major that you and he are old friends."

"We first met in England more than two years ago," she managed.

"Splendid. Then you two must have many things to talk over. If you will excuse me for just a few moments, I shall let Mrs. Allen know that the spare room is to be used again."

Rebecca nearly jumped from her chair. "I'll go for you, Mr. Kent."

"Nonsense, my dear. You make the major feel at home. I won't be more than a minute." And he walked briskly from the room.

The girl sank back, chagrin in every line of her face and body.

"You seem less than pleased that I am come to stay." Major Tyson stood looking down at her, a tight smile stretching the corners of his thin mouth.

"I have told you that I cannot feel pride in knowing a turncoat."

"When I have given my all for the crown? I merely wear my allegiance openly now. My constancy has never wavered. Can you say the same?"

Rebecca looked at him sharply. "What an absurd question."

"Is it? Do you mean to say that the dashing Colonel Meade did not manage to turn your head?"

"You know nothing of the matter, Major. I am here, am I not?"

"Indeed. And one wonders how you came."

"It was not easy. And it is none of your affair." The girl was breathing quickly now, her indignation mounting.

"Perhaps, but I make many things my affair, you will find. Your newest activities, for instance."

"What on earth do you mean?"

"I chanced to see you at the North Church only this morning. It crossed my mind to wonder what you did there.

267

Going to gawk at the prisoners, perchance? Or to visit someone you know?"

Rebecca regained her feet in a swift movement. "You talk in riddles, sir, and I'm afraid I have more pressing matters to occupy my time."

"Some ladies, I am told, receive a thrill at watching the half-naked men line up for food," he said conversationally.

Rebecca gasped. "You are insulting, sir."

"Such protest!" His eyes were mocking. "You play it well, Miss Blair, but I discover you have not yet answered my question."

Dim instinct told Rebecca never to mention Alex's name. "Nor do I intend to, Major. You will excuse me." She flounced past him, and when he put out a hand to stop her, she sidestepped neatly and sped out the door.

In the hall she nearly collided with Mr. Kent. "Ah, my dear. Perhaps you could discuss the menu with Mrs. Allen now. I am told there will be four more officers here this evening for the meal, and they will require the drawing room afterward for their own affairs. I know they will all be charmed to have you act as hostess at dinner."

Although she was still breathing quickly, Rebecca managed to control her voice. "I am taking my meal with Uncle Julian this evening," she stated.

"I'm sorry you feel you must, but I do understand. Poor Julian is not doing as well as we'd hoped, is he? Perhaps you can take him the news of Major Tyson's arrival. He should be pleased. The request for our spare room was signed by Sir Henry himself, you know." Mr. Kent's voice was almost conspiratorial. "And I have heard from your Charles Revington that the major is dealing with counterintelligence for the general, as well as attending to his regular duties. Quite a lot of activity I expect we'll see around here in future. This meeting tonight is to be very private, I understand."

Rebecca didn't even attempt a smile. "I'll inform Mrs. Allen of your wishes," she said stiffly, and left Mr. Kent looking puzzled.

True to her word, she took her meal upstairs with her uncle that night, and spent a deal of time cajoling the sick man to eat the soft foods prepared for him. He seemed barely able to sit in his chair, and was most grateful when his niece finally helped him back to his bed. She sat for an hour after that, reading to him from Smollett's *Roderick Random,* her voice growing hoarse as much from worry as from the strain of reading.

At last Julian Halscomb seemed to sleep peacefully, his labored breathing quieting, and she put down the book. If only she could make him well again! The doctors they had called in had little to say about his condition. They neither held out hope for his recovery, nor condemned him to the life of an invalid. Shaking their heads, they came and went, leaving sleeping draughts and medicines and urging them to keep him warm, but never did Uncle Julian improve.

How she longed to be able to talk to him, to tell him of all that had been happening, of all she felt and worried over. But he mustn't be upset in any way. So she spent her time with him smiling, playing chess, reading, occasionally talking of England, never of the future unless he asked about Charles. Tonight she'd assured him again that all would be well and that she would marry Charles whenever he'd have her. She wished she could feel as confident as she'd sounded.

Wearily, she snuffed the candles, checked that the heavy drapes were drawn tightly across the windows and retreated on tiptoe to her own room. Sylvie was not there waiting, and she stood by the bed, trying to decide if she should ring for the girl. Perhaps she wouldn't bother.

Far below her a door slammed with a hollow thud. Annoyed, Rebecca began to remove the loose jacket from over her crewel embroidered dress of pink linen. The officers had no thought, evidently, for people wishing to sleep upstairs. She wondered if they were drunk. Her hand was at the long sash tied around her waist when she heard a loud voice, then booted feet on the stairs. Worried now, as well as angry, she slipped the jacket back over her arms. The feet were mounting steadily. Soon they were in the hall outside. Quickly she opened her door.

Major Tyson was peering up and down the narrow hall. She slid out of her room and closed the door behind her. "Are you looking for your room, Major?" she asked coldly. "Allow me to direct you."

The man whirled at her voice. "Not at all, Miss Blair. I am glad to find you still up."

"It is difficult to retire when there is so much noise."

"The noise, Miss Blair, was due to your maid. If you will follow me, I will explain." Without waiting for a reply, the man started back down the stairs. Outraged, but curious,

Rebecca followed. When they were nearly to the main hall, he turned. "I caught her, Miss Blair, outside the door to the drawing room. Not a place for your personal maid to be at this hour, surely?"

Rebecca halted on the stair above him. "I can only suppose, Major Tyson, that Mr. Kent's fine brandy has been poured most liberally this evening. You *cannot* be saying you came all the way upstairs to fetch me only to tell me that Sylvie was in the hall a few minutes ago."

The aquiline face with its dark eyes looked angrily back at her. "That is precisely why I came after you. Your maid was eavesdropping, Miss Blair. She was directly outside the door when I opened it."

Rebecca remembered Mr. Kent's words about Major Tyson's meeting being a most private one this evening. Her mind raced, seeking an explanation for Sylvie's presence downstairs. "Just what made you fling the door open in the first place?" she asked, coming the rest of the way into the hall and looking around.

"I thought I had heard a stealthy movement outside. I was all too correct."

Rebecca walked into the drawing room to find the other officers standing in a pack before the small figure of her maid. Sylvie looked shaken, but calm. "Major," Rebecca said dryly, "if someone were intent on listening at this door, she would hardly make enough noise for you to hear her."

"I *told* them I was just looking for your gloves, miss." Sylvie wrung her hands and looked earnest.

"A bloody likely story," a fat officer said from behind her.

Rebecca gave the man a cold stare. "Nonetheless, it is one you will have to accept. My tan gloves are not fit to be worn at present, and I wanted them cleaned. I sent Sylvie in search of them. I often drop my gloves on the table by the garden door."

The man subsided behind a brother officer's shoulder, but Major Tyson stepped forward. "She had no business outside this door, I tell you."

"And I tell you that you are jumping to ridiculous conclusions." Rebecca rounded on him. "You have not been here often, Major. You are perhaps unaware that to get to the garden door you must pass this room."

"Not if you use the servants' stairs."

"But you wouldn't use the servants' stairs if you were

270

checking the other hall tables and the morning room first, as I had asked." Rebecca was extemporizing with an agility she hadn't known she possessed. Now she could only hope her story matched Sylvie's.

"That's what I tried to tell them, miss. They kept asking what I heard in here, but I explained I'd not been near the door till I tripped on that big Chinese chest outside there. They won't believe me." The girl looked as though she were going to burst into tears. "That's the sound they heard."

"Why didn't we hear you before that, if you were looking all over for the gloves?"

"I *told* you," Sylvie wailed. "I knew you were meeting with these gentlemen and I didn't want to disturb you. I only wanted to get the gloves and meet Miss Rebecca when she left her uncle's room."

Major Tyson opened his mouth to say more, but Rebecca cut in smoothly. "Thank you, Sylvie. I'm sure the question has been cleared up. You may go up now and set out my night things." A hard look in her eye challenged anyone to speak until Sylvie had darted gratefully from the room. "And now, Major, if you and these gentlemen will excuse me, I will retire at last."

"But surely not without those gloves which are so important to you, Miss Blair." The major was at her elbow, guiding her from the room, turning her down the hall. "Since Sylvie seems to have looked everywhere else, we'd best check that table you spoke of."

Rebecca's whole body went cold at his words, but she forced herself to walk casually beside him till they reached the rear of the house. The small half-oval table beneath a long gilt mirror was bare.

"Tsk, tsk, Miss Blair. Not here either." Major Tyson's eyes looked decidedly feline.

"Oh, dear." Rebecca stooped and looked under the table. "Then I *must* have left them in Uncle Julian's room." She straightened, looking the man in the eye with a composure she was far from feeling. "A great deal of trouble has been caused this evening by those gloves. I apologize for that, Major. And I assure you that no one in this house has the least interest in what you and your friends are saying now, or at any time." She swept regally past him.

"I look forward to seeing the infamous tan gloves on your beautiful hands," he called softly after her.

It was on the tip of her tongue to say she would burn them first, but she clamped her lips tight and ascended the stairs without looking back.

Sylvie was in her room when she came up, and Rebecca studied her as she latched the door. "Now that I have perjured myself for you this evening, I would be grateful if you would supply an explanation for the necessity."

"I really did stumble against that chest, Miss Rebecca. Those carved legs stick out at an awful angle." Sylvie's eyes slid away from Rebecca's gaze.

"I see. Now I'm forced to sound like the unpleasant major, and ask *why* you were stumbling around that chest."

"You heard me tell those men, miss. I was looking for some of your gloves."

Rebecca sat down at the dressing table and began pulling hairpins out of her coiffure. Perhaps if she weren't glaring at the girl it would be easier to get the truth. "Since the tan gloves I mentioned are tucked safely in the drawer beside me, I have to wonder which ones you were looking for." She glanced in the mirror and saw a desperate look cross Sylvie's face before the girl bowed her head.

"I thought it was the ivory kid pair you wanted cleaned. And I had not seen them."

Rebecca brushed her hair quickly. It was true she'd soiled the ivory gloves last week. She had mentioned the fact to Sylvie, too. But those gloves were near the bottom of her drawer right now. It was possible, she supposed, that Sylvie had looked for them in a sudden excess of zeal, and had not found them. But that hardly explained a night search for them downstairs. Slowly she stood up and began undressing. "Surely you could have looked this afternoon, or waited until morning."

"I should have, miss. I'm sorry." Sylvie came to help her disrobe.

Rebecca looked at her as she unfastened tiny buttons, and realized with a start that Sylvie, for perhaps the first time in all the years she'd known the girl, looked positively sullen. There was nothing else she was going to say on the subject, no matter what Rebecca did. With a sigh she gave up. Less and less did she understand her maid.

When she was ready for bed, Sylvie cleared the room efficiently and snuffed the candles. At the doorway, her soft voice floated back to the big bed. "Thank you very much, Miss Rebecca." Then she was gone.

The following afternoon, as Rebecca sat in Uncle Julian's room reading *Roderick Random* again, she realized he hadn't coughed for several minutes. She looked over at the bed and saw her uncle had fallen into another fitful doze. The book dropped to her lap and she put her head back to ease her tired muscles. Then slowly she turned her head to look out the window. It was one of those heavy gray days that spoke of an intense fall storm, and she watched the churning clouds with pleasure. She'd never seen such weather patterns before coming to America, and she'd delighted in the rapid, often startling changes the sky could display in Westchester. Here in New York the effect was not so great among the buildings, but right now the large patch of sky she could see was in fascinating turmoil. She stood up and went to the window.

Down in the street several matrons scurried for cover before the storm broke. A horse carriage rumbled past, its driver pulling the high collar of his coat close around his head as he slapped the reins on the horses' backs. Idly, she followed the carriage's progress to the far corner where it turned north. Beyond its big wheels a figure in gray moved, bending close to a much taller form wrapped completely in a drab cloak that looked as though it had once belonged to a portly gentleman.

With sudden interest, Rebecca leaned forward. The figure in gray was Sylvie. Who on earth was she talking to on the street? Whoever it was, he didn't wish to be recognized, for a large misshapen hat, such as a farmer might wear in the hot sun, totally covered his head and the collar of his cloak was pulled up to the hat brim. Still, there was something disturbingly familiar about the man.

As she watched, the two moved out of sight. Then Sylvie reappeared alone, walking slowly. Rebecca frowned. If Sylvie had a new lover in New York, it was no matter. But if this man she'd just met accounted for her odd behavior, it was something to worry about. Still, how to explain that the cloaked figure was vaguely familiar? A sudden thought jolted her. Could it be Seth who had somehow found a way to be near Sylvie here in the city? Was that why he looked familiar? But why wouldn't Seth come openly to see Sylvie? Her mind whirled as she watched the maid approach the house.

Then a splash of red in the corner of her vision made her look the other way. A scarlet-clad officer was crossing the street toward the house. The officer raised his head, and with relief she saw it was Charles. Quickly she checked that Uncle Julian still slept, then she slipped from the room to go downstairs.

"I'm sorry I couldn't come yesterday." Charles caught at her hand in the hall and pulled her into the drawing room, where he held her at arm's length. "You're looking more beautiful than ever, I think. So you really must be feeling better."

"Yes, yes, I am," she replied, laughing. "I'm sorry to have been such a bore these last days."

"Never were you that. You had me worried, though." He led her to the settee and watched as she arranged the skirt of her lilac dress. Sitting down beside her, his face sobered. "Now that I see you in good health again, I can tell you my news with less reluctance."

Rebecca met his gaze warily. "News? What news?"

"I'm being sent out of New York." The girl's eyes clouded, and Charles leaned over her solicitously. "It is nothing dangerous, I assure you."

Rebecca barely heard him. She was fighting to hide the relief she felt at learning his news had nothing to do with Alex or with last night's events here. "Where are you going?" She forced concern into her voice.

"I'm being sent with a special detachment to chase marauding rebels in central New Jersey. And from there we go on to join General Howe in Philadelphia."

Having conquered her fears, Rebecca could concentrate on what he was saying. "Oh dear, Charles. Will you be gone very long?"

"I don't know. We have waited for reinforcements here in New York. If they don't arrive soon, I imagine we'll be needed back here more than in Philadelphia. Sir Henry is preparing to march north. Someone will have to protect the city in his absence."

"Then you may come back within short weeks. I'm so glad. But you will be careful, won't you, Charles?"

"Of course I will. With you to come back to, any man would be a fool to take undo risks." She smiled at him then, and his breath caught in his throat. He looked as though he wanted to snatch her to him, but he coughed and took one of her hands. "You must take no risks either, Rebecca."

"Why, what risks could I take in New York?"

"I overheard Major Tyson and another man at headquarters this morning. They sounded angry over some incident that occurred in this house last night; something to do with Sylvie."

Rebecca snatched her hand back. "They are determined to make much of an innocent misunderstanding, and I've heard more than enough about it already." Charles looked hurt at her tone, and she relented. "It was an unpleasant scene, thanks to Major Tyson's suspicious mind. Sylvie had simply gone looking for my gloves, and that foolish man acted as though she'd been *spying* on him."

"I gathered it was something like that. And I am sure that it was perfectly innocent. But do not underestimate Warren Tyson, my dear. He is not a fool. He has moved into your house now, and it might be wise to get along with him."

"I doubt I can ever get along with Major Tyson."

Charles was exasperated. "So you made clear the other evening at the ball. You spoke then in a most unguarded fashion."

"He is a turncoat, Charles. He has betrayed men who trusted him."

"Rebels," he spat and stood up to pace in front of her. "He is *not* a turncoat. His allegiance has always remained the same."

"Then he should not have worn the uniform of the Continental Army," she snapped.

Charles threw up his hands. "He is a friend of mine, Rebecca. Have you forgotten that it was he and his men who carried me to Dobbs Ferry Road to get help when I was wounded?"

"No, I haven't forgotten. Nor have I forgotten he was acting under orders."

"Whose orders?"

Rebecca drew a long breath. "Colonel Meade's orders. I was there. I heard them."

Charles's face darkened for an instant. Then he shrugged. "Warren is fighting for what he thinks is right, as we all are. He is becoming powerful at headquarters. You would be well advised not to run afoul of him."

"I'll remember, Charles." She spoke softly, and he came to stand just above her.

Reaching out, he pulled her to her feet. "Oh, Rebecca, I did not come here to argue with you. I came to say good-bye."

"You are leaving soon then?"

"Tomorrow morning. And I must go now. There is so much to be done before we march. But I promise to return as soon as possible."

"I shall miss you, Charles." She looked at the firm lines of his familiar face and reflected that she really would miss him.

"I'm glad," he said simply, and kissed both her hands. "Knowing you are safe here is a thought that will sustain me. You won't let anyone turn your head while I'm away, will you?"

"There is not another scarlet uniform that could interest me seriously," she replied with perfect honesty.

Words seemed to fail him at that, and he gave way to his former impulse. Pulling her close, he leaned down and kissed her, holding her gently, as though she were fragile.

His mouth was warm on hers, hesitant and passionate at the same time. Rebecca longed to have him crush her to him. She wanted him to command her emotions, force her to forget everyone and everything else. But Charles, always the gentleman, had learned his lesson the other evening. He would not risk giving offense to her now. Reluctantly he raised his head and, gripping her arms, put her away from him.

"I'll be back," he promised huskily, and walked out the door.

The squall yesterday evening had cleared the air to a fresh autumn crispness, and had cleaned the cobblestones of dust and debris. It felt good to walk briskly through the noonday sun, Rebecca thought, as she lifted her skirts to avoid small puddles at the bases of buildings and between the stones of the paving. Now if only Sylvie, tramping along behind her through the crowds, would act less withdrawn, more like her old self. There had been a time when the girl would have scurried at her side, exclaiming over each sight they passed. But increasingly, it had become harder to talk to Sylvie, about even the most commonplace things. Today Rebecca didn't even try. The girl was more remote than ever, perhaps because Rebecca had questioned her last night about the man

276

she had met on the street. Sylvie had laughed, saying it was only a tradesman who was becoming too ardent, but Rebecca had thought there was a false ring to the words. She'd kept her own counsel, though, not wanting to upset the girl. And she'd wondered if she weren't becoming too suspicious anyway. Major Tyson's presence in the house had put her nerves on edge.

At the familiar corner of Fair and William, Rebecca turned toward the North Church and pulled the hood of her cloak closer around her face. In just the few days she had been bringing food to Alex, she could see the difference it had made. He was still gaunt, but the hollows in his cheeks were less pronounced, and his eyes had begun to look less glazed with hunger and suffering. If only he could get more exercise and some fresh air, too, he would lose some of that ghastly pallor the jailed men all had.

"Miss Rebecca!" Sylvie came up to her at the corner. From under her wide cloak she brought the narrow basket of ham and fresh carrots stolen from the kitchen this morning. "Will you go alone today? I have an . . . an errand I must do for Mr. Kent."

Rebecca looked her surprise. "Can't it wait until we leave the church?"

"He found we were going, you see. And he might think it odd if I am so long about it. I won't be gone more than a few minutes, honestly. It's just back there a way." She waved vaguely behind her. "A merchant's order, he said. I can be back at the steps before you ever come out."

Rebecca did not relish the thought of going to the prison doors alone, and would have argued, but she knew she was already late. Mrs. Allen had kept Sylvie from retrieving the stolen food this morning by standing right at the closet door to talk to one of the maids. "We can go together to this merchant," she said, but she was already taking the basket Sylvie thrust at her.

"I will be back in just a few minutes," the girl repeated, folding Rebecca's cloak over the little hamper. Then she turned and crossed the street before Rebecca could say any more.

Really, Rebecca thought, the girl had got completely out of line. Sylvie knew her mistress couldn't call out to her right here. Her new-found independence was becoming difficult to deal with. She turned and hurried toward the church steps, only to see visitors beginning to push back into the bright sunlight. The two soldiers lugged the barrels out the door as the sergeant swung his chain at a prisoner who didn't move back fast enough. Rebecca winced and darted forward, trying to reach the big doors before they were shut. But she was too late. Before she reached the top of the steps, they slammed with a resounding thud.

She stood for a moment, staring at them, wondering what Alex was thinking of her for not coming today. There was nothing she could do, though. She'd have to explain tomorrow. Already the sentries were pushing back the last of the crowd. She turned away, and remembered Sylvie. From where she stood she could just make out the gray cloak disappearing down Fair Street, nearly two blocks off. She would catch up to her, not wait here on the open steps for the girl to return.

She hurried across the intersection and nearly missed seeing the cloak turn off the street ahead. Hugging the basket and her hood close, she began to run lightly after. When she reached the place she'd seen Sylvie turn she was startled to discover it was an alley, not a shop. But she was sure this was the place. What was Sylvie doing going down an alley? All her suspicions about Sylvie's odd behavior floated up in her mind and she stepped into the narrow way determined to find the girl and call her to account.

Rebecca ran on in time to see her maid crossing the next street. More curious than ever, she did not call out, but moved even faster. They were at the edge of a ruined section of the city now, going toward the bay. What could Sylvie be doing? There were no reputable merchants anywhere around here.

As the thought went through her mind, the girl entered a doorway in a half-burned building. Rebecca looked up and down the street. An old man squatted by a shelter made of canvas across the way, scratching at his head. She could hear the shrill voice of a woman somewhere nearby scolding a child. But at the moment the short street was otherwise deserted. Cautiously, she stepped through the doorway Sylvie had entered and eyed dark stairs leading into deeper gloom above her.

She was wondering if she dared ascend those stairs when a hand closed over her mouth.

Chapter 26

A wiry arm went around her, pinning her arms to her sides, and slowly she was forced to move toward the stairs. She struggled for breath beneath the tight hand over her face, too frightened to resist the strong arm that dragged her along. Awkwardly they mounted to the floor above. In front of a battered wooden door, the man halted.

"Oh, no." From the gloom near the door Sylvie's horrified whisper seemed to bounce and echo off peeling plaster walls.

Rebecca twisted in the man's arms, straining to see in the dim light.

A hissing voice in her ear said, "Not a sound out of you, miss."

Sylvie came forward then. "Oh, Miss Rebecca, *why* did you follow me?"

Rebecca fought to answer but the hand clamped more firmly over her mouth. A booted foot kicked gently at the door panels. From inside the room Rebecca heard stealthy steps. "It's Davey, Mr. Corbet."

Sylvie stood, wringing her hands as the door opened just wide enough for her to slip through. Rebecca heard her mutter something. There was a low command, then Sylvie's voice. "Davey has Miss Blair. She followed me." There was an oath, and the door opened wider.

Almost limp with fear, Rebecca was propelled through the narrow opening. The room was shabby and small. A bare, splintered floor supported a table, two wooden chairs and a lopsided washstand. The one window filtered gray light through dusty panes, serving only to give harsh effect to the sparse furnishings. A big man dressed in a brown jerkin over a rough linen shirt hunched over the table, his back to them. Draped on a chair next to him was a voluminous drab-colored cloak. Beyond, another door led into an equally small room. He didn't turn around as Rebecca was forced to the center of the floor.

"Get her out of here," he growled in a hoarse voice. "Leave her on a street somewhere."

"I can't do that, Mr. Corbet." Davey's voice was little more than a whisper. "She followed Sylvie here. She knows this place now."

"We'll move. She hasn't seen you. Get her out!"

"What if she talks about Sylvie's coming here?"

There was a long silence. Rebecca tried to shake her head to indicate she wouldn't say a word. She saw the big man's fist clench on the table top, and his black head bowed lower. She stared at the hand, mesmerized.

Sylvie darted across the floor. "She saved me the other night, sir. She won't say anything if we explain."

The large hand descended on the table with controlled force, making only a hollow thump in the little room. "Get her out!" the strange voice grated.

Rebecca was still staring at the big form by the table, and her heart was beginning to pound with something more than fright. Davey began backing to the door as Sylvie laid an imploring hand on the man's arm. Rebecca moved close against her captor till he reached for the handle. As the door began to creak open, she kicked backward and threw herself against the arm that still held her. Caught off balance, the man stumbled and snatched at her. She twisted and heard her cloak tear. Tugging at the ribbons that held it, she pulled away and the cloak was stripped from her shoulders. Davey lunged, but she was already across the room.

"No," she cried, and both hands came out to hold the big man's arm. He tried to look away, but she pushed at his arm, turning him. "Gordon," she whispered.

Hard blue eyes looked into hers. Slowly he uncurled her fingers from his arm and stood straight. "You should have gone, Miss Blair," he said in his normal voice, but there was a cold edge to it.

Tears made her violet eyes glisten. She blinked, trying to hold them back. "You're alive. My God, you're alive." She could only stand, drinking in the sight of him, the wonder of it.

"A bitter disappointment to you, no doubt."

"How can you say that?" Her voice was as low as his.

"Or perhaps you envisioned only prison for me that day you joined the redcoats and discussed McHenry's farm with them."

"Discussed ... What are you talking about?" She felt hysteria welling as the cold eyes raked her face. He looked so angry, so ruthless.

As though some pent-up force was seeking escape, his hands gripped her arms. She winced under the pain and searched his face imploringly, but saw only fury and disgust. "Or perhaps you merely joined the army and let Tyson do the work of informing on us."

"Informing on you? Oh, my God," she repeated, feeling her legs begin to give way under her. "You think I told the British you were going to the farm; that I had you ambushed." Her knees buckled then, and she collapsed onto a rickety chair, his hands still digging into her arms. The tears wouldn't be stopped now, but she made no effort to brush them away. He'd thought all these long months that she had betrayed him, that she was *capable* of such an act, after what they'd shared at Halscomb. Mutely she stared into his opaque eyes.

"So you do know there was an ambush. Did you and Tyson plan it together, or did you go on your own?" he asked, but his voice was not quite steady now. He shook her lightly, as though he could spill the truth from her mouth.

Rebecca was still in shock at discovering Gordon was alive. The tears went on streaming down her cheeks, but she managed to hold herself up as she studied his face. "What did you do to your hair?" she choked, half way between laughter and a complete breakdown into screaming hysteria.

Gordon's eyes narrowed in surprise, and she noted the fine lines at their corners. He, too, looked older, she thought. Then he shook her again, and her head snapped back. "Answer me, God damn you."

"Would it matter what I said?" she whispered, and felt as though her voice were coming from somewhere downstairs.

"No." He let go of her so fast she slumped back and heard the chair groan.

Sylvie came forward then, looking scared. "Colonel ..."

His blazing eyes rounded on her, and she stopped in confusion. Davey stood behind her, an interested but wary spectator. "Mr. Corbet," she finally managed, "Miss Blair came to the village that day."

"After meeting the British on the Dobbs Ferry Road." Gordon turned away in disgust. When he looked back his voice was low and commanding. "Why did you follow Sylvie today?"

Rebecca saw her most secret dreams crumbling before her; the dreams she had locked away when she had thought this man dead. She had been right that morning last November; Gordon Meade had never cared, had used her as any hungry male might use an easily accessible female. And because he had never cared, he'd had no reason to assume he could trust her. Yet she had trusted him, until that moment in the meadow when he had sounded so callous about her fate. She had even made the tragic mistake of falling in love with him. Seeing him so suddenly just now had confirmed her fears on that score. She had never loved Charles, and perhaps she never would. She didn't question why Gordon was here now; she didn't take her thoughts that far. She thought only of the fact that he seemed to hate her and despite his hate, she loved him.

"I thought she was going to a merchant's. I didn't want to have to wait for her, so I tried to catch up," she said in a tired voice.

"Surely you realized quickly that she was going to no shop."

"Once she turned in the alley, yes." She didn't bother to say more.

"Who told you to watch Sylvie?"

"No one told me to watch Sylvie." Her voice seemed far away again.

"I'm sure that's true." The maid was between them now. "Miss Rebecca knew nothing of why I was downstairs when officers were at the house the other night, and yet she lied for me, made the men believe her. She saved me then." She backed up at the look on Gordon's face. "It's true," she said.

Rebecca smiled suddenly. "You *were* listening at that door. You were *spying*." Her voice cracked on a high note, and she giggled.

Gordon's hand shot out and slapped her so hard she nearly fell from the chair. Fresh tears started from her eyes and she covered her face, her head swimming with pain. Her hysteria was gone, and a healthy fear took its place. She huddled before him, waiting for the next blow. Rough hands jerked her to her feet and dragged her across the room. At the door to the next room, she felt her lacy fichu, tucked so modestly into her low bodice, being drawn away. She looked up, automatically trying to catch it.

Gordon whipped it into the air and smiled unpleasantly. "One more sound out of you, and I shall strangle you." He twirled the long scarf to make a rope of it, flicked it in front of her face and backed out of the room.

Paralyzed with horror, Rebecca stood still and watched the door close. A murmur of voices came to her through the thin planks as slowly her breathing returned to a normal rate. She looked around quickly then. She didn't want to wait for Gordon's return.

The little room was even smaller than its neighbor, she discovered; more like a cell than a room. And it was bare but for a lumpy pallet in one corner of the floor. A single window looked out on the wall of another charred building and appeared as though it had not been opened in years. She backed around the room, feeling trapped and desperate till she came once more to the door.

"Sylvie," she heard Gordon say. "I do not wish to discuss Miss Blair or anything else. I want what you came here to tell Davey, and I want it quickly."

Sylvie's voice was an indistinct mumble. It seemed to go on and on as Rebecca flattened herself against the door, listening. When Gordon had heard her out, what would he do then?

At last Sylvie stopped, and there was a long silence. Then Gordon's voice said, "Good." Another silence, as Rebecca strained against the panels, her heartbeat sounding loud in her ears. Then Gordon was talking again, and this time she could make out only part of what he said. It all had something to do with the back room of Mr. James Rivington's tavern. She knew Mr. Rivington to be the publisher of the *Royal Gazette*, a staunch Tory newspaper, and she'd heard he owned a tavern as well. What could Gordon have to do with such a man? It soon became clear, from the snatches she heard, that Gordon had less than nothing to do with Rivington, that he was interested only in the back room of that tavern, where he claimed, a new batch of counterfeit Continental money was being stored on its way from Long Island printing presses to British headquarters. From there it would be handed in bagfuls to any willing food suppliers who would carry it back to the areas outside New York City. Rebecca lost the next part, for her mind was riveted by what she'd heard. If great quantities of counterfeit money were to be let loose in the colonies, it would drive even lower the value of the already shaky Continental currency.

"It won't stop the flow of false money" she heard Gordon say now, "but at least we might make Mr. Rivington pause before accepting any more of the paper money for safe-keeping. And it has to be tonight. The money won't be there for long. I learned of it only this morning. I want it destroyed." She heard what sounded like a fist banging on the table, and jumped.

Davey and Sylvie both said something, and a moment later footsteps crossed the floor. Then the outer door creaked again. Were they all leaving? Panic at the thought of being left alone in this place made Rebecca snatch her door open, only to find Gordon Meade blocking her path. With a gasp, she fell back and tried to close it again, but his foot jammed the flimsy door and pushing at it firmly, he came on.

She backed before him, shaking her head. In his hands he held the scarf from her throat, and one hand was twisted in the material. Her foot struck the pallet and she stumbled, fetching up against the wall. For a horrible instant she wondered if her last sight was to be Gordon's harsh yet beautiful face as he wrapped the scarf around her neck. She closed her eyes and swayed.

A hand gripped her arm, and she tried feebly to pull away. Then she felt the chignon on top of her head being tugged. She jerked away and felt her hair tumble forward over her face and shoulders. Gordon's hand lifted her chin and her eyes flew open.

"Treacherous, but so beautiful." His voice was hoarse.

Her lips parted to speak, to deny his words, but her mouth was too dry with fear to form her thoughts.

"Becky," he said with a groan, and caught her trembling body to his broad chest.

She went rigid in his arms, fearing some new humiliation, some new pain. But then his hand cupped her chin again and his lips found hers. Surprise held her stiff until his mouth moved, brushed her cheek and returned to kiss her insistently. A warmth began to flood over her, a memory of his body, of his low voice, of her response to him long ago. And slowly, tentatively, her arms came up to circle his neck.

When he raised his head, his eyes were hooded, but the hard lines of his face were still there. "Damn you," he said very softly.

His fingers traced the line of lace on her bodice, leaving a trail of fire across her skin. "Oh, Gordon, you don't believe I had anything to do with the ambush, do you?" Her wide eyes held his, willing him to answer her.

"Why did you leave that morning?"

She shivered under his still-moving fingers, and tried to step back, but the wall blocked her. "I . . . I heard you say it would be better if I'd gone with Charles. I knew I was only an encumbrance to you. And then I began to worry about Charles, lying alone beside the road. I couldn't just leave him."

"So you galloped off to his aid." His hands were still now.

"I never found him. But the army was coming down the road. My horse bolted across it, right in front of a column of troops." She shuddered with the memory of her fright. "I had nowhere to go then but to the village. I went to Seth Adams's house, where Sylvie was staying." She felt him start, but she went on, the words tumbling out with more confidence now that he held her. "We learned Halscomb was taken by the British. I had nowhere to go. I knew you'd left the area. So Seth and Sylvie brought me into the city. I found Uncle Julian at Mr. Kent's townhouse, and we've been there ever since. All these months, wondering where you were. And then . . . then two months ago I heard you'd been killed that day."

"How on earth did you hear that?"

"I was at a party. Major Tyson was there. Oh, Gordon, did you know that awful man is here in New York, holding the same rank under Sir Henry Clinton?"

Gordon's face was grim. "Yes, I'd heard that."

"He told Charles that you'd been left for dead."

The man's arms stiffened around her. "So the revered Captain Revington is in New York also?"

Rebecca nodded. "Yes. He was transferred here in May."

This is your cue, Gordon thought. She is still being courted by her Charles, is thick with redcoat officers. He tried to let her go then, but her oval face, turned up to him so trustingly, held him like a magnet. He looked at the sensual mouth, quivering only inches away, and he was lost. Be damned to her Charles, he thought savagely, feeling his body's aching need for her. Dimly he was aware he was breaking every one of his own rules for survival in the dangerous game he was playing, and as her lips responded to his, he put his hands in the thick silk masses of her hair and drew her head closer.

Rebecca was as lost as he. Gone was her fear of only moments before; gone were the months of agonizing worry and of even more agonizing desolation. This was no dream. He was holding her, kissing her, and the war, the world of New York, even the shabby room, ceased to exist for her.

"Don't ever let me go," she whispered, and felt his hands tighten in her hair, drawing her head back, making her arch toward him.

His breath was ragged as he kissed the exposed skin of her breasts. Then he was undoing the buttons at her back, pulling the shoulders of her dress down her arms, pushing at the neckline of her chemise. She gasped as the bodice fell to the floor and his hands, then his mouth, circled her breasts, making the nipples taut with the desire that was spreading through her like wildfire.

They undressed hurriedly, and he pulled her down on the heap of her skirts. His urgency was infectious as he pressed the long length of his body to hers. She moaned when he touched her hips, then her thighs, and tried to hold him closer yet. He entered her slowly, and she wrapped her legs around his, writhing beneath him with abandon. She felt him bury his face in her hair and she threw her head back, biting her lip to keep from crying out at her mounting ecstasy, and thought she would fly apart if the waves of almost unbearable sensation didn't end soon. But their need was so great they could not have prolonged their love-making if they'd tried.

When they lay still again, Rebecca heard Gordon's chuckle as though it came from a distant place. She was floating in a hazy afterglow, but his first words brought her back to the squalid little room with a jolt.

"I've done even more damage to your face and breasts than I have to your clothing, I fear."

"What do you mean?" She raised her head and tried to peer at her chest.

"The pot-black on my hair . . ."

"Oh, dear. Is *that* what you used." She fell back, smiling dreamily. "Marked for life."

"Not quite, I hope." He got up then, and with the loss of his body head, she shivered, realizing the little room was cold. "Miraculously, there is some water in that crumbling pitcher out there. I'll try to make your face, at least, less smudged. The rest we can cover. Put some clothes on. You'll freeze."

Rebecca sat up and her eyes widened. "Gordon! Your chest!" She had not noticed before the great pale scar that angled from his shoulder across his collarbone and down to his ribs on his right side.

"A small memento of the day I last saw you." He pulled on his clothes and left for the water.

She wished she hadn't said anything. He'd withdrawn from her now. She could feel it, and the thought made her grow nearly ill with longing.

When he returned, Rebecca was almost dressed, and she knew as soon as she looked at him that she'd been right. His eyes, so tender only minutes before, were remote, his face set in the hard lines she'd seen earlier. With an expertise she remembered, he refastened her dress. Then he set to work washing her face without a word.

"I'm afraid it isn't perfect," he said at last, standing back to survey his handiwork. "And there's nothing to be done for your chic hairstyle, I'm afraid." He almost smiled. "Sylvie will be back any moment, though. She can cope."

Rebecca tried to match his casual tone. "How did you get into New York, Gordon?"

"Very quietly."

"Will you be staying here?" She looked around the room with distaste.

"No. I have to go back."

Rebecca felt her heart constrict. "Sylvie was giving you information, wasn't she? She's been spying for you."

"Not for me, precisely. I arrived only yesterday."

"Then who is she working for?" Gordon's face closed even more at the question, but she took hold of his hands. "All right. Don't tell me that, but at least tell me, if you know, how long she has been doing this."

"Why do you ask that?" His right hand pulled from her grasp and moved up to stroke her cheek. But his eyes were wary.

"It would explain so much, you see. She has been acting odd for months; forgetful, almost secretive. I thought it was

287

only that she was dreaming of Seth. But when I offered to send her back to Dobbs Ferry to him, she refused."

"She won't refuse much longer. She tells me that Tyson has moved into your house, that he nearly jailed her the other night."

"He suspects her, Gordon. I didn't realize at the time that he was anything more than angry at being disturbed. But now I understand. I'm not sure he'd let her leave, even if she was willing."

His hand had settled on her shoulder, but he was looking past her at the dirty panes of the window. Almost to himself he said, "She can't come with me. It is too dangerous. I'll ask Davey to find a way. Perhaps I can help before I leave."

"When do you go?"

"Soon. I have one piece of unfinished business first."

"The counterfeit money at James Rivington's?"

His eyes refocused on her face abruptly. "You heard that? Yes, there's the money. But Davey and others will see to that."

"*Not* Major Tyson?"

His hand, still on her shoulder, curled into a fist. "No, not the treacherous major. If I could get to him, I would . . . But I can't jeopardize my mission by killing one of Sir Henry's officers. Not yet."

"Is there anything I can do?" she asked quietly.

"You?" His hand dropped hers and he stepped back. "The one way you can help is to keep absolutely silent about all that happened here today." His face was suddenly harder than ever. "And if you don't, I will find you, and I will strangle you as I threatened."

Her eyes clouded, but she did not look away. Her body still tingled from his touch, and she knew suddenly she was set on an irrevocable path. His threat was empty. Hadn't he just made love to her with a tenderness, a passion that belied his cruel words? She longed to hold him, to somehow erase the harsh lines on his face. She was completely shameless, she thought, for she would do anything, use anything to have him. "I don't care about politics, Gordon, I care only about you."

He looked as though he'd answer her, but he turned away instead. "Go back to your Tory captain, Rebecca. Forget you ever saw this house or me."

"I like it better when you call me Becky."

"God damn it, girl." His fist smashed into the flimsy doorframe, making the wood jump and rattle. "I have to find Alex, and I have to leave New York. If I am discovered anywhere between here and Peekskill, I will hang from the first tree."

"Alex!" The name cut across his explosive words. Rebecca ran to him. "You haven't seen him?"

Bitterly, Gordon shook his head. "I don't even know where he is. But I'll find him."

Rebecca almost laughed with a sudden heady sensation. "You may not trust me yet, but if you will kiss me, I will tell you where he is."

Gordon spun around, nearly knocking her off balance. He grabbed her then, a wild light jumping into his bright blue eyes. "You've seen him?"

She nodded eagerly. "Nearly every day for a week."

He kissed her, hard and fast, but when he would have let her go, she held his face. "Not quite good enough, Colonel Meade." She pouted and stood on tiptoe to reach his mouth. He chuckled softly, and this time he kissed her thoroughly, taking her breath away. She felt his body tensing with desire again, and she wanted to respond with all her heart. But at last she drew away.

"He's in the North Church," she said.

Chapter 27

Gordon paced the floor. He'd be like a caged lion, if it weren't for his blackened hair, Rebecca thought, and smiled.

"The North Church is only blocks from here," he was saying.

"Yes. That's where I was when Sylvie left me to come here today."

Gordon returned to her. "What does he look like? How is Alex?"

"He's all right. But it's a dreadful place. Men die in there, and they just dump the bodies outside to be carted away the next day. All the prisoners are kept on starvation rations. Sylvie says that the men in charge of them take half their alotted food and sell it elsewhere for their own gain."

"A time-honored practice of kindly souls like the provost marshal."

"We've taken food to Alex. He's already looking a bit stronger." She savored the new light in his eyes, the softening of the deep lines by his mouth. "Today I was too late to see him. There's a basket somewhere in the lower hall that has ham and raw carrots for him." She would talk forever if it would keep him looking at her this way.

A noise at the door made Gordon move, shattering the moment. From thin air, it seemed, a knife appeared in his hand and he motioned her back. Quickly, he went to the door, heard something, and opened it. Sylvie walked into the room, behind her the man named Davey. He was a short man, Rebecca saw for the first time, thin and stooped, with a seamed face and rough curly hair only partially controlled by the tight ribbon at the back of his neck. He wasn't what he seemed though, as she had reason to know. For all his scrawny looks, he was as tough as a steel band. She wondered what he did for a living. Or was he in the army like Gordon?

The two men were talking in an undertone, and Sylvie crossed to her mistress. "We'll have to go back now, miss."

Rebecca saw her maid look at her loose hair, and she felt her face begin to burn. "My cloak will hide my lack of hairstyle, won't it?"

Sylvie nodded, keeping her face straight.

Rebecca flushed again, and tried to take her mind off Gordon. "Am I right in supposing you've been spying for the rebels for some time?"

"Ever since we came to New York. But not spying, exactly. Only passing on any information I could."

"Sylvie, that was so dangerous." Rebecca was horrified. "All those officers in the house all the time . . ."

"That was why I was needed. But it wasn't anything dangerous, until that Major Tyson arrived. Remember all that sewing I was always forgetting?" Rebecca looked mystified. "I left messages inside and a man would reach through the fence there at the arbor and collect them at sundown."

Rebecca sighed. "And here I thought you were just pining away for Seth."

"I have been that too, Miss Rebecca. But he needed me down here."

"You mean Seth Adams is in this business too?"

Sylvie put a finger to her lips. "We must go, miss."

"Wait a minute." Rebecca had only the haziest idea of what Sylvie and the men were doing, but she remembered Gordon's words about being lynched if he were caught, and she remembered Warren Tyson's dark suspicions and sly questions. Sylvie could not stay at Queen Street. It was too dangerous for her.

Gordon and Davey were still talking, but they broke off as Rebecca approached. Up close, Davey's face showed not only the seams of age, but scars from a long-ago case of smallpox, she noticed, and suddenly she had a crazy idea.

Gordon saw her examination of Davey's face, and his brow furrowed. "What are you thinking?"

"I just realized how we might remove Sylvie from the city."

He cocked his head at her, smiling indulgently. "Suppose you let us worry about that."

"You had any thoughts, Mr. Corbet?" Davey's laconic look shifted between the two of them.

"Not yet."

The stooped man nodded. "I don't want the girl around here any more. She's been pointed at, and once that happens it's just a matter of time."

"How much time is the question."

"Warren Tyson is a shrewd, self-serving man. If he thinks Sylvie is anything but a lady's maid, he will stop at nothing to pin the label of spy on her—gain himself a little glory. She wouldn't be the first woman who has helped our cause, and well he knows it. So the sooner she's away from Queen Street the safer we'll all be."

"If Major Tyson really suspects me, will he try to stop me?" Sylvie's brown eyes were nearly black with worry.

"Could be."

"But what if he thought she had a dread disease?" Three sets of eyes swiveled in surprise, and Rebecca went on. "If we can convince people Sylvie may have smallpox, they will *not* want her around."

"They'd send her to a ward in one of the hospitals."

"I could insist that she not be taken to one of those places."

"Even if they did send her, she could up and walk out of a hospital. Maybe I could get her away then." Davey rubbed his long chin. "Main thing is to get her out of Mr. Kent's house."

"I might even obtain a pass for her through the lines at Kingsbridge," Rebecca put in, "though who would drive her out of the city?"

No one spoke for several moments as Sylvie clasped her hands anxiously. Then Gordon's eyes looked hard at Rebecca. "How would you get that pass for Sylvie?"

"If I have to go to Sir Henry himself, I will. But I'm quite certain I can do it. We are a most respected loyalist household, remember."

"You certainly are." Gordon's mouth quirked and he fell silent again. "All right," he stated a minute later. "You get that pass for Sylvie and for a driver. Give him any name you like. Davey, are you still able to pick up messages at the fence at Kent's place?"

"No one's stopped me yet."

"Then, Rebecca, leave a message for Davey. Tomorrow'd be too soon. Two days from now. Sylvie will have her cart and a driver."

They talked for several more minutes, then Davey led the way out of the room. As he and Sylvie slipped through the door, Rebecca turned back. "Will I see you again soon, Gordon?" she asked in a whisper.

His face, under the plastered black hair, was sober as he touched her cheek. "I can promise nothing, Becky. You will find your life easier if you take my advice and go back to take tea with your captain."

She wanted to cry out that she couldn't do that any more, that she wanted only to go with him, but she knew it was useless to ask. "Will you send me a message?"

"No. I don't think so. Becky, I have to leave New York. I may never return. And you *must* forget you ever heard of me or of Davey once Sylvie is gone. Promise me that."

"How could I promise a thing like that?" Her voice was low and anguished.

Gordon flinched, but he took her shoulders and turned her. "You *must*, Becky." Then he pushed her after the two shadowy forms going down the stairs.

At a shop just three blocks away, Rebecca made several hasty purchases to account for her long absence from the house. What she would do with the homely ribbons and the yards of brown satinet she didn't know, but she was glad of the bundles she would carry into the house. Briskly then, she and her maid walked down Queen Street till they were nearly home. As they approached the door, Sylvie's steps faltered and she put a hand to her head. Solicitously, Rebecca took her arm and urged her the last half block.

At the door an interested footman watched the mistress support her maid into the hall and call for Mrs. Allen.

"Sylvie is unwell," she told the housekeeper when she appeared a moment later. "Please see she is taken to her room. I shall be along directly." She gave Sylvie over to the woman's care and hastened upstairs with her packages, hoping the hood of her cloak had managed to hide most of her dishevelment.

Inside her room she threw the bundles on the bed and stood, breathing deeply. The canopied bed with its gaily colored silk quilt rolled at the foot, the floral wallpaper, the pretty rosewood furniture and the yellow silk drapes were all so familiar, so comfortable looking. She felt she was waking from a dream. Slowly she removed her cloak, then she went to sit down before her mirror. The image that looked back at her showed that her memories were not imagination. Her hair was in complete disarray, and on her cheek and neck faint dark smudges still showed where Gordon's blackened hair had rubbed against her pale skin. Gordon! She touched her mouth and could almost feel his kiss. Her eyes glittered back at her with a brilliant new light. For a moment, she sat still, remembering. Then she shook herself and began brushing her hair. She had now embarked on a dangerous charade, and she must see it through.

Searching for a ribbon to tie back her thick hair, she allowed only a minute for the thought that she too was now in danger. She had done the unthinkable, had fallen in love with a rebel, a man opposed to the necessary order of things as she and all good loyalists saw them, and one who might be killed at any instant if he was discovered out of uniform behind British lines. Further, she had involved herself with rebel spies, and if she were caught, she would share whatever fate awaited such people. She tied the bow at her neck and tugged it tight. She'd told Gordon she would get Sylvie out of here, and that was what she meant to do. Thinking about consequences would make her hesitate, and hesitation could be fatal around someone like Warren Tyson.

Even Mr. Kent, usually so wrapped up in his business he scarcely noticed what went on around him, became aware of how abstracted Rebecca was at dinner that evening.

"My dear, you're only toying with your food. Is something wrong? I saw Julian this afternoon, and he seemed a bit better, I thought."

"Yes, I thought so too. It isn't that, Mr. Kent. I was thinking about my maid Sylvie. I've hardly ever known her to be ill. But she's feverish and miserable now." From the corner of her eye she watched Warren Tyson lift his wine glass and sip delicately. She'd been cool but polite to him tonight, and thought he was not looking at her suspiciously. She would have to be careful what she said, though.

"Dear, dear. Have you called for a doctor?"

"If she does not seem better in the morning, I will. Perhaps it is nothing, really." She made an effort to eat some of the trout and the candied carrots on her plate, thinking all the while of officers she might approach for the necessary pass. If only Charles were still here.

After dinner she declined to sit with the gentlemen in the drawing room, saying she felt it her duty to return to her maid, and glad of the excuse to avoid the major, she went up the stairs immediately.

At her next meal with Mr. Kent, a cold luncheon on the following day, her host was the one to look abstracted when he came in.

"Is anything wrong?" Rebecca asked, seating herself and wondering what new worry would now be put before her.

"Eh? Oh, sorry, my dear. No, nothing is wrong. I was just thinking. Did you hear there was a fire last night at Rivington's tavern?"

Rebecca's eyes flew wide and she nearly dropped her fork.

"No, no. Don't be alarmed. It did not spread. Only ruined a storeroom at the rear of the establishment. But it made me think I should see to having more buckets of sand and water at the warehouse. These old buildings, you know."

Rebecca agreed that would be a good idea, and turned away to hide the pride and amusement she felt for Davey's work. That was one printing of counterfeit money well accounted for.

"How is that little maid of yours today? Better?"

His question brought her back from her reverie. "No, I'm afraid not, Mr. Kent." She took a deep breath and plunged. "I had Uncle Julian's doctor look at her this morning. I'm afraid we have a difficulty."

"Difficulty?" Mr. Kent didn't look awfully interested.

"Yes. You see there's a chance that Sylvie may have smallpox."

"Smallpox!" The man's face whitened. "But how?"

"I fear she met a soldier, newly come from outside the city. . . ." She let her voice trail away suggestively. Smallpox was common among the troops, especially newly arrived recruits. If Sylvie had played loose with a foot soldier, anything might have happened. Rebecca almost smiled at the memory of hot bricks and heaped quilts that had produced the desired fever on Sylvie's brow. And the quavering confession of her maid into the sympathetic doctor's ear, had planted the suspicion that had taken firm hold in the worthy man's mind from that moment.

"Oh, dear. Has the doctor removed her to a proper ward?"

"I couldn't let him." Rebecca looked horrified. "Those dreadful overcrowded places. She would never get proper care there. I will nurse her myself."

"You couldn't." Mr. Kent half rose from his chair.

"I am told I had it as a small child. I'm sure I can't get it again."

"What if you're wrong? And many of us have not had it. Besides, you will not be able to sustain such an effort. No, no, she must go to a hospital."

Rebecca, into whose mind a new and dazzling idea had jumped, looked thoughtful for a moment. "A hospital is no place for my maid," she said firmly. "But I know of a family back in Westchester who could care for her."

"In Westchester? But how could she go back there?"

"I'm sure I could persuade some kind officer to give her a pass."

Mr. Kent, appalled at the prospect of smallpox in his house, did not stop to consider the ramifications. "If a pass would get her there, I'll obtain one myself."

Rebecca's heart jumped. A perfect solution. She'd been wondering how she could hide her request from Major Tyson. If it came from Mr. Kent, it would surely not arouse the officer's suspicions. "She will need to have some means of conveyance, and a man to take her."

"I will get the necessary passes, and then we will see about how to convey your maid."

Rebecca smiled warmly at her host. "Oh, thank you, Mr. Kent." She took her final plunge, trying out the new idea. "And I would like to go with her, to see she is safely settled."

Thomas Kent stared down his broad nose at her. "You go along? No, my dear. That is carrying duty too far. I won't have you exposed to the dangers of a journey through half an army and possible marauding bands."

Rebecca argued with him, pleading she would not feel right sending Sylvie off alone, but wrung from him only a promise to discuss the matter at headquarters. Fearing she might jeopardize the whole scheme if she pushed further, the girl abandoned the battle at that, and went upstairs to wait.

There was no word that day, though. Mr. Kent had gone to headquarters to find he had to return in the morning, and before dinner, had expressed his determination to do so. The subject was not brought up at the table, but Rebecca felt nervously that Major Tyson's eyes were on her more than was warranted by the light conversation. She spent a fretful evening with Sylvie, wondering if the girl would have to make a miraculous recovery in the end, for if Major Tyson began watching them closely, they would never get her away.

She and Sylvie decided to try to stall Mr. Kent on the question of driving the maid up to Westchester. Somehow Rebecca must convince him she'd found means on her own. They agreed that it was likely that Gordon himself would be the driver. It was a good way for him to slip unnoticed through the lines. And Rebecca meant to go with him.

Her hopes were nearly dashed the next noon, though, when Mr. Kent returned triumphantly from Sir Henry's headquarters to announce that he'd obtained the passes, but that the general himself had been shocked at the thought of Rebecca going north with Sylvie. "He said you were admired by too many of his officers to be allowed to do anything so foolishly dangerous," Mr. Kent reported with finality, and Rebecca bit her lip in chagrin. The main point, she reflected, was that Sylvie was now free to go, and she'd have to think of some other method of accompanying her.

An hour before sunset she wandered into the garden and went to sit by the arbor for a space. Looking up at the high windows of the house, she waited to see if anyone watched. Then she slipped a piece of paper down between the bench and the board fence behind. Slowly, she wandered back toward the house, admiring the fall flowers along the way.

Once up in Sylvie's room she clapped her hands like a little girl. "It's done," she announced in triumph. "Now let's hope it is picked up."

Sylvie smiled wanly from her sick bed. She looked pale, Rebecca thought, and wished she dared open the window and give her some air. It was as though the trappings of illness had begun to make the girl feel the way she was supposed to. Rebecca went and sat on the bed across from her. Until now Sylvie had shared the room with a maid, but the other girl had moved out precipitously once the word "smallpox" had entered her world. "I've been wondering about Alex. What must he think of us for not showing up for three days running?"

"I'm sure our Mr. Corbet or someone else took the little basket to him," Sylvie answered. She looked over Rebecca's shoulder at the sky. "You had best go and change for dinner, miss."

"I will eat with Uncle Julian tonight, so I needn't bother. I wouldn't face that major now for anything."

"Then do not go to your uncle until nearly dark. It is then that you must see if a message has been left by the bench."

"Oh!" Rebecca jumped up, studying the sky. "In that case, I will go and sit with my uncle a while now. I'll be back by dark." She gave the girl's hand a squeeze and left, glad of the excuse to do something besides sit and worry.

When it was almost night, Rebecca stopped in the kitchen to order trays for Julian's room, and made her way quietly through the garden again. Trembling with excitement and anxiety, she groped along the back of the bench until her fingers closed on a piece of paper. In the dark she couldn't read the writing, but she could see it was a long message. Smiling, she tucked it into her bodice and went back upstairs.

Sylvie sat plucking at the covers on her narrow bed when her mistress entered the room. "I'm going to starve before ever I leave this place," she complained as soon as Rebecca had closed the door. "One of the girls who's had the pox comes up several times a day and spoons thin broth into me. It's awful."

Rebecca laughed. "I shall bring you something from my tray tonight while they're all still busy downstairs. Meanwhile, I have something to lift your spirits." She went to stand by the one candle on a little table, and unfolding the message, began to read aloud.

My Dear Sir,
It is unfortunate, but we have never yet met. However, I am now the vessel of conveyance for a piece of news that may most felicitously be of heartening interest to you. . . ."

She stopped, staring at the bold, well-formed words. "Oh, Sylvie, this is no message for us. I've never read anything so flowery, but it is meant for some merchant or broker. It talks about a shipment ready for the warehouse. Someone must have dropped it." She turned to find her maid out of bed, groping under the mattress. "What are you doing?" Her heart felt like a stone that had dropped below her stomach.

Sylvie looked up, smiling. "I will show you." In her hand was a piece of black paper whose center had been cut out in the shape of a squat hourglass. She took the letter from

Rebecca's nerveless fingers and spread it flat on the little table. Laying the black paper over it, she moved it around until, from the center of the hourglass cutout, words practically leaped from the page.

we have
conveyance
be
ready tomorrow
evening

With a gasp of delight, Rebecca read the message. "How clever. When you look at the whole letter it seems so innocuous."

Sylvie smiled again as she held the paper in the flame of the candle, watching the corner begin to brown and curl. "These masks are effective," she said simply. Then, holding up the black paper, she burned it too.

A sense of awe swept over her as Rebecca scraped up the ashes and quickly sprinkled them out the window. She shut it firmly afterwards, and tucked Sylvie back in bed. This was no light game she and her maid were playing. It was an elaborate masquerade in which lives were at stake. Without a word she left the room and went down the stairs. As she walked to her uncle's door, a slow smile curved her full mouth. If the prize at the end was Gordon Meade, any danger was worthwhile.

Chapter 28

Rebecca awoke the next morning with a dazed feeling of anticipation. She lay still for a minute, wondering why she wanted to leap from the bed. She'd been dreaming of Gordon, she knew, and her cheeks flushed with memory of her fantasies. Then she jumped up. Today was the day Sylvie was to return to Westchester, and that meant she would see Gordon again. Hurriedly she dressed in a simple white morning gown and went up to see her maid.

Sylvie was lying stoically on her bed when Rebecca arrived, but her color had not improved. "I can't stand much more of this stuffy room, miss," she said and tossed restlessly when Rebecca sat down.

"It's not much longer now."

"Only all day. Has Mr. Kent said anything more about having me carted away?"

"Not so far. And I'll stall him. Somehow I'll think of an excuse for producing a wagon myself. You are all right, aren't you, Sylvie? The trip won't be too much for you? You're not looking well."

"I'm not used to lying in bed, Miss Rebecca. I hate it. There's nothing that could sound better to me than climbing into a wagon. Though I've been worrying about leaving you. I don't like to do that."

Rebecca patted her hand. "Perhaps you shan't," she said, smiling.

Sylvie sat up with a jerk. "You did say there were passes for only two, didn't you?"

"Yes, but . . ."

"Miss Rebecca, don't you start setting your chin now. There's no way we could get you through those British soldiers if you don't have a pass. You're going to have to trust the colonel and let him decide."

"He seems to have decided already," her mistress answered with a frown. "He told me to go back to my Tory captain." She stood up. "But I can't do that, Sylvie, not any more."

"I know. But you can't gallivant out of New York in what will probably be an open wagon, either. Besides," she added shrewdly, "you need to concentrate on keeping everyone in the house from becoming suspicious. The colonel is counting on you for that."

More discussion at midday brought inspiration to Rebecca on the subject of the wagon. Taking one of the maids with her, she journeyed to a livery stable Sylvie had told her about, and there she carried on a long private conversation with the owner. The maid could now verify that Rebecca had gone to the stable, and could say, if asked, that it certainly looked as though Miss Rebecca had been bargaining for the use of a wagon.

She then spent an hour with Uncle Julian, telling herself that he really did appear to have improved, so she needn't fear for him if she left. After that she could do little but pace and wait.

It was nearing dark once more as Rebecca stood at the front windows in the drawing room watching the street with nervous eyes. She was dreading the arrival of Major Tyson, who might be here any moment, and she couldn't understand why he was late this evening. Then she saw a dilapidated farm wagon clatter over the cobblestones and turn in beside the house. The driver was a tall man, she could tell, though he slouched on the wooden seat, looking awkward and gangling. A shapeless hat was pushed below his ears, hiding his face, and he had on a baggy brown coat that made him look formless.

Her heart pounding in her ears, she turned to Mr. Kent. "The cart I told you about is here. I will go to see Sylvie is handled gently." Thomas Kent nodded, looking worried. "I won't be long. It will be a relief to all of us to know she is on her way."

"Yes." The man sighed with heartfelt agreement.

Trying to walk normally, Rebecca made her way out to the narrow stableyard. In the dim light of a single lantern she could see a stableboy holding the horse's head as the driver of the wagon climbed down. "Thank you, Danny," she said, waving him away. "You'd best go back to your supper."

Tugging on his hair, the boy retreated, and Rebecca turned to the driver. He lifted his hat a fraction, showing only the bottom half of his face, and the girl drew in her breath sharply. "Alex," she hissed. "It *can't* be."

"In the flesh," he whispered back. "And glad to be here. Now go and get your maid. We have a long ugly journey ahead of us this night."

"How did you ever escape?" Her mind was reeling.

"Gordon had friends bribe two guards; the oldest escape route in the world. It was touch and go, though. Too bad the story is not one I can tell here."

"But where is Gordon?" She felt faint with joy and disappointment at the same time.

"Gone. He had his own method for leaving the city. He gave me this for you."

Something hard was pressed into her hand, but she didn't look down. "Gone," she repeated in a lifeless voice.

Alex stooped and peered into her anguished face. "I'm sorry, Becky." He look away at nothing in particular. When he turned back the hint of a grin tugged at the corner of his mouth. "The way things are going, he may be back."

"I'm not waiting." Her voice was low but forceful. "I'm coming with you."

The grin was gone now. "You can't. Your message said passes for two people. You're going to have to trust Gordon, Rebecca. You're safer right here than anywhere we're going."

The girl thought of Major Tyson. "I'm not sure. Anyway, I don't care."

"But we do." His mouth looked firm as he seemed to decide on something. "The war can't go on forever, you know. Gordon . . ." He stopped, then said with a rush, "If you have any *real* trouble over this whole affair, if you think you are in danger, you can go to Verona Drake. I don't know her, but she's a friend of Gordon's. She might be able to help." He muttered an address on Murray Street as his eyes slid past her. "Now hush. Someone is coming. Put that thing away."

He gestured to the narrow packet in her hand. "And don't speak to me again if you value our lives." He turned to the horse's head and stood holding the bridle lazily, for all the world a bored man hired to do a distasteful job.

Rebecca stared at his back, fighting down tears. Behind her she heard men emerging from the house. Mrs. Allen must have seen the wagon arrive too, and had sent upstairs for Sylvie. The girl was carried to the small wagon, and there a bed of old quilts was made for her. Mrs. Allen hovered, and Rebecca could do little but cling to Sylvie's hand as Alex climbed onto the seat again. "Take care, Sylvie," she whispered, brushing away moisture that blurred her view of the muffled girl on the wagon bed. An answering pressure on her fingers was all there was time for. Alex whipped up the horse and they clattered out of the yard into the night.

Turning blindly back to the house, Rebecca had a sudden sense of entering a prison. Then she remembered the thin hard packet still clutched in her hand. In the hall, when the others had gone, she slipped it into her bodice. There was no time to look at it now; she must finish the charade.

Dinner was an exhausting affair. Under the sympathetic eyes of Mr. Kent and the brooding ones of Major Tyson, she had to maintain the demeanor of a sad but relieved mistress aware she'd done her duty by a beloved servant. She did an admirable job, she thought, until the major, watching her closely, announced he'd come in late this evening because there had been an escape from one of the jails. Using all the willpower she possessed, Rebecca managed to look only mildly interested in his words.

"It was from the North Church," the major went on. "Someone you will remember, Miss Blair."

"Oh?" She looked puzzled as her heart hammered. "You are teasing, of course."

"Not at all. Alexander Meade *was* the young man you visited there, wasn't he?"

"Alex?" There was no sense denying it. Tyson had seen her at the door of the prison last week. "Yes. I knew him, as you are well aware. And I did go to see him once, to try to persuade him to give his parole." Inspired, she went on the attack. "Those prisons are a disgrace, not fit for human beings. Alex is a boy. He doesn't belong there. I can't be sorry if he managed to escape."

Major Tyson was taken aback, but he pursued doggedly. "He is an officer in the rebellious army. And we will catch him. He can't have gone far."

"It's a pity he can't fly, then," Rebecca snapped, and rose from her chair. She prayed her legs would keep her moving steadily as she left the room.

But upstairs she collapsed in a heap on her bed, overcome by the efforts of the past hour and by the strain of the last few days. It was then that she recalled the little packet. Sitting up shakily, she took it out. It was a heavy piece of paper folded around something thin and hard. Carefully she unwrapped it and stared in amazement at a small knife. She'd last seen it when it materialized so suddenly in Gordon's hand that day she'd stumbled upon Sylvie's deception. It was not fancy, just a small wooden handle chased with metal and a thin short blade. She looked from it to the paper, and with misty eyes read the few words written there in familiar bold letters. "All I can leave you—in lieu of the sword you have preferred in the past. Have your captain when he returns." She blinked. How had he discovered Charles was out of the city? "But meanwhile, take care."

That was all. This little knife and a few hasty words were what she was left with after the earth-shaking discovery that Gordon was alive, after sharing another glorious moment of love with him, and after two days of fear and hope that there might be a lifetime ahead of them. Gordon had departed as silently and as abruptly as he'd appeared, and he had no intention of being in any way responsible for her.

With great care she undressed, placed the knife and the paper under her pillow and climbed onto the bed. For a very long time she lay, dry-eyed, staring at the shadows on the ceiling.

During the next two days she functioned almost without knowing it. Her only defense against renewed desolation was not to think at all. Mechanically, she oversaw the house, discussed menus with Mrs. Allen or a new ship's cargo with Mr. Kent, faced Major Tyson's black eyes and made meaningless conversation at the table. But on the third day it was her uncle who pulled her thoughts out of herself, for when she went to see him that morning he looked very ill indeed.

Frightened, she pulled covers up to his chin, plumped up

304

his pillows and listened to rasping breath that seemed to fill the room. Only yesterday he'd seemed better than ever, had played another game of chess with her by the window. She could hardly believe this was the same man. His nose seemed pinched in the middle, his cheeks looked hollow and his eyes, when he opened them briefly, seemed to bulge with the effort of getting air. If only she could breathe for him! She was suddenly thankful for the twist of fate that had held her in New York. Nothing would budge her from his side now.

Rebecca sent for the doctor immediately, but when she came back to hold Uncle Julian's hand, she knew it was no use. Her own breath began to rattle in her throat as she watched him labor to fill his lungs. By the time the doctor arrived at noon, the fight was over, and Rebecca sat holding a thin hand that was already growing stiff.

There were no tears left in her, she thought, as she allowed Mrs. Allen to lead her away from the bedside. Uncle Julian was better at last; no need to cry for him. He'd lost most of what he cared about, and did not mind dying, she was sure. The only one to cry for now was herself, left alone again. But she was beyond tears at that prospect.

Gratefully, she let Mr. Kent make all arrangements and decisions. She didn't even register surprise when a suddenly solicitous Major Tyson detailed men for the burial. And after it was over the following day, she scarcely noticed that the major was watching her constantly, touching her hand more than necessary. His only words that registered in her mind were ones about his having to be gone for a day or two. With complete apathy she bid him good-bye and retired to her room to avoid any further discussion before he left.

That night, as she climbed wearily into her bed once more, her hand touched the little knife under her pillow. "You're going to have to trust Gordon," Alex had said. But Gordon had left her only the knife, had disappeared as though the grave had swallowed him truly this time. What she was to do with herself now she didn't know. Mr. Kent had been kind and generous, insisting that she remain in his house until the war's end or until Charles came back to claim her. But the thought of maintaining a period of mourning under this roof with Major Tyson's speculative eyes always upon her, made her head ache. If only Charles had snatched her away months ago, had married her and carried her off to another home . . .

She thought of Charles with a twinge of sadness. Twice now, she had betrayed his feelings for her, and she couldn't let him think any longer that she would marry him. She didn't love him, and it wasn't fair to allow him to go on hoping. A tiny voice of common sense told her few marriages were based on initial love, that she could still make Charles Revington happy if she chose to. But she knew that now she had seen Gordon again, it was too late. If ever Colonel Meade walked back into her life, she would betray Charles again, marriage or no marriage, and that one humiliation she would spare him.

Restlessly, she twisted on the bed, her grief for Uncle Julian and her worries drowned now in a yearning need for the one man beyond her reach, the one man who had treated her so cavalierly.

The hopeless longing was still with her the next evening as she sat in her room composing the letter to Charles she knew she must send. It was a harrowing job, but it was necessary, and she felt only relief when it was done. But now she was reluctant to go to bed and face another night of churning dreams. Nightmares of Gordon's capture, or of the discovery of Sylvie and Alex were beginning to haunt her days. At night it was worse, when her need for Gordon mingled with her fears.

So lost in her tortured thoughts was she that she was only obscurely aware of voices on the stairs and the tramp of heavy boots in the hall outside. For a while thereafter all was silent, and she stood up at last, supposing she must face the night without the constricting clothes she wore. As she reached for the top buttons of her dress, the latch of her door clicked and she spun around.

Warren Tyson entered her room in stockinged feet and stood looking at her with red-rimmed eyes that were nonetheless bright with determination.

Silently, Rebecca cursed herself. Every night since the major had come to stay in this house, she'd locked her door. Tonight, absorbed in her own worries, and thinking him out of the city, she had forgotten. "I had thought you away," she said irrelevantly, annoyed yet vaguely afraid.

"As you see, I have returned, though." The major closed the door very carefully at his back and leaned on it. He'd left his heavy coat in his room, and his fine linen shirt clung to him where he was perspiring freely, emphasizing the lithe, cat-like grace that had always repelled her.

"This is hardly the hour or the place to announce your presence." She eyed him warily and took a step back. She hoped she sounded distant, even haughty. The man had been drinking; she could smell his breath from here. And she had not forgotten the last time she'd seen him drunk, back at Halscomb.

"What better place than in my lady's chamber?"

"Very well. You have shown you are returned, and no doubt we will hear of your exploits tomorrow. But the hour is late, and I had hoped to retire. Good night, Major."

"Surely that large bed becomes cold at night, Rebecca," he said softly, eyeing the turned down covers and moving toward her.

"If you take another step into my room, I shall scream," she stated calmly, trying to hold his eyes with a look of defiance.

A slow smile widened his mouth. "Perhaps. But how fortunate that Mr. Kent is out for the evening. And the servants are still belowstairs. You see, it's not really so late."

She backed again before his hot gaze. Her heart was beginning to pound with fear, and she wondered wildly how strong he was. "What do you want?" she whispered.

"Want?" The man moved again. "I want you, Rebecca. I have always meant to have you. Ever since that first time I saw you in London. Very inconvenient it was that your father died and you had to remove from the city. But when we met again in Westchester, I knew I was fated to succeed . . . in the end."

"Never," she stated, her voice filled with revulsion.

"I have been most patient, you know. But I needn't be any longer." There was a hard look to his eye that made Rebecca's breath catch as she backed once more. "You see, I now have you alone, and right where I want you."

"What do you mean?"

"It cannot have escaped your notice that I have watched you a long time."

Rebecca shuddered, but said nothing.

"I tried to warn you when I first came to stay here that you should be careful. There is no Colonel Gordon Meade to protect you. But you persisted in activities that would be of interest to Sir Henry Clinton, and I can't believe you would like me to discuss those activities with him."

"What activities?" she asked in a small voice, praying he was talking only of her food for Alex.

"Helping a spy and an escaped prisoner is a very serious offense indeed, my dear. How painful it would all be for Mr. Kent. How much more painful for you."

Rebecca thought of the stable where she'd gone to supposedly hire a wagon for Sylvie. This fiendish man must have been there, discovered she'd never hired anything. She fought down rising panic. "You are talking nonsense, Major, mere conjecture."

"Am I? In that case you have nothing to fear from the authorities, and you may now try to scream the house down. I will take you either way."

He advanced one last time and Rebecca felt the panic welling. His long hands reached for her and she twisted, stumbled on the edge of the bed and went sprawling.

With a growl of triumph Warren Tyson fell on her, his hard mouth seeking hers as she turned her head from side to side. "Rebecca," he whispered, hoarse with passion.

Her name sounded suddenly vile to her ears. But when his lips bruised her neck and he called her "Becky," she went rigid with fury. The hatred that engulfed her cleared her brain. She tried to kick him, but he laughed as he began to grope for the neckline of her dress. She hit him with her left hand, heard him grunt, felt her arm being pinned to the bed. All the while she was sliding her right hand under her pillow.

He was mouthing obscenities now, but she shut her ears and her hand closed over the little knife.

"Gordon Meade's alive," she cried, and heard her dress begin to rip as he swore. She kicked out again and he gasped as her leg hit his groin. With his free hand he slapped her. Through the stinging pain she saw his leering face rear back. There was a frenzied look to it now that was maniacal. He was going to hit her again. She closed her eyes, and with all the strength she had, she slashed with the knife.

There was a sickening impact with flesh, and the knife was nearly jerked from her hand. She pulled it free as Tyson yelled and rolled back, clutching at his arm. Instinctively, she tumbled off the bed away from him, and crouched on the floor, watching with awe the red stain that spread between his fingers. The man raised his head, and she knew she should flee, but she was paralyzed with horror at what she'd done.

"Bitch," he screamed. "I'll have you, or I'll hang you, you whore." With his good hand out, he lunged.

Chapter 29

The burning eyes of the man as he spoke broke Rebecca's paralysis. Jumping up, she ran for the door. Like a creature demented, Warren Tyson staggered after her yelling curses, his slashed arm trailing blood across the floor. Beyond thought, gripped by the greatest fear she'd ever known, Rebecca flung the door open in his face, heard it smash into his lowered head and saw him reel backward. Then she was out of the room, running down the hall, screaming soundlessly.

She didn't stop until she was on the street near the corner where she'd once seen Sylvie meet a mysterious cloaked figure. There her footsteps faltered. One hand to her mouth, she looked around wildly. The dark streets stretched before her, broken occasionally by pools of light from lanterns on tall poles. She didn't know where to go, but she knew she couldn't go back. A vision of the jail where Alex had spent harrowing months swam before her eyes. Warren Tyson would see her in one of those places, if he didn't have her hanged. He might even now be coming for her.

Turning north, she darted along the street close to the shadows of the buildings, and it wasn't until her breath gave out a few blocks farther on that she stopped again. In the dim pool of light at a corner, she looked down and realized she still clutched the little knife. She jerked convulsively at the sight of it, choking on a sob. Then her hand closed over its length. This was all Gordon had left her, and it had served her well. No matter that it had also sealed her fate with the British. It had protected her from the man she loathed beyond any she'd ever known. She would keep it, a bloody talisman, close to her. Tucking it in her bodice, she looked around, trying to summon the words Alex had spoken when they stood together in the stableyard just five nights ago. Gordon *had* left her something else, though he didn't know it. He'd left her a refuge. What was the name Alex had given her? Verona Drake. On Murray Street. That was to the west, nearer the Hudson, but not so very far away. She stood a moment longer, sudden indecision gripping her. Who was Verona Drake? What was she to Gordon? What if she turned Rebecca away from her door?

Shadowed figures to her right emerged from the black depths of a doorway. They seemed to loom toward her, and Rebecca's indecision fled on new wings of fear. Running as fast as her skirts allowed, she zigzagged through the streets, always heading north and west. Several people tried to stop her, but alarm gave her strength to dodge them and go blindly on.

Murray Street, beyond the college, was not so dark as many she had traveled. Desperately she searched her mind for the number Alex had given her, unaware of the stares of passersby. At last she saw it, a tall brick house with lanterns on either side of the door. A man went up the steps as she approached, and was admitted by a pert little maid who smiled at him in a familiar way. Was Verona Drake giving a party? For the first time since she'd remembered the woman's name, Rebecca slowed her steps. But where else could she go? She had no choice but to ask for admittance. She looked down at her sea-green corded dimity gown. It was rumpled and undoubtedly stained from her flight, perhaps even had Major Tyson's blood on it. Shuddering, she almost drew back, but the memory of the major's contorted face as he screamed that he would hang her drove her feet forward.

At her knock the door was opened by the same pert maid, who looked almost comically surprised to see the figure on the steps. Rebecca smiled wanly at her. "Please carry my name to Mrs. Drake," she said. "I am Rebecca Blair, a friend of Gordon and Alex Meade."

The maid, who had looked as though she might turn her away, opened the door at that and admitted Rebecca to a red hall. The walls were hung with red damask, two gilded chairs covered with red velvet stood beside the door, and the floor was overlaid by an Oriental carpet in shades of the same red. Gilt wall sconces and mirrors bounced the candlelight about the space like clusters of stars. Rebecca had never seen anything like it, and for the first time in days had the urge to laugh.

She sobered, though, when she saw the maid appraising her in what could only be termed an insolent manner. Rebecca raised her eyebrows at the girl and drew herself up. With that, the maid scurried into a room to the right of the hall. There was a low-voiced exchange, and Rebecca's nerves began to fray as she waited. Then a throaty voice with a hint of a French accent said, "Show her into the rear parlor, Mary," and the maid reappeared.

Rebecca's thoughts churned as she followed the girl down the red hallway where the red damask gave way to a floral print on the walls. The lady of the house disdained to come out to the hall, and would not have a stranger ushered in before her guests. But after all, she was an unknown, unaccompanied female who had appeared out of the night without so much as a cloak wrapped around her shoulders. It was a wonder, she reflected ruefully, Mrs. Drake was willing to see her at all.

She entered the small rear parlor and stopped short. Like the hall, the room was opulent, almost gaudy in its decor. Richly patterned Chinese wallpaper vied for attention with brilliantly colored carpets, brocade-covered chairs, swagged silk curtains. Trying not to stare at her surroundings, Rebecca chose a chair and ignored the maid's giggle as she closed the door behind her. She folded her hands in her lap and looked at the myriad porcelain figurines that covered the mantle beneath an enormous Italian gilt mirror. Judging by what she'd seen so far, Gordon's friend was an eccentric woman, to say the least. Any one of the room's appointments would have done quite nicely by itself, but jumbled together as they were, the effect was almost dizzying. She wondered if this were a private parlor where the lady of the house indulged her whims and reflected her own special personality. She rather hoped so. The chaos of color *could* mean the lady was open, generous.

Her ruminations were cut short as the door opened and a tall woman dressed in lavender silk swept regally into the room. Rebecca stood up and blinked at the clash of colors the woman's dress presented against the deep blues and reds of the room. The gown was of the sheerest silk, swirling around her like a cloud. The short, close sleeves fell off at the elbows in large double ruffles of lawn trimmed with Dresden lace, and above the exceedingly low-cut bodice, three rows of glowing pearls rested on her long neck. But it was the woman's face, beneath elaborately piled masses of shimmering blond hair that arrested Rebecca's attention. It was a beautiful face, made of strong planes and hollows, but the slightly protruding gray-green eyes were coldly assessing above the voluptuous mouth that smiled coolly.

Rebecca smiled tremulously in return, overpowered by the sheer presence of the woman, feeling suddenly very small and very young. "Mrs. Drake?" she said in a shaking voice.

The woman came all the way into the room and closed the door, her eyes never leaving Rebecca. "I am Verona Drake," she said in the throaty voice the girl had heard before.

"I . . . I am so sorry to interrupt you at this hour, but I had nowhere to go, you see." Rebecca stopped and spread her hands helplessly.

The gray-green eyes narrowed in thought. "Mary said you used the name of Gordon Meade at the door, Miss . . . uh . . . Blair, was it?"

"Yes. Mr. Meade is an acquaintance of mine. But it was actually his younger brother, Alex, who gave me your name and said I might come to you if I needed assistance." Rebecca refrained from twisting her hands together with an effort. She was surprised when the woman chuckled softly.

"So the bear cub grows up despite Gordon."

"Excuse me?"

A long hand with pointed nails waved in the air. "It is nothing. But let me have a good look at you." The woman walked slowly around Rebecca, eyeing her like a horse at auction, the girl thought as she stood still, baffled. Then Verona Drake went and sat in a high chair and poured herself a glass of brandy from a decanter beside her, leaving Rebecca standing awkwardly in the center of the room.

"May I sit down please?" Rebecca felt her legs wouldn't hold her up much longer, and she was irritated by the woman's scrutiny.

There was a pause as Verona sipped from her glass, but at last she nodded and seemed to watch closely as Rebecca moved back to her chair and sat down, her back very straight.

Verona sipped again and her eyes narrowed further. "Where did you meet Gordon?" she asked abruptly.

Rebecca sighed. She supposed if she was going to ask for this woman's protection, she'd have to answer any questions, but the last few minutes had made her begin to wonder if coming here hadn't been a mistake. "I met him nearly a year ago at my uncle's house in Westchester," she said softly, seeing no need to go into the circumstances of that meeting. "Before that, we had been introduced in London."

"Ah, and Alex?"

"I met him for the first time in Westchester."

"Then what do you do here in New York?"

Rebecca folded her hands very carefully. "Our house was burned. My uncle and I managed to reach the city, and have lived since last winter with a friend in Queen Street."

Verona Drake nodded, as though Rebecca's words had confirmed a thought. "It was obvious to me you were not a girl off the streets. And yet you come to me for assistance. What do you want?"

The question, put that way, took Rebecca completely off guard. "Your protection," she blurted.

"You want to work for me?" The painted brows rose in a perfect arch.

Taken aback, Rebecca sought for words. She realized she had not made her position on Queen Street clear, but perhaps that was as well. If she were to ask this odd woman to take her in, she'd have to discover some way to earn her keep. She thought quickly.

"I have had good schooling," she said slowly, and watched the gray-green eyes widen. "Perhaps, if you have children, I could be their governess." A deep laugh disconcerted her and she rushed on. "I also sew very well." She shuddered inwardly. Sewing was not a skill she cherished or wished to use every day of her life. She stopped then, the look of pure mirth on the woman's face embarrassing her.

"Oh, my God." The throaty voice chuckled, completing Rebecca's confusion. "*Why* do you come to me?"

"M-my uncle died," Rebecca stammered. "I could not stay on at the house with his friend." She couldn't bring herself to tell what she had done to an officer of the king. Her disheveled appearance told more than enough of the story, she feared.

There was a moment's silence as the two stared at each other. Then Verona Drake stood up. "It is late," she said brusquely. "You may have the French room. Mary will show you the way. I suggest you keep to the room. Tomorrow I am busy, but the next day we will see what to do with you."

There was no further explanation, no words of welcome. The woman spoke with authority, was obviously unaccustomed to explaining herself. Rebecca's eyes threatened to fill with tears. Just like that, Verona Drake had given her a place to stay. She blinked back the tears and tried to thank Mrs. Drake, but the woman waved away her words, and after one last lingering look at her new guest, went out of the room.

The little maid reappeared a minute later, her eyes wide as she asked Rebecca to follow her. She seemed to be appraising her with a mixture of awe and speculation, and Rebecca grew uncomfortable in her presence. But she had no choice but to follow the girl up curving rear stairs to the end of a long hallway.

Mary led her into a small room furnished with fragile, gilded chairs, tables and bed. At least the colors in here were muted, Rebecca thought with relief, looking at the golds and whites and greens that glowed softly in the candles Mary was lighting. The girl turned back the wide bed's covers without looking at her, indicated the wardrobe and the washstand hidden behind a gilded chest panel, then left.

Rebecca collapsed onto a thin-legged chair and found it was sturdier than it looked. She began disrobing, feeling suddenly an overwhelming physical and emotional exhaustion. In her thin chemise at last, she crawled between the covers and prayed for the oblivion of sleep.

Her fatigue was greater than she realized, for when she woke the next morning, her one window showed the sun was already high in the sky. Her first thought was of food. She'd eaten little the day before, and last night's terrors had brought on a ravenous hunger. She got up and inspected her dress in the sunlight, all the while listening for sounds of the household. But silence seemed to envelope the place. She shook out the skirts, and saw there was only a faint stain beneath one fold on the side. Blood? She shivered. At the washstand she dabbed at the stain with cold water and watched it nearly disappear before she spread the skirt to dry. Then with determination, she retrieved the little knife from under her pillow and washed it too, trying not to look at it as she worked. She dried it carefully and put it back under her pillow, but still she heard no sounds from below.

When her dress was dry, she donned it, her stomach growling more than ever. She would have to make a foray to the kitchens if someone didn't come to her soon. Perhaps the family was all out for the morning, had left her here to rest, not thinking she'd awaken till noon. Mrs. Drake had said she'd be busy today. She might even have forgotten her unexpected guest. It must be nearly noon now.

Rebecca was bracing herself for an exploring expedition when there was a timid knock on the door, and she opened it to find Mary balancing a tray in the hall.

"Good morning, Mary." Rebecca smiled, gratitude that she had not been forgotten flooding her.

The maid's expression was sullen as she entered the room and put the tray on the white and gold table by the window. "Miss Drake said you were to be served up here today," the girl said and made to leave.

Rebecca stopped her. *"Miss* Drake? Then the lady of the house is not married?"

Mary's eyes widened and she almost looked as though she'd laugh. "Married? Not that I've ever heard." And she walked out.

Rebecca looked at the tray across the room, her thoughts rotating. Of course Mary must be resentful of her being here, for she added to the maid's duties, a thought that made her feel guilty. Nonetheless, the girl's manner was insolent. Perhaps that came from having no master of the house to keep her in line. What on earth was Rebecca to make of this newest revelation about the mistress, though? Was Miss Drake an heiress that she could live in this quite large and obviously expensive house? Did she make a hobby of taking in strangers with so little ado?

The girl sat down and attacked her scanty breakfast with vigor, and when she was done she felt better. There was little good to come of guessing what Verona Drake's motives were. Right now she needed the woman's help, and she mustn't let anything stand in the way of a possible friendship that might develop.

Thinking of being taken into homes brought Mr. Kent to her mind. What must the man be imagining right now, having discovered Rebecca had disappeared into the dark last night? Perhaps Warren Tyson had not told his host what had happened. It would hardly be a feather in his cap to admit he'd attacked Julian Halscomb's niece and she'd cut him with a knife before running away. So how would he explain her disappearance? She worried the question for some time as the fat from her bacon congealed on the plate and the little pot of hot chocolate grew cold. She hated to have kind Mr. Kent wonder about her. And if Major Tyson had made up some fantastical story about her running away, she would like Mr. Kent to know the truth of it, not think her ungrateful. Could she ask Mary to send the elderly man a message? She rather doubted it. Besides, what if the message fell into the hands of the vengeful major? Her skin grew cold at the thought. No, she'd have to abandon the hope of telling Mr. Kent anything for the present.

It was a long afternoon for Rebecca, and she paced the little room endlessly, growing heartily sick of the sight of the green and yellow birds on the wallpaper, the view of chimney pots and steep roofs out her window, the floral pattern of her carpet. She was actually glad to see Mary when the girl brought her dinner that evening, but the maid, in a fresh uniform and looking more lively than this morning, was no more communicative than before. And still there was no sign of Verona Drake.

Some time after dark she began to hear voices in the house, and wondered if she hadn't heard them earlier just because she had been so lost in thought. Her brain was tired now, refusing to think further, and she sat, listening to the tramp of male feet on the stairs, to the slam of a door down the hall, to a high girlish giggle nearby. What a contrast it was to this morning. Now the house seemed populated by dozens of people. Another party? She felt alone and left out, but knew she was being foolish. She wouldn't know any of Miss Drake's friends, and she didn't wish to be seen right now anyway.

At length she got undressed and climbed between the sheets, shivering with a new thought. What if there were a search for her? And what if there were British officers in the house at this moment? She snuggled down under the covers and tried to blot the horrible possibility from her mind. Instead, she let her thoughts drift to Gordon, as they had so often all day. Where was he now? Would he return to New York? Did he ever think of her, or had he put her as far from his mind as he had from his presence?

There was another slam of a door, a hoot of laughter, then muffled voices. She realized of a sudden that the sounds were coming from the next room. Who else lived in this house besides Miss Drake, and what would they be doing upstairs when there was a party going on? The voices stopped. There was what sounded like a loud slap, then a cry. But it didn't sound like a cry of pain. She sat up, all hope of sleep gone, and wondered if she should go and see if the occupants were all right. But all was quiet now.

She sat back against the headboard and drew her knees up to her chin. How was she going to get a message to Gordon? Surely he would find a way to help her if he knew she was in danger from the British. Perhaps this Verona Drake knew how he could be reached.

The silence of her little room was broken by a muffled cry. Rebecca hugged her knees, straining her ears. Now she could make out a strange squeaking sound, and suddenly her face grew hot with understanding of what the sound meant. Someone in the next room was making love on the bed. She tried not to listen, but the sounds seemed to grow louder. Her body began to tingle with the images her mind conjured and the memories she couldn't suppress.

Then suddenly another sound overrode that of the bed. A man was coming heavily up the stairs. She hoped he wasn't searching for the couple in the next room, and was relieved when she made out his steps passing that door, until she realized they were approaching her own. A quick dread took hold of her and she groped under her pillow even as her door flung open.

In the light from the hall her terrified eyes discovered the man was not in uniform. She was so relieved he wasn't a king's officer come to arrest her, she nearly fell back again. But the man was advancing into the room and she could see he was peering at the bed with a broad grin on his round face.

"You have made a mistake, sir," she said in a low, clear voice.

He stopped, hands on hips. He was a heavy man of medium height, dressed elegantly. His grin broadened. "Ummm . . . I think not." His voice was very deep, so deep it nearly muffled his words. "Looks like Verona's keeping you for something special. I assure you I am something special." He chuckled and hiccoughed loudly.

Rebecca couldn't think what he meant as he talked, but she

318

remembered the sounds in the next room. The man began to remove his coat, and it dawned on her what he intended. "If you come any closer," she said calmly, "I shall scream."

The man was pulling at his cravat as he eyed her. Light from the open door showed her clearly, huddled at the top of the big bed. "You like a tussle, eh? Well, that's just fine with me."

The girl's hand closed around the handle of her knife, and her gaze never left the broad form only feet away. She felt no fear, only a determination that no man would take her against her will. The knife had served her before; it would again. But she'd prefer not to use it on a guest in this house. "I warn you," she said as the man finished loosening his cravat and took a step forward.

He chuckled again. And she screamed.

The sound seemed to echo around the small room and bounce through the house. Frozen in midstride, the man glared at her. She could smell his brandy-soaked breath now. He moved a step nearer and she brought up the knife.

Feet pounded on the stairs, in the hall. Rebecca paid no attention to them. She never took her eyes from the furious man before her.

When Verona Drake reached the doorway, she found one of her frequent and prized customers facing a snarling form crouched on the bed like a panther, a short gleaming blade in one hand.

Chapter 30

In a swift movement Verona was between the man and the bed. Another girl appeared in the doorway, wide-eyed and giggling, but the woman ignored the sound. Her throaty voice soothing, she murmured about the gentleman's misfortune in thinking delight awaited him here, and steered him to the door saying the *front* room was the one he wanted. The man grumbled, but allowed her to lead him away. Throughout the exchange Rebecca had not moved a muscle.

When Verona returned a few moments later, and sent the girl in the doorway packing, she found Rebecca still crouched on the bed, but the knife had disappeared. The two women looked hard at one another without speaking. Then slowly Rebecca uncoiled and sat down.

"He . . . he was going to attack me," she explained, feeling inexplicably defensive.

"A mistake, I see." Verona lit Rebecca's bedside candle, then closed the door, leaning on it. This evening she wore a dress of heavy white satin shot through with silver and gold threads. She looked thoughtful and displeased. "We will have to talk more tomorrow. For tonight, no one else will disturb you."

"Thank you," Rebecca said stiffly. But as Miss Drake made to leave, she jumped up. "Will you send a message to Mr. Meade for me?"

320

Verona looked back, an expression of shrewd calculation in her eyes. "You want Alex to come and take you away?"

"Alex or Gordon. I'm sure they would help me if they knew. . . ."

"Knew you were in my house?" The protuberant eyes narrowed.

"No, it isn't that," Rebecca said hastily. "I think Gordon is the only person I know who can help me at present."

"You seem to forget, Miss Blair, that this city is in British hands. Gordon Meade is a colonel in the Continental Army. He cannot simply ride into New York and carry you off." No sense in letting the girl know Gordon had slipped into the city only last week, or that he might return now that General Clinton had not left the city on the twenty-eighth as even his highest staff had expected him to.

"Y-yes," Rebecca stammered, feeling trapped. She couldn't very well tell this woman she'd seen Gordon recently. She had no idea where her loyalties lay. Nor could she explain why it was so urgent that she get away from the city.

"You have no friends to turn to here?" Verona surprised herself by her soft question. She'd thought a lot about this girl today. She, who knew women well, was unsure if Rebecca Blair was a virgin. The trouble was the girl was obviously well-bred. She'd listened and watched her closely last night, and Rebecca had spoken, had moved, had even sat like a lady, using all unconscious the polish Verona had worked so hard to achieve on her own. Quite a prize she could be in this house. But her performance tonight indicated she was not eager to join Verona's girls in pleasing their male customers. Then why had she come here? Was it possible she didn't even know what sort of house she was in? Or was she as smart as she was beautiful and was holding out for only the highest paying men? To her mind, that was the most likely explanation. But she wanted to know more about this girl before she decided what to do with her. She'd need to ask more questions of more people. "No one?" she repeated.

"No one." Rebecca's voice was firm with conviction. She wanted to impress on Miss Drake that she needed her help, but watching those hard eyes by the door, she was almost sorry she had been so adamant.

A slow smile curved the woman's sensual mouth. "Then we will have to come to some sort of arrangement, won't we?"

Something about Verona Drake's tone made Rebecca shiver in her thin chemise. "I . . . I told you I would work for you."

The smile widened. "So you did, miss. So you did." She opened the door and was gone without another word.

It was only then that Rebecca realized there had been no explanation for the strange man who had blundered into her room. What did Miss Drake mean when she'd said he belonged in the *front* room? And why hadn't she shown more concern for Rebecca's state of mind after his attack? Of course, if she'd seen the knife, she may have decided the girl was in no need of consoling, might even have been a bit leery of approaching too close. Good, Rebecca thought with surprising satisfaction.

She sat still for a time, watching the candle sputter in its own wax. The sounds from the next room had ceased. Perhaps she could get some sleep after all. She'd need it if she was to keep her wits on the morrow with the formidable mistress of this odd house. Miss Drake had assured her there'd be no further intrusion, but she wished she had a lock on the door anyway. She eyed the thin-legged chair near the window. It had proved sturdier than she'd supposed. Perhaps it would do. Carefully she carried the chair to the door and wedged the back under the handle. That felt better. But the room was growing stuffy after all the activity here the last twenty minutes. She opened her window and discovered the night was pleasantly cool. Heavy clouds showed it might rain, but she'd take that chance.

At last she returned to her bed, and fell into a deep sleep.

In the morning there was no sound to indicate that there had been what could only be termed a riotous party the night before, no maids' voices as they cleaned up, no footsteps of the inhabitants. Everything was as still as it had been yesterday. Despite the gray clouds still hanging over the city, she could tell it was early. The alley that ran beside the house below her window showed small puddles of rain, but no wet footprints. Her room faced the narrow rear garden where a lime tree stood in the center of rows of neatly clipped grass and gravel walks. Beside a low fence ran the alley. By leaning out, she could see below her a sturdy grape arbor nestled against the house. The large spreading leaves climbed in tangled masses nearly to her windowsill. There were no sounds from this rear area.

She dressed once more in her sea-green gown and wished

she had the nerve to request a change of clothes so that hers could be cleaned. But nothing had been offered her and she felt she couldn't ask anything more of Verona Drake. Even though the woman had taken her in, she'd made it clear that somehow Rebecca would have to repay her hospitality. The idea soothed the girl's conscience, but it did nothing to aid her in her desire to leave New York, to find Gordon. And leave she must, she thought suddenly. If last night's revelries were an indication of the pattern of Verona's life, sooner or later, Rebecca would be confronted with a scarlet uniform on someone who knew her or who had been given a description of her. She didn't for a moment entertain the hope that Warren Tyson would forgive and forget. He was a hard, calculating, remorseless man, and he would see her captured if he could.

Quaking at the thought, Rebecca removed her barricade and opened her door, listening more closely for voices. Still, the house was wrapped in silence. Perhaps she could go to the kitchen and seek her own breakfast. Then she had an idea. Last night Miss Drake had as much as said she had no notion where Gordon was. And even if she did, she might be unwilling to imperil his life by asking him to return to the city. If Rebecca was to get out of New York, she'd have to find a way on her own. And there was just one other person she knew of who might be able to help. If yesterday's pattern were to repeat itself, she had well over an hour before Mary brought her a tray. There was no use sitting here waiting. She would see if she could help herself while still the city was quiet. Softly she closed the door behind her and tiptoed down the hall past several closed doors. The occupants of those rooms, if there were any, were fast abed, for no sound issued from any of them. Thank heaven the house had been well built, for no floorboard, no stair creaked under her weight. Down she went to the gaudy red hall with its high paneled front door. The locks were well oiled she discovered with satisfaction, and quickly she let herself out into the gray day.

Walking briskly, she reached Broadway and turned south. Here she discovered it was not so early as she'd thought, for the sidewalk was crowded with people. Every time she saw a scarlet coat she had to force her feet to keep moving steadily, not give way to the urge to run. A few blocks further, though, she realized she couldn't stand much more of the fright she felt every time anyone looked at her, and she dodged into an alley. By using only back streets and occasional short alleyways, she came eventually to the area below the North Church where she'd followed Sylvie that fateful morning ten long days ago. Several times she lost her way, but eventually she reached the tenement-lined street she remembered so vividly. It was not as deserted now, she noticed, hesitating. But there across the street was the same old man still squatting by the canvas shelter, and for some reason that gave her heart. Quickly she entered the gloom of the half-burned hallway and mounted the steps. The battered door stared at her as blankly as it had before, and with her heart jumping in her throat she tried the handle. It was unlocked. Swiftly, she pushed it open, whispering, "Davey? Are you there?"

The ugly little room gave back her whisper with an echoing emptiness. The lopsided washstand, the small table, the two rickety chairs were all there, but they had a deserted, forlorn look to them in the dim gray light. She went through to the next room to find the pallet still on the floor. Around it the dust motes swirled at the movement of the door. With her hand to her mouth, she fought the need to scream Davey's name and backed from the doorway. Desperately she searched the front room for some sign, but not a paper, not a scrap of food, nothing could she find to testify to the use of this place. Davey had disappeared as completely as Gordon.

She stood in the center of the room, her head in her hands. Her life had become one long nightmare ever since that day she had left Gordon in this building. But she had known, with a knowledge that went bone-deep, that if she could find him again, the nightmare world she lived in would dissolve. Now that sustaining hope was slipping away in black despair.

Only the knowledge that she must return to the house on Murray Street before she was missed made her able to retrace her steps. But perhaps it was her very despair that made her senses sharper now, her mind more acute. When she entered that bright red hallway again, she wondered for the first time what sort of single woman would have a house decorated in this manner, who gave boisterous parties every night of the week. Certainly Gordon's friend could not be very respectable.

She had ceased to feel surprise at anything, so she was not startled when she turned from closing the door and saw Miss Drake standing in the hall by the stairs.

"A morning constitutional, Miss Blair?" the woman asked with a look of distaste.

"Something like that, yes," answered Rebecca, feeling for once, no awe at all.

"Then you must have an appetite. You may share my breakfast with me." Verona Drake took obedience for granted. She turned and walked majestically along the hall, and Rebecca trailed apathetically after.

In the same dizzying parlor she'd seen the first evening, Rebecca found her hostess seated before a tiny table holding a breakfast tray. She motioned the girl into another chair and rang a bell. The two said nothing as they waited, and soon Mary appeared to receive orders. The silence dragged on and Rebecca folded her hands in her lap, determined to allow Miss Drake the opening gambit. She had no intention of explaining where she had been, and no good notion of how to discuss her future with this woman.

When Mary returned and Miss Drake motioned to her to eat, Rebecca found her appetite was wanting, but politely she picked at her food.

"I heard an interesting thing last night, Miss Blair," Verona said at last, her shrewd eyes fastened on Rebecca's face.

"Yes?" Rebecca took a sip of chocolate, wondering if she would now receive an apology for Miss Drake's guest's behavior last evening.

"I heard a certain major on Sir Henry Clinton's staff met with misfortune in a house on Queen Street two nights ago."

Rebecca felt the color draining from her face and willed it to return. Her hand was arrested on her cup, and she didn't try to lift it again for fear she'd spill chocolate on her dress. But she had to look down from those sharp eyes. "Oh? What sort of misfortune?" she asked, and was proud that her voice didn't quaver.

"It seems he was stabbed. No one knows quite how . . . yet. Rumors fly, of course." She lifted a piece of toast to her mouth negligently. "There is even some wild tale about a girl who was trying to discourage the major's attentions. Though some think she could not have done it herself, that it is more likely there was a lover who did the deed for her when the major came upon them unawares."

Rebecca surprised herself by saying, "It all sounds a bit like one of Mrs. Brooke's novels," and felt sure she was not fooling the woman. But she found herself reluctant, even now, to tell Miss Drake the truth. Seeing her again this morning with a new understanding of how alone she was and how precarious her position, she realized she didn't trust Verona Drake. Still, she needed the woman's protection until she could think what to do.

The older woman poured chocolate from a blue and white china pot. "I imagine much of life is stranger than any story Mrs. Brooke can make up. And often sadder. The captain who told me of the affair said there was talk at the hospital of infection having set in. He felt the major had waited too long to have the wound attended."

Rebecca swallowed hard, and with great concentration removed her fingers from her cup. "I am sorry to hear that," she said with a certain honesty.

There followed a thoughtful silence, and Rebecca began to feel her nerves giving way at last under the narrow-eyed scrutiny. She'd run screaming in a moment if she didn't turn the woman's thoughts. "I had hoped," she said slowly, "that you would have something for me to do today. I very much want to repay your kindness in allowing me to stay here."

Verona tapped a long-nailed finger on her chin. "You said you can sew?"

"Yes."

"Then you may certainly help me by mending some clothes this afternoon."

Rebecca was startled by the abruptness of the decision, but she was grateful for the change in conversation, and for the chance to do more than sit and stare at her hands. "Certainly. And I will try, Miss Drake, not to burden you with my presence any longer than necessary." While they were making abrupt decisions, Rebecca thought, she might as well make one of her own.

"You have somewhere else to go perhaps?"

"I ... I must try to find myself a position," Rebecca answered lamely, feeling foolish, and wishing she did have some idea of where else to go.

"Do not think you have to leave us, Miss Blair." Verona Drake's eyes seemed almost warm now. "I am sure we will manage to come to some amicable arrangement."

Only twenty minutes after regaining her room, Rebecca found Mary at her door, arms piled high with materials.

"Good heavens, it looks like your mistress's entire wardrobe," she said as she helped Mary deposit the heap on her bed.

"Oh, none of them belong to Miss Drake," Mary answered. "I'll go and get the sewing box."

Rebecca stared at the profusion of muslin, satinet and silk. "Just who *does* own these gowns, Mary?" she asked when the maid reappeared.

"The other girls. Miss Drake said I was to bring you dinner up here tonight. So I will return for these," and she waved at the bed, "in the evening."

Rebecca sat down with a sigh. What other girls? She picked up a floral muslin skirt and shook it out. It certainly was too short and too narrow in the waist for Miss Drake. Could it belong to the girl she'd heard in the next room? Her cheeks grew hot with the memory of the noises she'd heard, and she examined the material for the damage she must repair. Discovering it was only the hooks at the waist that had popped off, she set to work, glad of something to keep her hands busy while her mind whirled round and round her predicament. There was no one who could help her unless she could persuade Miss Drake to find a way for her to leave the city. And how was that to be done, with British boats on the rivers and a British regiment at Kingsbridge? Then she remembered she had entered the city pretending to be a farmer's wife. Why couldn't she leave the same way? But how?

During the long afternoon Rebecca heard voices in the house at last, all of them female. And in the evening the partying began once more. She had finished much of the mending before supper, and when Mary came with her meal she gave the girl the clothes.

Silently the maid sorted through the dresses. There were just two left to repair. She pointed to a deep blue silk still on Rebecca's bed. "That one is the dress Miss Drake says should fit you. If you'll give me your clothes, we'll have them cleaned," she said.

"Oh, how wonderful." Rebecca could hardly believe her ears.

"I'll come back for the tray, and you can give them to me then. I'll bring a robe for you to wear."

Rebecca ate her dinner hastily, eager to be quit of her dirty garments. When Mary returned she'd stripped off her dress, and was waiting in her chemise. The girl handed her a filmy silk robe and turned her back while Rebecca shed her last layer and wrapped the robe around herself. She was startled to find that it was like wearing the wings of a butterfly—soft and colorful, but nearly transparent, with only a simple tie at the waist. She had a hard time wrapping it far enough around herself to be decent, and was chagrined when Mary smirked at her efforts. Then the girl left, and Rebecca set to work with a will on the remaining clothes.

A simple muslin skirt with no bodice to it had a tear near the hem. She stitched that quickly, and at last turned to the deep blue silk, inspecting it critically by the light of the several candles she'd lit. The sleeve had been pulled half off the narrow shoulder, and she stared at it a long time, wondering what the owner had been doing to tear the dress so, when suddenly she remembered the cry she'd heard last night. The girl had not ripped the dress herself; some man had torn it in a passion. The material dropped to her lap, and her whole body went numb with the recognition, at long last, of just what this house was.

Dear God, how could she have been so naive? All the strange looks from Miss Drake, all the strange sounds, even the odd hours of the household made a horrifying sort of sense now.

After her devastating disappointment this morning at not finding Davey, she'd thought she was inured to any fresh shocks, but she found herself trembling violently under a new onslaught of fear. Verona Drake had guessed she was the girl who had stabbed the major in Queen Street. She could turn Rebecca over to the army at any time. Then why hadn't she? Because she expected to make money off her first by selling her to customers who came to this house?

Jumping up, Rebecca ran to her door and wedged her chair beneath the handle again. Never, never would she repay the woman *that* way.

It was an endless, demon-ridden night for the girl. She started awake at every noise, sweat drenching her at each imagined horror, and by the time the night began to pale toward dawn, she wondered how she would exist through another day in this place. Somehow she had to get out of here.

A thought had come to her in the small hours while she waited for the house to fall silent. Mary was the only servant she'd yet seen. If she was also the one who did the marketing for the household, Rebecca would ask to accompany her, and would discover a cart which had come from Westchester. She would beg a seat in that cart when it left the city. She had no money to entice a farmer to take that chance, but if the man could be convinced to take her to Dobbs Ferry, Seth would pay him, she felt sure. And some day she could sell the Halscomb land and repay the school teacher. Uncle Julian had left her his estate, and it was all she had for herself now, unless someday she could communicate with Mr. Bancroft again.

On that more cheering thought she had slept at last, and didn't awaken until nearly noon. Immediately she realized she might already be too late to go with Mary, and she leaped from the bed in a frenzy of worry. The only article of clothing she had was the blue silk gown, but she blessed the fact that it was a one-piece dress with hooks at the side and front. It was hardly appropriate for daytime wear, but she didn't care. She donned it hurriedly, and went to brush her hair, wishing the neckline of the dress were more decent. When she looked in the mirror, though, she blanched. The dress fit her beautifully, small stays sewn into the bodice lifting her breasts and pulling the waist into a becomingly small line. But the neckline was carved nearly off her shoulders, and plunged into a deep V in the front, exposing a shocking amount of flesh, she thought. On occasion she had reveled in wearing daringly cut dresses to balls and fetes, but this gown carried daring to an extreme she would never have contemplated. Desperately she searched drawers and wardrobe for a handkerchief, a piece of lace, anything to modify the line of the deep cleavage. There was nothing in the room. She'd have to borrow something from Mary, and she'd have to seek the girl out herself.

This time she used the rear steps, assuming that they would lead her eventually to the basement kitchen. As she rounded the bottom of the stairs, though, she found the door to the back parlor standing open and Verona Drake watching her with interest.

Sucking in her breath, Rebecca steeled herself to pass the door without a word, but the throaty voice invited her to enter, and she didn't see how she could ignore it. It didn't matter what Verona Drake was, she was the only thing between Rebecca and a New York jail at the moment. Resignedly the girl walked into the room, and was surprised to see the calculating eyes held something more this morning. A wariness? A grudging respect? Baffled, she halted inside the door.

"The dress is becoming," the woman stated.

"Oh. I . . . I must thank you for the use of it, but I confess I feel it is more suited to evening wear."

"Hmmm . . ." Verona inspected her narrowly. Rebecca felt her skin grow hot under the scrutiny, and wished desperately she had a shawl to put over her shoulders. "Do you remember that major I told you about yesterday?" Verona asked suddenly, shifting her attention back to Rebecca's face.

Startled, the girl nodded, feeling her hands begin to grow damp.

"He is dead."

Chapter 31

Shocked into immobility, Rebecca stood gazing at her hostess. She was powerless to speak, even if there were anything to say. She was a murderess, and she could already feel the heavy rope descending around her neck.

"Why, you look pale, Miss Blair," the voice across from her purred. "Perhaps you'd better sit down."

Dazedly, Rebecca shook her head. She knew she couldn't move without collapsing on the floor, and she wanted to be still standing when she heard what Verona meant to do now.

The woman sat back, preparing to be comfortable. "He didn't die of the original wound, of course," she said conversationally.

"Then of what?" Rebecca's voice was little more than a squeak and she hated herself for it.

"My informant two nights ago was right; infection had set into the wound. Major Tyson was taken to the hospital, where yesterday evening a surgeon finally amputated the arm."

Rebecca shuddered and closed her eyes.

"A drastic measure that some say was unnecessary, but you know how these sawbones can be. However, the surgeon was not only mistaken in his diagnosis, perhaps; he was certainly inept at his calling. He allowed the major to bleed to death under his hands."

"How horrible," Rebecca breathed, and put out a hand to steady herself against a chair back.

"Yes, rather. But it is done. And there is still speculation as to who gave the major the wound in the first place. However, that may die down . . . in time. And meanwhile, we have your future to consider, don't we, Miss Blair?"

"Yes," the girl answered in a faint voice.

"Tell me how well you knew Gordon Meade."

The sudden question startled Rebecca, and she tried to focus her sluggish mind on what it was Verona really wanted. "We were friends, of a sort," she stated finally.

"I see. And young Alex?"

"We were friends also."

"Have you had any lovers?"

Shocked, Rebecca drew herself up. "I cannot believe you are really interested in such a question."

"But I am, my dear, I am. It would make things simpler if I knew."

For an instant Rebecca let her dislike show before she lowered her eyes. She would not respond to a query like that.

"I see we have come to the point of being honest with one another, Rebecca." The woman chuckled. "And I am glad. The game was becoming tedious. You took refuge in my house, stating you wanted to work for me. But you are the first girl who's ever used sewing and other genteel accomplishments as a ruse to get in here. I have wondered at your motives. Did you think I would set you up in high style here, to lord it over the other girls, to make your own selection of customers because you presented yourself as a lady?"

Stunned into speechlessness, Rebecca gaped at the tall woman sitting so languidly before her.

"Oh, you're beautiful enough, I'll grant you. But are you practiced enough? No, my dear, you will have to start like all the rest and prove your worth to me, and to the men I allow within this house. Perhaps even tonight . . . No, tomorrow night there is just the right one coming here."

"If you think that I . . ." Rebecca began hotly.

"I think you do not wish to be seen in the city at present, Miss Blair," Verona cut in smoothly, "nor that you wish anyone here to contact Sir Henry's headquarters. But, of course, I plan to be most discreet. You will receive only the men I choose for you, and they none of them will be from the army."

The girl gasped, her eyes wide with horror, but Verona wasn't looking at her now. She was studying the porcelain mantel decorations thoughtfully. "Yes, that is how we'll do it, my fine lady. Today you will sew the remaining things we need. Tomorrow we will discuss what is expected of you, will practice what I consider the proper way for you to behave, will select a name for you, and then will introduce you to a very wealthy, and I may say, generous customer."

Rebecca had a sudden urge to laugh hysterically. "You expect me to sell my . . . to join your despicable calling?" she choked.

"I expect you to use your sense and realize that you can make a fortune for both of us if you'll do as I say. You'll never make it on your own." The throaty voice was as hard as a shaft of steel. "Your alternative, Miss Blair, is to be delivered to Sir Henry, and if you think you can just walk out of here, consider the fact that right now half of New York may be looking for you."

Rebecca ran then. She fled up the stairs in a mindless panic, wanting only to escape that hateful voice, those suddenly mocking gray-green eyes. She would kill herself before she'd let Verona Drake use her this way. And kill herself she probably must, she thought dully back in her room again, for there was no way out. She wanted to tear off the obscene dress she wore, but there was only the equally revealing and even less suitable robe to put on. Frantically, she paced her room, and at last decided that her chances on the streets were no worse than the fate that awaited her here. She went back to the door and opened it. In the hall a sultry-eyed blonde eyed her curiously. Quickly she shut the door again, shivering at the thought of what that girl did at Verona Drake's bidding. She looked wildly around her room, seeing only the delicate furniture, the wardrobe and the window. A vision of her cowering at the back of the wardrobe as Verona ushered a sweating customer into her room crossed her mind, and she had another urge to laugh uncontrollably. Then her eye rested once more on the window, and she remembered the grape arbor just below. If she could somehow get outside the opening, she might be able to climb down that heavy trellis to the ground. She went over and threw up the sash again. In the narrow garden behind, Verona Drake sat talking to a burly youth in ragged homespun. At that instant the protruding gray-green eyes lifted to the back of the house, and

Rebecca drew back as though she'd seen a viper. Frenziedly she threw herself on her bed and gave way to the useless defense of tears.

When Mary brought her food an hour later, Rebecca did not speak or even try to move from the bed. The maid had never shown the slightest interest in befriending Miss Drake's newest guest, had been nothing but sullen and insolent. There was no help to be had from her. But eventually Rebecca's hunger drove her to the little table, and the simple act of eating began to bring back rational thought. She had given in to despair again, and it would do her no good. She had no one to rely on but herself, and if she couldn't do that, she was lost indeed. Slowly she chewed and swallowed, emptying her mind of all the fearful images her imagination had conjured this past hour and more. Once she had accomplished that feat, the answer came to her with devastating simplicity. She sat very straight and mulled it over, savoring each aspect as though it were the choicest morsel.

She'd already discovered the routine of this household, had walked out once with no hinderance whatever. She would do it again. This afternoon, or this evening, Mary would return her cleaned clothes to her. Tomorrow morning she would rise very early, and she would simply walk away! That settled, she turned to considering where she would go. Now that Major Tyson was dead, did she dare return to Mr. Kent's house? Or was that just what anyone looking for her would expect? No, she decided, she could not return to Queen Street. Once more her mind conjured the perfectly simple answer. She would walk east, to the river. Surely somewhere on that long shoreline, she would come across a boat, a fisherman's dory, a boy's dinghy. She was capable of rowing that boat across the river, as though she were delivering something to the Long Island shore. She would then turn north, and if she had to, would get work along the way until she could pay for passage up to Westchester. The only thing she needed to do was avoid the British troops. Surely that was not impossible.

With an almost heady elation, she set to work sewing on the new dresses Mary brought her, glad of something to occupy the long hours ahead of her. By suppertime she could almost smile, and was merely annoyed when Mary explained that her clothes were not yet dry.

"They can finish drying up here," she stated with authority, already savoring her freedom.

"Perhaps," the maid answered sulkily, and left again with the tray.

Rebecca waited another hour, until it was dark outside, and finally decided Mary was too busy to bring the clothing back up the long flights of stairs. She would have to go and get it herself.

Dusk had given way to the somber shades of night when Gordon Meade made his way down the alley and unlatched the little gate into the garden. He crossed the neat gravel paths and cursed himself for being so late. Verona might already be in the front parlor, ready to receive the first callers of the evening, and he'd hoped to have a quick word with her before she went to work. He didn't want that fool Mary shrieking his name if she saw him first. He'd have to strangle the girl if she did it again. Briefly he considered staying in the garden, but the night was already growing chilly, and he was exhausted. He wanted only a few short hours' sleep before he set out on what had to be a fast and desperate journey.

Silently he opened the rear door to the tall house and let himself in to the tiny alcove off the back hall. The place seemed quiet enough. He stole around the corner and stopped short. A deep blue silk skirt was at the bottom of the rear stairs. Very carefully, he flattened against the wall and slid his left foot back around the corner. In the instant it took to slither back out of sight, he caught a glimpse of the girl now standing uncertainly in the hallway. The shock of that instant nearly made him careless, and he had to draw a shuddering breath to hold himself very still. Leaning his head against the hard wall, he realized his exhaustion must be almost complete. He wished he could rub his eyes, but didn't dare move until the apparition had left the hall.

Damn his reeling senses. It was bad enough that Davey had greeted him with the news of Warren Tyson's death and the speculation about what had happened to Rebecca. It was worse that the two of them had wasted precious hours today trying to discover her whereabouts. But now to come into this house, looking for rest, and have his eyes project the one image he wanted to see in this cursed city was the outside of enough.

The grim decision that had been taking shape for nearly two weeks stood in the center of his mind with a force that jolted him. He had no choice but to leave tonight, to return upriver and deliver the last intelligence about Clinton's move north. But when that deed was done, he would resign his commission for a time, leave the army and return to New York as a civilian. He would find Rebecca if it was the last thing he did. The thought went little further than that. Motives didn't concern him at the moment. He'd left the girl to fend for herself after risking her life to help Sylvie and Alex, to face alone the one man he knew she feared the most, to run alone after being forced to defend herself against that man. At the time he'd had no choice but to leave her, but the burden of guilt was still his. Rebecca might be anywhere. She might even be dead. By God, he would find out.

Verona's deep voice cut into his thoughts then. She was coming from the front of the house, along the hallway. The softest rustle of silk indicated that the girl who had startled him in the hallway was retreating fast. He waited a moment to be sure Verona was going to her private parlor, and wondered why the girl would run back up the stairs. She had been dressed in the most enticing gown he'd seen in some time, obviously ready for the evening. He smiled grimly to himself, wishing he could take more pleasure in the deep décolletage he'd glimpsed. If some day Verona were to offer him *that* beauty . . . It annoyed him to realize he'd turn down the offer, and he wondered why. The girl had the most exquisite profile, and masses of long gleaming hair . . . He did rub his eyes now. Damn it. The trouble was, she'd looked just like Becky.

Verona's dress swished along the narrow hall. There were no other footsteps and Gordon finally judged it safe to emerge. Silently he walked into the colorful parlor, his mind still maddeningly on the girl he'd seen.

Verona had come to pick up her fan, and was startled when she turned to find Gordon filling the doorway. "God, you frightened me," she said in a stage whisper, and for just a second Gordon thought he saw a look of anxiety cloud her big eyes.

"I didn't mean to do that," he said softly, "but I didn't want to linger in the hall until you noticed me. Too much traffic out there."

Verona gave her throaty chuckle. "The girls are all up dressing. I came down first in case an early arrival became too eager. You've nothing to worry about yet."

"You may think all the girls are up dressing. But I very nearly walked into one by the back stairs just now."

Again there was that strange, fleeting look on her face. But it disappeared in a dazzling smile. "Then you'd best shut the door."

"I won't keep you. I wanted only to beg a bed for a few hours."

"A bed by yourself, or shared?" his old friend asked with an arch look.

"Definitely by myself. I have a long trip ahead of me."

"So you have breezed into New York again only to disappear nearly as quickly as the last time."

"More quickly, I'm afraid. May I use the rear room until midnight?"

Verona made a fuss of opening her ivory fan. "I'm sorry, dear, but that room is occupied at present. You will have to go to the top floor and use mine. Perhaps I could even sneak away for a while later."

Gordon tried to look sorrowful. "I can't tramp around the halls, so I will have to decline your kind offer. May I just stretch out here?" He indicated the long cushioned window bench at the end of the room.

Verona hid her chagrin. "Yes, I suppose so. No one would dare come in here if I am in the front parlor."

Gordon bowed. "I don't know what I would do without you, Verona. Though I am sorry not to have the comfort of that wide bed." He moved away from the door. "Is it a new girl you've given that rear room to?" His question was idle, but her reaction, swiftly hidden, made him wonder.

"Yes, in fact. But she is not yet receiving anyone."

Gordon patted his mouth to hide a yawn, and his half-closed eyes studied the woman. "Oh?" he asked indifferently. "Then she is newly arrived. Where'd you find her?"

"She came to me, actually. Said she wanted to work for me. I'm afraid she has much to learn, though."

The man walked to the window bench and lay down. "I didn't think you took them off the streets, Verona."

The woman's laugh had a faintly hollow ring to it, he thought. "I have not gone soft yet," she said. "This one is as clean as the snow. Perhaps someday when you return and have more time I shall introduce you." She laughed again and left the room.

Gordon lay on the hard cushions trying to rid his mind of

337

her words and of the image he'd thought he'd seen in the hallway. It didn't work. The more he tried for sleep, the more awake he became, and the more obsessively Rebecca's beautiful face floated before his eyes. It was crazy, but he couldn't stop thinking about her, worrying over her fate, and he couldn't stop wondering who the girl was who had reminded him so forcefully of her. At last, swearing softly, he got up and walked to the door. He'd get no rest until he'd seen for himself that the girl in the deep blue dress was just another tramp from Verona's stable.

There were soft voices in the front parlor now, hiding his stealthy progress the few feet down the hall to the narrow back stairs. Swiftly he mounted them, pausing once near the top to listen for anyone in the upper hallway. When he was sure there was no one about, he bounded the last three stairs and turned to the door on his right. He knocked softly, but there was no answer. Very quietly he turned the handle, but the door gave only a fraction before it was stopped by something behind it. He pushed harder, but whatever was holding it stayed put. The girl inside did not want intruders, apparently. He'd have to risk calling to her.

He hesitated, naming himself a fool for his persistence, and then it was too late. Down the hall he heard the click of a door latch, and it sounded like a gunshot to his stretched nerves. He was back down the stairs before the door came fully open.

This time he walked into the gaudy parlor, threw himself full length on the window bench and slept.

Chapter 32

Rebecca was furious with herself for waiting too long to go down and collect her clothes. Verona had reached the bottom floor first, and now she'd missed her chance. There was nothing for it but strategic retreat, she decided after an agonizing minute in the center of the back stairs. Footsteps that seemed to be a man's had joined Verona in the little parlor, and the door was still open. She'd never get past that entrance. She'd have to wait till dawn.

As she climbed wearily toward her room, she heard the man's low voice say something very softly, and for a breath-catching heartbeat she thought she'd recognized that voice. But even as she wondered, she heard Verona say that her girls were all upstairs dressing, and panic swept over her. What if the soft-spoken man were the one Verona had decided Rebecca was to meet? She raced up the remaining steps and barricaded herself into her room again, this time adding an overturned table to the chair beneath the door handle. Then she sat in the dark, staring at the thin sliver of light that forced its way past the door edges.

Because her nerves seemed to be exposed, standing outside her body to be rubbed raw by each air current, she heard the stealthy movement on the back steps before the feet reached the top. She had to jam a fist in her mouth to keep back her screams as she knelt and added her own weight to the crude fortification at her door. When the light knock came, Rebecca could not have answered if she'd wanted to. Her throat was wholly closed in fear. Something pushed against her barrier, and then, as suddenly and as quietly as the intruder had arrived, he went away. Dimly she heard voices in the hall after that, and feet on the stairs. But she didn't move. She stayed where she was for a very long time, crouched like a wild animal who is cornered but will turn to face his death with teeth bared for the last fight.

The girls and their visitors came upstairs and went down again, but still Rebecca didn't move until she felt quite sure no one else was going to stop at her door. Then her cramped muscles made it hard to light a candle and undress. She put on the filmy silk robe, opened her window so she could breath again, and went to bed finally wrung dry of emotion.

She must have fallen into a deep sleep, she realized later, for it took her some time to become aware of noises in her room. Even then she thought she was dreaming and had to force open one eye to get her bearings. She was turned on her side, her back to the piled-up door and she stared at a blank wall, hoping her imagination was all that was at work. Then she saw the dim shadow move on the wall, and heard a small thump. Very carefully she lowered her head and looked at the window. A monstrous form filled the opening.

Rebecca felt such a brain-numbing terror she couldn't move, couldn't cry out, couldn't wake herself from this newest nightmare.

Then the form moved, put its long legs down to the floor and stood up. Stealthily it groped over the little table by the window, and its movement brought back her senses. Clinging to her sanity by a very slim thread, she groped silently for her knife. The figure stayed by the table, and she closed her eyes, her arm sliding beneath the pillow. At last her fingers found the little handle and slowly she pulled the weapon out and down near her chest. She heard a spark struck, and through the taut membrane of her eyelid she saw light spring up in her room. The light grew brighter. Her intruder was coming toward her. She could hear the whisper of steps on the carpet, the soft scrape of the candle being set on her night table. She waited until her every fiber was screaming for release, until the terrifying figure was so close she could smell the musty odor of old clothes.

Then she uncoiled like a rattlesnake, and struck out blindly. She heard the searing tear of heavy cloth at the same

340

instant she felt the blow to her arm. A heavy weight crashed into her, pinning her down, and strong arms sought to catch her flailing limbs. The room seemed filled with the hoarse rasp of panting breath. She fought like a thing possessed, clawing her way up for air, but when her head finally emerged, and she steeled herself for the blows that would follow, she heard only the harshest of gasps.

"Sweet Jesus, it *is* you," a low voice said.

She twisted so quickly he rolled to the side and her violet eyes flew open to see Gordon's drawn face only inches away. So filled with fear was she that she could not feel relief. She could only gaze at him, her eyes growing darker until they were midnight pools.

The hard lines of the man's face didn't relax either as he sat up, still looking at her with disbelief. "I thought I was having hallucinations," he said at last, a catch in his voice. "I glimpsed you in the back hall and wouldn't believe my eyes."

Rebecca pulled herself further away from him on the bed. She was shaking uncontrollably. "Why did you come through that window?" she asked, her voice quavering. "Who did you expect to find?"

Gordon almost smiled then. "The door was locked when I tried it earlier," he explained. "I nearly didn't come back. But when I left the house, I couldn't get rid of the feeling that you were here somewhere. And I knew someone was locked in this room." He glanced at the door as he spoke, and at sight of the propped furniture, his voice stopped on indrawn breath. He looked back at the huddled form in the thin robe. "My God, Rebecca, what *are* you doing here?"

Rebecca was still shaking, but now that the first terror was past and her heart had resumed beating, she felt its pumping was filling her whole body with unbearable sound. "Have you ever noticed, Colonel," she said, knowing hysteria was in her voice, "that we rarely observe even the most basic good manners when we meet?" She giggled, and Gordon grabbed her shoulders.

"Stop it," he said roughly. He shook her then, and she let her head fall back toward the wall. She stared up at the ceiling, and at last felt relief begin to flood over her.

"I came here," she began in a more normal voice, "because Alex gave me Verona Drake's name as a place to go if I was in danger." She felt the shaking stop and was almost sorry.

"Alex!" He swore and released her, and at that she lifted

341

her head again. "And after you arrived, you found this sort of life not quite to your liking?" He nodded toward the door, avoiding her eyes.

Rebecca laughed softly, bitterly. Always Gordon would deliberately misunderstand, would insist to himself she acted from base motives. Long ago he had told her he'd never met an honest woman. Forever, apparently, she would be explaining herself until she won his trust. "I was so naive that it wasn't until last night that I realized what sort of . . . establishment this was. Alex told me Verona Drake was an old friend of yours. You don't pick the nicest friends, Gordon."

The brilliant blue eyes fastened on her face with a look of horror, and she noticed with pleasure that he had not blackened his hair this trip. But she was given no time to savor the sight, for suddenly his arms were around her and his head was buried against her chest. "Oh God, what have they done to you, Becky?" His voice was muffled and very deep.

"Nothing, Gordon, nothing." She felt she was soothing a child as she stroked the golden head. "Though your Miss Drake is not at all a good hostess."

He laughed then, low and long, and at last lifted his head. "I imagine she's not," he choked.

Rebecca smiled, and was amazed at her ability to do so. Then she sobered. "She threatened me, to keep me here, and today she said I had only one way to repay her hospitality. She already had some awful man picked out for me." She looked away, indignation mixing with returning horror. She felt the arms that held her go hard at her words.

"The bitch! How could she . . ." Gordon moved restlessly, dropping his arms.

"No, Gordon, don't let go of me. I shall fly to pieces if you do."

Immediately his hands were back, holding her arms, steadying her. "Is it true you came here because you were running away from Warren Tyson?"

"H-how did you know?"

"Davey and I have turned the city inside out looking for you. He greeted me with the news of Tyson's death today, and said no one knew where you'd gone."

"Yes, it's true. Major Tyson tried to attack me after Uncle Julian died. I was so frightened. But I had that knife you'd given me, you see . . ."

"Rebecca, I love you." Gordon shook his head, half laughing. "Do you?"

His face sobered, and he looked past her shoulder. "Why didn't you go to your Captain Revington? He might have been able to protect you."

"He is out of the city." She touched his face gently. "And he is not my Captain Revington."

He pulled away from her touch. "It was made clear to me that you were nearly betrothed."

Rebecca sighed. "That was before I knew you." She could talk and talk, she knew, but it wouldn't matter. As once before, the battle was his to fight.

This time his eyes met hers squarely, and grew nearly as dark as her own while his hands tightened unconsciously on her arms. He tried not to look at her beauty, at the tumbled mass of black hair, the moist sensual mouth, the half-exposed body beneath the revealing robe. He wished he knew what was inside the perfectly molded exterior of this girl. But all he could think of was what could have happened to her at the hands of Warren Tyson and the British, at what had nearly happened to her in this house. The thought suddenly overwhelmed him and he snatched her to him, wanting to protect her from the imagined horrors. Be damned to Charles Revington. He hadn't protected Rebecca from all that had happened to her. He didn't deserve the prize.

It took all of Rebecca's willpower not to cry out as she watched Gordon at war with himself again. And she knew if she could find the words to make him believe in her, she'd give up her martyr role and use them. But if Pamela Jenkins and Verona Drake were the sort of women Gordon had known in the past, there was little to say to convince him she was different. She had to trust to her own blind instinct to keep silent and let him come to her. When he snatched her against him, she began to cry.

"God, Becky, don't do that. Not now." His voice was nearly lost in her hair, and he began to smooth it roughly. "You've got to hold on until we get out of here."

She rubbed at her eyes and looked up. The hard planes of his face were softer now, and she had to fight back fresh tears. He smiled at her effort and she smiled tremulously back at him.

"In fact," he said in the most normal voice he'd used yet, "if we don't leave soon we'll be marooned in this place." And he let go of her.

Rebecca jumped to her knees. "You are leaving New York tonight?"

"Yes. And you are coming with me. Verona will have to find another new attraction for her best customers." He eyed her straight little form before him, the flowered silk robe outlining every curve and crevice, the deep V of the crossed neckline exposing most of her beautiful breasts. "That is," he added huskily, "if I can manage to get us out of here at all."

The girl saw his look and felt her whole body tremble in response to it. After the events of the last few days, she'd thought never again to be able to want a man, yet here she was growing hot under his eyes, needing Gordon more than she ever had before. She reached up and touched his face, trailing her fingers along his cheekbone. "I'm so very glad you found me," she whispered.

Gordon groaned. "You won't be glad if you don't get dressed quickly. I can't stand looking at you this way much longer."

With a wantonness she'd never known, Rebecca held his eyes and very slowly untied the light sash at her waist. The filmy material parted, and her breasts tingled as she felt the soft silk slip away from them.

"Becky!" Gordon's whisper was close to a growl. "Don't do this to me. This is no time . . ."

"But what better place?" she asked very softly, and put her head back as his lips burned her throat.

He kissed her shoulders, then her breasts, all the while running his hands along her body as though he would explore and map every part of her. When he'd pulled the silk robe free and she'd stretched out catlike under his caresses, he stood up and took off his own clothes, his eyes never leaving her. "I would even feel it fitting if Verona managed to get in here and find us." He almost chuckled.

She looked languidly at him. "Verona Drake accused me of wanting to pick my own men. She was right."

"Wielding that little knife as you do, a man would be a fool to try to take you unwilling."

Rebecca sat up with a jerk. "Oh, Gordon, I didn't stab you, did I?" Her eyes searched the rippling muscles of his chest and arms.

"No, hellcat, you didn't manage that. Though Davey's coat will never be the same."

She sighed. "I am sorry. But you scared me so. It was like ... like that night. ..."

"Tyson?" Gordon's face was grim again.

"Yes. And the man who came in here the second evening ... but he was frightened off more easily. Oh, Gordon, I've killed a man," she wailed, suddenly overcome with a new horror.

Gordon sat down on the edge of the bed. "No, Becky, you didn't kill Tyson. Though I wouldn't have minded at all if you had. He killed himself with his greed and his hatred. Davey managed to learn the whole story, and it seems Warren was so hellbent on finding you, he ignored a bad wound too long that night. A butcher of an army surgeon did him in in the end, and I wish I could shake the surgeon's hand. It was a most fitting end for a despicable man."

Rebecca shuddered. "To think I might have done the same thing to you! I'm so sorry," she repeated.

"Don't be sorry. I'm glad to know you can defend yourself. Though never again against me, Becky."

A tentative smile played at the corners of her full mouth as she tried to hide the sudden light that leaped to her eyes. She felt his hands reach for her, and she closed them completely. "Never," she whispered to herself.

His long body stretched beside hers, and she lay back in his arms with a feeling almost like contentment. But the feeling was short-lived, for now his hands and his mouth were setting her on fire again, and she was absorbed in her body's response to him. She sensed his urgency was greater than ever before, and she moved her hands over him, wanting to erase everything in the world but what they shared. When he pushed her thighs apart gently, she arched her back. She knew to what heights he could carry her now, and she scaled them rapturously.

It seemed tragic to her afterward that there was no time to savor the healthy langor and intense closeness she felt. With an apologetic smile, Gordon had pulled free and gotten up. "Come on, hellcat," he said now and slapped her round bottom. "We'll miss our boat if we don't go."

Rebecca rose slowly from the bed. As always after their love-making, doubts began to assail her. He was going to get her out of this awful house, out of the dangerous city. But would his concern end there? Would he then ride off into the night, as he had before, leaving her to make her own way and wait for a day when their paths might cross again? Only a few minutes ago she'd felt in the very bottom of her heart that he loved her, but now she was unsure.

He didn't see her hesitancy, was gathering up her clothes and dumping them on the bed. Then he went to undo her barricade at the door.

She donned the indecent dress silently, wishing she could hide more of this body that had betrayed her love for him so wantonly. But when he turned back to help her, she saw his smile widen. His face looked more relaxed than it had in all the time she'd known him, and for the first time she thought he looked young and full of arrogant strength.

"Where in the name of all that's holy did you get that gown?" he asked.

Flushing, she explained, and watched him come closer. She might as well have had no clothes on at all, she thought, seeing his expression and feeling the tip of one long finger trace the plunging neckline of the dress.

"I am very, very glad no other man has seen you in that," he said softly. "For the first time in her rigidly controlled house, Verona might have had brawls in the hallways. It's too bad it's so late, or I'd take pleasure in tearing it off you myself."

Rebecca could do nothing but blush more furiously, and he laughed at that. "The two of us are a fine pair, forced into doing things that suit us not at all. You would never make a proper whore, dearheart, if you blush every time a man looks on you with lust. And I will never make a proper spy, for I find that at the first opportunity all the painfully gathered intelligence that I must report goes out of my head when I am faced with a desirable and available woman."

Rebecca raised her fist. Was that all she meant—a desirable and *available* woman?

He caught her arm easily. "We don't even have time for fighting. Do you have a cloak?"

She shook her head, defeated. "I don't even have a piece of material." She looked down at her exposed flesh with disgust.

Gordon's eyes twinkled. "Much as I wish to enjoy the sight, I'll have to be a gentleman and aid you in your distress." He pulled from his pocket a large handkerchief and handed it to her with a grin.

Trying to be businesslike, Rebecca took it with a nod and wrapped it around her neck, tucking the ends across each other into her bodice. She felt much better. "How, Colonel Meade, do you propose to walk out of here now?" she then asked. "Verona's parties go on nearly till dawn."

"Very true. So we do not walk. We climb." He snuffed out the candle as he said it, and without giving her a moment to protest, he swooped her into his arms and crossed to the window. Rebecca had to suppress a squeal as she felt herself being shoved unceremoniously through the opening until her feet dangled in space. Desperately she gripped his arms.

"You proved once before you were good at this sort of thing. There's a solid top to the arbor right below you. From there climb down it like a ladder."

She clung to him shaking her head in sudden fright.

"Do it now!" His low voice held the old note of command, and she didn't dare disobey. He might simply push her off the window ledge.

Frantically, she grabbed the sill and let her feet fall straight. To her surprise, she touched the arbor instantly, and only moments later she was on the ground.

When Gordon joined her, he tucked her hand into his arm, patted it once, and said simply, "Walk."

For half an hour the two strolled through alleys and up dark streets, working their way north and west of Murray Street. Whenever they met others walking home, Rebecca knew she should feel familiar twinges of fear, but she could summon none as long as Gordon held her arm.

When they crossed to the west side of Greenwich Street, Gordon hurried the pace. They were near the banks of the Hudson now, heading for the northern limits of the city. Soon they were among trees and fields, walking fast.

At last he allowed low-voiced conversation, and it was then that Rebecca learned what she'd wanted to ask since leaving the room at Verona's house. Sylvie and Alex had gotten out of the city safely, though they'd been badly frightened several times on their journey. Alex had taken the girl to Dobbs Ferry, and there had discovered that Royalists had burned Adams's house. Sylvie had been wild with worry until they'd found Seth and his mother living with friends a mile beyond the village. All was well, and the talk was of a wedding next month. As for Alex, he had followed his instructions, and had joined Gordon in Peekskill within twenty-four hours. "He's changed a deal," Gordon said when he'd finished the narrative. "He aged in that jail, learned a lot about surviving. I wouldn't have had him go through that experience, but he has grown up in the process, and I confess I feel better about his chances of surviving this war now."

"I know what that feeling must mean to you," Rebecca replied softly, and saw him look at her with surprise, and then warmth. If only he felt about others as he felt about Alex, she thought.

Another mile and Gordon turned off the road, dragging her over a fence and between rocks and bushes. When they could see the banks of the river below them, he stopped and looked around at last. A white moon drained the earth of color, giving the narrow fields a ghostly, shimmering gray tone. The trees stood black and ominous against the luminosity.

"Damn that moon," Gordon breathed softly. He pulled her back from the low bank and wound through thickets and bushes until at last she protested. His big hand came out and clamped over her mouth. They were standing in a small grove of trees, and twinkling between the trunks could be seen the lights of a house ahead. Putting his mouth to her ear, Gordon spoke. "Not a sound. These banks are lined with British sentries. Boats patrol the water. Let your damned dress tear, and let your face get scratched. If you speak again we'll both hang from these trees at dawn."

Rebecca nodded, feeling her stomach rise at his words, and wondering if she'd now have the strength to go on. She felt his lips brush her cheek then, and his hand grasped hers more firmly. She staggered after him.

Another agonizing mile and then Gordon stopped at last. Below them was one of the many little coves that dotted the shoreline of the rocky island. He pulled her down beside a boulder and squatted, his eyes searching the narrow shore. At last he raised his head.

"There he is," he said very softly, his hand pointing to what looked like a tumbled mass of boulders beside a narrow stream mouth.

Now Rebecca could make out the outline of a small boat, and a shape sitting beside it. She felt the first fear she'd experienced since leaving Verona Drake's house. Here was their escape route, and their chance for freedom. Would Gordon take that freedom and use it to be clear of her as well as of New York?

As though in answer to her thoughts, she felt his arms go around her. "We will have no more chance to talk. On the river we must be absolutely silent, and even then a sentry or a boat may spot us. We have no choice though, and no chances but this one. It is the final risk Davey can take. So I'll tell you now what will happen if we make it. There are two men waiting on the New Jersey shore. They have horses for us. One will go to General Washington with the information I have. That information is that General Clinton will march north on October third, in two days' time. Remember that if anything happens to me."

She began to protest, to cling to him, but he put a finger to her lips. "The other man," he went on, "is Alex. He will come north with us and will take us back across the river to the Westchester shore. We will then go to Peekskill, where Alex will see you are safely with General Putnam by dawn tomorrow."

"And you?" she asked, her heart hammering. "Where will you go?"

"I'll have to go on to Fishkill and maybe even north to General Gates."

"I see." Her voice was remote. "Gordon, how am I ever to get a message to Mr. Kent? He must have worried about me for days, and I would like him to know I am all right."

"Davey can get a message to him. From what I gather, Mr. Kent understands full well why you left his house. But you have your Charles to consider, too."

Rebecca was lost in her own dismal thoughts. She didn't even hear this last. Gordon planned to leave her with some strange general while he disappeared again. And except for going to Sylvie and being a burden on the Adamses she had no choice.

"Becky!" His voice was urgent now. "Did you hear me? Are you having second thoughts about Charles?"

Rebecca felt leaden, but she managed to shake her head. "I left him a letter days ago. Mr. Kent will see he gets it. I think I could never have married him even if I hadn't met you."

Gordon's hand groped for hers in the dark. "I will travel easier for knowing that."

"Will you? And what will *I* do, left behind at your General Putnam's headquarters?"

Gordon hesitated. "Would you rather I had Alex take you to Dobbs Ferry to Seth and Sylvie?"

She shook her head, knowing he'd say she couldn't come with him if she asked, and with that knowledge not caring where she went.

"Then stay with Putnam," he said at last, "where I'll know you are safe. I will come back for you." He enunciated each word slowly.

Rebecca looked up sharply. "And where will you take me then?" She tried to see his features in the leafy shadows. She thought he was smiling slightly.

"I don't know, Becky. This could be a long war, and I may never know from one week to the next where I must be. But when I return from this job I have to do, I will not let you out of my sight again. You do nothing but get into trouble when you're on your own. Wait for me."

"Is that an order, Colonel?" Her heart was soaring, and she wanted to leap up and shout.

"A request, Miss Blair."

"Granted, Colonel Meade."

He kissed her then, deftly and quickly. Then he pulled her down the rocky bank to the waiting boat.

Davey was surprised to see two figures emerge beside him, but grinned as he received instructions. For a long time they all sat, waiting for the slow moving clouds to finally obscure the too-bright moon. At last the shimmering water was plunged into darkness, and they shoved off from the shore.

Rebecca sat in the stern of the boat, clasping her hands very tightly, watching the rhythmic swing of Gordon's powerful arms on the muffled oars. She knew that if they survived the river crossing, made it to the New Jersey shore, there might still be years ahead when she would be separated from this man. She might fear for his life many times yet, but never again would she live with the fear of not knowing if he would come back to her. For a fleeting moment, there in the limitless expanse of slapping black water, she realized that some day she would return to live beside this river she'd grown to love, and she smiled for pure joy. No matter that the house would not be Halscomb. At Laurel Manor she would make her final fresh start in life, in Gordon's arms.